She jerked the tip of her rod up to set the hook. She felt the tug again, stronger this time. Her eyes widened with surprise. She had actually caught a fish! The contact was like a jolt of electricity straight from the fish to her heart.

Her giddy elation quickly changed to panic. Her feet slid over the slippery river rocks as she followed the fish downstream. Dipping her hand in the water, she lowered and grasped the beautiful olive green brook trout in her palm. It was gulping and gasping wildly for air. The trout had fought too hard and was too young.

"I'm as scared as you are," she told the fish. . . .

MARY ALICE MONROE

was awarded the 2008 Award for Writing from the South Carolina Center for the Book

TIME IS A RIVER

**was a *USA Today* "Summer 2008 Pick"
for best summer books,
an Indie Next Pick,
and a *Woman's Day* "best beach read"**

Time Is a River is also available as an eBook

More acclaim for *Time Is a River*

"This is very good writing. . . . The story is so compelling. . . ."

— *The Asheville Citizen-Times* (NC)

"[A] novel of strong Southern women . . . the author's love for her characters is palpable throughout."

— *Publishers Weekly*

"A thoroughly restorative book."

— Laura Hansen, Bookin' It (Little Falls, MN)

"A soothing and rare treasure of a book. Monroe has really outdone herself. . . . A very powerful story of forgiveness, redemption, and new birth. Vitality flows through this book just as surely as the river flows next to the cabin. Any woman who believes—or at least longs *to* believe— in second chances should read this book."

— Tattered Cover Book Store (Denver, CO)

Mary Alice Monroe

Time Is a River

A NOVEL

POCKET BOOKS

NEW YORK LONDON TORONTO SYDNEY

Pocket Books
A Division of Simon & Schuster, Inc.
1230 Avenue of the Americas
New York, NY 10020

This book is a work of fiction. Names, characters, places, and incidents either are products of the author's imagination or are used fictitiously. Any resemblance to actual events or locales or persons, living or dead, is entirely coincidental.

First Pocket Books paperback edition February 2009

POCKET and colophon are registered trademarks of Simon & Schuster, Inc.

For information about special discounts for bulk purchases, please contact Simon & Schuster Special Sales at 1-800-456-6798 or business@simonandschuster.com.

Cover design by Susan Zucker
Cover photo by Stephen Wisbauer/Jupiter Images

Manufactured in the United States of America

10 9 8 7 6 5 4 3 2 1

ISBN-13: 978-1-4391-4177-9
ISBN-10:   1-4391-4177-0
ISBN-13: 978-1-4391-4998-0
ISBN-10:   1-4391-4998-4

*This book is dedicated to
my mother, Elayne Cryns,
my grandmother, Alice Monogue,
my friend, Carol Martino,
and to all our loved ones
who have lost the battle
with breast cancer.*

And to all the valiant survivors.

Acknowledgments

Each book is a journey during which I meet so many helpful, inspiring people. For this novel, especially, I have been humbled by the willingness of the following people to step forward to share their knowledge, offer much-needed information, support my work, and help me in any way they could.

First, I feel so fortunate to have my editor, Lauren McKenna. We worked shoulder to shoulder with enthusiasm and respect, and it was a delight to see our ideas come alive. I look forward to many more books together. Thank you to Louise Burke for all your input and support. Many people at Simon & Schuster worked hard to produce and promote this book, and your work was invaluable. Thanks to all.

My literary agents, Kimberly Whalen and Robert Gottlieb, deserve stars beside their names for advice and support that is much appreciated. Thanks, also, to my audio agent, Alanna Ramirez, and my foreign rights agent, Lara Allen at Trident Media Group. You're a great team.

For ideas that sent my mind soaring and my fingers tapping, I send thanks to my sister, Marguerite Martino. Here's to the Dream Machine! And to my friend Martha Keenan—the lowcountry awaits your next visit.

I had a marvelous experience recording the audio book with Brilliance Audio, and hugs and thanks to Eileen and Bob Hutton.

The world of fly-fishing is filled with wise and generous people eager to share their knowledge, insights, and experience. In particular I want to thank Starr Nolan of Brookside Guides, Asheville, North Carolina, for not only being my favorite teacher and guide, but for being the inspiring and dedicated leader of the North Carolina chapter of Casting for Recovery. I am indebted to Starr for reading my manuscript and making corrections, thus saving this novice from embarrassing errors like calling a fly rod a pole.

Thank you to Dana Rikimaru for her book, *Fly-Fishing: A Woman's Guide*. It is, indeed, everything you need to know to get started—and keep going—and was very helpful to me in writing the chapter headings. Thanks for your work with CFR, too.

Casting for Recovery is a national, non-profit program for women who have or have had breast cancer. The weekend retreats provide free counseling, educational services, and the sport of fly-fishing to promote mental and physical healing. I met many glorious, strong survivors and thank them for their time and courage. I especially want to thank the guides who gave so tirelessly and inspired me: Charity Rutter (and her fabulous book *Rise Rings & Rhododendron*), Caroline Hassell, Linda

Michael, Trish Dumaine, and Mary K. Jenkins. Thanks to Caroline Rhodes and Sarah Manucy at the Charleston Angler, and my fellow "Reel Women," Catherine Rhea, Dawn Johnson, Sheila and Hadley Northen, Judy Boehm, Paula Skinner, Martha Dean Miller, and Susan Smythe. A special wave to my first fly-fishing teacher and dock pals, Clay and Martha Cable.

I am indebted to the many women who came forward to talk about their experiences with breast cancer. I continue to be impressed by their strength, courage, and honesty. A special thank-you to my dear friends Julie Beard, Brucie Harry, Mary Pringle, Terri Sword, and to Rosalind L. Connor and Ann Caldwell.

I appreciated more than I can say the support (and baked goods) from M. Fitzgerald, Lynn Noyes, James and Patti Frierson, and all the Kruesi, Brock, Frierson, and Killebrew family in wonderful Chattanooga. Thank you, Leah Greenberg, for readings with a view! The town of Watkins Mill and all the characters in this novel are strictly fiction. However, I did use the names of Betky, Skipper, and Katherine Shaffer and Charlie Aikman in this book with their permission. My writer friends, James Cryns, Patti Callahan Henry, Marjory Wentworth, Ciji Ware, Lindy Carter, and Sue Monk Kidd talked the story through with me and helped create magic in my mind. Thank you all so much!

A special farewell to beloved author Robert Jordan (James Rigney). His inspiration lives on through his words.

A nod to the incomparable Cornelia "Fly Rod"

Crosby ("Fly Rod's Notebook"), Joan Wulff, and to the many women in the history of fly-fishing who were an inspiration for the development of my character Kate Watkins, and who have shown the world that fly-fishing is a sport for women.

Thanks to the team at *All You* and Walmart for their wonderful support.

As always, I conclude with those who come first in my life—my love and thanks to Markus, Claire, John, Jack, Margaretta, and Zack for more than I can say here.

HOLDING EACH OTHER UP
Mark Nepo*

Let's be honest
which doesn't mean
being harsh, but gentle.

Let's be clear
which doesn't mean
being dispassionate, but
holding each other up
in the face of what is true.

Let's be enduring
which doesn't mean
being important or famous,
but staying useful like a wheel
worn by rain in the same place
after years of carrying
each other's burdens.

Let's be in awe
which doesn't mean
anything but the courage
to gape like fish at the surface
breaking around our mouths
as we meet the air.

*www.MarkNepo.com

Time Is a River

Chapter One

The charm of fly-fishing is that it is the pursuit
of what is elusive, but attainable—a perpetual
series of occasions for hope.

—ANONYMOUS

The river was spawned high in the Appalachian Mountains formed of sedimentary rock and ancient ocean floor. Fed by rain and melted snow, rivulets of cold, clear water gush over boulders and between rocky ridges to lace the mountainsides. Thousands of miles of freestone streams run unchecked, cascading down to form the mighty rivers.

Mia Landan followed the river as it wound in a serpentine manner, deeper into the woods. To her right, the sienna-hued wall of rock was dotted with patches of bright green moss. To her left, the river raced on, rushing forward in a confident current. She reached over the passenger seat of her car to clutch a wrinkled sheet of paper from under a torn road map. Scribbled across the page of directions she read, *Follow the river.*

"I am not lost," she said aloud, though she doubted her words. She was following the pebbles in the river like Hansel and Gretel, believing that they would lead her through the dark forest to a safe haven. Except Mia Landan no longer believed in fairy tales.

Thunder rolled overhead, threatening rain. Back home in Charleston, South Carolina, the spring rain had already given way to scorching heat and humidity. Here in the North Carolina mountains, however, the air was still cool and the forests aflame with wildflowers. Around each bend in the road she encountered a cluster of rhododendrons blooming scarlet or white. A little farther on, the paved road ended to become a rutted bed of dirt and gravel, as worn and filled with holes as a pauper's coat.

A few fat drops of rain splattered against the windshield, turning the dust to long streaks of mud. She turned on the windshield wipers and her heartbeat matched the metronome click. She leaned far over the wheel, clutching it tight, peering through the sudden deluge at the sliver of road ahead. Where was the cabin? she worried as she peered through the rain and fog. Could it be this far off the beaten track? Just when she thought she should turn around and head back, the river tumbled over a ridge of rocks to a large pool. Beside it on a high bank, nestled between a pair of towering hemlocks, sat a rustic log cabin.

Mia released a ragged sigh, slumped her shoulders, and loosened her grip on the wheel. She had found it. It had been a long, circuitous drive with directions scribbled in haste. But she'd made it. Her wheels hit soft grass and mud as she parked as close to the cabin as she could.

Turning off the engine, she was immediately immersed in a deep mountain silence. The miles still raced in her veins. Her clothes clung and the car seat was littered with empty water bottles and candy wrappers. The stale air reminded her of hospital rooms. She lowered the window enough to let the fresh air awaken her after the long journey. The rain sprinkled in and she lifted her face to it, tasting its cool sweetness.

Mia looked again to the cabin. It lurked, isolated and foreboding, under the canopy of the trees and mist. The woods seemed to close in around her. She felt a shiver of loneliness. But hadn't she wanted a faraway, secluded place? A sanctuary? Rolling up the window she cast a worried glance at the clock on the dashboard. It was half past six. Belle had told her she would pick up supplies and meet her at the cabin no later than seven. There was nowhere to go. The cabin was locked and the rain was coming down in sheets. She was trapped in this car, in the wilderness, to wait as the night closed in around her. Relentless rain coursed tracks down her foggy window, mirroring the tears flowing down her cheeks. Mia brought her hands to her face and wondered how she got to this place.

It had all begun with fly-fishing. She'd never had any interest in the sport. She was a public relations director for the Spoleto arts festival in Charleston. Though she lived by the ocean and mountains, she didn't have any connection to either. Her idea of a good time was drinks and dinner at a restaurant with friends. If she went on a boat, it was docked for a party. A trip to the mountains meant a few days at a ski lodge. Nonetheless, her sister, Madeline, had signed her up for a three-day fly-fishing retreat designed especially for breast cancer survivors. Casting for Recovery provided spiritual and physical therapy, and Madeline believed Mia needed both.

So that spring Mia had driven hours from her home in Charleston to the Casting for Recovery retreat in the foothills of North Carolina. She'd agreed to go only to keep Madeline from nagging. Some of the women at the retreat were still early in their treatments. Others were ten, twenty, or more years post-diagnosis. At thirty-eight years old, Mia was the youngest. She was reticent at first, but Belle would not allow her to remain aloof.

Belle Carson was their fly-fishing guide and the leader of the retreat. Belle was a tall, straight-talking, sensitive, and big-hearted woman who had chucked an academic career at the University of Virginia to move to Asheville, North Carolina, and open her own fly-fishing business. Belle gently coaxed Mia out of isolation into group discussions and taught her how to cast a dry fly. Mia was drawn into the group by force of the women's brutal honesty and their wise understanding. It was an intense three days that felt like three weeks, so much had transpired. They laughed, they cried. They were sister survivors. By the end of the retreat she'd joined their feminine solidarity formed by a shared history.

But it was in the river that Mia felt the first glimmer of life since the shock of her diagnosis had left her heart as numb as the white scar on her chest. Belle Carson had taught her how to cast a thin line from a rod onto the shallow waters of the Davidson River. To her amazement, she found hope rising in thin wisps of speckled silver. She might not have believed in fairy tales, but she believed in that spark of life she felt at the other end of the line.

Eager to share her new excitement with her husband, she'd hugged the women farewell and drove back a day early to Charleston. Closing her eyes, Mia saw again the lurid image of her husband and that unknown woman lying on *her* marriage bed. She'd stumbled down the stairs, climbed back into her car, and started to drive, her eyes blind and her mind numb.

Mia Landan of two years ago would have stood her ground and confronted them. Then, she was confident in her career, her beauty, her self. *That* Mia would not have run to the mountains with her tail between her legs. But two years ago Mia had not yet found the lump in her breast.

The wheels had hummed beneath her on the highway. The green road signs passed in a blur as she put miles between herself and her husband's infidelity. She'd driven for forty-five minutes before she realized she didn't know where she was. When at last she focused on the signs she saw she was on Interstate 26.

Her instincts were acting as her compass, guiding her north, back to the mountains where she'd felt safe.

By the time she'd returned to the retreat, the sun had lowered far to the west and the placid water of the lake had darkened to a deep purple. A few dimples disturbed the glassiness. *Rises*, she'd learned they were called, were created by trout when they rose to the surface to sip an insect. She drove past the wall of tall firs and hemlocks that surrounded the lake to the row of cottages that she'd shared with the eighteen other women at the retreat. Now they all stood empty and quiet. One by one, each woman had returned to a husband, a family, a partner. For them, life had gone on post-cancer. At that moment, Mia saw with clarity that she was not a survivor.

She couldn't go back to Charleston. She could not start the engine and drive. She had nothing and no one waiting for her. She'd brought her trembling hands to her face and began to sob.

Perhaps if she hadn't felt such hope on the river, she could have maintained the hard shell of apathy that had sustained her for the year of treatment and recovery. But the spirit of the river, the rhythm of the cast, and the tenuous connection to life at the end of a thin line had broken through her shell. It had filled her with silvery light, lifted her up and made her feel whole again. To lose that now . . .

Belle Carson had been walking down the road and saw Mia crying the hoarse, ragged sobs of a desperate woman. She opened the car door.

"Mia? What are you doing here? Are you all right?"

Mia swung around, lifting her face. "I can't go back," she cried in a broken voice.

Belle bent to look in the car. Her long braid slipped over her shoulder. "What happened?"

"He's left me. I have nowhere to go."

Belle took Mia's arm, then gently but firmly drew her from the car. "Come with me," she said, putting her arm around Mia's shoulders. She guided her inside the lodge which, mercifully, was deserted. Belle treated Mia like she would an injured animal, gently and with a calm voice, giving her time to settle until the panic faded from her eyes. She offered Mia coffee, then rummaged through the camp fridge to prepare a plate and set it before her. When Mia sat slump-shouldered and looked at the food with a dazed expression, Belle didn't nag at her to eat it. She'd sat across from Mia and waited while the sun lowered and the geese honked by the lake, calling their young. When the grief trickled out, Belle handed her tissues, and later, when it gushed, she listened patiently before asking questions.

It was Belle's dark brown eyes that Mia remembered more than anything she'd actually said. They were calm waters, like the lake, and in their depths she'd felt hope rising.

Then Belle offered Mia what she needed most—safe refuge.

"I have a place," Belle told her. "A cabin not too far away. It's not much. It's been abandoned for years and

I haven't checked on it in months. But it's yours, if you want to stay there."

So Mia had returned to her car with Belle's hastily delivered directions and found her way to this remote cabin. And here she was, still sitting in her car, waiting once more to be rescued.

Thirty minutes later the rain dissipated and from the distance Mia heard the sound of tires and the hum of an engine. She stepped out of the car to see an old green Blazer inscribed with the words *Brookside Guides* roll to a stop beside her.

"Belle!" she called out.

Belle Carson stepped out of the truck, wearing a green rain jacket with her company's logo over the pocket. She was somewhere in her fifties but still as narrow in the hips as a girl. Her red hair fell down her back in a long braid under her forest green baseball cap.

"Hey," she called. She bent to grab a large box from her truck and hurried up the muddy path to the porch with the same sure-footed steps she'd taken in the rushing stream earlier that day. Once under the porch roof they shook the rain from their jackets. They stood eye to eye while Belle surveyed Mia's soaked clothes dripping from her thin frame. Strands of reddish blond hair plastered across Mia's forehead.

Belle's lips twitched. "You look like a drowned rat."

"I feel like it."

"Let's get you warm and settled," Belle said as she handed Mia the large box. "See you found the cabin all right." Belle pulled out a key affixed to a yellowed, water-stained paper tag that had the name *Watkins Cove* written in an old-fashioned script. "This here is the original. I'll have to make another copy so take good care of it."

Mia thought she had never heard a more beautiful sound than the click of that lock turning over. Then, taking a deep breath, she stepped inside the cabin. Instantly she was assailed by the scents of wood smoke and mildew. She wrinkled her nose. Her hand fumbled against the wall, groping for a light switch and praying some animal didn't dart at her from the dark. "Thank God," she whispered when she heard a click and yellow light poured from a hanging fixture that looked like a converted kerosene lamp.

She laughed out loud. All that was missing was a bunch of old men and their fishing gear. She could almost smell the tobacco. It was a compact space with one main room dominated by a fireplace made of river rocks. The dark wood walls were bare. She imagined this was where fish stories were shared on cool nights as unshaven men smoked pipes and clustered around the fire in rocking chairs.

In the pale light, the room appeared ghostly with sheets covering heavy pieces of furniture and threadbare curtains loosely draped around paned windows. Motes of dust rose in the stirred air as her boots left muddy prints across the floor. She couldn't shake the feeling that she was disturbing the peace of the ancient anglers that still hovered here. When the door clicked shut behind her she startled in the tomblike room.

"Well, let's take a look," Belle said, grabbing the box from Mia and setting it down on the table across the room. She turned slowly, lips pursed as her gaze swept around. When she faced Mia again she set her hands on her hips and shrugged. "Could be worse." After cracking a wry grin she shook her head. "But not much. I told you it hadn't been used in years."

"It's not that bad," Mia replied, but her voice lacked conviction. "Mostly it's just dirty."

"It's filthy. A haven for spiders and mice, looks like to me. I'd understand if you changed your mind. It's too late to head back to Charleston but you can stay at my place tonight."

"Really, it's OK."

Belle looked at Mia with the same intensity as when studying the waters. "You ever spend time up in the mountains? Alone?"

Mia shook her head no.

Belle rubbed her jaw, struggling with her reply. "Let me show you around. You haven't even seen the whole place yet. It's pretty rugged. There's no central heat, not to mention air conditioning." She turned and walked to the small kitchen. "This is an add-on to the original cabin. At least they made the ceilings a little higher," she said, craning her neck to look at the wood trusses and beams. "I don't imagine those old codgers gave much mind to cooking back when this place was built. It was updated in the nineteen thirties, I figure. Electricity was added, gas, some more modern appliances. All relative, keep in mind. Look at this old stove, will you?" she said, walking to an antique cast-iron and enamel stove. "This has to be an original."

Mia warily eyed the black iron behemoth that dominated the small kitchen. "Is it safe?"

"This thing? As far as I know it's in working condition. No warping or cracks. This one was taken care of, you can tell. Though it sat here for a long while." Her face softened and she spoke with a tone of reminiscence. "My mama had a wood-burning stove in our house in Virginia. We also had a modern one, of course, but she had a soft spot for the old ones. She used to claim a biscuit tasted best when baked in an old cast-iron stove. I'm kind of partial to them myself. Nothing better to keep a house warm on a cold night. I intend to keep this beauty. It's a collector's item." She patted the cast iron and said, "They just don't build 'em like they used to."

Belle opened the enamel oven door, then let it slam shut with a grimace. "Looks like some mice and critters took up residence in there. Just needs a good cleaning out. This oven will burn with some dry wood."

"I'm never cooking on that thing."

"Never say never. When the electricity goes out, and it will with every big storm, you'll be glad to have this old wood-burning stove around. Otherwise, this here gas stove might only have two burners but it'll do the job for you. Same with this old fridge."

She pointed to a small enamel fridge with rounded edges. Both it and the stove looked like they were bought after the war. Which war, Mia didn't dare guess.

Belle opened the fridge. It was heavy but swung easily. The inside was clean. "It's a bit rusty. But it's cold. A guy I know comes in to check on the place to make sure everything is in working order."

"With my cooking, it won't make much of a difference. But I *am* curious about the bathroom."

"You mean the outhouse?"

Mia's face froze.

Belle laughed. "Sorry, it was too easy. It's over here."

The small room had only one undersize window and was hardly a place for a luxurious soak. The porcelain commode was minuscule, the tiny sink had a nasty crack, and the claw-footed tub was badly stained. "There's only cold running water. That's spring water. So when I say cold, I mean cold."

"As long as I can pee without something coming up to bite me in the ass, I'll manage."

"I hear that." Belle shook her head and chuckled. "I'm installing a new hot-water heater. I'll prod George to get going on that right away. Until then, you'll have to heat water on the stove. OK, let's see what we got in here." She moved on to the small room next to the bathroom and opened the door.

Perhaps it was the whisk of wind from the opened door. Or maybe it was the pale white linen against the window, but something made the hairs along Mia's neck rise when she stepped into the bedroom.

"There should be a light switch somewhere," Belle said, fumbling along the wall. Finding none, she walked to the small bedside lamp. "There, that's better," she said as soft light filled the room.

"Why, this is a *woman's* room," Mia said, surprised. She'd expected to find rotting waders and boots, red and black checked wool blankets, and other masculine items. Instead the black iron bed was made up with a linen quilt and shams boldly embroidered with flowers and the dark green initials *KW*. A jewel-toned hooked rug lay beneath the bed, and over a long mahogany dresser was an elaborate Venetian mirror that was out of place against the rough cabin walls.

Belle's face was sober. "It was." She turned on her heel and walked out. "Let's see what's upstairs."

Mia had a thousand questions lingering on her tongue to ask about the woman who loved fine, feminine things but lived out here in the wilderness. But she refrained from asking even one and, instead, silently followed Belle up the steep, narrow stairs. This was a gaunt room, barren of furniture save for a window seat under a row of dingy, small windows. At one end sat another fireplace, smaller than the one downstairs. An old wooden toy lay beside it. Curious, Mia went to pick it up.

"It's a toy caboose! Someone carved it from a single piece of wood. It's beautifully done." She handed it to Belle. "Odd that it's here in a fishing cabin."

Belle took the toy and lifted it in her hand as though weighing it. "Back when, this would have been a garret where they put the bunks for fishing trips." Then, handing the caboose back to her, she added, "But my mother was raised in this house, so I guess it's likely she played in here."

"Your mother grew up in this cabin?" It seemed impossible that any child would be brought up in such a remote place.

"That's right."

"Was that her room downstairs?"

Belle shook her head. "My mother married young and left soon after. She never came back. I never knew my grandmother. That was her room." Belle spoke through tightened lips and her tone implied that she didn't want to discuss this further.

When they returned to the main room Belle appeared restless. She walked around pulling the sheets off the few pieces of furniture. The Victorian pieces were large and cumbersome, more fitting a grand room than a small wood cabin. An ornate, blue velvet sofa was badly faded and worn. The pedestal mahogany dining table was too large for the small space even with all the leaves removed. Most imposing of all was an enormous armoire adorned with the carving of the head of a stag with antlers.

"Wow," was all Mia could say.

"They look ridiculous in here."

"They're beautiful. Just . . . out of place."

Belle scowled as she looked at them. "Everything about this place is, well, never mind." She rolled up the sheets with a punching motion. Then she turned to face Mia.

"I'm sorry. I shouldn't have offered this place to you. It's really rough and I'm worried whether you're up to staying this far out on your own. This isn't some romantic getaway. You can't pick up the phone and order room service. I care about you but I'm not going to be able to be at your beck and call. I'm going out of town soon and I won't be here to look out after you."

"I'm not asking you to," she replied defensively. Though in her heart, that was exactly what she hoped for.

"This part of western North Carolina has high mountains, small towns, and a lot of wilderness in between. Your cell phone is unreliable if you have an emergency. If you get a lot of rain you'll need a four-wheel drive to get out. You're probably stuck right now. And what are you going to do if the power goes out? It gets cold up here. Do you even know how to start a fire?"

"I was a Girl Scout. And I've got matches."

Belle's hand slid to her head and she scratched. "Can you shoot?"

Mia laughed lightly. "A gun? Good God, no."

"It'd be better if you did. What are you going to do if some animal comes knockin' on your door?"

"Human or other?"

"I'm serious. I'm not just talking about little raccoons. There are bears and venomous snakes to deal with. Maybe a sick or rabid animal. They're dangerous and you've got to know how to recognize them and deal with them. And you have to know your way around. You can get lost in these mountains and no one would know."

"Are you trying to scare me?"

"I'm trying to tell you what's real up here. Nature isn't always pretty. It can be damned heartless."

Mia's heart began pounding as a knot of pressure caused her throat to tighten. "I know about cruel and heartless."

Belle shook her head and looked at her boots. "Shit. Mia, I didn't mean that."

"I know what you meant." She hated the tears that were welling in her eyes. "Belle, I know I'm not a mountain woman—far from it. I've got a lot to learn. But hey. You called me a survivor. Doesn't that count for something?"

"Mia, it does. Of course. But be realistic."

"I am. My reality is pretty harsh. I'm thirty-eight and I've lost my left breast, my hair, my job, and my husband. I haven't any money to rent a place. This is my only chance! I have to stay. Belle, I have to find out what the hell I'm surviving for."

She was embarrassed for the flash of pain in her eyes that compelled Belle to turn away. She lowered her tone but her voice still trembled. "So much has happened so fast I haven't had a chance to make sense of what's happened to my body . . . to *me*. A survivor? I've never felt so lost or afraid. But I'm more afraid of going back home than anything I might face here."

Belle shifted her weight and crossed her arms in thought. Mia knew that as a guide Belle took inexperienced men and women into the wild every day. She'd seen some pretty stupid things damn near get folks killed, and it made her cautious. Mia also knew that Belle saw her as weakened, damaged. It would be against her nature to leave someone wounded and inexperienced alone in the wilderness. Yet Belle had witnessed the courage of the survivors at the retreat.

"Please, Belle. Let me stay."

Belle looked at the rain splattering the glass. When she turned again to Mia, she saw that the woman's mind was made up.

"You'll have to return home someday, you know. You can't hide out here forever."

Mia took a breath, unaware that she'd been holding it. "Even Sleeping Beauty had to wake up sometime."

Belle returned a commiserating smile. "This is a far cry from a palace. But it's a start." She took a deep breath, resigned to her decision. She leaned against the table and uncrossed her arms. "Mia, I inherited the cabin only last winter after my mother died. Like I said, she and my grandmother had a falling out and didn't communicate, not once in my lifetime, so I never came up here, never saw the place." She stopped. "Truth is, I never wanted to come." She pursed her lips, holding in words.

"After the funeral I got the deed and the keys," Belle continued, her dark gaze sweeping again the cabin. "I felt duty bound to take a look. It gets pretty cold up here in the winter. The roads were icing up and I didn't spend much time. It was really nothing more than a walk-through. Maybe it was grief that blinded me, I don't know, but it didn't look so bad back then. My plan was to clean it up this summer, maybe get the place rewired, make a few improvements, and add that water heater. Get it ready before the fall hunting and fishing season kicked in. Then I figured I'd rent it." Belle looked at her boots. "But I don't have money to pour into it and I'll be in Scotland most of the summer."

"But that's our deal. I'll clean it for you in exchange for rent."

"I think I'm getting the better end of the deal." ·

"Doesn't matter. You're a lifesaver. And I'm a hard worker. I'll get it done." She smirked. "Even that old stove."

Belle whistled softly, acknowledging the battle that task would be. She walked over to the box and pulled out a bottle of white wine. "You're going to need this."

"Bless you."

Next she took out a down blanket, fresh sheets, several candles, a big bar of soap, white towels, rolls of bathroom tissue, and lastly a bag from a fast-food restaurant. The scent of greasy French fries and hot coffee wafted into the air. When she was done she turned to Mia, studying her again.

"This isn't some wager, Mia. You don't have to prove

anything to me. I don't want you to think you're failing if you decide it isn't working for you up here."

"I won't," she said, and felt enormously grateful.

"Tell you what, friend. Let's take it a week at a time. No commitments. You might get antsy up here all alone, or come face-to-face with a bear and commence running."

Mia chuckled softly. "I just might. Week by week it is."

"And you know I have to rent it in the fall," she said in warning. "If you want to stay longer, it'll cost you."

"One summer," Mia agreed. "Right now, that feels like a lifetime."

Before leaving, Belle helped Mia put the fresh sheets on the bed and lit a roaring fire that warmed the cabin and took the edge off the stark sense of isolation. Belle also gave her a local map of Asheville and its surrounding areas and marked the location of the cabin with a big X. Then she drew the unmarked road that would lead her from the cabin to Watkins Mill, the nearest town.

Belle turned at the door and hugged Mia fiercely. "I care about you, kiddo. Fighting demons is all fine and good. But sometimes you just have to have a good time. Be good to yourself up here. And remember. Trout live in beautiful places."

Chapter Two

The river has taught me to listen; you will
learn from it, too. The river knows everything; one can learn everything from it. You
have already learned from the river that it is
good to strive downwards, to sink, to seek
the depths.

HERMANN HESSE, *SIDDHARTHA*

Night falls heavy in the mountains. Once settled, the darkness has a presence that is palpable.

Mia sat on the ancient velvet sofa, wrapped in
a wool blanket that smelled of must and smoke. She
should have fallen asleep in exhaustion, yet her mind
would not rest. It kept traveling over the same rugged
terrain of memories, carrying her, an unwilling passenger, along.

It was a dank night and the old cabin was cob-
webbed and filthy, more fit for bear than human. Across
from her the logs smoldered in the fireplace. She idly
stoked the embers and watched the flames lick and
snap at the wood. Mia was acutely aware that she was
utterly alone, without a telephone, television, radio, or

any man-made distraction to deflect the night's power. She felt an overwhelming loneliness. It was so strong it felt like a sickness. It made her head pound and her body shiver, no matter how tight her thin arms held the blanket around her shoulders.

Perhaps Belle was right after all, she thought. What was she doing here? Was she clutching to some romantic notion of a cabin in the woods? Of being alone in the mountains so she could sort out her life? But that was just it—*she was alone in the mountains.* Be careful what you wish for, she chided herself. This wasn't some silly notion any longer. It was all very real. The dust and dark were real. The hoots and snaps and rustlings outside the window were real. No one would come running if she called for help. The power could go out at any moment, and then what would she do?

Outside the wind continued to blow and the hovering trees scraped their branches against the glass, like bony fingers tapping to get in. Her mind started playing tricks on her and she wondered wildly if that tapping wasn't a tree, but a bear . . . or a man? She'd read *Deliverance.* She knew what could happen in the wild of these mountains where men with bad teeth and worse lineage roamed. Three eerie, mournful hoots of an owl broke the silence, ending with a catlike snarl.

The last time she was in the mountains she was at the retreat with eighteen other women. There had been comfort in camaraderie. Here, the blackness outside felt too big, the unknown too threatening. Blood drumming in her ears, Mia jumped up to close and lock each of the windows, then tugged the thin curtains shut.

She crossed the creaking floor to the kitchen. The old wood stove was a hulking beast in the corner. She skirted around it and commenced opening the drawers, her spirits sinking further at the mice droppings and medieval-looking kitchen appliances she found. She pulled out a ten-inch carving knife with a thick, wooden handle. It was heavy—probably used to skin a bear—but it made a very serious weapon. She carried it with her as she checked again the lock on the front door, and then for good measure wedged a chair under the door handle.

In the bedroom she repeated the ritual. As she tugged closed the wafer-thin curtains, a large, black spider crawled out from the corner, scurrying across the pane. Mia screamed and ran across the room to stare back, frozen, knife at the ready. She was terrified of spiders. Where was Charles? she thought wildly. He was the one she'd call now to be the hunter and catch his prey.

He was gone, she told herself. There was no one to call. Up here, there was only her. She clenched the knife at her side and willed her heartbeat to steady. There was no way she was going to be able to sleep with a spider crawling over her head. Mia prowled the cabin and found a broom. Rolling it in her hands, she mustered her courage. In her mind the spider had grown to a big, hairy tarantula lying in wait behind the curtains. With shaky hands, she stuck out the broom and moved back the curtain. The spider was gone. Cursing, she shook out all the bed linens, poked the cobwebs from each window, then got on her knees, dust rising as she swept under the bed. The spider had disappeared.

The wind gusted outside, rattling the windows. It sounded to her like the cabin was laughing at her. With a resigned sigh, she set the broom against the wall beside the bed. She undressed quickly and pulled on a pair of thick flannel pajamas. Weary, she sat on the mattress, surprised at how soft and comfortable it was. Good for you, Mountain Woman, she thought, relishing the first real comfort she'd felt that day.

The bottoms of her socks were sooty from the floor. She hated wearing dirty clothes, but it was so damp and cold in the cabin, and her toes felt like ice. So she rammed her feet under the fresh sheets and pulled the down blanket high up around her ears. The pillow was lumpy but Belle's linen smelled of fabric softener. Lumpy or musty, it didn't matter to her. This bed held no memories of her marriage. She lifted her head once more to check that the knife was on the small bedside table. She kept the light on. Then she lowered her head and clutched the pillow, grasping small comforts where she could find them.

Mia lay with her eyes wide open. The wind whistled and she tensed at every snap and crackle from the fire. She was sure she heard something small rustling in the other room. Whatever it was, she wasn't going after it.

Time passed and the rain slackened. Mia lay awake, clutching her blanket close to her neck. Every time her lids grew heavy she saw Charles again and snapped them open. No matter how she tried to train her mind on something else—anything else—the memory pushed itself back, forcing her to see again the painful images. The branch tapping on the window was like a finger tapping on her shoulder—*remember, remember, remember.* Tired and beaten by despair, Mia fell into her memories.

Just yesterday she had been standing in the river with Belle, bubbling over with joy and hope for the future after catching her first trout. Mia didn't want to wait to share her joy with Charles, the man whom she'd thought would stand by her through the long years of recovery. She decided to leave the retreat early. She woke and drove straight from Asheville to Charleston. It was Monday morning and Charles would be at his desk at the firm he'd joined directly from law school.

While driving she thought of how they'd shared some lean times in the early days of their marriage. But they were so happy they didn't seem to notice. Spare dimes went for a bottle of wine or a movie. Sometimes he'd surprised her with a bunch of daisies when he returned from work. She'd told him daisies were her favorite flower, knowing they were cheap. So she'd picked up a bunch of daisies from a street vendor en route. She planned to shower, primp, and then surprise him for lunch.

It was she who was surprised when she saw his car in the driveway at home. Instinct flared, warning her to call out his name as she normally would when she walked into the house. Yet some inner voice told her to be quiet as she wound her way through the empty living room and up the narrow, carpeted stairs to the bedroom they'd shared for nearly ten years. The bedroom door was closed, and from behind she heard the muffled moans of a man and a woman. Her body tingled with adrenaline. Time slowed and her mind balked at accepting what was already ridiculously obvious. This couldn't be happening to her . . . to them. It was too banal, too much of a cliché.

Her hand shook as she raised it to the paneled door. She gave a single push and with a whisper of air it swung open, revealing by degrees two pairs of feet, long legs entangled, a man's naked form clutching at a pair of scarlet panties riding high along a perfectly tanned and rounded ass.

It was the woman's breasts, however, that riveted her attention. They were creamy white and firm with large, rosy nipples as if from a seventeenth-century painting. She watched as her husband burrowed his face in their softness, groaning, obviously relishing the feast of the woman's perfection. Mia wanted to run but she could not tear her gaze from the woman's breasts. They were so round, so large—and they were real, not some fabrication of silicone inserted beneath the skin.

What hurt the most was that Charles had not merely cheated on her, but he had chosen a woman with beautiful, unscarred, perfect breasts.

"It's not what you think," he blurted out when he finally sensed someone watching. He'd startled at the sight of the tall, waiflike figure standing at the bedroom door, expressionless, her arms limp at her sides, a bunch of daisies dangling from her fingers.

"In three more minutes it would have been exactly what I think," she replied in a calm voice that belied the shaking in her gut.

Charles tossed the sheets over the woman's nakedness. The woman's long, black hair cascaded over her shoulders as she raised herself on one elbow. A rosy tint spread across her cheeks and breasts, like dawn on the mountains.

He rose from the bed, unconcerned with his own nakedness. Her gaze dropped to his flagging erection pointing outward like a drawn sword. She turned away in disgust.

"Mia, wait—"

"Get away from me!" She threw the daisies at him, then turned and ran down the stairs. She was shaking violently now, feeling the bile rising in her throat. All she wanted now was to save some shred of her dignity and get away.

In her haste, she tripped over Charles's golf clubs, catching herself on the fender of his BMW before hitting the garage floor. The titanium clubs were Charles's pride and joy. They'd cost a fortune and he used them only when he wanted to impress someone. He used to joke that in case of a fire he'd have a hard time choosing whether to save her or the clubs. A fulcrum of fury whipped through her, crazy and irrational. She picked up the golf bag and dragged the clubs across the floor to toss them into her trunk. It was senseless but she had to take something precious away from him, as he had ripped away something precious from her. The clubs landed with a satisfying crash. She drove off just as Charles came trotting barefoot from the house, calling her name and tying the sash around his robe. She could still hear his voice calling her name.

Mia pushed back the covers, rising up from the mattress and gasping for air. Her heart was beating wildly. She climbed from the bed and paced the room, pushing her palms flat against her feverish face. The memory of Charles's betrayal burned so hot that her body was sweaty. She felt nauseous and dizzy. Oh God, she thought. Her face felt like peach fuzz. Was she going to faint?

She went to the bathroom, splashed icy water on her face, then held on tight to the rim of the porcelain sink and took deep, calming breaths. No, no, no, she thought, exhaling slowly. She knew what this was. This was not a heart attack. This was what it felt like to have your heart broken.

Gradually her breathing came back to normal. Mia slowly rose and pushed back her damp hair from her forehead. Wake up, she told herself, looking at her pale face in the mirror. Charles was not the good husband, always by her side during each step of her cancer recovery. Why had she convinced herself that he was? Was it easier for her to make excuses for him than to face the truth?

Mia pushed her hair from her face, determined not to think about him. She needed to set her mind on something else. Her socks shuffled across the dusty floors to the bookcase. She pulled out the first book she touched: *The Awakening* by Kate Chopin. Books had always been a comfort to her and this one was an old friend. She carried the slim volume back to the black iron bed, depending on the words to be her solace through the long, lonely hours till dawn. Outside the cabin, the rain was still coming down but the thunder had retreated to a soft rumbling in the distance. The storm was passing.

Mia fought sleep, reading until her eyes grew heavy and the words blurred on the page. It was very late when she relinquished and closed the book. She set it beside the knife and the diminutive, milky white lamp on the table. Behind it rested the wood-poled broom. They were a pitiful arsenal against the terrors of the night. Before turning out the light, she looked across the bedroom. The walls, the iron bed, the mirror, every splinter of wood felt hostile. Belle had told her that she was the first to sleep in this house in many years. She couldn't shake the feeling that she was invading a private space. Yet Belle had given her permission to stay.

Then she thought again of the woman who had lived here before, the woman who brought fine things to the wilderness, who chose isolation as Mia had, whose room this once was. This woman had not granted permission for a stranger to stay in her home. So Mia offered the same words that she'd said to Belle, saying them aloud for no reason she could articulate.

"Please. Let me stay."

A soft breeze fluttered the curtains, though the windows were closed. Mia's breath hitched and she closed her eyes tight and burrowed deep under the covers. Enveloped in the scent of cedar, caught in the eddy of memories, she knew that sleep would not come easily.

Mia woke to the piercing light that poured in through the narrow slit between the curtains. Her body was sweaty under the blankets and, kicking them off, the heat from the closed room felt like an oven. She turned to her side, tucking her clasped hands beneath her cheek, feeling the remnants of her bleak despair. It had been an arduous night of tossing and turning in the stifling room. She'd been haunted not by some woman's ghost, but by memories of Charles and her during happier times. It felt like he was dead, only worse. She grieved the loss of all the trust and love they'd shared for nearly ten years. To have that relationship cut off so quickly, so cruelly, left her bleeding. She felt the pain like a phantom limb.

Awakening fully, she slowly rose and shuffled into

the main room. The hems of her flannel pajamas dragged a trail in the dust. The fire had died and the scent of cold ashes lay heavy in the air. This little cabin—a living room, a bedroom on the left, a narrow kitchen and eating area on the right, an upstairs room—would be her home for the next few months. Pale light attempted to pierce the yellowed, gauzy curtains at the windows, giving the room an aura of gloom. She unlocked one of the windows and pushed hard. The old wood rattled up the frame.

Immediately she heard the soothing sound of rushing water. A soft breeze that felt like liquid cooled the perspiration from her body. The rain had stopped, the birds were chattering noisily in the trees, and the earth was green and ripe. Why, she wondered, couldn't she feel the newness of the day?

Restless, Mia began to prowl. In the kitchen she eyed the farm sink balanced on wobbly pipe legs. She imagined calloused hands expertly wielding a filet knife, separating sweet meat from guts, heads, and bones. She shuddered at the thought. How long had it been since water flowed through these old pipes? With a firm yank, she turned the faucet. The old pump moaned and clunked loudly. She took two steps back, ready to bolt to safety if it blew. With a slow hiss the pipes released a trickle of water the color of fish blood. She waited, watching, till it changed to a clear flow. She splashed some water on her face, gasping at its iciness. Then she tentatively tasted the spring water. It was cold and delicious. She drank her fill and ate the remains of a health bar she'd found at the bottom of her purse.

The rough-hewn cabinets held a miserly group of dented pots, a heavy cast-iron frying pan, chipped, brown pottery dishes, and mismatched silverware. It was a depressing collection. The neglect of a room as personal to a woman as a kitchen signaled that whoever had lived here had long since given up caring.

Wiping the dust from her hands, Mia glanced at her watch. Her stomach was rumbling and the faint caffeine headache in her temples told her it was time to stop snooping and head to town for supplies.

She dressed quickly in jeans and a wrinkled cotton sweater pulled out from her small, black suitcase. After washing she dried her face, catching her reflection in the small mirror over the sink. Mia avoided looking at her reflection. It was deeply unsettling because she no longer recognized the woman staring back at her.

Only a year ago Mia Landan was a tanned, sophisticated, and well-dressed young professional in Charleston. She was never seen in public without her hair and makeup done. She had a dancer's body with long, slender arms and legs and a swan's neck. With her hair upswept and pearls, she used to imagine herself a young Grace Kelly.

The woman staring back at her now was gaunt and pale, like she'd not seen the sun in months. After chemo, her straight blond hair had grown back reddish blond and curly. She reached out to run her hands through the unruly wisps floating around her head. She liked the color—so full of fire and life. She didn't have the heart to cut it so the curls stuck out from her head in different lengths. Her heart-shaped face ended with a deeply dimpled chin under full lips.

She looked at her face dispassionately. In PR it was her job to sum up people quickly. She thought she looked like a scarecrow after being hit by a bolt of lightning.

Mia turned from the mirror and flicked off the light. Then, grabbing her purse, she headed outside. She came to an abrupt stop on the front porch. Last night the darkness had cloaked her surroundings. Looking out in the early morning light, she was struck with the magnificence of the landscape.

The cabin was sheltered by a mountain ridge to one side covered with tall trees and lush vegetation in every shade of green imaginable. Yards away the river cascaded over white rocks, tumbling in its mellifluous music into a deep, bluish green pool.

Belle had told her this area was called Watkins Cove. Mia had said that she'd thought a cove was a bay in a body of water. Belle explained that a cove was also a sheltered recess in a mountainside. "Both," she'd told her with meaning, "were protected areas of refuge."

Beyond those mountains, farther to the east then down south to the coast, the city of Charleston was just awakening. She saw in her mind's eye the narrow, charming streets; historic buildings; and spired churches that made up the city of her birth. Charleston was for her like a sophisticated, sweet-scented great-aunt, one who was never without her pearl necklace, attended church services regularly, knew her place in society, and dutifully performed the responsibilities that position demanded. Mia was grateful for the culture and refinement that she'd learned from her. Yet sometimes, especially when times were hard and her obligatory smile was brittle, she chafed under the expectations she felt, mostly from within herself.

Here in the mountains, she felt free. No one had any expectations of her, and in turn that liberated her to explore desires sprung from deep within herself. She felt grounded here in the rich, loamy earth. By the sea she'd felt as unfixed as the sand. Charleston had always been her home, but she was beginning to wonder if the historic city should be her home in the future.

Regardless of her decision, she would have to return to Charleston at summer's end. Mia leaned against the porch railing, lifting her face, and breathed deep. She felt the freshness swirl through her veins and sweep the staleness from her body in one long exhale. This small pocket in the mountains would shelter her while she healed.

The journey to Watkins Mill was no better or worse than she'd expected. The countryside was green and lush after the rain. She passed small farmhouses with tidy gardens and a dog or a goat standing near; open fields dotted with grazing horses or steers; and imposing new log homes peeking out from mountain ridges. The road twisted and turned, yet Belle was right that the trip to town would be quick. Before long she reached a paved road that led to the small town nestled in the mountains. At first glance, she thought it looked like a town that time forgot.

Mia parked her car in a small lot in front of the old train depot. It was a charming wood building with a flared roof; wide, overhanging eaves; and big barrels of flowers along the walkway. From signs on the building she learned that the once popular train had ceased service years earlier, but the town had revitalized the station and it was now the home of the historical society.

Main Street made up most of the town's shopping area and was only a few blocks long. The train depot sat at one end of a long stretch of compact, one. and two-story buildings of red and yellow brick. A spired church sat at the other. In between, cheerful awnings interspersed with trees spread out over the sidewalk, and beneath them sat more barrels of colorful geraniums and bright green, chubby shrubs. It was, she thought with a stab, the kind of town that she and Charles used to love to visit together on a weekend holiday.

Belle had told her that the townspeople were a friendly group, close-knit and reliable. Most of them had grown up in Watkins Mill, as had their parents and grandparents. So they knew just about every intimate detail about one another. More than likely, Belle teased, they were hungry for some fresh gossip.

Mia felt battered and raw inside, incapable of small talk. She wanted nothing more than to be invisible as she slipped through town and gathered her supplies. Ducking her head, she began walking briskly along the sidewalk. She passed a library, the town hall, and a restaurant. When she passed a women's clothing store, she thought about her small, black suitcase at the cabin packed only with the few clothes she'd needed for a three-day fly-fishing retreat. She grimaced and thought she would have to buy some more.

There was a time not long ago that she relished the chance to shop for new clothes or browse through an antique store. Her closet at home held several fine wool suits and crisp white blouses that had looked good on her tall, lean body. There were shelves of silk tops, and neatly stacked boxes each filled with designer shoes, her one extravagance. They didn't have much cash flow and she didn't desire jewelry like so many of her friends did. She was satisfied with her channel set diamond wedding band—by agreement there had been no engagement ring—diamond studs in her ears, and the pearl necklace that Charles had given to her on their first wedding anniversary. They were lovely, lustrous Mikimotos in graduating sizes. The double strands were still in her jewelry box on top of her dresser.

She looked at the mannequin in the window wearing a pleated tan skirt and an unremarkable cotton blouse, then walked on. Clothes or her looks no longer captured her attention. She'd buy what she needed later, when she had to.

The scents of freshly baked bread, cinnamon, and coffee lured her to a small restaurant bakery. A big chalkboard on an easel in front announced the day's specials. Today's was cinnamon rolls. A little bell over the door chimed when she walked in.

"Be right with you!" The bobbing blond head below the counter rose up to smile perfunctorily toward the door. The head was attached to a robust, middle-aged woman in a pale pink uniform bursting at the buttons against her hourglass figure. Her face was pretty, pink-cheeked, and friendly, but her spectacular blue eyes that sparkled with life drew Mia's attention.

"Welcome to Shaffer's," she said with the drawl of the North Carolina mountains. "What can I do for you?"

Mia's hungry gaze devoured the rows of freshly baked doughnuts and pastries in the glass display case. There was another long glass case behind it to form an L down the restaurant, and this one was filled with all kinds of bread, cakes, pies, and cookies. Her knees almost buckled at the smell of hot coffee brewing.

"Do you take credit?" she asked.

The woman scoffed. "Cash only, I'm afraid."

Mia nodded, painfully aware that she only had a few singles in her purse. She glanced up and checked the price of coffee.

"I'll have a cup of black coffee, please. Large." Her fingers danced on the glass as she tried to choose. "I'll have a plain doughnut," she said, pointing. "No, wait. Make that a cinnamon roll."

A knowing grin stretched across the woman's face. "You sure about that?"

Mia returned a hesitant grin. "They all look so good."

"Looks like you can afford to fatten up a little, sugar," she said, grabbing the metal tongs and pulling out the pastry. "Not me. I eat one and it goes straight to my hips and stays there. Will that be for here?"

Mia looked to several small tables covered in pink and white checked tablecloths. "Yes, thank you."

The woman put the pastry on a plate and poured the coffee in a thick white mug. "That'll be two sixty."

Mia took out her wallet and carefully laid out three dollars. She reflected on her state of mind when she fled her home yesterday. She hadn't even realized she had almost no money in her wallet. "Is there an ATM nearby?"

"Over at the bank. Turn right when you leave here and it'll be at the end of the block. You can't miss it. Here you go . . ." She paused before calling her *sugar* again. "What's your name?"

She hesitated. "Mia."

"You visiting our little town, Mia?"

"Yes." She glanced down at the name tag that was pinned to the woman's chest like a billboard on a mountain. "Becky," she replied, taking her coffee and pastry and moving over to the table. She picked up the local real estate brochure from a pile by the door and began leafing through it to discourage Becky from asking more questions. Becky went back to polishing the glass, and Mia knew she was being sized up as just another tourist with dreams of owning a cabin in the mountains.

Mia bit into the pastry and her eyes closed with pleasure. It was so delicious and the coffee so hot and rich Mia almost purred as she lapped it up. She hadn't realized how hungry she was.

"They're addictive," Becky said from the counter.

Mia looked up to see Becky smiling. "I bake 'em fresh every morning." She patted her belly. "Skipper doesn't care, though. Says there's more of me to love." She laughed again and polished more glass. "Come on back tomorrow morning. I'm making custard doughnuts. I open at seven sharp. I have to be ready for the anglers before they head out. They like their coffee hot and their pastries sweet. You know, I've got a little post office in the back," she said, pointing to a small counter. "You can do your mailing here. You staying in town?"

"No, I'm up the road a bit."

"Renting? Or do you own the place? Lots of new homes sprouting up on these mountains."

"Renting," she replied, looking again at her magazine. She hoped the woman would catch the hint. But it was clear Becky was interested in small talk. Mia suspected that this coffee shop with a post office in the back was the hub for news in the small town.

"I'll bet you're renting the Murphy place," Becky

continued. "That's a fine old house. In need of some fixing up. Mostly cosmetic, though. I heard they were putting it up for rent. Maybe for sale. It would be a good buy."

"No. I don't know the house."

Becky mulled this over, then shifted her weight and asked, "So where *are* you staying?"

"Actually, I'm staying at the cabin of a friend."

"Oh. Who's that?"

"Belle Carson."

Becky idly polished the glass counter, her lips pursed like she was sucking a sour candy. "Name sounds familiar. Is she from these parts?"

"She lives in Asheville, so . . ." Mia wiped her fingers with the tiny paper napkin and rose to leave.

"Don't forget about those custard doughnuts. I'll put your name on one," Becky called out in her friendly manner. Mia waved, then headed out the door, the little bell ringing as she left.

A few cars slowly passed, and a young couple with two children prancing at their heels eagerly entered Shaffer's. Mia smiled to herself when she heard the bell chime and Becky's hearty hail.

Next door, the hardware store was a sharp contrast to the cheery, feminine pink of Shaffer's. This was a male bastion filled with utilitarian steel shelves overflowing with cardboard boxes, tools large and small, and rows and rows of plastic bins filled with nuts and bolts and nails and God only knew what else. She wrinkled her nose as she passed; the smell of dust and motor oil was pervasive. She would make a stop here later in the week.

A few stores farther down, Mia stopped before a small shop that carried an eclectic selection of stationery, crafts, paintings, and handcrafted jewelry by local artists. What caught her eye was a sign: *We carry a full line of art supplies.*

Mia felt a long-buried love of painting tugging at her. She had been an art major in college and had painted a lot then, fearlessly experimenting with different styles and mediums. After she graduated she found a job, then got married, and she never found time to paint. Since her breast cancer surgery, however, she had been looking to do something creative in her life. The myriad blues and greens of the river and the quality of fractured light on water had her itching to pick up a brush. If the river could elicit some spark again . . .

Mia pushed open the door and stepped into the smell of perfumed candles and oils. She walked through the aisle letting her fingertips run across brushes, tubes of paint, and canvases, not really knowing what she wanted but finding the textures soothing. A young woman about Mia's age approached her. She was tall and slender, like Mia, and as pale as milk. Her white blond hair floated around her head like a nimbus.

"Hello," she said, smiling in welcome. "I'm Maeve MacBride. Can I help you?"

Mia's eyes scanned the long shelf filled with tubes of paint. "I don't know where to start."

"Well, what's your medium?"

"It's been a long time."

Maeve sensed her hesitation. "Watercolors would be a good place to start. They're not as toxic as oils."

"Perfect," Mia replied, leaping at this. After her cancer treatment, anything toxic was an anathema.

It turned out Maeve was the owner of the quaint shop. She helped Mia choose a Sennelier starter kit of small squares of color, brushes, and a block of thick watercolor paper. Mia gathered her bundle, cradled it under her arm, and left the shop feeling the first stirrings of possibilities.

Next door was a twin redbrick building that housed the grocer. It looked like the kind of grocery store she'd walked through with her mother in Charleston as a child. Local produce was arranged in big baskets at the front, a butcher in a stained white apron worked in the back, and in between were narrow aisles with original wood shelving carrying everything from salad dressing and cereal to fishing poles and bait.

Becky was standing near the entrance, leaning against a little pushcart that held two paper bags of groceries. She was talking in the manner of old friends to a stout woman in a greengrocer's apron. They looked up when she approached and from the look in their eyes, Mia guessed that she was the topic of conversation.

"Hey there, Mia," Becky called out as if they, too, were old friends. She waved her over. "Come meet Flossie," she said, indicating the woman beside her.

Flossie was middle-aged and plain with a pale, flat face and small, thoughtful eyes. Her graying blond hair was pulled back into a ponytail as though in afterthought. Yet when she smiled the lines at her eyes made her face appear warm and wise. She was clearly someone's mother, someone's aunt, someone's friend. The kind of woman who would wrap solid arms around you in a hug, knowing when you needed one.

"I'm Flossie Barbieri," she informed Mia. "I own this place, or my parents do. They're retired but can't let go of it, if you know what I mean. Everyone just knows the store as Rodale's, which is my maiden name."

"Nice to meet you," Mia replied, and began walking away. "Oh," she said, turning to Flossie. "Do you take credit?"

"I prefer cash when I can get it, but I'll take your credit, too."

She was careful, buying only what she thought she needed for a few days. It must be hard to make a go of a family-run store, she thought, when farther down the road a giant supermarket with flowers and wine selections offered many more choices, and at a cheaper price. She preferred the smaller store and the slower pace. She felt far removed from the city, not just in miles but in years.

As she wheeled her cart toward the checkout, she heard Becky's voice calling her name. Mia warily turned to see Becky waving and using the pushcart as a walker. Her legs moved awkwardly and she leaned heavily against it. Flossie was a step behind her.

"I knew I'd heard that name before! Belle Carson, you said, right?" Becky was breathless from the exertion and her eyes were bright. She brought a hand to her chest as she caught her breath. "Belle is such a pretty name, not one you'd likely forget."

Mia waited with an increasing sense of dread.

"She owns some fishing business in Asheville, that right?"

Mia nodded.

"Yep, that'll be her," Becky said to Flossie, nodding her head in affirmation.

"I knew I was right," agreed Flossie.

An old woman with a floral triangle scarf over snowy white hair walked up to them, already a part of the conversation. "Carson, you say? I remember that name. I went to school with a Carson. Isn't she the one that up and left town soon after she graduated? Ran off to get married. Surprised some, but not me. I'm older than you so you wouldn't remember. What was her first name?" She tapped the cheek of her wizened face. "Theo . . . Theodosia something?"

"Theodora," Flossie replied, and the old woman's eyes shifted from puzzlement to recognition. "She was a friend of my mother's, or as much of a friend as anyone could be stuck out there in that ol' cabin far from anything. My mama still says how she feels badly that she didn't go out there more often to pay a visit. But it was such a dark place. Not welcoming."

"I guess it's no wonder, with what her mama done," added the old woman.

"What did her mother do?" asked Mia, suddenly interested.

"She killed her lover, that's what. Some say she done it right in that cabin," replied Flossie.

"Theodora killed her lover?" Mia asked, struggling to get the story straight.

Becky shook her head. "No, her mother, Kate Watkins, did. She's the woman who lived in the cabin. The one you're staying at."

Flossie sighed with agreement. "Theo quit the place when she got the chance. Never came back, not once in all these years. Not that I blame her none."

"Belle Carson," the old woman said, rolling the name on her tongue. "She must be Theodora's child."

"That'll be the one," Becky said with authority. Then she turned to look again at Mia, her face filled with wonder. "So she's gone ahead and opened up her grandmother's cabin, has she?"

The old woman said softly, "I was of a mind that place should be left closed up."

Flossie nodded. "Let the spirits rest."

The three women turned their attention to Mia, looking at her with renewed speculation. Mia was unnerved and felt that old tingling on the back of her neck.

Flossie's eyes glowed from deep in her cheeks. "Imagine. Kate Watkins's place is opened up. And you're staying in that cabin *alone*?"

Chapter Three

Fly-fishing starts with paying attention. It's about being a good observer.

—BELLE CARSON

Mia sat on a bench at a scenic overlook on the outskirts of Watkins Mill. It was a spit of land just off a narrow road that afforded a breathtaking view of the mountains beyond. The vista seemed to go on clear to the ocean where her sister, Madeline, lived on John's Island. She had a comfortable marriage with Don, a professor at the college, and their teenage children: a son and a daughter. Mia always thought that Madeline should have had more children. It might have redirected some of Maddie's worry from her. Her sister had been more a mother than a sister since their mother had died of breast cancer when Mia was thirteen. Once Mia's cancer was diagnosed, Maddie had rarely left her side.

It had been her sister and not her husband who had taken time off from her job to go with Mia to each chemo cocktail party. It was Maddie, not Charles, who held her hand in the sick green hospital room while the nurses poked her veins. Maddie who bore Mia's complaints and who took her to an upscale wig shop when her hair fell out. Big sister Maddie had watched over her as an adult with her cancer just as she had when she was a child and skinned her knee. It was always Maddie.

Mia leaned back against the creaky wooden bench and dialed the number she knew by heart. She said a quick prayer of relief that there was phone service here.

"Mia!" Madeline screamed with relief when she heard Mia's voice on the phone. "Oh my God, where are you? I've been so worried!"

"I'm fine," she replied, feeling guilt for causing her sister worry. "I'm in North Carolina. I came home after the retreat but I turned around when . . . I drove right back." She paused, then blurted out, "Maddie, I found Charles in bed with another woman."

Shocked, Maddie launched into a long tirade against Charles and how she couldn't believe the no-count scum could be so heartless and underhanded. Mia let her carry on, feeling a vicarious pleasure at hearing her husband so vilified.

"Where are you now?" Maddie wanted to know.

"I'm staying at the cabin of a friend."

"I can understand you needing to escape but it's not healthy for you to hide out too long. When are you coming back?"

"I don't know."

"What do you mean, you don't know?" Her voice rang with worry, a tone Mia had heard many times before.

"I just don't know," Mia said again. "I only know that I can't come back now."

"OK, well." She paused. "I'll come up there with you."

"No. Please don't."

"Why not? You don't want me to come?"

"Not yet. I just need to be alone for a while."

"Oh." She sounded hurt.

"Maddie—"

"It's just that I'd think you'd need your friends now."

"My friends? What friends? Most of them disappeared the minute they caught the first whiff of cancer."

"That's not fair. They're just afraid."

"Afraid of what? Me?"

"No. Some people just don't know what to do when someone they care about gets cancer. Watching you deal with it makes it real. If it can happen to you it can happen to them."

"Do you know what the survivors at the retreat called friends like that? Tupperware friends."

"I don't get it."

"Because when they hear you have cancer they cook up a sympathy meal and bring it over in a Tupperware dish. By the time you eat the food, wash the dish, and try to return it, they're long gone. You never see them again."

"I hope you don't include me in that group."

"Never, Maddie. Not even once. I'll always need you. You're my sister."

"I have to tell you something. Sometimes I feel you cut me off, too."

"How?"

"You don't confide in me."

"Yes, I do. All the time."

"For little things, yes. But not in the things that really matter. Mia, don't you trust me?"

Mia paused, acknowledging that what her sister said was true. "It's not that I don't trust you."

"Then why?"

Mia looked out to the vista beyond the short stone wall that bordered the overlook. Her eye was drawn to the broad horizon of rugged mountains covered with rich forest.

"Maddie, it's not you. It's me. No matter how hard I try to explain, I know you could never understand what I'm going through. I know you love me, but you can't fix this. Being at the retreat with the other women made me realize only I can fix my life." She laughed softly. "Even though I would love for you to fix it all and make it better. I want to try to make it up here on my own. Just give me a little time. Please."

Madeline tsked in frustration, unable to let the bone drop. "Just because that ass of a husband of yours couldn't keep his family business in his pants doesn't mean that you have to run off and leave your life in tatters. Let him hightail it to the mountains. He's the one at fault here. My God, he abandoned you while you're going through all your cancer and—"

"Maddie, I see this as my first real step out from

that darkness. I just need time to think." She paused and stretched out her long legs in the grass. "You know, for a long time I didn't think about . . . well, anything. I just reeled from disaster to disaster. I blamed it on chemo brain, but in truth, I just couldn't face what had happened to me. When I was at the retreat, it helped me stop and reflect. Thank you, by the way."

"For what?"

"For arranging for me to go."

"You mean for nagging and bullying you to go."

"You're good at that." After they chuckled, Mia continued. "It was so much more than just fishing. We talked about random things. Like what happened to us with the cancer and after, during recovery. Some women never got any counseling at all. Not even about medical problems." She paused, seeing in her mind's eye the women seated in a circle, tired but flushed with contentment after a day fishing, all feeling the powerful bond forged on the river.

"But the one thing that I was most struck by—I mean it really, profoundly floored me—was when the ladies talked about how, after diagnosis, husbands fell into two extremes. One is the hero. The good guy who stands by you, loves you no matter what, calls you beautiful every day. These women, they're so grateful, so madly in love with their husbands, blushing like girls." She paused. "The other is the one who takes one look at the scene and says adios. Unfortunately, Charles falls into that category. I just refused to see it. I was weak."

"No, you were sick."

Bless her heart, Maddie was always her greatest defender. "OK. I was both; how's that?"

"You sound so blasé about it," Maddie said, her voice indignant. "You should be mad as hell."

"Mad?" Mia took a breath and looked at her wedding ring, its diamonds catching the light. "I'm not mad as much as I'm hurt. Deeply hurt by his betrayal. It was like getting kicked in the gut when I was already sprawled out on the floor."

"Don't sell yourself short. There's a lot waiting for you here at home. People who care about you. A lot of people like you and respect your work. They'd hire you back in PR, or maybe you want to do something else."

Mia winced, feeling again the embarrassment of losing her job. *"Something else."*

"You could. You're young yet."

"Hardly young, Maddie," she replied, feeling ancient. "I've thought about it. My life in Charleston was wrapped up in my life with Charles. I took on his values and goals. His future was my future. Even my job in PR had a lot to do with making contacts for him. All that's changed. My job is gone. My husband is gone. The woman I used to be is gone."

"I happened to like that woman."

"I did too. But I have to find out who I am now."

"Can't you find yourself at home?"

Her gaze drifted again to the valley that stretched below the Blue Ridge Mountains. She couldn't bear to return to Charleston, where the details of her sordid story would be common gossip. One more sad chapter in Mia Landan's tragic life. If she went back to Charleston now, she'd have to endure again the looks of pity and the well-meant, murmured condolences.

"Maddie, what I went through was too profound. I faced my mortality. I can never be the same person. This is my opportunity to find out where I fit in, what I really want to do with my life. For however long or short that life may be."

"Oh, Mia . . ." There was a long silence on the line while Maddie gathered her composure. When she spoke again, the bossy tone was gone. "So, what are you going to do up there all on your lonesome?"

Mia's relieved smile eased across her face. "It is lonely, I grant you that. There isn't any television. The only radio I have is in my car. And believe it or not, I can get phone reception only here in town. But it's a good lonely, if you know what I mean. It'll be sporadic, but I'll call you."

"You'd better. A lot."

"Actually, I'm not really alone after all. Apparently the cabin I'm in is haunted."

"What?"

"I just found out that it belonged to this old mountain woman by the name of Kate Watkins. She was involved in some kind of scandal. They think she murdered her lover."

"Oh, great. That sets my mind at ease."

"It happened decades ago. Anyway, she went to live alone in this cabin for years, barely speaking to anyone.

She had a child. A girl who ran off as soon as she was old enough to get married. Kate stayed on in the cabin alone. She became a real hermit. After she died the cabin was locked up and no one's stayed in it since."

"Sounds like a right cheery place."

"It's not. It's quite gloomy. Filthy, in fact. Terribly neglected. I guess I can understand why Belle never went there."

"Can you blame her? That's quite the sordid family history. How can you stand to stay there alone?"

"Oddly enough, I like it. From what little I know about her, I like Kate, too. And the fact that she murdered her lover is not a negative for me right now. Somehow I can get behind that."

Madeline laughed but her tone turned serious. "Really, Mia, how long do you figure on staying up there?"

"I've agreed to take it week by week. I can come home anytime. But for sure, no later than September. Belle will be putting the place up for rent."

"What are you going to do about Charles?"

"Nothing. Let him do something."

"Do you want him to know where you are?"

Mia thought about that for a moment. Being away from Charles was what she needed most. "No."

"A judge can construe what you're doing as abandonment."

Mia released a bitter laugh. "That's rich." Then she said with resignation, "What does it matter? We have no money to speak of."

"That was my next question."

"Let's just say when I took out a few hundred dollars from the ATM today I practically closed the account. The medical bills continue to run us dry."

"Jesus, Mia! How are you going to live? Do you need some money? I can send you some." Then, with a burst of worry she exclaimed, "Come home. Stay with us for as long as it takes to get your life in order."

"Maddie, that's exactly what I'm doing," she replied, believing it. "One day at a time."

Before she left the overlook, Mia made one more phone call. Her hands trembled as she dialed the number of her home in Charleston. She knew Charles would be at the office. The phone rang four times before the answering machine picked up. The sound of his voice on the recording stung like a slap. She drew in her breath, then tried to speak as calmly as she could.

"Charles, it's Mia. I'm safe. I'm in the mountains. I don't want to talk to you now. Don't worry and don't bother Maddie. I'll call again when I'm able to talk."

Mia closed the phone and let her hand fall into her lap. She leaned far back into the chair, feeling to her marrow the hurt of the broken connection. Crossing her arms she let her gaze wander aimlessly across the greens and blues of the horizon.

The weather had warmed and the afternoon was sunny when she returned to the cabin. Mia gathered her purchases like a general would an army and planned her attack. Then she set to work.

She dragged the carpets outdoors and shook them, sending decades of dust to the winds. She swept up small hills of dust from the floors, then washed them with oil soap till they gleamed. She gagged as she cleaned mouse droppings and dried insect carcasses from the cabinets. Then she scrubbed the wood with disinfectant and hot water boiled on the stove. She boiled more hot water, then washed the tiny gas stove, refrigerator, and all the pots, pans, and dishes, then set them back in the fresh-smelling cabinets. She couldn't scrub away the ancient stains in the toilet and tub, but she was satisfied that they were as clean as they were going to get.

She enjoyed cleaning the cabin. It made her feel more that she belonged here. Seeing her own food in the fridge, flowers on the table, and a few of her own possessions here and there made the place more her own. A wicked smile formed at her lips as she thought of how Charles's fabulously expensive golf clubs turned out to be a worthwhile investment after all. Mia had used a five iron to knock the abandoned swallow nests from under the eaves of the porch and a six iron to smash spiders. The putter made an acceptable poker for stoking the fire. She didn't have a hammer, but she'd discovered that with proper aim, the driver did the job of driving a nail into wood. She was sure she'd find more uses for the other clubs and kept them handy in a corner by the door.

While dusting the fine mahogany and marveling at the magnificently carved stag's head on the armoire, she wondered what memories the old pieces had elicited in Kate as she had polished. She tugged at the brass knobs but they wouldn't budge. She jiggled it again, but the armoire was securely locked.

Mia scanned the room, trying to figure where someone might have hidden a key. Like a child on a treasure hunt, she went from drawer to drawer in the kitchen and through each cabinet and closet. Next she went through the bedroom drawers, pulling open each one and moving her clothing around lest she had missed the key when she had unpacked. Not there. Her fingers tapped the sides of her legs as she glanced around the bedroom. The black iron bed, the maple dresser, the mirror . . . When her gaze fell on the small writing desk beside the window, she spotted a narrow drawer just beneath the desktop's surface that she'd not noticed before. She walked directly to it and tugged at the drawer handle. The wood was slightly swollen and she had to pull hard, but the drawer slid open. Inside was a small brass key.

Feeling like Alice in Wonderland, Mia grabbed the key and hurried back to the armoire. The key slid neatly into place and with a turn of the wrist, the treasure chest opened.

Mia gasped at the finery she found sequestered there. It was like she'd leaped from a world of minimal comforts to one of comparative luxury. Reaching out, she lifted a china plate from a tall stack of at least a dozen. She blew off a coating of dust and lifted the plate to the light. The delicate fronds of a wildflower graced the center and light flowed through the creamy porcelain. Each plate was hand-painted with a different wildflower. Mia grew up in a home where formal dinner parties were common. Her experienced eye knew that this china was priceless. As was the heavy sterling silver tableware, each piece engraved with a bold *KW*. A fine, vintage evening gown of royal blue taffeta hung beside a long, white silk scarf, the kind gentlemen of certain wealth used to wear to formal dinners or to the theater. Again, hardly mountain gear.

Tucked in the back, behind the dress, were two bamboo fishing rods; a battered wicker creel, its leather straps cracked from heavy use; and an old fly-fishing wallet. The brown leather was very soft and supple, and opening it she found over two dozen hand-tied dry flies.

Mia closed the armoire doors at a thoughtful pace and let her hand rest on the wood. Why, it was more a memory chest, she thought. She was beginning to form an image of the woman who once lived in this cabin. She was obviously much more than a common mountain woman of her time—this woman was educated and well born. These items that had seemed so incongruous to a rustic cabin she now saw as a collection of this woman's most precious possessions. Brought, no doubt, from another home. A few personal items that she could not—or would not—live without. Did she marry below her station?

There were no photographs in silver frames, no albums filled with family portraits, no clues of a personal nature. Why wouldn't a woman so sentimental about furniture and china keep a single photograph of a husband . . . a daughter . . . a granddaughter? Mia shook her head, bewildered. The woman was an enigma.

Belle would know more about her, of course, but Mia recalled her reticence, even aversion, at so much as the mention of her grandmother. Still, did Belle know that these treasures were here? If Belle sold them, they could go a long way to paying for the improvements she hoped to make on the cabin.

Night began to fall and darkness descended upon the small cabin. Outside the song of insects began to swell. Mia went from window to window, closing each tight and drawing the shabby curtains to create a safe cocoon. She ate a meager dinner of a rotisserie chicken she'd purchased at Rodale's and a few stalks of celery. Too exhausted to heat water on the stove for a bath, she sat on the edge of the tub and wiped her body down with cool water and a cloth.

When she went to bed that night, she crawled between the cotton sheets and fell into a deep sleep.

Morning broke a long dream that Mia could not remember when she opened her eyes. She awoke clutching her sheets and filled with yearning for something she couldn't name. She padded slowly across the creaking floor to the kitchen and made a pot of coffee in the four-cup coffeemaker she'd purchased in town. It was the kind she'd find in any motel room but the coffee tasted strong and performed its magic when she took her first sip.

She raked her damp hair from her forehead, surprised to find beads of sweat. The cabin was stifling hot with all the windows closed. In the light of day she felt silly for having shut them all tight, but knew she would do it all over again that night as well. She went out to the porch and stood in the cooler morning air to drink her coffee and gaze lazily out at the deep blue pool. She felt tired and groggy. Bits of the dream flitted through her mind like a mosquito with a high, annoying hum.

She had been in a forest, lost and following a scraggly path deeper into a dark place. She wandered with her arms outstretched. She came across another figure in the dream, a woman Mia sensed was herself, only she was a whole and contented self. The woman looked at her, then she smiled, waved, and walked away. Mia tried to follow her but she got lost again. There was no moon or pebbles to guide her. She was crawling on her hands and knees, holding on to the grass for dear life as she mimicked the sounds of the forest in her throat.

Mia couldn't guess how long she'd stared at the water cascading gently from over the cluster of white rocks, but eventually her body complained and her coffee cup was empty. She roused herself and dressed in jeans and a pink Casting for Recovery T-shirt, donned rubber gloves, and confronted the cast-iron stove.

It was a fearsome, filthy, chilly-looking monster and she squared off before it armed with soap and hot water and rags. She held her breath and cautiously opened the metal oven door. It was a cavelike box that had been home to mice and some other varmints for years. But at least they all seemed to have vacated the premises, she thought with great relief. She set to work with broom and pan. There were no surprises. Just feces, dust, and bits of rust. She swept and scrubbed the oven, then ran her rag over the six burners, somewhat rusty but not bad considering the old girl's age. The porcelain needed a hefty amount of elbow grease. She swore and sweated and when she was done, she tossed the rag into the bucket, and wiped a damp strand of hair from her face.

The massive beast of steel and porcelain was tamed. She stroked it lightly, pleased with her efforts. But she'd paid a price, she thought, bringing her hands to her lower back and massaging the ache blooming there. Her poor hands. She lifted them up to her face. They were roughened and scraped. But what drew her attention was the sight of the channel set wedding band on her left finger.

She tugged the gold from her finger. Her finger was swollen, but she twisted the ring until at last it slid off. Mia went to the front door, swung it open, and brought back her hand. She was tempted to throw it into the night, but common sense held her arm back. Instead she went to the bedroom and tossed the ring into the top drawer, wondering what a diamond wedding band would fetch on eBay.

Later that evening, the sun had set, the fire was lit, and the cabin gleamed with that radiance that only came from a good scrubbing. The air was heavy with the scent of burning wood, pine soap, and oil. At the windows the threadbare curtains hung stiff from drying in the sun. Now this cabin felt more like home, she thought. The freshness in the air made her feel it was a new start for her. She smiled and felt, for the first time, a little less afraid up here.

In honor of the clean cabin, Mia thought it was time to clean her body. Her poor skin and bones had been through a lot these past few days, so she would take Belle's advice and be good to herself. Tonight she deserved pampering. While the water heated up on the stove, she gathered the candles that Belle had brought, lit all five of them, and set them around the cramped bathroom. In the glowing halos of light, the room did not seem so shabby. She went to the kitchen and filled a glass with chilled white wine and set it beside the tub. Finally, she carried the steaming water from the stove to the bath, poured it in, and closed the door.

In the dim light she stripped the dirty clothes from her body and pinned up her wayward curls. Slowly she eased into the hot water and stretched out her tired legs as far as she could against the porcelain. Then, reaching for the bar of soap, she brought it to her nose and sniffed. Ah, it was lavender. Her favorite. "Bless you, Belle," she said as she gently rubbed sweet-scented soap over her body, then rinsed off the day's grime with tepid water. She groaned softly with the pleasure of it, leaned against the high back of the ancient tub, and sipped her wine.

The candles flickered yellow and blue in the darkness. The quiet was profound. Mia took a deep breath and told herself, *I can do this*. This small cabin would be her sanctuary. She would tend her broken body and wounded spirit here until she grew strong again.

She swallowed another sip of wine and set the glass aside. At the retreat the therapist had told them to face their fears. It was a first step toward healing. Her heart quickened. You can do this, she said again, gathering her courage. Hesitatingly, she moved her head to look down at her chest. Where once her left breast had been now stretched a wide, white scar like a seam of skin sewn with jagged stitches. She took a long breath, then tentatively brought her fingers up to gently touch the edges. Slowly she traced the horizontal line across her chest, feeling the sensation in her fingertips but not on the breast.

This was her body. She knew she should let go of her old self-image and make peace with the way her body was now. Yet she still felt as betrayed by it as she did by Charles. Perhaps more. Looking at the scar, she couldn't help but wonder if the cancer was still in there, a minuscule cell that was missed. The doctors just gave her a clean bill of health and sent her on her way, saying they'd see her in three months. The cancer could grow in that time. It could come back.

Even now her shoulders were aching, and though common sense told her it was from all the scrubbing, in the back of her mind a menacing voice whispered—could that tenderness be cancer? The lurking fear of cancer hung at the fringe of all her aches and pains. She felt her body was a walking time bomb.

She squeezed her washcloth over her tender shoulder. The water trickled a cool course down her body to the tub. With a firm yank, she pulled the plug. A small whirl of water circled the drain. Mia closed her eyes and said a small prayer for strength. She had to let this fear of cancer go down the drain with the dirty water. To live fully, she had to believe she would live.

Chapter Four

A good cast is essential to fly-fishing. It can be frustrating for the beginner who gets tangled in line or can't get the fly to go in the right direction or catches all things with the hook but a fish. Good casting requires patience, practice, and peace of mind. Not a bad recipe for life as well.

—BELLE CARSON

Mia had always heard that it took three days to get your sea legs. She figured it took as many days to get your mountain legs, too.

As it turned out, it took more. She needed a full week for her rhythm to change from the harried, fast pace of the city to the quieter, unhurried one of the mountains. Every day she felt a bit more of her strength returning, yet she still didn't feel at home in the mountains. She'd thought being surrounded by nature would comfort and inspire her. It was the opposite. Her isolation grew as thick as kudzu around her heart. The forest beyond her little cabin felt dark and foreboding. Since she'd arrived, she hadn't ventured alone into the woods.

Mia sat on the sofa reading. Outside she heard the calls of the birds as they busily tended their nests. Here she was, sitting inside again, while just a few steps away the great wilderness was alive and bustling. She dragged herself from repose and decided it was past time to leave the confines of the cabin and explore.

She put on jeans, sprayed mosquito repellent, and armed herself with a bottle of water. Squaring her shoulders, she closed the door behind her and took off down the dirt road. Her heels crunched loudly in the dirt and gravel, sounding like an army on the move. As she walked she enjoyed the patches of wildflowers that filled the air with sweet scents. It felt good to stretch her legs. After ten minutes, the road turned away from the river and descended deeper in the woods. The air grew cooler and the shade dense. Glancing up, she saw the branches of the large, primordial trees stretched high over the road like the ribs of Jonah's whale.

The farther in she walked the deeper the shade became. From somewhere in the brush she heard a scuffling, then the loud snap of a twig. With each step farther from the cabin she felt increasingly vulnerable. When she paused to tie her shoe the silence descended on her and she felt swallowed by the woods. Her heart began pounding in her ears and she felt a familiar rush of panic. Wild-eyed, she turned on her heel and marched back at a brisk pace to the cabin, trying not to run.

When she reached the porch, Mia ran up the stairs

and leaned against the railing, catching her breath. She felt ridiculous for being so afraid. She wasn't always scared of the dark. She used to love turning off all the lights and going outdoors to lie under the dark sky and marvel at the stars. One August, she'd driven far out from the city lights to some inn in the country where she could watch the Perseid meteors appear to rain into the atmosphere.

After her cancer, however, she couldn't bear to be alone in the dark. She sometimes woke up in the middle of the night, sweating in a panic. Her therapist had explained to her that her fear of the dark was more a fear of death and the unknown.

Looking out at the wall of trees, Mia thought nothing was more unknown to her, or darker, than the woods.

She straightened and crossed her arms as she looked out over the river. The moving, musical water seemed so inviting. What was most disappointing to her was that she felt disconnected up here at the cabin—not only from the people in Charleston but from the landscape around her. She wasn't a nature girl. Not that she expected to instantly become a mountain woman, either. It was just that she didn't feel like she belonged *anywhere* anymore. Here, she had nothing and no one but herself.

Staring at the water, Mia asked herself if that wasn't exactly what she was most afraid of. The one person she truly had no connection with was herself.

What was she doing here? For the hundredth time

since she'd arrived, she asked herself why she didn't just grab her car keys and drive home.

Something was holding her back. Some expectation, some anticipation of an enlightenment that she believed was just a breath away. What *was* it, she asked herself, bringing her hand through her hair. Where was this epiphany? She felt like a dry well surrounded by water.

Mia removed her shoes and walked through the soft grass to sit at the riverbank. She dangled her feet listlessly in the water. It was cool and refreshing. The sun was warm on her shoulders and in time the quiet settled over her. She didn't think of the woods or her fears. She didn't think of Charles, or what she should do next. She sighed and let her mind drift.

She heard the melody of water over rocks and felt the movement of the river swirl around her legs, nudging her in its current. Lifting her gaze, she watched how the river captured the light and held it, shimmering on the surface. The colors of the river changed depending on the water's depth and movement. In the deep pockets the still, shadowed water was the color of green tea. The shallow water rushing over pebbles with noisy splashes sparkled in the sunlight like shards of crystal.

Mia felt the colors of the river seep into her skin to race in her veins. She rose and with a light step hurried to the cabin to capture the energy she felt inside before it flowed from her. She scrambled to grab her paints, paper, and brushes and carried them to the table. Then she took a glass, filled it with water, and stuck a brush in it.

She smoothed the blank piece of paper with her palms then took a step back, wringing her hands, feeling daunted by the blank, white space waiting to be filled. When she was young, colors had exploded in her mind and she was fearless. She prayed for the colors now. She took a deep breath, then with a step forward, she dabbed the brush into blue. Slowly, she laid the pigment down, letting the paper absorb the hue. Layer after layer she added colors. She wasn't seeking to make any form. She just let the blues and greens and yellows and browns intermingle and flow like the river.

When she set the brush down again she stepped back and looked at her work. The watercolors dripped across the paper. A small smile curved her lips. It didn't matter if it was great art. It wasn't. But she'd covered the blank page with her vision of the river. It was her first connection to nature. It was, she knew, her first step out from darkness.

"Hello! Is anybody home?"

The sound of a voice broke the omnipresent silence of the cabin. Mia was washing her underwear in the bathtub and swung her head around toward the door.

"Belle? Is that you?"

"Who else? Can I come in?"

Mia scrambled to her feet and grabbed a towel.

Drying her hands, she hurried from the bathroom. Belle was standing in the front room carrying waders, a rod, and a box of supplies.

"What a surprise!" Mia exclaimed, beaming from ear to ear. "I'm so glad to see you. Come in, come in. Here, let me take that box."

"No, I got it," Belle replied, grinning. She carried the box to the table and set it down with a thunk.

"What is all that stuff?"

"Surprises," Belle said, her dark eyes sparkling. She looked around. "The place looks good. Smells good, too. Last time I was here all I could smell was mice droppings and mold." She sniffed loudly. "Lemon oil. Nice."

"Thank you very much," Mia replied with mock hauteur. "My nails are a wreck but I won the battle with the oven."

"Never doubted it for a minute." She tilted her head. "You look good, too. You've got some color. I'm glad to see it. I tell you it was a struggle not to come here right off. I was worried about you but I wanted to give you a few days on your own to figure things out. But I was also afraid I'd find you curled up in the fetal position on that big ol' sofa."

"If you came the first day, you would have. But it's hard to be too lazy up here. Nature is a strict taskmaster."

Belle chuckled in agreement. "I like that." When Mia's eyes moved to the box, Belle reached out for the waders. "Here, try these on."

Mia approached them with reverence. Stepping into them was like stepping into a pair of footie pajamas. She slid her feet into the waterproof socks of the waders, then tugged the garment up over her shorts and T-shirt to fasten the suspenders at her chest. Next she put her feet into the felt-soled boots, wiggling her toes and tying the laces tight. Over this she put the tan vest. It was one of those she'd worn at the CFR retreat, with multiple pockets of all sizes filled with bottles, pliers, and tubes. She didn't know one whit about how to use them but she was charmed by the way the gadgets dangled from the vest. It made her at least feel like she knew what she was doing out there on the water.

She caught a glimpse of herself in the armoire mirror and chuckled. "I look like a model for an Orvis catalog."

"Yep, and looks like they fit." She walked over to the rod and held it in her hand, testing its weight. "I think this will be a good rod for the river out front. It's a nice all-'round rod if you don't go catching any monster fish. But you know what they say. *The least experienced fisherman always catches the biggest fish.* Ready? Let's go out and see how it feels."

Mia's heart gave a fish leap of joy. She had come to the mountains not to clean but to feel again a tug of life at the end of a line. She hadn't had time yet to get outfitted and out fishing. She followed Belle, giggling at feeling fat in all the layers after being thin for so long and hearing the fabric swish loudly as she walked to the bank of the river. It was early evening and the water in the pool looked like green glass, broken only by occasional rise rings. Mia smiled with anticipation.

Belle finished tying a dry fly on her line, then handed her the eight-foot fly rod. "OK, let's see you cast a few."

Standing on the bank dressed to the nines, Mia felt nervous with Belle watching beside her. It had been a week since she'd held a rod in her hand, and all of Belle's instructions were a jumble in her head. She lifted the rod, getting a feel for it. Her hand clenched the rod tight. The dry fly dangled in the air as she tried to remember how to cast it out there on the water. Something about a four-count rhythm.

Taking a breath, Mia thrust the rod back to her shoulder. She heard the line snap loudly behind her. Then, with a jerk, she extended her rod far forward like a sword toward the water. The line soared wildly in the air, then came falling to the ground to land at her feet like a pile of spaghetti.

She could hear Belle's voice behind her. "Don't bend your wrist! Try again!"

Gritting her teeth, Mia reeled the loose line in and tried again. Again, the line fell in a sloppy mess on the water.

Belle chuckled softly. "It's that wrist again."

Over and over her little fly flopped forward in a heap of line, or got caught in her pants, or twisted around her rod like a ribbon around a maypole, making knots that would try the patience of a saint. Her spirits were sinking with the sun.

Belle came over to gently take the rod from her hand. "You're trying too hard," she told her. "Look at you. Your shoulders are tense and your nails are digging into your palm. You're clutching that rod in a death grip. You're only going to get tired out that way. Stretch your hand out and shake it. That's right. Loosen it up."

She put the rod back into Mia's hand, guiding her thumb on top of the rod and the reel below her wrist.

"Now listen to me because this is the most important lesson I'm ever going to give you about fly-fishing." She paused. "Mia, fly-fishing should be fun."

Belle met Mia's gaze with a sweet smile. "Coming to the river is coming to nature at her best. It's your time away from the pressures of work and life. When you fly-fish you get in touch with that wild, instinctive part of you, my friend. Let her loose!"

Mia whooped, then laughed self-consciously.

"That's the spirit! Now let's try it again. First, get yourself comfortable. Take your time, this isn't a race. There's no prize for most fish caught, OK? Now just think where you want that fly to go. Then imagine that big clock again and go from nine o'clock to one."

Mia gathered her composure for a final cast before quitting for the day. You can do this, she told herself. In her mind's eye she saw Belle gracefully cast her rod back and forth, the long line in a tight S loop. Focused now, Mia held her rod parallel to the ground, imagined a big clock face, and brought the rod back in a quick motion.

The line sailed back. Then she tried to thrust forward but she felt a tug from behind. Looking over her shoulder, she followed her line to see it tangled up in the tree branch that hung above the water. Her little brown fly was dangling with a bright green leaf she'd been admiring earlier.

"Noooo," she groaned, and tugged at it. The tip of the rod bent in a curve, but that fly wasn't budging.

"Careful of that rod tip," Belle said, then laughed softly as she walked to the tree. Reaching up on tiptoe she tugged the branch closer till she could bend it down and clip the line free. The little brown fly sprang back, still wound on the branch. "We'll leave that victory to the tree."

"I'm hopeless."

"No, you're a beginner." She took the rod and began reeling the line.

Mia felt frustrated, ready to toss the rod into the river. "Some of the other women at the retreat were naturals."

"This isn't a competition, you know. Go at your own pace."

"Can you possibly come up to teach me a lesson?"

Belle sighed and grimaced. "I wanted to talk to you about that. Remember I told you I was going to Scotland? Well, I leave in a few weeks and I'll be gone for a lot of the summer. So I'm really slammed right now just trying to tie things up with the business. I wish I could give you another lesson before I go but I just can't promise it. Hey, don't look so crestfallen. I brought all this gear up so you can practice on your own."

"I don't know what to do out there."

"Oh, yes you do. You learned all the basics at the retreat. Now you just need practice, patience, and confidence. And the only way to get them is to get out on the water. Get yourself a local guide if you want to explore other rivers and streams."

"I don't want another guide," Mia said petulantly. "You're the best."

"Well, thank you, but there are some really good ones right close. And you don't have to rely on a guide, you know. The main thing is to get off the couch and get out on the water." Belle hugged her, then gave her a sisterly shake. "You'll be fine. And Mia? Have fun."

Mia went back to the cabin, removed her fishing gear, and carefully put it in a closet. Her waders hung with the feet attached like a dress form. She'd heard some folks just took to fly-fishing and others never did. She feared she was in the latter category.

"Maybe I'm just not cut out for this," she said with disappointment as she closed the door on her gear.

She quietly and perfunctorily went through the motions of preparing a meal in the little kitchen, thinking about what it meant to be up here in the mountains without Belle in shouting distance. The thought that it was a good thing she didn't buy more supplies formed in her mind as the concept of going home took root. The rotisserie chicken looked like a skeleton in the plastic container. She sliced bits of dry chicken, a tomato, the last of an onion. She put a piece of bread into the new toaster oven she'd bought in town, then pushed down the lever. The silence was rent by a loud, snapping spark. Then the lights went dead.

Mia's mouth dropped open as she stared at a thin curl of smoke at the outlet. A sooty stain blackened the wall. This couldn't be happening, she thought as she opened the fridge. It, too, was dead. Cursing, her mind whirled with questions. She didn't have a clue what to do. On a whim she looked out the window, but Belle was long gone. Mia stood in the middle of the room feeling utterly helpless.

She was an intelligent woman. But nowhere in college did she take Fix It 101. She figured that she blew a fuse, but she didn't know how to change it. She didn't even know where the damn fuse box was.

Night was falling fast. Mia felt panic compounding her fears as an owl hooted from a nearby tree. She hurried from window to window, slamming them shut and locking them. Soon after she finished, the cabin was plunged in blackness. She grappled in the dark, searching for the flashlight, and released a ragged sigh when the narrow beam of light pierced the black. She hurriedly lit a fire with the last of the wood, feeling her panic subside with the soft glow of the firelight. She pulled one of the rocking chairs closer to the light and rocked, back and forth, while she ate a dinner of melting chocolate ice cream.

Staring into the flames, Mia couldn't remember

ever feeling so desolate. She wanted to weep. She'd
endured so much in the past year, only to be defeated
by a toaster oven. Someday, she would tell this story at
a party and everyone would laugh, including her. At the
moment, though, it was really too pitiful. It wasn't just
that she hadn't learned how to do common household
repairs. She didn't think she could name one friend
who could. She suddenly realized that she couldn't
take care of herself. Out in the wilderness—even in the
city—she'd come to rely on others to take care of her.
Up here in the mountains, her independence needed
to be redefined.

She set the ice cream aside and went to the library
shelf. Books had always been a source of comfort. The
narrow beam of her flashlight traveled across the titles.
She'd read *The Awakening* and *A Room of One's Own*
hoping to be inspired by these great feminist authors.
She'd had no great awakening up here, and the only
inspiration she had from Woolf was to fill her pockets with rocks and walk into the deepest point of the
river.

She moved her beam of light to another shelf. It
was filled with books on fly-fishing. A safer topic, she
thought, given her frame of mind. She pulled out six
books. They were very heavy and coated with a thick
layer of dust. Wrinkling her nose, she balanced the
weight of them against her chest to get a good grip. As
she hoisted them up, her flashlight slipped. She twisted
to catch it. The stream of light illuminated the back of
the bookshelf.

The dust on the shelf was streaked where the six volumes had sat, but in the open space on the left she spied a single volume covered in dust, lying flat against the back. Curious, she set the stack of fly-fishing books on the table and returned to the bookshelf and brought the light close for a better look. The slender, leather volume was wedged behind the row of books. Wiggling it, she found it was also stuck in the shelf. She pushed aside the other books and gently tugged, easing it out, careful not to tear it. Once free she brought it closer to the light of the fire. The navy leather was soft and lustrous in the rosy light. She brushed a layer of dust from the cover with her palm. In gilt lettering, surrounded by a circlet of gilt acanthus leaves, were the initials *KW*.

"Kate Watkins," Mia whispered.

She eased back in the rocker and laid the book on her lap. The pages seemed pressed tightly together, probably from so many years wedged in the bookcase. With great care, she opened it.

The pages were as thin as butterfly wings. Mia drew her breath and studied the neat, careful script written on the lines of blue. It was the penmanship of a child.

June 12, 1912
Dear Diary,

Mia's breath caught in her throat. This was the diary of young Kate Watkins.

She sat back in her chair and stared at the thin volume in her hand. She was hesitant to read it. These were just the innocent writings of a child, true. Almost a hundred years old. What harm could there be? Didn't libraries treasure such historical pieces? Yet she had come to feel the presence of Kate Watkins in this cabin. Would it be a transgression as her guest? A diary was someone's private thoughts.

A gust of wind fluttered the thin pages. Mia felt goose bumps spring up along her arms, knowing the windows were shut. She told herself she was acting as childlike as the girl who wrote these words, but remembering the gossip that the cabin was haunted, she scooted her chair a few inches closer to the fire. Looking again at the diary she spied something in the middle. Skimming the pages, she found a photograph. The sepia-toned photo showed a man and a young girl. They were standing outdoors by a river. On closer inspection, it looked like the very pool outside this cabin. The man wore a tweedy three-piece suit and was carrying a fishing rod, a wooden net, and an impressive string of large fish. A wicker creel hung from his shoulder on a wide leather strap. His posture was relaxed, as was his smile. He appeared a man who was quite pleased with the day.

Mia shifted her attention to the girl standing beside him. She looked to be on the precipice between girlhood and teens. She wore an old-fashioned dark skirt over high-buttoned boots and a white blouse with a

wide collar that fell over her shoulders. Her long, lustrous dark hair was drawn up at the sides and gathered
in the back with an enormous bow, typical of young
girls at the turn of the century. The girl stood straight,
proudly holding a fishing rod that was taller than she
was. She was a beautiful girl, unusually so. But it was
something in her eyes—intelligence—that gave her
the aura of not a child but a young woman. She seemed
to be looking straight at Mia from the photo—from
another time—with a small smile playing at her lips
as though she were thinking, I know who you are and
what you want.

The minx, Mia thought as she turned the photo
over to see if there was writing on the back. In faded
pencil she could barely read *WW and KW, 1912.*

This was young Kate Watkins. WW, she assumed,
was her father. They looked rather alike in the long
forehead and the dark eyes. He was a gentleman. That
much was obvious in the style of his clothes and his
posture. So, she thought with a small smile of discovery, ol' mountain woman Kate Watkins was a gentleman's daughter. Interesting, she thought as she set the
picture aside.

She would read the diary, she decided. She sensed
that there was something in these pages she was meant
to read. Perhaps one of the answers she was searching
for. Leaning back in her rocker and raising the flashlight into position, she opened the diary to the first
page and began to read.

June 12, 1912

Dear Diary,

I am alone in my room. Mrs. Hodges thinks to
punish me and told me to write in this diary. It will
teach me not to draw on the walls. She was very
angry and said I was not the lady my mother was.
That was very hurtful of her to say. I don't remember
my mother.

I don't see what the fuss was all about. After all, it
is my room isn't it? And my drawings are quite lovely.
I spent a very long time on the Turk's cap lily. It is a
very difficult shade of red-orange to get right. There
are so many different kinds of wildflowers. Lowrance
knows the names of all of them. I hope that by
knowing the names and habits of things wild, I shall
feel a little less afraid of the woods. I do not wish to
be afraid.

Daddy says that fear is our greatest enemy. He
also tells me that we are most afraid of what we do
not know. I believe this, too.

So that is why I painted wildflowers on the
walls. Not to be headstrong or selfish, like Mrs.
Hodges said. Not at all! I thought if I painted the
flowers on the wall, I would see them each morning
when I awoke and each evening before I fell asleep
and I would learn their names.

I do hope Daddy won't be angry at me. My
Daddy is the handsomest man in the county,
everybody thinks so. People tell me we both have

the Watkins dark eyes. His eyes have so much love in them that seeing them makes me want to try harder to be a good girl. I don't think Daddy ever sins like I do. I wonder, can ministers sin?

I won't write any more in this silly diary. I shall lie in bed and read *Wind in the Willows*. I wish I could escape from this stuffy old house and live with Rat and Mole at Toad Hall. When I grow up I shall live deep in the woods and fish and hunt and do whatever I want to do—even if I am a girl.

So, this is good-bye Diary!

Kate Watkins

Mia finished the entry and stared into the fire. What a precocious girl, she thought. Mia could almost hear her voice. She reached over to pick up the picture and looked once more into the girl's face. She saw the challenge in the lift of her chin. There was a maturity to her writing—even wit. Most certainly, there was stubborn will. She smiled ruefully as she set the photograph aside. Wasn't it amusing that both she and Kate were afraid of the woods, Mia thought, feeling a bond with the young girl.

And what a lovely idea of hers to paint the wild-flowers on the wall. She had once read how Whistler had painted the walls of Lillie Langtry's drawing room with gold fans because she'd found the room so dull. Mia thought that Kate's choice of indigenous wild-flowers was much more clever. Her mind went to the china she'd discovered in the armoire. Each plate was hand-painted with a wildflower. Mia smiled, making one more link.

Eager for more, she tucked a leg beneath her and turned again to the diary.

June 13
Dear Diary,

It is because of Daddy that I have decided to write again in this diary. I would do anything for him. He is more than just my father. He is my teacher. My fly-fishing companion. My best friend.

Last night he walked slowly along the wall, hands behind his back, studying my paintings. Then he stopped before my painting of the Turk's cap lily. "A very good rendition," he told me. "But there should be six segments, not five." He told me if I was going to be a serious student of nature, then I had to pay attention to the details. He said, "Nature is nothing if not a miracle of details."

When Daddy asked me why I had painted on the walls I told him about my plan to learn the names of all things that live in the woods. He liked that idea a lot. I could tell by the look he got in his eyes. It was the same look he gets when he catches a fish. Then he called me his own little naturalist. Me! I've never heard him call Lowrance a naturalist. He went to his room and brought back his fishing diary. Its binding looked like the heavy tweed of his outdoors suit. There were neat black lines that were filled with my father's tidy script and pencil drawings of trout and the flies he used to catch them.

I never even knew there was such a thing as a fishing diary! But I knew at that very moment that someday I was going to make a fishing diary of my very own. I looked up at Daddy and he laughed and said I looked like a trout on a hook! Daddy told me to take pains to be accurate with my entries. He said it is better to write one entry carefully than to write a dozen willy-nilly. In life, he said, I should trust my own eye and not rely on what others tell me.

This is my plan. I will begin with wildflowers. Then I will move on to trees. Then critters. By the end of summer I will know as much as Lowrance. Maybe more. Most of all, I will not be afraid. I will make the woods my own!

Very truly yours,
Kate, the Brave

Mia leaned back and rocked for a long time. Gazing at the fire, she thought of the words she read and the spirit behind them. Even though just a girl, Kate had confronted her fears. Children were innocent of their own mortality and it made them fearless. Yet Mia felt that spirit still lived in all women's souls. Don't we all need to go bravely into the woods? she thought.

As she rocked, Mia stared into the flames and saw herself lying on the gurney, waiting to be rolled into surgery. She was pale and thin, looking up into the fluorescent lighting, trying to be brave knowing that in a short while her body would be cut in a battle to save her life. She was offering her breast as a sacrifice to the gods with hope they would be appeased and let her live. Mia remembered the fear she felt when the oxygen mask was placed over her mouth, wondering for one black moment if she would ever wake up.

She had confronted death, and hadn't she found her way back from that darkness? Wasn't that brave, Mia asked herself?

Mia stopped rocking, rose from the chair, and went from window to window, opening them wide to the dark. What, she demanded of herself, was she afraid of? The night had no hold on her. Every moment of her life was a victory over death. Standing in the middle of the room with her arms outstretched she called out, "I am Mia the Brave!"

Chapter Five

Dear Diary,

Today I begin my life as a naturalist! Isn't it a lark? I am beginning a nature journal and will go into the woods to gather wildflowers. I adore them! When I walk into a mountain meadow and see bursts of pale pinks, shimmering white, deepest reds, I am certain I am entering a fairy land. Or when Daddy takes me with him to the river early in the morning, I see the daintiest blossoms peeking at me through the rocks. I think I've never seen anything more lovely.

Every day I will go a little bit farther into the woods. Day by day, until I am no longer afraid.

Very truly yours,
Kate, the Naturalist

Mia hummed as she drove down the dusty road. She should be tired. She'd read Kate's diary until the wee hours of the morning and woke when she heard the early birdsongs outside her open window. She laughed aloud. How wonderful it was to let the music in!

She'd never slept so well. Certainly not since she'd

arrived in the mountains. Before going to bed she'd put that ridiculous, humongous knife back in the kitchen drawer where it belonged. With the window above her bed open, Mia fell asleep to sounds she'd found frightening earlier: the melodic calls of a night bird, the hoots of an owl, the stirring of trees in the wind lulling her to sleep with whispered rustling. She'd slept without a single bad dream or haunting memory. And when she woke, she wasn't sweaty and groggy. She felt deliciously refreshed. Looking up at the sky, she saw it was a brilliant cerulean without a cloud in sight. Mia tapped the wheel in time to the music on the radio.

She went first to Shaffer's for coffee. The little bell clanged as she came in, and Becky called out a welcoming hello.

"You're back!" she exclaimed from behind the counter.

This time Mia wasn't aloof; she smiled warmly and ordered a coffee and a powdered-sugar cruller. Then she pulled out a second chair at her table. "Care to join me for a cup?" she called out.

Becky's brows rose. Then she smiled wide and came around, limping slightly. Gripping the sides of her chair she eased gracefully, though slowly, into the chair.

"How are you?" Mia asked, concerned about her leg.

Becky adjusted her seat and shrugged. "There are good days and bad days. Today's a pretty good one." She waved her hand, eager to change the subject. "Anyway, how are you doing up there in the Watkins cabin? Any good ghost stories to share?"

"Not unless you consider the lights going out a ghostly event."

"Really? They just went out?" Becky slapped her hand on the table and her eyes gleamed. "I knew it. The place is haunted. What did you do? Whooee, I'd've been out of that cabin and in my car in two seconds flat. Gimp leg or no."

Mia laughed and shook her head. "Sorry to disappoint you, but it wasn't a ghost. It was the toaster oven. I blew a fuse."

Becky laughed heartily, enjoying the joke. "Damn. And here I thought all those stories we heard about Kate haunting that house were true." She wiped her eyes, chuckling again. "I'm thinking you might do best to keep that bit about the toaster oven to yourself. It's good that folks think that place is haunted. Keeps the kids from going up there if it stands empty. They're always looking for a place to hang out."

"Becky, what do you know about Kate Watkins?"

Becky took a sip from a mug of steaming coffee.

"Not too much. She used to be kind of a legend in these parts. I guess you could say she went from famous to infamous. Why?"

"Living in her cabin makes me curious. That's all." She set down her cup and put her chin in her palm. "What was she famous for? The murder?"

"No, no, that mess all came later. Our Kate used to be famous for fly-fishing."

"Really?" she said, inordinately delighted by this.

So Kate made it as a fly fisherwoman after all. She noted that Becky had referred to the woman as *our* Kate.

"I didn't think women did much fly-fishing back in the nineteen hundreds. Wasn't it a male sport? All clubbish and no-women-allowed kind of thing?"

"It still is in some parts. When anglers come in to pick up their coffee and doughnut, I still hear some old farts grumble about women in the streams, like they have no right to be there." She harrumphed. "But it's changing. We've got groups of women coming up here to fish now, same as men."

"So Kate was a pioneer."

"I guess. Of course, she had the social standing to back it up. When you got money, you can get away with a lot and no one gives you grief. At least not to your face."

"Oh? What social standing?"

Becky looked at her sideways. "She was a Watkins."

When Mia still looked at her with puzzlement, Becky said, "You know this town is called Watkins Mill, don't you? She was one of *those* Watkinses."

"I'm not from these parts so I don't know the family. Are they like the Vanderbilts?"

"Well, hell, honey. There aren't many that can stand with the Vanderbilts. You ever been to the Biltmore? Who hasn't, eh? Such opulence! Some two hundred and fifty rooms in that house. And I complain about cleaning my eight. Famous people from all over the world came to visit them back when." She reached over to help herself to a piece of Mia's cruller. "The Watkins house isn't too shabby, though. Did you ever see Watkins Lodge just up the road a piece?" She popped the doughnut into her mouth, sprinkling her chest with powdered sugar.

"I've seen the brochure." Mia recalled the impressive Queen Anne mansion on the rolling grounds. She had thought Kate came from money. The diary photograph indicated a certain lifestyle, and her father had a housekeeper and a cook. But she didn't expect the level of wealth that would have been required to live at an estate. "That's quite a grand place."

"It's been added on to over the years, of course. All the new buildings, the lodge, the spa—none of that was there back when Kate lived there. But the main house, that's where she grew up."

Mia smiled, thinking of the little girl's bedroom walls painted with wildflowers. She wondered if the child's paintings were still there, lighting up the plain white walls. Probably not. They undoubtedly had been painted over by new owners. Made into the dull and proper hotel room.

Becky took another sip of her coffee, getting a little caught up in the topic. "The Watkins family owned a chunk of land hereabouts, too. Thousands of acres. But then the Depression came and they went under."

"That's when they sold their house?"

"It was a common enough story back then. Lots of estates were sold off."

"The loss of a fortune is hardly a scandal or a mystery."

"No, but the thing is, Kate became a recluse. A one hundred percent, genuine hermit."

A young mother came in with a girl in tow. The girl let go and ran to the glass cabinet, flattening against it and declaring which pastries she wanted to buy. Becky rose but before she walked off she turned to Mia.

"And don't forget, there was that little matter of a murder."

She wanted to ask more questions but another customer came in, jingling the bell. The more Mia learned about Kate, the more intrigued she became. She paid her bill and left.

She went first to Clark's Hardware. A small-framed man with wisps of gray hair on the top of his head stood at the cash register. He wore an apple red apron with the name *Clark's Hardware* in bright green letters.

"Can I help you?" he called out in a flattened voice.

"Yes, thank you." She looked at the aisles of tools and gadgets and felt lost. "I'm not sure I know what to ask you for."

"Don't be shy. That's what I see as my job, hear? To help the customers, especially the ladies when they get confused. We're a small bread-and-butter kind of place and service is our middle name." He stuck out his hand. The bones were delicate and he had a soft grip. "I'm Clarence Clark, the owner of this store."

"Hello," she replied. "Mia Landan."

"You from around here?"

"I'm from Charleston."

"We get lots of visitors from Charleston. Pretty city. I go there often. So, what can I do you for?"

"Well, Clarence, if I may call you Clarence?" He nodded emphatically. "I have a problem."

Clarence removed his glasses and polished them briskly. "Ask away. I'm your man."

Mia told him how the cabin had lost power when she'd plugged in the new toaster oven she'd just purchased in his store.

"Blown fuse, no doubt about it. I'll bet that electrical system is ancient. Did you bring a fuse with you?"

Mia shook her head. She was embarrassed to tell him she couldn't even find the box.

He put his glasses back on and pursed his lips in thought. "Probably just as well. Those old fuse boxes can be tricky. I wonder what size fuse it would take?" He thought, drumming his fingers on the counter. "Was it the kind you screw in?"

"Honestly, Clarence, I have no idea."

"Do you know where the fuse box is?"

Mia shook her head.

He sized up the situation quickly. "I'll have to come up and have a look-see."

Mia bet he'd love to be the first to see the inside of Kate Watkins's cabin. "All right, yes, thank you. That would be fine, if you can spare the time. It's a drive."

"I'll get Joe to come in and cover for me while I'm

gone." He could barely restrain his enthusiasm. "I'll just be a minute."

"Before you go . . . I need some wood for the fireplace. Can you tell me how I can get that?"

"You've come to the right place. Do you want a cord?"

Mia sighed and shrugged. "What's a cord?"

His eyes widened. "Why, uh, a cord is the measure by which wood is sold." He leaned closer and spoke in a tone of confidence. "You've got to be careful where you buy your wood. I hate to say it, but there are some less than honest people who'll take advantage of a pretty girl like you. You don't want to get burned buying firewood." He laughed at his own joke.

"A cord is a hundred twenty-eight cubic feet. That measures about four feet high by eight feet long. You want to buy it stacked, too, or you might find you bought less wood than you bargained for. And you want wood that's been stored off the ground."

He droned on about the proper cutting, stacking, and storing of firewood, and all Mia could think to herself was that this was one more area she never studied in college.

"Anything else?" he inquired, all business.

"I need some basic tools. Nothing fancy. Just enough to do a few tasks or repairs. You know, maybe a hammer and nails, that sort of thing." Mia was determined to learn to be self-sufficient.

The little man lunged forward with alacrity, eager

to tackle the task. She followed him as he darted from aisle to aisle pulling tools out of bins and muttering, "Phillips head, flat head, pliers, wrench, staple gun." He came to an abrupt stop. "Maybe even an electric drill. Yes, definitely." He persuaded her to buy a small yellow toolbox and as he filled it, he explained to her in great detail why she needed each item. Mia listened in a daze.

At the checkout counter she found a selection of fix-it manuals, and again with Clarence's assistance, she selected one with lots of photographs and bought that, too.

The total was more than she'd expected. She pulled out her credit card and handed it to Clarence, thinking how Charles would have a fit.

She went from store to store along Main Street, purchasing what she felt were essentials. At Rodale's she bought groceries; at Maeve MacBride's she purchased more tubes of paint. She also stopped at the women's clothing store to buy a few pairs of shorts and tops and a swimsuit to get her through the summer.

When she was working in the city she spent more on one suit than she did on all the things she bought today. During their marriage she and Charles made a good living, but they were cash poor. Other than a few stocks and bonds and their riverfront condominium, saving for the future had never been part of their budget. What little money they did have set aside had been devoured by her medical bills. Mia knew Charles deeply resented that. He'd never actually told her that in so many words. It was more in the exaggerated sighs when the medical bills came in, and comments like, "Well, I guess there's no vacation this year . . ."

Before going home she stopped at the overlook park again. This little bench had become her favorite spot for making and receiving phone calls. Pulling out her cell phone, she saw she had several messages. She dialed voice mail and heard Maddie's increasingly irritated phone messages, each demanding that she call immediately and how it had been six days since they'd talked, and if Mia didn't call soon she'd call the police to send out a rescue squad. There was a message from Belle, something about the hot water heater being delivered. She felt sucker punched when she heard Charles's voice.

"Mia, it's me. Charles. Please call me back when you get this. We need to talk."

She closed the phone and stared out at the view, seeing nothing. Hearing his voice made her physically ill. Her heart was pounding in her ears as she stared at his name on her phone. Charles. Not Chuck, Charlie, Chas. Even in bed he didn't like her using intimate nicknames. His family was old Charleston. This gave him a sense of entitlement that had once attracted her. He believed that it didn't matter how successful he became or how much money he earned; his honored forebears had fixed it so every door and every coveted event in the city would be open to him and his issue till the end of time. Maybe knowing that was why he had so little ambition. Charles rested on his ancestors' laurels.

Every instinct in her body screamed out for her to ignore the call. Yet despite the cold knot forming in her stomach, Mia knew there was no point in delaying the inevitable. Without thinking more, she jabbed his number into the phone.

After the fifth ring she thought she might catch a break and be able to leave a voice message. A simple hello, she was all right, she would call again next week. She wasn't so lucky.

"Hello." His voice sounded tense.

"It's me," she said coolly.

"I called a dozen times. Don't you check your messages? Where the hell have you been?"

"Why the hell do you care?"

"That's not fair."

She could only laugh, but there wasn't a trace of humor in it. "So now you're telling me what's fair?"

"Mia, you've been gone more than a week. Where are you?" he asked again, insistent.

"I'm in North Carolina," she replied, begrudging him that morsel.

"What are you doing up there? You should be here. In Charleston. This is such a mess. We've got to talk."

"I'm not ready to talk."

"Look, Mia. I know you're hurt. God, I'm so sorry. I didn't mean for you to find out this way."

"You mean you didn't mean for me to catch you

fucking that girl on my bed? So, which way did you mean for me to find out?"

"You don't need to be crass."

She blushed. Mia hated foul language, rarely used it. But she was so hurt, so angry, it felt good to strike out. If only with words.

"Me crass? I would have thought you'd at least have the decency to take her to some cheap motel that you pay for by the hour. Isn't that the way it's usually done?"

"She's not that kind of girl."

Mia was taken aback. She had expected him to say he was sorry that he brought the woman into their bed. That he was sorry for hurting her. She did not expect him to defend the girl.

"Just what kind of a girl is she? Aside from the kind that sleeps with a married man."

"I didn't call to talk about her."

"Then why did you call? To talk about me?"

"Yes. And us."

"Well I'm fine. So you can cross that off your list."

"Fine isn't running out of the house and disappearing for a week. Fine isn't not bothering to call to let me know you're alive. And fine sure isn't taking my Titleist clubs!"

"Oh my God, Charles. You're not calling to check on me. You're calling to check on your golf clubs!"

"Don't be ridiculous. Listen, Mia, let's not start getting nasty. I've seen that happen with my clients and nothing gets accomplished. We need to remember how we once felt about each other and move forward from that point."

Mia's blood chilled as she heard the divorce lawyer come into his voice. He had already made up his mind. He saw her as a client. She cleared her throat.

"Why don't you tell me what's going on."

He took a long, ragged breath, the first sign of true emotion she'd heard. "I want a divorce."

Despite the fact that she knew deep in her heart that this was coming, hearing the words caused her to suck in her breath.

"I'm sorry, Mia. I didn't want to drop it on you like this, on the phone. It's been coming for a long time. You must have felt it, too."

"No. I didn't actually." That made her feel all the more the fool. "Then again, nothing's been quite the same for the past year."

"Exactly."

She felt suddenly defensive. "It's not like we planned it. We didn't wake up and say, hey, how about you get cancer so we can test our marriage to the nth degree."

"I know. Mia, I do. But plan it or not, it happened. It did test our marriage. And frankly, Mia, it failed."

"How can you say that? We had some great years."

"Had. Not anymore. We don't go out. We never talk."

"I know I haven't been myself."

"We never make love anymore."

"That's because you don't want to," she cried back. "I know it can be difficult for husbands after surgery. But you won't touch me. You can't even look at me."

There was a long pause during which Mia closed her eyes and saw in her mind's eye the night she had dared to show her husband the scar after her breast surgery. She'd never forget the look on his face before he turned his head away.

His voice cracked. "I'm sorry, Mia. Really I am. I know it makes me shallow. I've told myself a hundred times it shouldn't matter. But it does. I . . . I just can't get past it."

"In time . . ."

"It's not just the breast or the scar. It's *you*."

He flung the word at her accusingly, as though all of their problems—the cancer, the scar, the affair—were her fault.

"You're not the same person I married."

"No, I'm not. How can I be? I've been through hell and back."

"I know. I'm sorry. But things are different now and I can't go back."

"Who said marriage is easy? Marriage is for better or for worse. This was *the worse* part. But we have to hope for *the better*."

"Mia . . ."

"You're my husband," she exploded, hearing the finality in his tone. She knew he didn't call to talk about it. His mind was made up. The hurt was scathing. "You should have been there to help me get through this.

But you weren't there. Charles, you were never worried about how the cancer was affecting me. All you were worried about was how the cancer was affecting you. When would you have told me if I didn't come home early?"

"I was waiting till you were stronger."

"So you were going to do it again?"

"I'm sorry."

"Stop saying you're sorry when you're not!"

"But I am sorry," he shouted back. Then, skipping a beat, he repeated more softly, "I am. I never planned for this to happen. I still care about you. But it's over."

"I hate you for doing this to us," she said, her voice breaking. She brought her fingers to her forehead and squeezed her eyes shut while she rocked back and forth, willing herself not to cry.

"I was hoping we would be able to work the divorce out ourselves." He spoke in the voice she'd heard him use in court. "We don't have a lot of property and we have no children. We could save a lot of money, given we have so little to divide."

She dropped her hand, incredulous. "So now you want me to trust you to be fair to me? After what you did?"

He sighed with resignation. "Fine. Do it your way. You need to get a lawyer. I can recommend a few, if you like."

"Screw you. Screw that girl. And screw—"

She heard a click.

Mia flushed. He'd hung up on her. How could he

be so callous? How could he care so little to ask for a divorce without discussion, without even waiting until she came home. Why didn't she see it coming? She let her hand drop to her lap. Charles wanted a divorce. She couldn't quite get that concept clear in her mind. Her marriage was over and in walking away he took from her all that she had so willingly given of herself. And for all his saying "I'm sorry" over and over, he never really apologized.

She took a breath, then picked up the phone and dialed her sister's number. It was a reflex action.

When she heard Maddie's voice on the line Mia blurted out in a rush, "I talked to Charles."

"Damn. I've been trying to reach you before he did. Don't you ever answer your phone?" She paused, then said cautiously, "He told you?"

"Yes."

"What did he tell you?"

"He wants a divorce."

"Is that all he told you?"

Mia tensed again, sensing another blow. "Isn't that enough?"

Maddie sighed heavily. "I'm just going to spit this out so you hear it straight and you hear it from me." She paused, then blurted out, "He's going to marry that bimbo."

Mia's mind stalled. "Who? That woman?"

"She has a name," Maddie said softly. "Do you want to know it?"

Mia felt her blood ice in her veins. She wasn't sure

she wanted to give the woman an identity. It made her real.

"Yes."

"Julia Barnes. She's a law clerk for the same firm. Did you know her?"

"No," she blurted out, regretting her decision, seeing again her face; her long, dark hair flowing over her beautiful breasts. "And I don't care what her name is. She doesn't deserve my recognition."

"OK, then," Maddie drawled.

"How did you find out he wants to marry her?"

"He told me. God help me, Mia, he's been calling me every day, bending my ear about this and that, like I'm some ambassador between the two of you. He seems to think if he can make me his ally this will all end neatly and without scandal. He's going on about how he'll divide everything equally and how you can both get on with your lives, make a new start, that kind of crap. My bet is he's more than a little worried about how his law firm will react to any gossip about how you found him in bed with Julia at lunch hour. Not a classy scene. Wouldn't look too good for him."

"So. It's going to happen. The divorce."

"I'm afraid so, honey."

She swallowed the news, though it had a tough time getting down her throat. "I'll have to think about it more."

"Think fast. Charles seems hell-bent on it happening. He's putting it on the fast track."

"Why the hurry? I'll be up here for the summer. Let him sit on the hook for a while."

"Oh honey, bolster yourself. There's more."

Mia stiffened. "What more could there be?"

"She's pregnant."

Mia felt numb and could only sit for a moment, dazed and speechless. The first emotion that pushed through the shock was hate.

She and Charles had talked about having children early in their marriage, but they were both ambitious with careers blooming and they'd decided to wait. When Mia neared thirty-five, she wanted to begin a family but Charles didn't want to talk about it. He'd said he wasn't ready. He was still young and wanted a few more years of freedom, he called it. Time while they were still young to enjoy going out when they wanted to, to travel and not have to worry about being tied down by rug rats and diapers and that whole lifestyle.

The following year, Mia was diagnosed with breast cancer. The chemo had poisoned her body, possibly her eggs, and now it was questionable whether Mia could ever have children. How did that woman get pregnant so fast? she wondered. Had it been an accident? Could she be so manipulative as to try to trap Charles in that age-old ploy?

But Charles wanted to marry her. He wasn't the kind to get trapped.

"Honey, are you still there?"

Mia nodded, then croaked out, "Yes."

"I'm so sorry to be the one to tell you all this. I thought you should know."

"Hey, Maddie," she said, her voice soft and shaken. "You know how I said I didn't want you to come up here? How I needed to be alone?"

"Yeah."

"I lied. I'd really love it if you came up."

"I'll be there," Maddie replied. "Let me work out a few things here so I can take some time off. I need to get the kids taken care of. I have a big meeting next week. I can try and come after that. Are you OK till then? You won't do anything stupid?"

"No, of course not. I'll be fine. Settle it at work and with the family and come up when you have a spare weekend. Really, I'm OK. It'd just be nice to see you." Her voice broke.

"I'll be there as soon as I can. Call me every day, OK? Even if you have to climb a mountain to get reception, call me."

Chapter Six

Dear Diary,

Here is a secret. I was lost in the woods. I never told anyone.

I had followed a stream to its end deep in the forest. It dried up in some rocky crevice surrounded by a hillside of glorious fern. I've done this before. It has always been such an adventure, and when I reached the stream's end, I followed it back home. But I must have made a wrong turn because I was soon in a part of the woods I did not recognize. Nothing looked the least friendly or familiar. I wandered for a long time, calling out over and over for Daddy. Only the birds returned my calls. The trees, the wildflowers, the rocks, the critters, all things that I loved hours before suddenly made me afraid. My mind began playing tricks on me. I imagined bears and snakes and all manner of evil lurking where the trees grew thick. I've never been such a ninny before. I'd heard talk of children wandering off never to be seen again, that must have been what made me so fearful. I was embarrassed for my tears. Lowrance would tease me if I told him.

It was the river that saved me. I heard it before I saw it. The sound of rushing water was like hearing an old friend calling my name. I followed the sound over the mountain. My dress and stockings were torn and I was very thirsty. But my heart near burst at the sight of the most charming stream I'd ever seen. The water ran swift over the dearest waterfall and led to a deep pool. Just beside it sat a cabin. I knew instantly it had to be the one my father had built after my mother died. From time to time he went off for short trips alone in the woods. He never invited me to join him on these trips, though I'd often begged him to. He said that there were times when a man had to be alone with his God and his thoughts. I sat in a rocking chair on the porch of the cabin and waited, knowing he would come.

Afraid. Scared. Timid. Fearful. Terrified Frightened. Lonely.

I write these words down because I do not want them to come back into my heart. By writing these words down I must face the feelings. It is strange how I feel a shiver of the feeling when I say the word aloud. I shall read the words over and over until that feeling is gone. These are the feelings of the lost. I am not lost.

Kate, the Fearless

Clarence arrived at the cabin a few minutes after Mia did. She felt wounded and raw after her phone call with Charles. She crossed her arms and leaned against the porch pole as she watched

Clarence's shiny red truck pull up to the cabin, its enormous tires digging deep tracks in the mud. It was a giant four-wheeler and she wondered, when he jumped from the cab, if it didn't have something to do with compensation. A second, rusted truck ambled along behind, loaded with firewood. He directed the two men where to stack the wood, giving orders like a Napoleon, and then turned to join her on the porch.

"I made it in pretty good time," he called out as he walked up to the porch. He climbed the stairs and, tucking his fingertips in his pockets, looked out over the view of river, and beyond, a glimpse of mountaintops. "A right pretty spot it is," he said with a sigh. "I came here once as a boy, you know. Just to look at it. Most children hereabouts think the place is haunted. Old Kate was already long gone when I came up. I didn't mean any harm, just curious. Never went in, of course. Wouldn't do that. Wouldn't dare. Mrs. Minor kept the place locked and you never knew when that old harridan would come bolting out and chase the rascals out with a broom. True story. It happened to a friend of mine." He laughed and shook his head. "About scared the tar out of Bill Morgan."

"Who is Mrs. Minor?"

"She looked after this place after Kate Watkins died. She lived at the next house down the road. She was very loyal. I believe she was the only one Kate kept up with after she came out here. Course, Mrs. Minor's ancient now. In her nineties if a day. She doesn't come by to check on this place anymore, of course. I wouldn't be surprised if she's the one what started the ghost rumors. Just to keep the kids away. She's quite a character. Lives in town now where her folks can keep an eye on her." He wiped his palms on his chinos, then headed toward the door. "Well, let's see what we've got with this fuse box of yours."

Clarence gave the cabin a thorough once-over, commenting as he saw fit to Mia what could be done in repairs. He was enamored of the cast-iron stove, declaring it in mint condition and how he'd like to take it off her hands. Mia reminded him several times that the cabin did not belong to her, but he chose to ignore that and continued to make suggestions. To her relief he was able to fix the fuse. She didn't miss his smug smile when he showed her its location by the back door. Clarence didn't stay long, sensing her mood. She watched him drive away, no doubt in a hurry to report to the town the status of Watkins Cove. A little gossip was a small price to pay for a cord of wood properly stacked beside the house and the power restored.

"Day by day," she said softly, allowing Kate's words to become her mantra.

That evening, Mia flicked on a switch and yellow light filled the room. It was comforting, and she'd never take easy access to light for granted again. She wouldn't need to light a fire tonight, thank heavens. Summer had taken a hold in the mountains and the nights were warming up. The sun was setting on another day.

She went to roost on the blue sofa, bringing her knees up and wrapping her arms around them in a tight ball. Charles had hurt her today, this time so deeply she had to compartmentalize the pain and tuck it away to deal with when she was stronger. She had to see clearly now that she had made poor choices over the past years of her marriage. She had given up herself to be what he wanted—the trophy wife, the socialite, the perfectionist. Not that it was wrong to like pretty things, but she'd neglected to make choices for her inner self as well. She'd given away too much.

She uncurled her legs and sat up, feeling a surge of determination. Her life with Charles was over. She would be a child again. This was her second chance. What difference did age make? She would get up early in the morning and paint. She would take long walks and read and find what it was that made her happy and build an authentic life. It would take work and discipline. She'd never been afraid of that. She had to stay positive. She had to let Charles go. She had to let the fear of cancer go. If she dwelled on the divorce or disease she would lose the slim shred of serenity she'd struggled so hard for up here in this cabin. This was her sacred space. Up here in these walls she'd promised to be good to herself and not let the negative thoughts in.

She rose and prepared a light dinner with a glass of white wine, taking pains to set a pretty table. After she ate, she went to the bookshelves. On top was Kate's diary. She picked it up and held it in her hands. The leather was soft and familiar.

"Hello, friend," she said aloud. She'd read and reread the young girl's diary countless times. Kate Watkins's words had filled her like a rich wine did an empty decanter.

Tomorrow she'd try her hand at casting again, she decided. She wouldn't give up that dream so readily. First, she needed to learn how to knot a dry fly. She pulled several books on fly-fishing from the bookshelf and carried them to the table. She opened the first to discover that it was a series of essays on the art of fly-fishing. She closed this to read later.

The next two provided practical instructions on the basics of fly-fishing, more a twentieth-century how-to book. Always a good student, she dove in. For the next hour she studied diagrams and practiced tying a series of knots on the line that Belle had given her. When she was satisfied she could make a decent clinch knot, she idly opened the last book on the table.

This one had a heavy tweedlike cover. Something about it niggled in her memory. Opening it, her mouth slipped open in a silent gasp of recognition.

The heavy lined paper filled with neat script and charcoal sketches was exactly as Kate had described. Mia flipped back to the first page. She found the name

Walter Watkins written in the same tight script. Her mind flashed to the initials on the photograph. *WW.*

But of course Kate would have wanted to keep her father's fishing diary! She would have brought it with her to the cabin along with her other favorite books. It would have been one of her greatest treasures. Walter had written his entries in a tight and tidy script. On the right was an open space for comments. He had an incredible sense of detail and order. As she studied the pages, she remembered young Kate's rapture at seeing it.

Mia's head snapped up as words from Kate's diary rang in her memory. *Someday I was going to make a fishing diary of my very own.* If Kate had preserved her father's fishing diary, she thought . . .

Mia hurried to the bookcase and with excitement pumping in her veins scanned the titles for all the fly-fishing books. There were four more. She opened each one eagerly, one after the other. Each was another text on the topic of fly-fishing. No diary. Disappointed, her fingers tapped the table. She had felt so sure. Undaunted, Mia returned to the bookshelf and let her fingertips skim again over all the titles on all the shelves, reading each one carefully. There were many classics and a wide selection of early southern and feminist authors. She traced the titles by Henry David Thoreau, William Faulkner, Thomas Wolfe, Eudora Welty, Virginia Woolf, Kate Chopin, Zora Neale Hurston, and several about Amelia Earhart.

On the bottom shelf she found a narrow, burgundy leather box, tied in shipping string. With a flicker of interest, she pulled it out and brought it to the table. On the cover of the box the outline of a fish was etched into the leather in gold.

Mia untied the string. Then, with something akin to reverence, she opened the box. She sucked in her breath. Inside she found a burgundy, leather-bound book. It was thick and bulky, filling the box, which Mia knew was made especially for the book. The leather was well worn, burnished in some spots, and scratched deeply in others. In the center of the cover, in the same gilt as the fish, were the initials *KW*. Mia wiped her palms on her shirt, then very carefully lifted the book from the box. The book's bindings held strong. Mia held her breath and opened the book.

Her breath released with a laugh. Did she call this a fishing diary? This was a far, far different book than WW's neatly recorded journal. *This* was a marvel! It was a glorious explosion of creativity and color.

The design of the pages was exactly that of her father's diary. There were the classic black lines that marked the same categories: date, fish caught, location, rod, fly. But where he had neatly recorded the information like a banker in a ledger, Kate had embellished her entries with impeccably rendered watercolors.

Mia hurried through the pages to get a grasp of the book. The dates spanned from 1920 to 1951—so many years! The colors of the paintings had not faded. These were not the cheerful paintings of a child. These were the entries of a mature and accomplished angler and artist.

On the left side were the categories, and her entries were written in a serious, tidy script. In between her entries, however, she filled all the empty spaces with sketches, some quite whimsical, of objects that must have caught her eye while out in the wild. An eagle's head, a crested grebe, a barn swallow; there a rabbit, a bear, a deer—each carefully identified. On the right, where the diary provided a page for remarks, Kate filled the space with her shining watercolors of the spots she fished—the rivers, waterfalls, and mountains. And everywhere were fish—rainbow trout, brook trout, and others, large and small, swimming, leaping, on the fly, in the creel, even on the plate. Mia was enthralled. It was almost too much. She knew how an archeologist must feel when he opens a tomb for the first time to discover the marvelous treasures hidden there.

"Oh, Kate!" Mia exclaimed, bringing her hand to her cheek. "You wonderful girl. You queen of fly-fishing. You did it. Just as you said you would. You made the woods your own!"

Morning broke the stillness of night, stretching her pink and gold rays over the eastern mountains, then yawning wide and spreading her light down across the valley. In the forest, myriad birds shook their feathers and sang dawn songs to the new day.

Mia rose to begin her new routine. She hummed as she scooped coffee into the machine and reached into the cabinet to take out her favorite blue pottery mug and bowl that she'd found in Maeve's shop. The scent of coffee tantalized her senses and her fingers tapped a beat on the counter while she waited for the coffee to brew. Then she poured the steaming coffee into her mug, topped it off with milk, and began her day with her first sip. Her breakfast was always a bowl of oatmeal and blueberries, prepared just the way she liked it.

After breakfast, Mia set up her painting environment, mimicking the pleasure she found in preparing her breakfast. She'd found an old wooden table in the woodshed that was perfect to hold her paper and supplies. Preparing the paper, soaking it, watching the water spill off, then its placement on the waiting watercolor board was a careful task.

These quotidian movements were her version of tai chi exercises—free-flowing, continuous routines for health and longevity. Every morning Mia would take care of herself, following her natural cravings, falling into a healing rhythm.

Mia began exploring. She took Kate's words to heart and every day walked a little deeper into the woods, gaining confidence in steps. Today she felt braver and left the dirt road to follow the river, staying close to its winding curves. She traveled light, carrying only a bottle of water and the old fishing creel she'd found in the armoire. When she'd first put it on, she was keenly aware of the way the wide leather strap fell against the flat space on her chest. Now the strap was soothing, as if it were Kate's guiding hand on her shoulder.

The sky was deepening to a periwinkle blue. She walked a little farther, enjoying the gurgling of the river, when she caught sight of a patch of brilliant orange. She hurried toward it, pulling the creel from her shoulder. As she drew near she recognized the three-foot-high, regal Turk's cap lily. She smiled, remembering how Kate had painstakingly painted the orange color with the reddish-brown spots on her wall.

Mia reached into the creel to pull out her note-book and charcoal pencils. In the ancient, brittle wicker she collected specimens of trees and wildflowers instead of fish. She'd done sketches of bee balm, cardinal flower, and touch-me-nots. And now she had a Turk's cap lily. Her sketches weren't very good, but she wasn't collecting them to show to others. She was learning the names, as Kate had.

Young Kate Watkins was Mia's inspiration. The girl had shaken Mia's fear of her surroundings and replaced it with a childlike curiosity. How, she wondered, had she lived a lifetime and not taken the time to learn the names of the trees that lived beside her? Or the sweet wildflowers, the birds, the animals? What blind arrogance was this? They were her neighbors. They made up her world. Not knowing what they were or what to call them, how could she help but feel disconnected when she looked at them? Each step she took into the woods was a step away from her old life. Was it any wonder great fairy tales took place in enchanted forests?

Up here in the mountains with the forest closing her off from the world, Mia felt far from the life she'd lived near the ocean. The betrayal and hurt, the hectic lifestyle, the medical worries, the omnipresent bills, the stink of hospitals, the honking of horns, the crush of people . . . She knew they were out there beyond the perimeter, but they did not exist in the forest she was living in now.

In this new world Mia vowed that she would be like Kate. Fearless, adventurous, curious. Going out a little farther each day, with Kate as her guide, she was not lost. She was making the woods her own.

June 21, 2008
Charles,

I've given your suggestion of divorce mediation a great deal of thought. I agree that it is time for us to move forward with our lives, albeit separately. I suspect that the only real value we have accrued in our ten-year marriage is the condominium and a few stocks. That seems a rather sad statement, doesn't it? Of course, I am not speaking in terms of money. I would have liked to think that in the past ten years of our lives we have accumulated something of personal value. Perhaps in the fullness of time we will mine out that gold, but for now, I am resolved to settle for bits of gravel.

Please move forward with mediating the divorce. I trust you will provide an accurate and thorough accounting of our possessions, such as they are. I intend to remain in the mountains for the duration of the summer. If there is something that you need to discuss with me, leave a message on my cell phone or e-mail and I will contact you as soon as I am able.

Mia

Chapter Seven

I went to the woods because I wished to live
deliberately, to front only the essential facts
of life, and see if I could not learn what it had
to teach, and not, when I came to die, discover that I had not lived.

—HENRY DAVID THOREAU

On the eve of the solstice Mia stood on the
rocky bank of the river angling for the big
trout she saw cruising in the depths of the
pool. She'd seen that giant rainbow rise several times
to slurp down an insect, then dive again with a flash of
his silvery tail, as though to tease her.

She was dressed in waders and boots, and was casting the dry fly she had painstakingly attached to the
line. It had taken her hours. Back near the cabin she
heard the low rumble of an engine. Turning, she recognized the green Blazer that pulled to a stop. She waved
her arm in an arc and called out. "Over here!"

Belle heard Mia's call and waved, then detoured
toward where Mia was fishing. The day had been
hot and the early evening wasn't much cooler. Belle's
deeply tanned legs were cloaked in olive green hiking

shorts and boots. Her long braid slapped against her back as she walked with a steady gait.

"Look at you!" she called out as she walked toward her. An easy smile stretched across her face. "All geared up and casting like a pro. Catch anything?"

"Caught a big one but it got away."

Belle raised her hands in a victory sign and made an exaggerated face of surprise.

Mia confessed, "I caught a tree."

While Belle laughed, Mia recalled reading in Kate's diary how her father had taught her never to admit when she didn't catch a fish. She should say she caught a big one but it got away. The listener would simply assume that *it* was a fish.

"There's a big rainbow in there I'm anxious to meet," Mia said.

"Oh, yeah? Let me see you cast to it," Belle said, coming closer.

"Aren't you going to get your rod and join me?"

"There's no hurry. The sun is just lowering and the fish will start biting. This is a good spot. Go on, cast a few."

Nervous, Mia's wrist began to roll forward and the line did its trick of falling in a pile in the water. "It's my wrist, I know," she said with a groan. She expected some retort or correction from Belle but it wasn't forthcoming. Turning her head, she saw Belle standing still with her eyes wide.

"Where did you get that rod?" she asked in a stunned voice.

Mia looked at the bamboo rod in her hand. "I found this in the cabin," she replied hesitatingly. "I was having a hard time with the rod you gave me. The handle didn't feel right. So I thought I'd give this one a try. I've been doing much better with it."

"Where in the cabin did you find it?"

Mia heard tension creep into Belle's voice. She navigated across the river rocks closer to Belle, who was already reaching for the fishing rod. "It was in the armoire. There are two in there. This was the smaller. I didn't think you'd mind if—"

"There's another in there? Like this one?"

"Yes. Didn't you know?"

Belle shook her head. She was still eyeing the rod in her hand as if she didn't believe what she was seeing. "Show me."

Mia removed the boots and waders, then stood clenching and unclenching her hands as she watched Belle push aside the blue taffeta gown with annoyance to get to the second bamboo rod. She pulled out the bag and tube and let out a soft yelp of excitement when she saw the small hanging tag. "Look at this, Mia! It's a Payne!"

Mia watched Belle draw out the rich-looking rod as though it were made of glass.

"My God, it's a beauty," she said in an awed tone, inspecting all its details. "Jesus, Mary, and Joseph help me. There it is, his name on the butt cap. I've heard of them, of course. But I've never held one. And this one's in mint condition. Absolutely incredible."

Mia stood anxiously by her side, wishing there was something she could say to alleviate her wrong in taking what was obviously a valuable rod from the armoire and using it.

"I was alone and cleaning and I didn't think you'd mind if I opened the cabinets and closets. You told me to make myself at home. Everything had coats of dust and dirt to be wiped off. Anyway, when I found these bamboo poles I didn't think they were worth much. I used to see bamboo poles in the dime store growing up. I had no idea . . ."

Belle turned her head and looked at her with a searing gaze that seemed to question Mia's sanity. She gave a short laugh, the kind that said *I don't know where to begin.* She raised the bamboo rod like a wand in her hand, something magical and otherworldly.

"First, you never call a rod a pole. Second, Mia, this is not just some bamboo rod. This is a split cane rod. It's made from bamboo, true. Though not just any bamboo. This is from a bamboo called Tonkin, imported from China over a hundred years ago by master craftsmen as respected and revered in their day as any great watchmaker. They began as apprentices, and then maybe, if they had the magic in their hands, they'd be allowed to create rods. For it *is* magic, Mia, to split the stem of the bamboo, then to put it back together, stronger and more flexible than before. Each craftsman had his own secret method which he guarded jealously. State secrets were not so well protected. The names of the great rods of this era are still spoken in awe today. A split cane fly-fishing rod is a piece of art. And a split cane rod made by Payne is a museum-quality piece."

"And that's a Payne."

"It is."

"And I fished with it."

"You did."

Mia closed her eyes and felt sick to her stomach. "But aren't the new graphite ones better? They're lighter and stronger."

"You might think that. But you'd be wrong. Granted, not all bamboo rods were created equal. For every magnificent one, like this one, there were thousands of cheaper, mass-produced ones that are better left in basements than used. Some people think of these old rods as antiques, mere relics of the past. Well, I tell you those people never held a rod made by Payne in their hands. Are the new rods better? I guess it'd be like comparing a handcrafted watch with a machine-made digital." She shrugged. "They both tell you the time."

Belle lifted the rod and gave it a quick forward cast. A smile of satisfaction eased across her face. "Slow and smooth," she said in a long, easy drawl, her eyes revealing her appreciation for the rod's flex.

"I'm sorry I took it out," Mia told her, feeling the gravity of the situation. "I should have asked. Really, Belle, I had no idea of its worth."

"No harm done." She cocked her head. "How did it fish?"

"It was . . . different."

Belle looked disappointed in her lackluster response.

Mia opened her mouth, trying to find the words to describe the change she felt within herself using this rod. It wasn't so much about how she might catch a fish with it. It was more how she and the rod became one instrument.

Mia cracked a small smile. "It was magic."

Belle's chest swelled and Mia saw she was satisfied with that answer.

"You should take a look at the other things in the armoire. There are some real treasures in there."

"Yeah?" Belle put the bamboo rod carefully aside, then came back to the armoire and began rummaging through it with a businesslike efficiency.

Belle picked up the leather wallet filled with dry flies, pausing to admire one or two. Mia could see she was enthralled, but she closed it up and tossed it back into the armoire saying, "Help yourself. Someone should use them." She lifted a china plate, giving it little more than a cursory glance, then moved on to the silver. She picked up a knife, felt its weight, and replaced it in the box.

"Actually, the silver is sterling," Mia offered. "It should be quite valuable. And the china is hand-painted."

"Lord, Mia, I don't know squat about silver and china. Can I sell it?"

"I'm sure you can, but you should be careful not

to get taken. There are lots of dealers out there who'll tell you what's wrong with it and give you a fraction of its value." She almost laughed, thinking of Clarence's comments about firewood. "My sister is coming up for a visit this summer. I could have her take samples to an antique appraiser in Charleston. This furniture is good, too. If you'd like, we could take photographs of them for the appraiser. At least you'll have a ballpark figure."

"Thanks, I'd appreciate that," Belle replied with obvious relief. She stood and looked around the room. "Tell your sister it can all go. I'm only interested in the property. I don't want anything inside. If it was *hers*, then I want to get rid of it. Maybe then I can exorcise the ghost forever."

Mia froze and glanced nervously at the bookcase. "What about the books?"

With a bored sigh, Belle walked over to the library and scanned the books. She pulled out a fly-fishing text and leafed through it. Then another. "These books on fly-fishing are interesting. I'll keep these."

Mia's eyes darted to the bottom shelf where she'd put the diaries. She suddenly was terrified that Belle would find them and take them away. Her chest tightened as she watched Belle scan the bookshelves, pulling out a volume or two, perusing the pages then putting it back. Mia realized that she wasn't ready to give up the diaries. She needed Kate's voice. Feeling traitorous, she waited in pained silence and volunteered nothing.

Belle looked inside the armoire again, closed the

doors, then turned her back on it. "OK, that should do it. I'll keep the fly-fishing books here in case you want to look at them. But I'll take these bamboo rods. I still can't believe it," she said, handling the rods delicately. "I assumed my grandmother fished with a fabulous instrument, but I never figured it'd be a Payne. This was a pricey rod, even in her day."

"From what I've heard, Kate could have afforded about any rod she wanted."

Belle's eyes flashed. "You're hearing stories about my grandmother? How do you even know her name?"

Mia crossed her arms over her stomach as it tensed. "Well, the people in town figured out where I was staying. They told me it was Kate Watkins's house."

"I'll just bet they did." She turned back to the table and disassembled the fly rods with quick movements. "Damn gossips. What else did they tell you?"

"Not much, really."

"You're not a very good liar."

"They weren't gossiping, really. Just curious. Mostly about the fact the cabin has been opened up. I gather Kate Watkins was a celebrity when she lived."

"A celebrity? Is that what they call her now? Did they tell you what she was famous for?"

"Fly-fishing."

Belle snorted.

Mia felt suddenly defensive. "I heard about the murder, if that's what you mean."

Belle went still, then slowly turned around. Mia saw bitterness darken her eyes. "I'd hoped that damn story would have died with my grandmother. Why can't they just leave it alone?" Leaning against the table she asked more softly, "What's it going to take?"

"I don't think anyone meant any harm," Mia said in a small voice. "It's a fable. A small-town story."

Belle looked at Mia with a drawn expression. "This town drove my mother out with their stories and gossip."

"I'm sorry. I didn't know."

Belle pulled out a dining chair and sat in it, resting her elbows on her thighs. Mia moved to a rocker and began rocking slowly.

"Mama never told me the details," Belle said, "other than to say 'Kids can be cruel.' I always knew she had this history she refused to share with me. I mean, we all ask questions when we're kids. Like, Who's my grandmother? My grandfather? Where did you grow up? Right?"

Mia nodded. "I can remember asking my mother those questions."

"My mother just clammed up when I asked until I just stopped asking. Even as a child I figured it must've been pretty dark and deep that she couldn't even share the basics with her daughter. I only know that she lived a rugged existence with her mother in isolation in a cabin."

Belle's eyes scanned the room with a haunted expression. "She really hated this place," she said with feeling.

Mia followed her gaze and saw the hewn and polished logs of wood piled one on top of another with precision. She'd always thought that this was a place built with intention. How could anyone hate it? she wondered.

"She ran off when she was seventeen, barely old enough to get married. I don't believe she ever loved my father. She saw him as a ticket out." She shrugged. "Who knows about him? He left us when I was three. I don't remember him.

"But the irony is, she never really escaped this town. All her life she tried to be herself—Theodora Carson—not Theodora Watkins with all the baggage that name carried. She was haunted by the worry that someone in Virginia would discover her past. They might see her maiden name on her birth certificate, or she'd slip and say something that would tie her to this town and to that crazy Kate Watkins of Watkins Mill. Then they'd attach her to the stories and she'd be right back in this cabin, unable to be anyone but the daughter of Kate Watkins."

"So she never came back?"

Belle shook her head. "Never. Would you if your mother was the local Lizzie Borden? She warned me not to come back here, either. 'Don't stir up the mud,' she told me. 'Let the dead lie.'"

"But Kate was her mother. Didn't she ever write to her?"

"I don't know. I doubt it. I don't think she ever told her I was born."

Mia felt a stab of empathy for both women. "That's so harsh."

"Who's to say? The name Kate Watkins was rarely spoken in our home, and when it was, it was with contempt. I grew to hate her myself."

"Why? You never even met her."

"I didn't have to know her for her name to bring me pain." She straightened her shoulders and sat back in the hardwood chair. "My mother was an alcoholic." She sighed. "I can say that now, after years of therapy. My mother was an alcoholic," she repeated slowly. "Of course, I didn't know that big word when I was a kid. I only knew that whenever my mother drank she became mean and surly and that was the only time she'd talk. I used to tremble in my bed when I heard the ice chink in the glass at night, knowing she'd come and wake me and make me listen. When she was drunk she always wanted to have someone to talk to, and that someone was me. I didn't like her very much when she drank. She said some pretty horrible things about Kate. And about living out here."

Mia felt for the young girl woken up from sleep to hear that abuse. "Didn't she have any friends? Someone her own age she could confide in?"

"That's the sad part. She blamed her mother for not having any friends when she was growing up. But she never had any friends after she left, either."

Mia rocked and thought of the sadness and bitterness that Belle had grown up with. Right or wrong, it sounded like Kate Watkins was the scapegoat for all of Theodora's unhappiness. She thought about the optimism and spirit she'd discovered in the diaries. She couldn't match the cruel harridan of Theodora's story with the girl who wrote those words. There was something amiss in this perception, but Mia didn't know what it was.

"Aren't you curious about your grandmother? What she was really like? Don't you want to know her?"

"No," Belle shot back like a bullet. "She's nothing to me but a shame to get past."

Mia felt a stirring in the air, a breeze from the open window.

"Belle, if you feel that way, why didn't you sell the cabin?"

"Who'd buy it? Folks around here say it's haunted."

"Not everyone believes in ghosts. It's a beautiful spot. Someone from off would buy it. I'd buy it if I had the money."

"Goddamn, it should be easy for me to sell this place. It'd make my life easier, I can tell you that. But I . . . I never had much family. My mother had turned her back on the Watkins name but she never met the Carson family, either. So she was pretty much alone. She did her best, but she wasn't a very strong person and she didn't have much education. She read a lot, mind you, but she never had the money for college so she worked as a waitress, then got promoted to a manager. But she never made much money."

Belle wiped her face with her palms. "So it was a shock when she died and I found out I inherited this cabin and the eighty-seven acres it sits on. My mother always was short of cash and my first thought was, Why she just didn't sell it? She'd held on to it all those years, paid taxes on it when she didn't have a dollar to spare. I had to ask myself, What she was holding on to? That's why I'm going to hang on to it for a while, at least until I figure out the answer to that question."

Mia stopped rocking and studied Belle's face. Her brown eyes, usually so calm, were full of sorrow, and lines she'd never noticed before creased her forehead. Mia hadn't known Belle all that long but she knew Belle was the person everyone went to when they needed support. She was more a mentor than friend. It could hardly be anything other than that, considering Belle was the guide and the leader of the retreat, and now her landlord. Yet somewhere from then to now they had crossed some line toward friendship. She was glad Belle felt able to confide some of the hurt of her past. Now, at least, it wasn't all about Mia's pain. For a friendship to develop, it took two equals.

Mia gripped the sides of her chair and raised herself to standing. She went to the fridge and pulled out a bottle of white wine. Grabbing two small glasses she poured a liberal amount in each, then carried them back to the table. She handed one to Belle.

"Cheers," Mia said, raising her glass.

Belle clinked glasses with her and they both took a long drink. Mia thought Belle looked a little uncomfortable for having opened up so much of herself.

"Maybe," Mia ventured, "some of your answers are here in this cabin. In this town. Maybe you should be staying here. Not me."

"No way."

"Why not? Are you ashamed of being related to Kate?"

Belle looked incredulous. "Wouldn't you be ashamed if your grandmother was considered a murderer?" She took another long sip of wine. "Besides, this place gives me the creeps. Maybe it is haunted, after all."

"If it is haunted," Mia ventured, "the spirit isn't angry. She's . . ."

Belle's eyes narrowed. "What? Did you see a ghost?"

Mia wanted to laugh. "No, nothing like that. It's more a feeling I get sometimes. I sense a presence in the house, especially her bedroom. It's Kate."

Belle looked around the house with an uneasy expression. "I don't put any store in that crap. You're just alone too much up here. You've been through a lot, Mia. Facing death can sometimes make you dwell too much on death and dying. Careful, lest you lose your balance. It could be that's what happened to my grandmother out here."

"Or your mother."

"Maybe," Belle conceded. "I'd hate for you to become more unhappy. You're kind of on my watch, you know."

"Don't worry. I'm not dwelling on death at all, Belle. Quite the opposite. I'm focusing on living."

Belle came to her side and took hold of her hands. "I'm glad. Really glad. You look better than when I left you here that first night, that's for sure. Did you contact your husband?"

"Yes. We had a rather unpleasant phone call. He wants a divorce."

"I see," she said without surprise. "And what about you?"

"I don't have any choice. He wants to marry the woman I saw him with. Apparently they've been having an affair."

Belle squeezed her hands. "That's not what I'm asking. How do you *feel* about getting a divorce?"

Mia took a deep breath and in that space of time heard a birdcall outside her window. She recognized the strident cry as that of the Carolina wren. Belle released her hands and crossed her arms, waiting.

"My feelings have run the gamut from fury to hurt to finally just wanting to move on. That's the good thing about being at a place like this. There are no distractions. No television or Internet and e-mails. I've had a lot of time to think about me. Not just about the divorce but all that existential stuff—my emotions, ambitions, beliefs. I've had the rug pulled out from me in so many ways."

"Are you coming to any conclusions?"

"Oh, I've a long way to go yet," Mia replied with a wry smile. "But I've come to terms with the fact that

Charles's betrayal was just one more betrayal. Far worse was the betrayal of my body."

"Have you forgiven it?"

"I'm making friends with it. I'm eating better, taking long walks. And fly-fishing."

"Glad to hear that."

"I've told Charles to go ahead with the divorce."

"Glad to hear that, too."

"So is my sister."

"I feel badly that I'm taking off so soon. I feel like I'm leaving you on your own up here."

"When do you leave?"

"In two days. I'm meeting the group in Edinburgh on Saturday."

"It's a dream trip. Six whole weeks fly-fishing in Scotland."

"Will you be OK while I'm gone?"

"Oh, sure I will. I'm getting used to the place. I have my routine. I'm fishing more and I'm making a few friends in town."

Belle's gaze sharpened. "You are?"

"You know, at the shops and restaurants. It's inevitable."

"I'm going to ask you the same thing my mother asked me. Don't stir up the mud while you're up here."

"I can't help going to town."

"The townsfolk might ask you questions, but keep telling them you don't know anything and the gossip will die down again. I just want the story of Kate Watkins to die."

Mia felt a shudder but nodded her head.

Belle turned and took hold of the fishing rods, her eyes gleaming at the sight of them. "At least my grandmother left me something of value."

"Are you sure you don't want to take the books?" Mia ventured. It was a small offering of the truth.

"No, you should read them while you're here."

"I'll help you carry the rods out," Mia offered. She suddenly wanted Belle to leave before she changed her mind.

As Belle loaded up her car with her treasured rods, she paused and swung her head around. "Mia, go on and get that rod I lent you. The one with the handle that didn't feel right."

"Oh, it's OK. I'll get used to it."

"No, go get it. You don't want a rod that doesn't feel right."

When Mia returned she saw that Belle had pulled out a different rod from her car and held it out to her. Mia recognized it immediately by the rosy coloring. It was a Temple Fork rod created especially for Casting for Recovery.

"I remember you liked this rod."

Mia took the rod and held the slim, cork handle. It fit comfortably in her grip. She gave it a quick forward cast. "Smooth," she said, repeating Belle's word about the Payne.

"Hang on to it, then. See how you do."

"Are you sure? But, what if I should hurt it? With my luck I'll break the tip tugging my fly from some tree."

"Hey, no big deal. So I'll get another one." She paused to look at her feet, then raising her head said, "I didn't mean to snap at you in there. Whenever I get to talking about *her*," she jerked her chin, indicating the cabin, "I get riled. We can't choose our families, can we? We can only try to get past some of them."

"Do you want to stay for dinner? I can't promise a feast but I can rustle up something."

"Wish I could. I have so much to get done before I go."

"Of course." She walked with Belle to the driver's side of the car and stood by as Belle climbed in and shut the door. She put the key in the ignition and fired it, then turned her head to smile up at Mia. For such a strong, sometimes intimidating woman, Belle had the sweetest smile.

"Thanks for the rod," Mia said, then chuckled self-consciously. "And the waders and the boots and the vest and everything else."

"You bet. And I wanted to tell you that the cabin looks real nice. I can tell you worked hard. I didn't want to leave with you thinking I didn't notice." She pulled out a cigar from her pocket and set it between her lips. "Scotland, here I come."

That night Mia lay in her bed feeling that she was caught in a river with several strong currents. The diary, the journals—they were part of a long, running story of a family. One that had deep pools and pockets. Belle might not be aware of it, but there was a connection waiting for her here in this cabin. From father to daughter to granddaughter they were tethered to a common line—a love of fly-fishing. That wasn't coincidental. It ran through their bloodline as sure and strong as the currents in a river. Belle sensed it, which was why she couldn't sell the property. Yet she was wary of it. Theodora's version of the truth couldn't be the whole story. Nor was the town's version of the truth.

And what was her role in this story? Mia wondered. She had one, she felt certain. From the moment she'd stepped foot into this cabin she'd felt she was supposed to be here. Or perhaps she was granted the boon of staying in exchange for . . . what? Was she to be the historian? The narrator? A bit player?

Forgive me, Belle, she thought, but she could only find out by immersing herself in the story. To find out who Kate Watkins was and what had happened to lead her to a life of isolation she had no choice but to dive into the river.

Or perhaps Belle's mother had said it right after all. To stir up the mud.

Chapter Eight

Women can make better fly fishers than men.
They hold their body with more control,
they follow directions well, and they have an
ability to finesse the line. And they don't try
to overpower the fly rod. Fly-fishing is more
about skill than strength. Of course, it helps
that women are smarter, too.

—KATE WATKINS'S FISHING DIARY

The Watkins Mill library was a two-story, tawny
brick building with white-trimmed windows.
Mia enjoyed walking along the tree-shaded
street and catching the mouthwatering scents emanating from restaurants catering to the tourists. Summer
was kicking in and the charming Victorian town was a
popular vacation spot for people seeking respite in the
mountains.

She stepped inside the library and welcomed the
blast of cool air conditioning. Though cheery light
poured in from the front windows, the rest of the
library was muted and dim. Only a few patrons sat at
the long wood tables or across the room in the comfortable collection of sofas, upholstered chairs, tables,

and lamps designed to look like a family room. Book clubs likely met there, she thought, and it would be a marvelous place for her to sit and read when she came to town.

Mia had come to do research about the woman young Kate had become. She walked around the few rooms of the library, making herself familiar with the space. There were two computers for the public and her heartbeat accelerated at the chance to check her e-mails. Old habits died hard, she thought as she settled into a chair and eagerly hooked up to the Internet.

She had seventy-two e-mails. As she scrolled down the list, she was disheartened to find that most of them were spam. The few others were from Maddie and a few friends. There were two from Charles, one dated prior to their last phone call asking that she call. This had an urgent red flag attached. The second was dated yesterday, also with a red flag. She took a breath and opened it.

GOT THE VISA BILL. WHAT ARE YOU DOING UP IN WATKINS MILL, NC? THIS IS NOT VACATION TIME. DO YOU EXPECT ME TO PAY THESE BILLS? CALL ME.

It was just like him to shout at her in capital letters. Mia puffed up her cheeks and exhaled. Well, Charles knew where she was now. What did it matter, really? Except it was unfair of him to imply she was living in luxury, spending wildly. It'd be different if she'd flown off to some great hotel and he was getting whopping bills for room and food and spa treatments. Hardly the scenario. She'd spent a few measly hundred dollars on enough food and supplies to live on for weeks. And no rent! If she returned home, then he would have to leave. What difference did it make who left? Meanwhile he was undoubtedly still living his lifestyle of eating out most nights, going to bars, and playing golf. Of course, he'd consider that spending essential. But everything she spent on cleaning supplies and groceries and a few pairs of jeans he viewed as over the top. If she ate leftover chicken again she thought she'd gag.

He always knew how to boil her blood, but flying off the handle was not going to help the situation, she decided. She composed herself and replied with an e-mail that she had to rewrite several times to delete any nasty tone that crept in. In the end she whittled it down to a few unemotional lines.

Charles,

I thought we'd come to an agreement. You are staying in OUR house. I am living rent free at a friend's house. I will necessarily accrue some bills but will continue to be frugal. I expect that you will be as well. If this is unsatisfactory, it is clear you cannot mediate the divorce and I will seek my own representation immediately. If this is acceptable,

I expect my living expenses here to be paid by our
joint account. I cannot call you readily as phone
service is nil. We can leave messages.

> Please advise.
>
> Mia

Before pushing the send button, she affixed a red
flag. Along with the e-mail she sent off all the anger
bubbling in her veins into cyberspace. She harnessed
her attention and focused on her new quest.

"Who are you, Kate Watkins?" she murmured as
she typed the name into the search engine.

It felt good to have a project that she could sink her
teeth into. Her mind needed to work again and deflect
her thoughts from herself for a while. Her fingers
clicked rapidly on the keyboard as she hunted through
several results, following trails: Kate Watkins. Katherine Watkins. She was disappointed to find so little
information. The Watkins family apparently was not as
illustrious as she'd first thought. There were references
to the historical family but most of the information
was repetitive, offering similar document sources. She
kept copious notes in a notebook.

After two hours she shut down the computer and
yawned, stretching her arms over her head. It wasn't
all that fruitful a search. All her digging revealed
was that the Watkins ancestors had settled in western North Carolina in the 1740s with a land grant of
three thousand acres. Mia had to pause as she read
that number. Those were the days of enormous land

grants delivered from governments with a flick of the pen. Could she even imagine owning so much land today?

The family remained prosperous until the Civil War, when North Carolina seceded from the Union and the Watkins sons marched off to battle. She traced their war records, discovering that all four sons had joined a company called the Buncombe Rifles and marched off to war behind a flag made from the silk dresses of town belles. One son died as a prisoner of war and two other sons died in battle. Mia felt a stirring of sympathy for the mother who had lost three beloved sons. Only one son, the youngest named Robert, survived. He had returned home, injured and sick, to his grief-stricken parents. They died soon after, leaving Robert to face alone the trials of the Reconstruction era. He had fared better than his Watkins relations. Their homes and plantations had either been burned to the ground or sold.

Robert Watkins had hung on to his parcel with tooth and nail. He had strength of will and tenacity that Mia thought was passed down to his granddaughter, Kate. He sold off most of his land in parcels to support the rebuilding of the mill business. Eventually he married and fathered a son, Walter, and a daughter, Ann, who died young. By the turn of the century Walter Watkins owned less than five hundred of the original three thousand acres. Walter became a minister and married Isobel Rogers and had a daughter, Katherine. This last parcel of land and the estate house was lost in

1930, apparently due to heavy losses in the stock market crash of 1929.

The reports ended here.

Mia closed her notebook, feeling half full. As she tapped her pen against her lip she wondered about the loss of the family estate. Kate's father had been her hero as a child, yet he'd lost the family land and home to the stock market crash. Odd, she thought, that a minister who loved to fly-fish would also love to play the stock market. It seemed out of character for the gentle, retiring man she'd read about in Kate's diary. But, Mia thought, it would not be out of character for adventurous Kate.

Mia's mind was pressing with questions as she rose and walked to the librarian sitting behind the counter. She looked exactly like Mia thought a town librarian should look: a prim, elderly woman, slight in build but straight-backed. Her gray hair was severely pulled into a French twist but errant wisps floated around her head as she bent over the computer keyboard.

"Excuse me," Mia said, coming to the long wood counter.

The woman's hands paused from typing and she lifted her gaze. From behind horn-rimmed glasses, steel blue eyes delivered a cool appraisal. "Yes?"

"I need some help finding information, please."

The woman straightened with the air of someone being disturbed from some important task to deal with something no doubt trivial. She rose and clasped her hands on the counter and said archly, "How can I help you?"

"I'm looking for information on the Watkins family."

"Oh? What kind of information?"

"Anything I can find."

"Well," she said with a condescending laugh. "It's an old family."

"I know," Mia replied in an even tone. "I did some initial research. I have the genealogy. I know that they owned the mill that gave the town its name and that they lost their money after the crash in nineteen twenty-nine. I'm especially interested in Kate Watkins. I've heard she left town to live in the cabin at Watkins Cove and stayed there until her death in nineteen fifty-two."

The woman surveyed her with more interest. "Why, may I ask, are you interested in Kate Watkins?"

"Let me introduce myself. I'm Mia Landan. I'm staying in the cabin at Watkins Cove."

A flicker of recognition flashed in her eyes. "Ah yes, I heard someone had opened up the cabin. After all these years." Her gaze sharpened. "Are you a relative?"

"No. I'm staying with the permission of Kate Watkins's granddaughter."

"Oh? I didn't know she had a granddaughter. What is her name?"

"Belle Carson."

She nodded her head as though in recognition. "I see. What do you want to know?"

"Well." Mia stopped. "Excuse me, but I don't know your name." Mia thought that turnaround was fair play in this town.

"Phyllis. Phyllis Pace." She said the last name with a ring of pride.

Mia smiled, recognizing the name as the same she had seen carved in granite over a redbrick building on Main Street. "It's nice to meet you, Mrs. Pace."

"That's Miss Pace," she said, lifting her chin a tad higher. "Not Missus."

"Sorry. Miss Pace." Mia opened her notebook on the counter and went through her notes, all business now. "I can't find any information about the family after the stock market crash in nineteen twenty-nine. The trail ends with how Walter Watkins lost everything."

"That's not entirely true. It puts unfair blame on Reverend Watkins. In fact the Watkinses' fortunes began their downfall much earlier, after the Civil War. Back when they had the mill. I don't remember exactly when the mill closed, but by the time it did, the railroad had come to town. Instead of the mill, money came in from tourists. The Watkins family, well, their money just sort of dwindled. They sold their land, bit by bit. Then there was the stock market crash. Everyone lost their shirts in the Depression. The Watkins were like many of the other great families of that era, I suppose. The library has boxes of letters and correspondence of the family that were donated."

"Really?" Mia felt the thrill of the hunt pumping in her veins.

"They're not of a personal nature. These are largely business papers and household accounts. They're important in an historical sense, of course. But I warn you, it makes for some pretty dry reading."

"Thank you, Miss Pace. I'd love to see them."

"Well then," she said, and Mia caught a flash of interest. "Do you see that reading room in the far corner? If you wait there, I'll go get them and be back."

A short while later Phyllis carried in two boxes to Mia's table in the reading room. After instructions on the proper handling of the materials, Phyllis came back into the room several times, eyeing Mia, obviously nervous over the handling of the collection.

Mia set down her pencil. "Phyllis, perhaps you'd like to help?"

"Well, if you think I could." Phyllis gratefully took a chair beside Mia's and together they sorted through the documents.

After an hour of sorting and reading bank statements, household records, financial holdings, address books, and assorted photographs, Mia leaned back in her chair and rubbed her eyes. "You were right," she said morosely. "This was tough reading."

"Again," Phyllis replied with a hint of a teacher in her voice. "These documents have great historical value. You saw how much of the documentation was what was considered women's work. In those records we can mine so much rich cultural information. The library was most fortunate that the Watkins family donated their collection to us."

"I now know how much they paid for a slave. But I still don't know anything more about Kate. Not even a photograph of her."

Phyllis sighed deeply and her face relaxed. "Ah yes, Kate . . ."

Mia's attention sharpened at the change in Phyllis's tone. "Did you know her?"

"Me? Heavens no. I'm not that old. But, my father has told me so many stories about her. They were friends, you know. Oh, what a time it must have been when they were young. This area was a Mecca for the la-di-da types. The trains brought the glamorous out-side world into our sleepy hollow. In fact, it was the trains that changed this town. Even before my father's time, my grandfather told us the whole town used to sigh with relief each time they heard the train whistle blowing, because that signaled the train made it up the steep incline to town. They'd all come running to see what celebrity stepped off the train."

"What brought them here?"

She leaned back in her chair and steepled her fin-gers under her chin. "At the turn of the century thou-sands of people came for the curative powers of the spring water. *To take the waters* was how they phrased it. A lot of them came from Charleston. But then the railroad came, and by the twenties folks came from all around seeking more than wellness. They came to breathe the fresh mountain air, to fish in our rivers, and to escape the miasma of city air in the summer. Fancy hotels sprang up everywhere. And along with them the businesses that cater to the tourists. The mill wasn't important in Watkins Mill anymore."

"What happened to it?"

"The same thing that happened to the sanitariums. It closed its doors as businesses often do."

"What happened to Walter and Kate if the mill closed?"

"Walter Watkins was a minister. That was a proper profession for an educated man of a certain wealth in those days. He had enough money to maintain a secure but perhaps more modest lifestyle for himself and his daughter. He kept the estate as best he could. Though the property did fall into some disrepair over the years."

"What became of Mrs. Watkins, Kate's mother?"

"Isobel Watkins? She died in childbirth. I thought that would have been in the records."

Mia shook her head. "So Kate was raised by Mrs. Hodges."

"How did you know about Mrs. Hodges?"

Mia fumbled for an answer that would not give away the diaries. "I must have heard her name from someone."

Phyllis mulled that over, looking doubtful. "It's been a long time since I've heard that name. Helena Hodges." Then she snickered like a child. "My father used to call her Hellsafire Hodges."

Mia chuckled, thinking Kate no doubt cast that line

many times as well. She leaned forward on the wood table, cupping her chin in her palm. "What else did your father tell you about Kate?"

Phyllis's eyes kindled. "Oh, there are lots of stories about Kate Watkins. Most everyone has one. I haven't thought about them for years, though. Kate Watkins, Lord, Lord, Lord . . . She was something. To be honest, I always wished I'd known her. She wasn't like most women of her time. I guess you could say she was a tomboy as a child and never changed. I'll tell you this. She loved to fish, that's for sure, and she didn't care one whit if the men around these parts liked it or not. And a lot of them did not, let me tell you. They considered it an affront that a woman would despoil their waters." Her eyes took on a faraway look. "That she would stand in the face of male opposition and follow her own call was a spirit I always found inspiring."

Phyllis Pace blinked, then, catching herself, smiled tightly. "But she was a Watkins and could do about anything she wanted and no one would dare speak up to her. Not to her face, anyway. She had her admirers, too. Scores of them."

"Can you tell me one of your father's stories?"

Phyllis steepled her fingers and deliberated. Then she placed her palms on the table and rose from her chair. "I have a better idea." She picked up the two boxes. "Come along. I always say a good researcher goes to the original source. My father's in the next room. He's in his nineties but fit as a fiddle. I bring him here once or twice a week, mostly for a change of scenery. He'd love nothing better than to tell you one of his stories." She led Mia from the room, muttering softly, "God knows, I've heard them enough."

Mia couldn't believe her good fortune. She quickly scooped up her notebook and pens, grabbed her purse, and followed Phyllis to the comfortable seating area she had admired earlier. Sitting in a cushy armchair under a large window was an elderly man slumped slightly in the shoulders, bent over a book. When they approached he lifted his eyes from the page. They were a very pale blue, almost opaque.

"Hello, Daddy," Phyllis said in a voice more tender than Mia would have thought possible from the stern woman. "I'd like you to meet someone." She turned and waved Mia closer. "Speak loudly," she said in a whisper. "He's hard of hearing and never wears his darn hearing aid." Turning back to her father she said with respect, "Mia, this is my father, Phillip Pace. Daddy, this is Mia. She wants to hear stories about your old friend Kate Watkins."

At the name of Kate Watkins, the old man's rheumy eyes sharpened. "Kate Watkins, eh?" he said after they'd shook hands and Mia took a seat beside him. "I won't be talking ill about her," he said in warning. "Nor about that damn nonsense about the investigation neither. Let it lie, I tell you. You won't hear a peep from me about *that*." His face grew stern and Mia saw immediately the family resemblance to Phyllis.

"No, sir," she quickly assured him. She made mental note of the word *investigation*. She'd not heard that mentioned before. "I'm more interested in the young Kate. Phyllis tells me that you were a friend of hers?"

His face relaxed with memory. Seeing him settle in, Phyllis gave a quick wave of her hand and hurried back to her desk, where a patron was waiting.

"I was that," Phillip said with a slow nod.

He looked out the window for a moment and went very still. Mia thought for a moment that she'd lost him. But he turned his head back and his eyes had a new clarity of vision.

"It was a long time ago," he began. "The summer of nineteen sixteen, if memory serves. I was younger than Kate by some years. More a tag-along friend, if you will. It was my older brother, Eddie, who was part of the gang. But she was good-natured about it. They all were. We fished together, you know. Me and Eddie, Kate, Henry Harrison, and Lowrance Davidson. Didn't matter if she was a girl. Hell's bells, she could outfish all of us. 'Cept maybe Lowrance." He rubbed his jaw, smiling to himself at some memory. "Nobody in the county could outfish or outshoot Low."

Mia seized on this, remembering Kate's diary. *Lowrance knows the names of all the plants, of course. But he's older than me.*

"I heard that name before, Lowrance. Who was he?"

"Low was her cousin!" he snapped, surprised she didn't know such a basic fact. "Everybody knows that. Low and Kate, they were like two peas in a pod. Always jotting notes down in their journals. Always with their heads together over something. Low, he had a microscope and sat bent over that thing for hours on end. He said how he was going to be a . . . what's the word? A botanist, that's it. Those two went collecting leaves and critters and you name it. She liked the critters, especially. Said it helped her be a better fisherman. I never got into that. I mean, I know how to read the water just fine without having to draw some critter in a book! Pshaw . . ." He worked his jaw like he tasted something unpleasant.

"I reckon I was just a mite jealous of Low getting so much of Kate's time. Lowrance, you see, he was more than just her cousin. He looked out for her, same as Eddie did for me. I guess you could say he was her best friend. We all knew none of us had a chance with her. By the time she grew up, just about every man in the land of sky was in love with her. Yes, me too. Even though I was wet behind the ears. But that Lowrance," he said more loudly, jabbing a digit into the armrest of the chair to make his point. "That's a man that well and truly loved Kate. And I daresay she loved him, too." He shook his head with sorrow. "It's a damn shame how it all ended. Things would've turned out different for our Kate if he lived, that's for sure."

"Tell me about him," Mia said, and moved to the edge of her chair.

Phillip Pace sat clutching the armrests, lost in his memories. Then, gradually, his face eased and he loosened his grip on the chair. The leather creaked as he leaned back against the cushion.

"Ah, Kate," he said in a faraway voice. "I was just a kid. Hardly big enough to tag along with the boys—but I did. I don't remember much, but I remember Kate. Did you hear the story about how she used her dancing lessons to help her cast?"

Summer 1916

War was on everyone's mind that summer. In the barbershop the men talked about nothing else 'cept the battles and death tolls in the trenches. The wives and mothers in town were worried sick about conscription. They spoke of little else in the beauty salon. My mother didn't allow war talk at the dinner table, though. She said it upset the digestion and from what my friends told me, their mothers banned the topic, too. Maybe mothers throughout the county—maybe even the nation—laid down the same law. We boys used to laugh that our mamas thought war talk would give us mustard gas.

On one hot summer afternoon, we fellas were playing soldier in the woods. We were marching in single file like a troop, using our fishing rods as guns, that sort of thing. Just fooling around. But in our hearts, we were ready to sign up and go to war. We thought it would be an adventure and we could fire real guns and be heroes, like in the movies.

We'd been waiting on Kate to meet us. She had dance class every Thursday, which never sat well with

her. Her Aunt Grace and Mrs. Hodges had ganged up
on the Reverend and told him in no uncertain terms
that Kate needed to learn to be a lady. I guess they
thought dance lessons were part of feminine schooling.
That summer she'd turned sixteen, almost full grown.
For years she'd taken dance lessons and for years we'd
waited for her.

Anyway, we were out playing soldier when all of a
sudden we see this rock come flying at us and hear a
voice calling, "Bombs away!" First we ducked, then we
swung our heads around, fists at the ready.

Kate was standing on a rise a few yards back with
her hands on her hips and her face red and scowling.

"You boys quit playing soldiers, hear?" she called
out. "You're not going to some stupid ol' war. President
Wilson said so. Not ever!"

Lowrance straightened and began walking toward
her. He was the undeclared leader of our troop. He was
also the tallest, which gave him the edge. And the oldest. But mostly, he had this even-tempered way about
him that made folks want to listen to what he had to
say. His thick hair was the color of sand but he had the
dark brown eyes of the Watkins line.

"Kate! You're late," Low called out.

Low was the only one who could talk to Kate that
way. She just smiled in a sly way that made my heart do
a little leap whenever I saw it. I knew Low felt the same,
too, 'cause I could see it in his face. It'd always been
that way between them. Like they had some secret

that only they shared. Then Kate sat on the ground and pulled off her stockings. This wasn't anything unusual. She liked being bare-legged in the summer.

Mrs. Hodges told Kate she was prone to what she called "moments of excess exuberance." But sometimes Kate just liked to show off. Kate came running and when she got near the small creek that separated us she went and hitched up her skirt and cried, "Look at me! I'm a ballerina!" She leaped across the creek, throwing one leg ahead and the other behind, stretching them far out and flinging her arms out to the side. We all watched agog and damn if she wasn't just like a dancer I've seen in some magazine.

She landed on the other side of the creek, laughing and catching her breath. Low's face had grown still and his smile was gone. He leaned close when she came up and put his lips near her ear.

"You ought not to be flinging your dress up like that, showing your bare legs. Not in front of the boys."

Kate looked over at us. Henry and Eddie ducked their heads and kicked their feet in the dirt, embarrassed. I started looking at anything I could as long as it wasn't at her bare legs.

"Aw, Low, you know I hate it when my stockings pick up beggar's-lice from the prickly weeds. Besides, they're not boys. They're just Phil, Henry, and Eddie."

Eddie looked stricken but Henry snickered and said, "Why are you taking those stupid dancing classes anyway?"

"Yeah," Eddie said. His ears were as red as his hair.

My brother was seven years older than me. I was the youngest of eight Pace children and each of us a red-head. Yet I was only the second son. With six sisters, was it any wonder I clung to my older brother like a kudzu vine? So if Eddie took a side, I did, too.

"Why're you doing that?" I asked Kate. "Dancing is for girls."

The boys flicked their eyes at Kate before they threw back their heads and commenced hooting and hollering. Most girls would've glared at them, but Kate tossed her head back and laughed as hard as the rest of them. Then she came up and ruffled my hair. I was only a boy, but I felt special being singled out by Kate like that.

"I am a girl," she told me like it was an admission. "But I'm not like any girl you've ever met or are likely to meet."

"She's one of a kind, our Kate," Eddie said. We all knew he was head over heels in love with her.

"But she still is a girl," Henry said. "And silly girls have to do things like learn to dance and cook and play the piano so they can catch a husband. We all know girls aren't supposed to go catching fish. So maybe you better dance on back home, little girl, and let us men go on to our fishing."

Now Henry was nice enough, but we knew he was the type that liked to egg someone on. He had shrewd little eyes and when he taunted someone, he always made me think of a snake.

Kate spun around to face him, her face coloring. "At

least I don't go marching around playing soldier like you boys. I saw you poking and jabbing in the air." She crossed her arms and said in a haughty tone, "I might be a girl but I know the difference between a rod and a gun."

"We weren't playing, we were practicing, just so you know," Henry said, coloring. His small eyes got smaller. "There's a war going on and we're going to be fighting soon. Not play fighting, either, but real combat. With real guns. And you won't be able to come. Do you know why? Because you're a girl, that's why."

"Well," she sputtered, balling her hands in fists at her sides. She looked ready to fight us all to stop us from leaving Watkins Mill and going off to war. "I may be a girl. But do you know what you are, Henry Harrison? You're a boy. Not a man. A boy! And everybody knows you have to be eighteen to join the army."

She lifted her chin high and looked at the other boys, her eyes blazing, daring them to challenge her. Henry's face turned beet red because he couldn't refute that he was only sixteen and all his bluster wouldn't make any difference because we all knew he would have to wait until he turned eighteen before he—or any of the other boys—could enlist.

"Besides," she said, twisting the dagger. "That ol' war will be over by the time you're old enough."

"It will not!" Henry fired back.

"Henry," Lowrance said in a warning tone. "You're talking crazy. We should all pray that the war is over soon."

Eddie nodded his head in agreement. I took a step closer to my brother and leaned against his leg.

"I'm not talking crazy," Henry shouted. "They say the war is going to sweep across Europe like wildfire."

"Fine. Then go on and fight fires in Europe," she said, exasperated with the whole conversation. "I'm going fishing."

"She's right," Eddie said, picking up his gear. "The fish will be biting."

"I don't know if I want to fish anymore with a girl," Henry said.

We all knew he was a sore loser, but Low puffed up his chest and told Henry to take it back. Things got a little tense then on account of Henry was a big fella, even as a boy, with a quick temper. Low was slow to rise, but when he did, look out. So if they fought they were evenly matched. It was going to be a whopping.

Kate would have none of it. She stepped smack between those two roosters. She was a fearless creature to behold, standing there with her long, dark hair blowing in the breeze and her eyes blazing. She was almost eye to eye with Henry but as lean as a reed. Kate glared and said she was a better fly fisher than he was.

Henry snorted and said something stupid, like "Let's have a match right now."

Kate put her hands on her hips and told him she would meet him at the Fly-Fishing Tournament being held the next week in Asheville. She was fixing on competing in the distance category. She figured that would shut up not only Henry but all the men who looked at her funny each time she cast a fly in local water.

Phillip chortled then and slapped his knee. Mia laughed a bit herself, enjoying the memory. Mr. Pace was a natural storyteller and had her wrapped around each syllable.

"So what happened at the tournament?" she asked.

"What do you think happened?" he asked, astonished. "She won, of course. Just like we all knew she would. Tradition being what it was back then, the angling clubs were for men only. They didn't even allow women in their building for meetings. Her daddy, the Reverend Watkins, was so well respected a fisherman in these parts that they let his daughter enter the fly casting distance competition on his behalf. More a courtesy. Land alive, were they surprised when she beat them all!"

Phillip's face softened and his pale eyes grew misty. "I tell you, Kate was a picture that morning as she stepped out in the field. I can still see her in that kelly green skirt and stout shoes, and over her long hair she wore her favorite tam-o'-shanter hat with dry flies stuck in it. There was grumbling, to be sure. More from the fine Asheville ladies than the men. I mean, it simply wasn't done. But I tell you this slip of a girl walked onto that field of men with the confidence of a queen. She parted the waters. You know, she used to tell me that she had the blood of Scottish royalty in her veins. My brother, Eddie, didn't think that was true but he said it didn't matter, because in our town, just being a Watkins was high enough.

"Now here's the thing and I don't want to miss telling you that's most important. It's not just that she won, but *how* she won that stole our hearts—men and women alike. Bear with me because I'm old and I know I'm not going to explain this right."

Phillip shook his head and worked his jaw a bit in thought. "I can see it in my mind clear as day, but my words won't do her justice. When Kate Watkins cast that rod, why it was like watching her dance. Does that make sense? I mean to say it was pure grace and timing in motion. Yes, ma'am, watching her extend her arm forward and pointing her foot behind, her long line slicing the air in a tight loop to land far, far off in the water, she was as dainty as any ballet dancer. You could hear the whole crowd gasp.

"And that's when it hit me. I laughed out loud because I remembered how Kate leaped across the stream that day and cried out *'Look at me! I'm a ballerina!'* Our clever girl was using her dance lessons to create her own style of casting. Not a man's casting or a woman's casting. Just better, because any fool could see she was more than a fisherman. She was an artist.

"I was just a kid back then and didn't know nothing, but I learned what great casting was by watching her." His eyes misted and he looked down at his shoes.

"They took the award away from her. She set a record for man or woman, and they went and disqualified her because she was a woman." He shook his head. "That never set right with me and I hold a grudge against the club even still. The whole town did. From that day forward no one gave Kate Watkins the business when she fished in a river. Truth be told, I don't think the award mattered to her much. She told me later that it meant more than the award that Henry came up to her straightaway and apologized. 'Bout killed him to do it, but it honored her."

"So Kate Watkins never earned the recognition she deserved?" Mia asked.

"I didn't say that," Phillip said, bringing his head up. "Our Kate was famous in her time! Why, folks use to come in on the trains just to meet her and fish with her. They'd all read her articles, I reckon."

"Articles? What articles?"

Phillip screwed up his face and cast Mia a doubt-ful glance. "You sure don't know your history, do you? I'm talking about Kate's newspaper articles. The ones that went out all across the country." He scratched the back of his neck, muttering, "Now what did she call it?" He dropped his hand and his eyes lit up. "'On the Fly.' That's it. Never missed a copy. It was published right here in our own newspaper, too. I'll just bet they have copies of them lying around somewhere."

Mia was electrified by this new lead. She made quick notations in her notebook. Yet her mind kept coming back to Lowrance and Kate. She couldn't reconcile the sweetness between Kate and her cousin as children and the tragedy that would come later. There seemed to be such love there. What could have happened that led to murder?

"Forgive me, Mr. Pace, for asking. But I'm confused. What happened between Kate Watkins and Lowrance Davidson? They seemed so devoted to each other."

His eyes grew cloudy and his expression sad. "Yeah. Well, the war brought tragedy to so many families."

"The war? I don't understand."

"Lowrance Davidson went off to fight in World War I along with my brother Eddie and Henry Harrison. They all enlisted together, just as soon as they turned eighteen. Got sent over in, oh, the spring of nineteen eighteen, I believe. I remember Henry was nervous the war would end before he got there. Well, he got there, all right. They all did. My brother was wounded. He made it back, but the influenza killed him like it did my sister and my mother. Henry Harrison lost his arm. It was his casting arm, too. It soured him, but that's another story."

"And Lowrance?"

The old man sighed heavily, his chest sinking. "Lowrance Davidson died in the trenches in the fall of nineteen eighteen. Kate was never the same. I reckon Kate's life would've turned out different if he'd lived. Who's to say? But the fact is Lowrance never returned to Watkins Mill."

"Then who did Kate Watkins murder?"

Mr. Pace drew back in his chair and his mouth fell

open in outrage. "Murder? Kate never killed anybody. I thought you knew that or I wouldn't have spent five minutes with you telling you my stories."

Mia drew back, stunned and confused. "I'm sorry. I only heard—"

"Lies, that's what they are. A pack of lies. You best not be saying things like that to me, young lady. I'll set you straight. You got that?"

Chapter Nine

Catch and Release is the practice in fly-fishing of catching a fish then returning that fish unharmed to the water. In some places it's mandated for conservation. But I always figure it's more satisfying to choose life over death. Plus, the fish you release to reproduce will create more angling opportunities in the future.

—Stuart MacDougal

One camp in fly-fishing believed that the sport was all about casting. Another camp felt that catching the fish was what brought anglers back to the water. Mia was in the dawning stage of learning the sport and she was happy just to go to the river. It was easy to stay indoors where it was comfortable. For months after her chemotherapy, complacency had become too familiar. Occasionally when she was alone in the cabin, Mia caught herself sinking under the black pool of depression where Charles's betrayal and the divorce lay at the murky bottom.

Thus for Mia, the river was like Ariadne's thread. She followed it out from the darkness of depression's labyrinth to the light of the river. In the river she felt warmed by the sun, cooled by the water, filled with hope each time she cast her line onto the water.

On one of her treks along the river trail she'd discovered a breathlessly beautiful pocket where swift water broke over scattered white rocks. Mia intended to return this afternoon.

It was a hot day in late June and the water of the river was warming. She'd waited for the late afternoon when the fish would start biting, and she'd packed light, going wet wading. She found she could stand comfortably in the shallow water in her shorts and boots, just not for too long or her legs became numb. In her backpack she stuffed the felt-bottom boots, a bottle of water, and a peanut butter sandwich wrapped in cellophane.

In her zipper pouch she carefully packed all the fishing supplies and gadgets that she'd at last learned to use: a dry fly, floatant to dry the fly during fishing, snips that looked like fingernail clippers to trim the line, forceps to press the barbs flat and to help remove hooks, and polarized sunglasses to protect the eyes and to help see the fish through the water's glare.

She walked through the forest, following the river and enjoying the gentle breezes along the shaded trail. As the trail journeyed deeper into the woods, the ferns grew thick, lush moss cloaked the rocks, and her shoes became damp with dew. She passed a familiar cluster of rhododendron and felt a surge of excitement, knowing her secret spot was just around the bend. She walked another twenty feet, then came to an abrupt stop.

A strange man in waders and a tan vest was standing on her favorite bank. In a relaxed stance, he studied the water. His focus was intense; he did not stir or look over his shoulder as she approached.

Mia was indignant but held back. She knew it would be bad manners to barge in too close. Yet this was her special spot. She felt her sanctuary had been invaded. Scowling, she folded her arms while she deliberated what to do.

From the moment he raised his rod into the air it was clear this man was no beginner. His masterful casts fell into a natural rhythm, back and forth, allowing his line to unfurl longer and longer in a ballet of tight loops. She'd never seen his equal. Not even Belle. While watching this aerial dance her mind flew back to old Mr. Pace's description of Kate's casting at the tournament so many years ago. Mia knew this was what it must have been like for those people watching her. She was experiencing the same wonder and awe at poetry in motion.

Mia found herself moving her arm in sync with his, eager to absorb his seamless motion if only by some cosmic osmosis. Her lips moved as she counted the beats—*throw back the line, skip a beat, thrust forward, ease down.* When enough line had been released, he allowed the fly to touch the water delicately, as natural as a live insect. A trout rose to take the fly, leaping and splashing in a tremendous display.

Mia warred between resentfulness and admiration. He made it look so easy. She'd fished here for two days, spent hours on the river, and tried an array of flies, but she never caught anything but moss. It hadn't mattered to her before. She was content to stand in the river and practice casting. Yet now, suddenly, she felt desperate to catch a fish.

He reeled in the line; then, with a smooth sweep, he captured a large, glistening rainbow trout into his net. The angler removed the hook efficiently and released the beautiful fish back to the river.

Mia realized she had no choice but to relinquish her spot to this man. She walked forward and called out, "Hello! Excuse me. Do you mind if I fish upstream?"

He turned his head and looked at her over his shoulder. She couldn't see his eyes behind his polarized lenses, but he seemed as surprised at seeing another person this far into the backwoods as she had been.

"Go on ahead." He turned back to the river.

Mia had grown accustomed to the townspeople hailing out friendly greetings and coming up to introduce themselves. She should have appreciated his being aloof, but instead it annoyed her. Her boots crunched the gravel loudly as she passed, and she hoped she scared every fish in the pool away. Serves him right for taking my spot, she thought, well aware that these were not the thoughts of the serene sportswoman she hoped to become. A moment later she heard the swish of the water as her uninvited companion caught yet another trout.

Farther up the stream rushed quickly in riffles. Another nice spot, she thought, but not *as* nice as the one she'd forfeited. Trees and shrubs were heavy along the water at this stretch. She didn't want to feed the greedy trees her dry fly. She sneaked a look downstream at the stranger. He was casting toward a different spot in the river now, using short roll casts. The roll cast was nothing much more than a short push forward and then letting the line fall into the water. Mia figured even she could do that.

She cast a few in one riffle, still not able to get the fly quite where she wanted it to go. She tried casting a few around a large rock. The wily trout were not tempted by her poor presentation. Was she dropping her wrist again, she wondered? Was she extending too far? She grew petulant and wondered why the fish didn't like her little brown dry fly. The sun was slowly lowering but she didn't want another day to end without a strike. She cast again. From down the river she heard the stranger's excited "Good one!" Looking over she saw him bring in another trout to the net. She tugged the visor of her baseball cap lower. She was clumsily hitting the water so hard with her fly that she was like a fool drummer chasing all the trout right to him, she thought meanly.

Then she laughed at herself. What did it matter? She couldn't let some man she'd never met rattle her so badly. Come on, Mia, she scolded herself, thinking of Belle's advice to have fun.

She relaxed her shoulders, then walked across

slippery pebbles and silt to stand in the middle of the river. The current was strong and the water cold but shallow. Looking over her shoulder and seeing that there was no tree branch waiting to grab her fly, she let loose a full cast. It felt good to hear the line slice through the air as it went back. She didn't hurry. This time she waited a beat as she'd seen the man do, then pointed the rod to where she wanted her line to go. Her line slowly unfurled, then dropped the fly on the water without a splash. The current caught her fly and she saw a gray shadow in the water bolt for it. A second later her fly was sucked under the water. A fish!

She jerked the tip of her rod up to set the hook. She felt the tug again, stronger this time. Her eyes widened with surprise. She had actually caught a fish! The contact was like a jolt of electricity straight from the fish to her heart.

Her giddy elation quickly changed to panic. Her heart beat fast and her feet slid over the slippery river rocks as she followed the fish downstream. In her mind's ear she could hear Belle shouting, *Keep your rod up! Give it line!*

Where is Belle? her mind cried out. Mia stripped the line, pulling the tired fish in. When it got near she reached out to pull it close. At the end of the line was a sweet brook trout, not more than eight inches long. Dipping her hand in the water, she lowered and grasped the beautiful olive green fish in her palm. It was gulping and gasping wildly for air. The trout had fought too hard and was too young.

"I'm as scared as you are," she told the fish as she tried to remove the hook, but her hands were shaking so badly she could barely hold the fish, much less maneuver the tiny hook. The fish gave a hard wiggle, its mouth gasping for air. Mia looked up in a wild panic.

"Help!" she cried out. "I need some help!"

She lowered the fish so that it was in the water, and she tugged at the hook, but she couldn't get it loose from the fish's mouth. The fish gave a shudder, then lay limp in her hand. Its fish eye seemed to stare at her, imploring her for mercy.

"Can I help you?" said a deep voice from behind her.

Mia swung her head around. The man from down river stood beside her. His back was to the sun, cutting a long, dark silhouette against the glare.

"Please, I can't get the hook out! Can you take it out?"

He lowered beside her and wet his hands in the river. Then he took the trout. Cradled in his hands, the brookie looked small and fragile.

"Is the hook barbless?" he asked, referring to the cardinal rule of crushing the barb. A barbed hook would rip the fish's mouth.

"Yes," she replied, eyes on the fish. Its mouth opened in weaker gasps. She'd held it out of the water too long. "Hurry!"

He had long, slender fingers and he removed the

hook from the mouth with a surgeon's dexterity. Then he gently lowered it into the water. The fish didn't move.

"Oh, God, I killed it," Mia cried. She had come to the river to find peace after narrowly escaping death. That she could bring death to this sweet, glistening trout crushed her spirit.

"No, you didn't," he said, and his tone was gentle. "It just needs a minute to revive." He turned his head to look at her. Without his sunglasses, she was struck by the directness of his gaze. "I take it you've never done this before?"

"Not alone."

"Watch closely. What you have to do is hold the fish facing upstream in the current . . . like so. It forces oxygen back into its system. See the gill plates opening and closing? OK, let's see how he does."

He opened his hand but the slender fish did not dart away as Mia expected. She clutched the man's arm. "It's not swimming!"

"Give it a minute."

He repeated the gliding motion, a kind of CPR for fish. He released his hands. This time the trout twitched its tail, swam slowly to the left, then darted off and disappeared.

"There he goes, off to live another day."

"Thank God," she exclaimed, exhaling a ragged sigh. "And thank *you!*" Mia looked down to see she was still clutching the man's arm. She released him quickly and wiped her eyes, a bit ashamed for her emotional display. "Sorry."

They were still crouched low, shoulder to shoulder, at the water's edge. He turned his head to smile at her and it lit his eyes. "No problem."

She'd thought his face was ordinary, but she'd been wrong. She didn't remember that his nose was straight or his chin rounded or that his upper lip was thinner than his lower. The pieces came together in an attractive whole, but it was his eyes that seared her memory. They were a remarkable shade of blue, and their intensity against his tanned skin transformed his appearance from ordinary to memorable.

She felt a zing of attraction and it flustered her. Her body, which hadn't felt desire in over a year, suddenly sprang to life with one spark from those electric blue eyes. She rose on unsteady feet to a stand and looked downstream.

"Your first catch?"

"No, I've caught a fish before. An eighteen-inch rainbow."

"That's a big fish."

"Yeah, but it was with Belle, my guide. She told me where to cast and did all the hooking and unhooking."

"Ah," he said, and it was clear he understood that scenario completely. "So this was the first fish you caught solo?"

"I guess it is."

He nodded and said, "Well then, congratulations."

"I don't feel congratulations are in order," she said. "I shouldn't have been using a hook if I didn't know what I was doing. I know this sounds naïve, but I could feel its life in my hands and I was terrified I was going to kill that poor fish."

"Do you think you could remove the hook next time?"

"I don't know if there will be a next time."

"Don't let this spook you. You just need experience. It's not hard, you know. Just back the hook out like you were taking out a pin. It doesn't hurt the fish."

"My hands were shaking too much."

"Do you fish here often? I didn't expect to find anyone so far in the backcountry."

"I do. To be honest, I was surprised to see you here today. This is my favorite spot."

A wry grin eased across his face. "And I stole it from you?"

She shrugged, hiding her smile. "I was annoyed at first. Especially when you started catching all those fish. But now, I'm so glad you were here."

He put out his hand. "I'm Stuart."

She smiled, liking him more, and took the hand. His palm was smooth and he had a good, firm grip.

"I'm Mia."

"Well, Mia, I best be going. I've caught some fish and rescued a fair maiden in distress. My work here is done. It was nice meeting you. See you around." He turned and started walking downstream.

Mia, too, was done for the day. She slipped out from

her boots, then stuffed them into her backpack. Gathering her rod and reel, she saw her weary, shaggy fly still dangling from the leader. It was amazing that little brookie had even gone for that beaten fly. She remembered the excitement of the tug and the incredible feel of the smooth, slippery fish in her palm. She would fish again, she decided. Tonight she would practice removing a barbless hook from an oven mitt until she was confident. She just needed experience; isn't that what the man had said? His beautiful blue eyes flashed in her mind.

She turned her head and looked downstream, but like the brook trout, the man was already gone.

The following morning Mia gathered her notebook and pen and headed to town. Becky waved her over when she entered the bakery and handed her a large mug of steaming black coffee.

"I heard you met Phyllis Pace and her daddy."

"Mmm-hmm," she replied, sipping the rich brew. "Nice lady."

"Nice? That's the first time that word's been used to describe Phyllis. Don't get me wrong, she'd give you the shirt off her back. But she'd expect it washed, ironed, and folded without a wrinkle when you returned it, if you get my meaning."

Mia chuckled in her coffee.

"The Pace family is one of the oldest families in town, too. Used to be they owned the department store, but it closed a long time ago. They still own the building, though. Their name's carved right into the stone."

"She was a great help. But her father was a gold mine. What a storyteller. I could listen to him for hours."

"And he could tell you stories for hours. He's one of our oldest living citizens. Him and Mrs. Minor."

"I heard about her from Clarence. She knew Kate Watkins, right? Is there any way I could meet her?"

"Maybe, but she's ancient like Mr. Pace. She lives up on the hill on Sunset Street, right behind the train depot. Used to be she lived out in the backwoods near Watkins Cove. She was well known for fly-tying. Time was people came from all over to buy them. But her eyesight's gone. She tries, but can't make the flies like she used to. Her granddaughter took her in a while back. Mrs. Minor put up a fuss, but in the end she couldn't make it way out there all alone anymore. She's a tough old bird. It's kind of sad to see her cooped up."

"She might enjoy a visit."

"She might. I don't know if you'll have much luck. Sometimes she's clear as a bell, and other times she just sits there and stares out at nothing. You could try but I wouldn't get my hopes up."

Mia wrote the information down in her notebook. She tapped her pencil on the paper. "Becky, Mr. Pace got very upset when I asked who Kate Watkins murdered. He told me Kate didn't murder anybody. That it was all a lie."

"Really?" She shrugged. "Well, he was her friend, don't forget."

"I know, but he seemed so sure. It threw me. Up till him, I never heard anyone dispute it."

"Go figure. I grew up hearing that Kate Watkins killed her lover. It happened such a long time ago. When you find out something will you share the wealth?"

"Sure. When I get some to share. Mr. Pace also mentioned something about Kate Watkins having written articles for the newspaper. Do you know anything about that?"

"Nope, sorry. Did you try the *Gazette*? It's just down the block."

Mia nodded. "The girl I talked to didn't have a clue. She was just some receptionist, probably a summer temp, who had never heard of Kate Watkins and couldn't care less. I'm going back there later today. I have an appointment with the woman who keeps the archives."

"That'll be Nada Turner. She would know if anyone did. She also runs the historical society. She's a widow and lives in that pretty yellow house at the end of Main Street. She talks about turning it into a bed and breakfast, which would be nice, but I doubt she ever will. She spends too much time with the historical society and fighting to preserve our town. She's the one to go to with questions about the past. Nothing has ever happened in this town that she doesn't know about."

"Really?" Mia skipped a beat and sipped her coffee. Then a small smile curved her lips. "I thought that was your specialty."

Becky had the grace to laugh. "Tell you what. I'll

call Lucy Roosevelt. That's Mrs. Minor's granddaughter. See if she can arrange a time for you to meet her grandmother."

"Thanks, Becky. I feel like I'm unraveling some mystery."

"You're Sherlock Holmes and I'm that Watson fella."

"Well, Watson, I've another mystery I need to solve. I met someone today. Out on the river."

"Who's that?"

"That's what I want to ask you. His first name is Stuart. I didn't get his last name. He's around forty, I'd guess. Tall, dark hair."

"Oh yeah, him. He came in here a few times. Not often. I guess he doesn't have much of a sweet tooth. I know the local guides are none too happy with him."

"Why not?"

"He's bringing a big outfit like Orvis in. He keeps a pretty low profile. Kinda like you did when you first came. But we warmed you up." She took a long sip of coffee, her eyes dancing over the rim of her mug. "He's a good-looking fella."

She tried not to smile. "Is he? I didn't notice."

Becky laughed short. "Sure you didn't. You know, I hear he's single."

Mia was inordinately glad to hear that. "Don't get the tongues wagging, Becky. I'm not. At least not yet."

Becky seized on this, leaning forward across the table. "I didn't want to pry but I don't see a ring. So, what's your story? Are you getting a divorce?"

Mia looked into Becky's sympathetic eyes. She was the kind of woman people told their life stories to, and often did. Mia nodded her head. "As soon as I can."

"And that's why you're here?"

"It's what brought me here, but not why I'm here, if that makes sense. I'm getting strong and healthy, doing a little soul-searching. You see, I'm a . . ." Mia hesitated, feeling the words on her tongue. "I'm a breast cancer survivor."

Becky stared at Mia, taking that information in. Then she looked down at her coffee. "I'm glad to hear you pulled through. You know my leg?" She looked up again and searched Mia's face. When she nodded Becky said, "I have ALS."

Mia's confusion must have shown on her face because Becky went on to explain, "That's Lou Gehrig's disease."

Mia's heart sank. She knew it was a degenerative disease. That it involved the neurons of the brain and spinal cord. She also knew there was no cure. She opened her mouth to speak but she couldn't find the right words. She had a sudden sympathy for her friends who'd slunk off when they heard about her cancer.

Becky saw her struggle and added quickly, "I just got the diagnosis. Me and Skipper, we've got hope."

Mia saw that hope shining in her eyes and was only ashamed at her own self-pity after her recovery. She reached out to put her hand over Becky's. "Then I do, too. Listen, I have loads of time. If you want to talk to someone, or you just want to watch TV or drink a glass of wine with a pal, anything at all, you'll let me know, won't you?"

"Oh, sure," Becky said in her breezy manner, cutting off all sympathy. "Don't worry about me, though. I have Skipper. He comes to have lunch with me every day. And he brings me flowers like he did when we were first married. Can you believe what a sweetheart he is? You let me know if you need me for anything, too."

The *Gazette* was housed in another redbrick building on Main Street. The white-trimmed windows held posters of historical issues of the small-town newspaper dating back to the early 1900s when the railroad brought celebrities to town.

The young receptionist with the vacant smile was on the phone when she walked in, and it was obvious the call was personal. She hung up, took a sip of coffee, then rose to announce her arrival to Mrs. Turner. A minute later, a tall woman in a pale gray suit with a high-collared, white cotton blouse came into the reception area. Her graying hair was cut short with full bangs that fringed her thick tortoiseshell glasses. She was a formidable woman. Mia thought she had to be six feet tall in her stocking feet.

"I'm Nada Turner," the woman announced, putting forth her hand. "How can I help you?"

Despite her imposing appearance, the woman's manner was open and straightforward.

"Hi, I'm Mia Landan."

"Yes," Nada acknowledged, and Mia knew she'd heard all the recent gossip. "Missy tells me you're interested in Kate Watkins."

Mia looked over to see the receptionist listening intently and thought *Missy* was a perfect name for the flighty girl. "That's right."

"May I ask why you're interested in her? Are you writing an article about her?"

"No, nothing like that." Mia realized she had to get past another of Kate's gatekeepers. "Do I need a reason?"

Nada Turner's expression turned speculative. "No," she replied at length. "The articles are a matter of public record. But to be perfectly frank, I'm not inclined to assist anyone in digging up the old scandals about one of our past citizens. The Watkins family holds an important role in our town's history, and I believe that scandal has overshadowed the family's significant contributions to our community."

"Let me assure you nothing could be further from my mind. This is strictly personal. You know I'm staying at the cabin, I assume." When Nada nodded she continued. "I'm learning to fly-fish and I find her inspiring."

Nada's eyes sparked with interest. "You fly-fish?"

"I try. I'm not very good but I have to admit, I'm hooked. No pun intended."

"Well, why didn't you say so? That's a different story altogether. Come on back," she said, leading the way through the reception room door.

Apparently fly-fishing was a tight club, she thought. It certainly opened the doors to Nada Turner's heart. She followed Nada down a narrow hall lined with more posters of the *Gazette* front pages. At the end of the hall she opened a door to a stairwell.

"The basement is dedicated to the archives. It's my private bastion," she said with a light laugh. "I don't even allow Missy down here. I'm afraid she'll spill something."

The basement was wall-to-wall shelves chock-full of books and boxes with typed labels indicating dates and content. The hum of dehumidifiers was omnipresent but they did their job well, for the space was clean and dry. Fluorescent overhead lights provided ample light.

"There's a method to my madness," Nada said as she led Mia through the maze. "Our methods are old-fashioned by today's standards but we're a small paper with limited funds. The only way I can afford to keep all these historical records is through a grant from the historical society." She paused and her gaze swept the room. "It's my passion, you know. The town hall might keep the birth and death records, and the library has a few collections of significant families. They were donated to them," she said in a huff that Mia guessed was sour grapes. "But I collect the daily records of the lives of our everyday citizens. Each old photograph, each personal letter, each diary is an important link in the history of our town. Young people today don't know what to do with all the boxes of stuff they find in their parents' attics.

They're only too happy to dump them off with me. Each load is like Christmas for me, I can tell you. I've found some real treasures."

Mia thought of Kate Watkins's diary and the two fishing diaries and how Nada Turner would go wild over them. But they were not hers to donate. Besides, Mia knew that if she so much as mentioned them the pressure to give them up would be too much.

"Here we are," Nada said as they came to a small room. She opened the door and flicked on the light. Inside was a vintage microfilm machine. Nada ran her hand along the large monitor. "This is my baby. I don't know what I'd do without it. Not everything has gone digital. The Internet is a great tool, but there's still a wealth of information hidden in places like this. Anyway, let's get you started."

"I didn't expect you to help me," Mia said. "I'm sure you have your own work to get done."

"I do. But I'm curious about those articles myself, now that you brought it up. I haven't looked at those in many years. Did I tell you I fly-fish?"

Mia shook her head though she'd guessed as much.

"It used to be a passion of mine but I don't have the time I used to. We have some of the best trout fishing in America right under our noses. We sometimes get groups of women renting a house for a week of fly-fishing. Does my heart good to see it. You can bet Kate Watkins would have been right there with them, giving them pointers. She was a guide, you know. One of the best. She knew every inch of the backcountry. If there was a stream or a creek with fish in it, she'd been there and could tell you all about it and what fly to use. She did just that in her articles. What were they called?" She scratched her head. "She had a title for them . . ."

Mia quickly scanned her notebook. "Here it is. Mr. Pace said it was called 'On the Fly.'"

"That's it! Has a ring to it, don't you think? I know about when the articles were printed but she wrote for about four or five years, so that's a lot of film to search through. It's going to be a hunt. I hope you're not in too much of a hurry."

"I'm here for the duration."

Nada smiled broadly. "Good girl. OK, then. Why don't you pull in a couple of chairs from the other room? Then go up and ask Missy for a couple bottles of cold water while I begin searching for the microfilm." She turned to leave, then stopped and said with a burst of passion, "You know, when I was young, I was inspired by Kate Watkins, too. This is going to be fun."

Mia had two chairs set up by the microfilm machine and two bottles of water waiting by the time Nada came back bearing a box of small rolls of film. With quick, efficient movements she loaded the first roll onto the machine and began to scroll through.

"I wrote a paper on her myself," she said, a little self-consciously. "I'll get that for you, if you like. If I recall correctly, she didn't start writing for the paper until sometime in the nineteen twenties. But she published one article as a girl. Well, it wasn't an article so much as it was an essay. It was different from what the men wrote about, and by that I mean they like to tell you whether to use a number eighteen or a number fourteen for a quill hatch or what rod they used for what river. That sort of thing."

"What brought about her writing 'On the Fly'?"

"The timing was right. You see, fly-fishing was in its heyday in the mid–nineteen twenties. More and more wealthy sportsmen discovered there was mighty fine fly-fishing in our mountain streams, and with the railroad making a trip from the East Coast cities easier, they came in numbers, bringing their families along to enjoy the balmy climate.

"At that time, it was Kate's father, Walter Watkins, who was best known for his fly-fishing. He was a gentleman's angler, quiet-spoken and polite. I've read countless letters and diaries from local people and I never read a mean word spoken about him. Isn't that an amazing thing? Not one word. You know, I've always thought that when my time comes, if a bad word was never said about me, well, I can't think of a better eulogy."

"Kate was a lucky girl to have him as her father."

"That respect and affection the town felt for the Reverend transferred to his daughter, Kate. He taught her everything she knew about fishing. There are some who believe she grew to be better than him. We'll never know for certain. Reverend Watkins never entered a tournament. It wasn't his style."

"And Kate did?"

"Oh my, yes! I'll find you articles about the tournaments she won. Dozens of them. By the time she was twenty-five she was considered one of the best anglers in the country. Our own Annie Oakley, if you will. How could the town not love her? The more her reputation grew, so did the town's. Today you'd call her a public-relations dream. Imagine a woman fly fisher—and one who could beat the men, too!"

"I love it," Mia said.

"Yep. She was something. Truth is, though, reporters back then were not always, well, shall we say they didn't always check their facts. They puffed things up a bit. Her name sold newspapers, though. Sort of like those young girls in movies sell newspapers today with the press blowing up all their naughty antics. I swear, I'd rather the press today play up a lady fly fisher than some floozy who can fill out a dress and get drunk. Well, never mind. What I'm getting at is the editor of the *Gazette*, not being born a fool, asked Kate if she would write a column. And she did. I'm sure it gave her a nice income, too. Sometimes she wrote about fishing, sometimes about the streams and rivers she fished. Sometimes, though, it was more a gossip column about the big-name celebrities and financiers who came to fish with her."

"How did the celebrities and high rollers find out about her? Even with a female angler, this is a small town. No offense," Mia added.

"None taken. We like it small and aim to keep it that way. But that's a good point. At first it was word of mouth. I guess being in the elite of New York City is like being in a small town, too, eh? I don't know how it happened but after a few years a New York paper picked up her column, then one in Boston and who knows where else."

"Really? That's amazing," Mia said, trying to imagine the magnitude of such an accomplishment in the 1920s. "To be picked up by a New York paper in any time period is a feat. I thought she just had a small column here in the town paper. But I didn't see any record of it when I did my Internet search."

"That was a long time ago, honey. And like I said, not everything is digital. But you're lucky, because every article she wrote the *Gazette* printed, too. So if you've got the time, we've got the articles. In fact, here's one. It's dated 1925. I'll move over. You come take a look."

Chapter Ten

The Gazette
April 1925
Kate Watkins, "On the Fly"

Spring has come to western North Carolina and with the migrating birds come the visiting anglers looking for a fine rainbow trout, or a big brown, or maybe even the elusive brookie. Some are expert at casting and others are as new as the spring green shoots sprouting up and down the mountains. Yet whether experienced or a beginner, when the water warms and the fish are biting, both are eager to get to the river and start fishing. Before you make that first cast into our streams, I'd like to share with you a lesson I learned from a master fly fisher—my father.

Slow down. Get comfortable in the water. When you come to the river, don't jump right in and start tying flies and casting like a drummer with a tom-tom. Most anglers learn straightaway how to read the water. My father, however, taught me to listen to the river. Especially in the spring when the waters are swollen with high expectations and fractured light sparkles through the greening leaves. Take a moment to look in the early morning mist that curls from the water like smoke and you will see countless butterflies fluttering. Along the graveled banks, the rocks and wild grass harbor telltale insects, and just beyond, the bright reds and yellows of wildflowers color the landscape. Elusive gray shadows swim upstream, barely visible against the pattern of river rock.

Stand a moment longer and listen to the music of the water. Breathe deep and soon you will catch its rhythm and your blood will pump its heady beat. As your body hums, your mind releases the nagging worries you carried with you to the river—thoughts of business and family and work and future slowly drain from you to be picked up in the current and dragged away. You now feel lighter, freer. You see with fresh eyes. You hear the secrets of the river. You are the river.

Now you are ready to connect with the fish.

Mia glanced at her watch and silently groaned. It was her nature to be like a terrier with a bone. Once she latched on to a subject it was hard to let go. She pushed back from the copy machine and stretched her arms over her head. She was making copies of each of the articles they found. "I can't believe how late it's getting. We worked right through lunch. And then some."

Nada was sitting across from her at a long table, culling through dozens of rolls of microfilm. She lifted her head and checked her own watch, then brought her palms to her face to rub weary eyes. "I'm going to catch hell. I have two stories I need to follow up on to make deadline."

"Nada, please don't let my quest interfere with your work at the paper."

"This *is* my work at the paper. Sort of." She looked in her coffee cup, frowned at the contents, and set it back down. "Mia, I can't help but get sucked into it."

Mia's lips curved in a knowing smile. "I know. But," she said, turning off the screen, "I've got to go. Can I come back tomorrow?"

"Tomorrow, the next day. Whenever."

Mia gathered her notebook and supplies and helped Nada close up the research room. After setting a time to return the following day, she left the building to do her shopping in town. She kept an eye on the clock.

It was an outstanding summer day. The sun was high and bright in a clear blue sky and there was no humidity. The breeze felt fresh on her cheeks, especially welcome after a morning spent in a basement without windows. It was midweek and the town had few tourists strolling.

She went first to the art shop on Main Street.

"How is your painting coming along?" Maeve asked when Mia walked in. She was wearing a long, flowing skirt of vivid colors and rough, hand-hewn jewelry.

"I don't know about the quality, but I love the process. I can't seem to stop myself. I get up in the morning, drink my coffee, and grab my brushes. Every day."

"Good. Are you still painting the river?"

"For the most part. I'm fascinated with how the water changes—in sunlight and in storms, in the early morning and at twilight. It's mercurial. When I wake up I can't wait to go out and see what the river will look like." She smiled. "I guess you could say it's my way of reading the water. I've been trying my hand with flowers and birds, too. My problem with birds is they're not very good models. I can pick a wildflower and it will stay still for me to draw. A mockingbird isn't so accommodating. I don't know how Audubon did it."

"He likely killed it, stuffed it, and then mounted it. Not a method I'd recommend you try."

They chuckled. Then, with Maeve's help, Mia selected more watercolor paints and paper.

"Please, bring some of your paintings down next time," Maeve said. "I'll critique them. Don't be shy."

"I'm not shy as much as plain embarrassed," Mia replied modestly. "I'm such an amateur. I should throw them out."

"Never say that. You must honor your creativity. Think of your art as a journey from a place of wholeness inside of you. You move through your center to renewed sensitivity to the world around you."

Mia thought that was how she felt with her rod while on the water. In truth, she took her painting very seriously. But she didn't want to share them. Mia wasn't painting for an observer. These daily watercolors were her entries in a diary—not a fishing diary but a painting journal for herself.

Mia left with a large bag filled with paint, paper,

and brushes, and returned to the sun shining on Main
Street. Her stomach was growling and she cast a longing glance at the café as she passed. It was midafternoon
and only a few diners sat near the window eating what
looked to be luscious pieces of quiche. She looked at
her watch and kept walking. If she left town now, she
could be at the river by four.

Mia arrived at her favorite spot on the river as the sun
was beginning its slow descent in the western sky. It
was her favorite time in the mountains. A bewitching
hour when the sky grew dusky and a mantle of blue and
purple settled around the mountains in a silken mist.

When she arrived at the spot she was breathless.
The sound of rushing water seemed louder in the twilight. Standing on the grassy bank she felt the large
pebbles dig into the rubber soles of her tennis shoes.
She looked upriver then downriver, but she didn't see
anyone else. Her disappointment surprised her. Mia
had no reason to expect he'd be here. It was highly
unlikely. Yet she still felt the fluttering of attraction in
her gut when she thought of those astonishingly blue
eyes. She hadn't felt that emotion in a long time. She
didn't believe it had been one-sided.

She felt the old insecurity sweep over her, forcing her to ask herself why an attractive man like Stuart would be interested in her. The days when a man
might be attracted to her were over. Feeling more than
a little sorry for herself, Mia stuffed her feet into wad-

ers and felt-bottom boots, then walked to the water's edge. In the water she saw dark shadows that made her heart skip. But by a large white rock over which water tumbled noisily, she saw a large fish come up for a sip before disappearing again. That was the fish she wanted.

She carefully made her way from the shallow water of the bank toward the deeper middle. The current was stronger here and her feet slipped along the bottom. She took her time settling her feet and getting her balance in the water. Only when she felt comfortable did she begin to cast. She started fishing the shady bank. Her casts were clumsy but at least the fly was hitting the water in the right area. Feeling better, she moved to cast as close to the big rock as she could, hoping to get the fly to fall smack dab in front of where she thought the big fish sat. On her third cast she was admiring the way her fly fell softly on the water when she felt the hoped-for tug on the line.

A strike! She jerked her pole high, setting the hook, and let loose a high squeal of excitement. The way her rod bowed and the weight on the line told her it was a good-size fish. The fish dove. She pulled back on the rod. Snap! The line went loose. She looked at the slack line in the water with a puzzled face.

"You didn't give him line."

Mia swung her head toward the bank to see Stuart watching her. His hat was off and she saw that his hair was dark and worn quite short. He wasn't wearing his fishing vest, either, but a pouch hung around his neck from a lanyard. On this hot day he looked infinitely more comfortable than she was in her sweaty waders. He eased his face into a wry grin and his eyes crinkled in humor.

Mia returned a rueful smile, inordinately glad to see him. "I was lifting the rod to set the hook," she called back.

"Well you did that just fine. But look where your finger is."

Mia looked down and saw that her index finger was holding the line taut against the rod. "I was holding on to him."

"You want to give a big fish like that plenty of line to run."

She began walking toward him with as much grace as she could plowing through water on slippery rocks. She didn't want to end this display of ineptness with a fall into the water. When she drew near he held out his hand to help her up the bank.

"Thanks," she said, feeling self-conscious. When she was on dry ground she said, "I thought I was supposed to keep my finger on the rod so I wouldn't let the line go loose."

"When your fish takes off you want to keep your finger off the line. Let him go. When he slows down you reel him in and if he pulls again, give some line. You give a little, you take a little. It's how you play him."

Mia thought that was an apt description of what girls did at bars and parties throughout the country. It was called flirtation, and she wondered if she remembered the rules of that sport as well.

"So, when do you reel him in?"

"You don't want to play him too hard and tire him out. You have to sense when it's time to bring him to the net. But if you don't let him run when he wants to, he'll swim away with your fly in his mouth."

"Like my fish just did."

"Yep."

Mia looked down the river knowing somewhere in that current her fish had swum off before she could take out the hook. It would come out in time, but she felt sorry for the fish.

"He took my only fly so I guess I'm done for the day."

"You don't want to quit so soon. I've got lots of flies."

"You'll share them?"

He turned his head. "Sure. It's not a big deal." He pulled a small plastic case from his pouch and opened it. Inside were dozens of flies, some so small they were no bigger than a gnat and others that looked like large ants and fuzzy furries. He looked out over the water again, then studied the flies in his case, finally settling on a small, brown, furry one.

"OK, is that a Woolly Bugger or a Mighty Mite?" she asked with a grin. She loved the funny names some of the flies had and wondered if she'd ever get them straight.

"No, this here is a number fourteen Hare's Ear."

She laughed again. "I love the names. Really, who thought up *Bitch Creek* flies?"

His lips twitched. "I've always liked *Humpies*." When Mia burst out laughing, he chuckled and added, "Or *Booby Nymph*?"

Mia laughed harder, thinking she could hardly wait to tell Maddie that one.

While their laughter subsided Mia realized how much she'd missed just laughing so hard she got teary. She glanced at Stuart. His head was bent as he attached the fly but he was chuckling. It was nice to be with someone with a sense of humor, she thought. He looked up and caught her gaze. From the way he looked at her she wondered if he was thinking the same about her.

"Maybe I should start painting flies, too," she said. "To help me remember their names. That's what I do with wildflowers and insects."

"Why paint them when you can tie your own flies?"

"Make them? Me? Isn't that hard?"

"Not really. I made these."

She laughed, then felt sorry for it. He seemed a little offended. "No, it's just that, isn't that a little like sewing? I don't think I've ever met a guy who, well, made flies."

He looked at her askance. "Then you don't know many fly fishermen, do you?"

She shook her head with another light laugh. "No, you're my first."

His brows rose. "Really?" He paused, then said with a wry smile, "I guess it's an honor to be your first."

Mia's cheeks felt heat and she realized with a start that she was blushing. They were playing the flirtation game. And she was enjoying it. Good God, she thought as her blush deepened, was she supposed to let him run or reel him in now?

She looked at her rod, nervously averting her gaze. She decided to let him run. "Would you mind tying my fly on? We'll be here for hours if I do it."

"Sure," he replied, and reached out for her fishing rod.

She enjoyed watching him. His expression was serious, and short wisps of dark hair fell over his forehead as he bent over the extremely fine fishing line. Standing close, she saw a few equally fine gray hairs interspersed with his darker ones. His long fingers worked quickly as he attached the fly; then he brought the line to his lips, the upper one disappearing over the fuller bottom lip as he moistened the line before tightening the knot. The cuff of his shirt slipped back and she noticed that his wrists were slender and tanned, too. She also noted that he did not wear a wedding ring. She looked down at her own hand and self-consciously rubbed the small pale line on her tanned left hand where her wedding ring used to be.

"All done," he said, then held her rod out before him, inspecting it. "It's a nice rod. It's one of the Temple Fork rods designed for Casting for Recovery, isn't it?"

She felt her stomach drop and took a breath. "Yes."

He slanted his gaze toward her. "Are you a survivor?"

There it was. The gauntlet thrown. And so soon.

"Yes." She reached out for her rod, feeling the giddy joy of the moment sink as rapidly as the sun over the water. "Thank you," she said in a soft voice. "And thank you for moving upriver tonight, by the way." She turned to leave.

"Seemed only fair," he continued.

He seemed unaware of her quick change in mood as he reeled in his line. Or perhaps, she thought, he was very aware and determined to press on.

"It's your favorite spot, after all. I did a little research and apparently we're standing on your land."

She looked up, surprised.

"This is your stretch of river. I hadn't realized I'd hiked in the backwoods so far and was trespassing. So, I should say both *I'm sorry* and *thanks* to you."

"No need. It's not my land. I mean, I'm staying up at the cabin but the land is owned by my friend Belle Carson." She saw a spark of recognition in his eyes. "Do you know her?"

"By reputation. She's with a guide service in Asheville, right?"

"She owns the business. Brookside Guides."

"Ah, yes. I remember. It's a small world up here. So, Belle Carson is one of my competitors, then."

"I'd heard you were a guide."

"Oh? You were checking up on me?"

Her face burned. "Your name came up," she replied.

"Someone was saying that you are setting up an Orvis store at the Watkins Lodge."

"Guilty as charged."

"That will shake things up a bit locally."

"In a good way. We've done our research. Western North Carolina has one of the most elaborate networks of trout streams in the nation. There are hundreds of streams all gorging with ample rain from high up in the mountains. Some of the best fly-fishing in the country is here and more and more people are getting involved in the sport. Orvis will be attracting a lot of people to the area, bringing them into the lodge. There's plenty to go around."

"Are you from around here?"

"Yes and no. I'm from the Tennessee side of the Blue Ridge Mountains. I know the big rivers around here but I'm getting familiar with the backwoods streams. Seeing as how I'm competition, I doubt many guides will want to show me their secret spots. I thought I'd found a winner with this pocket but now I see I've wandered off the lodge land. I doubt Ms. Carson would appreciate the competition fishing her stream."

"You never know, but I'd definitely ask first. So the Watkins Lodge property abuts this piece, does it?" Looking out, Mia asked, "Whereabouts?"

Stuart turned and pointed to the west. "Just on the other side of that ridge."

Mia looked up at the mountain ridge beyond and realized just how far young Kate had wandered lost in the woods before she found the cabin. "This here is Watkins land, too," Mia told him. "Belle Carson is a Watkins. She inherited this land from her mother, who inherited it from her mother, Kate Watkins."

"That explains it. I knew the family kept a chunk of the estate for themselves, and from looking at this stretch of river, I'd say the best fishing chunk, too. No surprise there. I understand that the Watkins family has a long, illustrious line of fly fishers."

"I heard that, too," Mia answered evasively.

"You say there's a cabin?" he asked.

"Yes. It was the fishing cabin for the Watkins family back when they still lived in the main house. They've kept it in the family."

"I love old fishing cabins. They have such character. And they're usually sitting on the sweetest spots for fishing."

She did not invite him to see it.

There was an awkward pause after which he looked off at the river again. "Well, I see the fish are biting. I'll leave you be. See you, Mia."

"Wait," she called out. "I'm sorry, but I don't know your name."

He put his hand to his heart in mock pain. Mia laughed and said, "Your full name, Stuart."

"Stuart MacDougal."

"Well, Stuart MacDougal," she said, repeating his name to cement it in her brain. Since chemotherapy, proper nouns had a way of slipping through her mind like water through a sieve. "Please don't run off. I'd like it if you stayed. Watching you fish I might actually learn a thing or two. If that's OK with you," she quickly added.

His smile came slow and easy. "I'd like that. Mia . . ."

She cracked a smile. "Mia Landan."

For the next hour they fished the pocket, or rather, Mia fished and Stuart gave her pointers. He was, she discovered, an excellent teacher. Belle had told her that each guide had his or her own style, and she found this was true. Belle was enigmatic and encouraging. She had watched Mia's every move and was right there to correct her. Stuart was laid-back and his voice was never sharp or frustrated, even when she did what she knew were some incredibly bad casts.

They fished till it got so dark they could barely see the fly on the water, but Mia didn't want to stop.

"Stuart, I can't stop now. I'm just getting the hang of it and I haven't caught a fish yet."

"That's why it's called fly-fishing, not fly-catching." He chuckled as he reeled in his line. "Some days are good ones and some days you have to accept you're going to be denied. Fly-fishing to me is just showing up. It's about being here—your head, your heart, your senses—all of it."

"Listen to the river," she said halfheartedly.

"Exactly," Stuart said in all seriousness. "Whether or not you catch a fish today is not important." He reached out for her hand and helped her up the bank. "I can see you're going to be one of those fishers who'll need to be dragged from the water." He stretched his shoulders and took a deep breath. "As for me, I caught fish this morning and fish this evening and I've got a long, fast walk out ahead of me. Time to call it a day."

Mia looked toward her path home. The woods were already dark. "I didn't realize how late it was getting."

They stood side by side on the bank packing up gear. The twilight deepened around them. Mia shouldered her backpack, then stood looking at the path with worry etched across her face.

"I didn't bring a flashlight," she said.

"How far is it to your cabin?"

"Not too far, but the path goes through the woods." The path was as steeped in black as tea. She looked up. "The moon hasn't risen."

"Do you want me to walk you back?"

She turned to face him. Once again he was a silhouette in the dark.

"Would you mind?"

"No, I will."

"When we get there, I'll drive you to the lodge."

"You don't have to. The road is well marked."

"It's a long walk and I'd feel better if you let me drive you. Deal?"

He laughed softly. "Deal."

They didn't talk on the trek back. She was apprehensive about missing a marker on the trail or falling down or not seeing where a copperhead might be lying along the dark path. Their footfalls sounded heavy in the night as they crunched and cracked across the forest floor.

Stuart kept up with her as she led the way along the river. When they passed a narrow bend Mia came to an abrupt halt. She felt Stuart come up close behind her and heard his intake of breath. Ahead, a fog of insects was swarming over the water. The fish that had been sitting quietly with an occasional sip were now thrashing at the surface.

"Stuart, what is that?"

"A hatch!" His whispered voice was heated with excitement.

"I've never seen one before."

"It's the hatching of insects over the water. The fish go wild for them. Follow me. And don't spook 'em."

They made a beeline to the river's edge. The air was alive with insects. Stuart tied a nymph fly to her line with swift fingers.

It was a magical, mystical evening. Mia wouldn't remember how many fish they caught but she would always remember the spontaneous outbursts of laughter and whoops of joy as the fish leaped at the flies, taking whatever they offered in their frenzy. When the hatch finished and the water quieted, their laughter subsided into silence. A surreal calm fell upon the river.

Stuart came closer and took her hands in his. He was a dark shadow. She couldn't make out his eyes.

"Your hands are cold."

"The water was icy."

Her gaze was trained on him as he lowered his mouth to her hands and blew on them. She felt his warm breath on her skin. She closed her eyes and felt her blood warm.

He pulled back slowly. "We should head back."

"All right," she replied, breathless, and turned to lead their way along the path. She walked in a daze, filled with the heady euphoria of the evening. Before too long, she saw the broad outline of the cabin sitting dark and shuttered across from the green pool.

"There it is. Watkins Cove."

Coming closer she saw it as he would. The moon was rising and the sloping metal roof mirrored its silver light. The still water of the pool beside it was a reflecting pond.

"See, I was right," Stuart said as they drew near. "Those old fishermen always claimed the prettiest spots."

Mia felt a surge of pride for the little cabin, though it wasn't even hers. By virtue of her relationship to Belle and Kate, she claimed a bond. They walked across the spit of land to the other side of the river where a flight of wood stairs led to the front porch. Mia began walking up.

"What would you say to a cup of coffee?" she asked in a companionable way.

Stuart stopped at the bottom of the porch steps, his hand on the railing, and deliberated. Mia turned her head, perplexed.

"Thanks. But I'd better head right back."

"Oh," she stumbled out. "OK."

"Maybe another time."

"Sure. I'll just get my keys."

Mia's head was spinning as she dropped her gear at the door and went inside to grab her purse. She felt a fool for inviting him in for coffee. Did he think she was making a move on him? She was just trying to be polite.

She came back out quickly, locked the door, and walked swiftly to the car where he was waiting. They climbed in wordlessly. The doors closed and immediately she felt an odd tension settle between them. Mia fired the engine and shifted into gear. The gravel crunched noisily under the tires as they took off, her high beams revealing the dirt road and tall, rugged trunks of trees in a ghostly light.

The night air was cooler and they rolled down their windows. The compartment felt fresher and the tension between them eased somewhat. They'd fished together so companionably, she thought. This new awkwardness confused her. It was because of her invitation for coffee, she scolded herself. He wasn't interested in her. Not in that way. Of course he wouldn't be. She'd misread his kindness.

The road to Watkins Lodge was a straight shot down over the mountain ridge. In ten minutes she saw the beautifully elegant roofline of the great old house atop a grassy hill. She pulled up in front of the low, sweeping portico.

"Thanks for the ride," Stuart said.

"A deal's a deal," she replied with a tight smile.

He climbed from the car and closed the door. Then

he leaned against the car and looked through the window at her.

"I was thinking," he said with hesitation. "I'm going to check out a stretch of the Green River tomorrow morning that sounds promising. It wouldn't be for long. Would you like to come along?"

"Why would you want me to come? Wouldn't I just get in your way?"

A small smile eased across his face and in the brighter light of the lodge she saw the faint shadow of stubble across his jaw. "You did pretty good out there today. But I thought you could use another lesson."

She laughed shortly. "That's pretty obvious."

"Come on. You can be my test case. I can evaluate how a classic beginner does on that strip of water."

It wasn't a date, she realized with relief. They would simply be helping each other out. "Well, that's me. A classic beginner," she said with sarcasm. "All right. Where do we meet?"

"I'll swing by tomorrow morning. Seven sharp." He rose to a stand, tapped the top of her car with the flat of his palm, and waved her off.

Though the night was warm, Mia lit a fire in the cabin's hearth. She heated pots of water on the stove and poured them into the claw-footed tub. After her bath, she moistened her skin with perfumed lotion, taking special care with her scar. Clean and scented, she wrapped herself in her robe and walked barefoot into the main room. It was dark but the fire cast a rosy, sensual glow. The royal velvet of the mahogany sofa was inviting and the jagged points of the stag's antlers on the armoire cast long shadows across the floor.

Mia still felt the sting of Stuart's rejection to come into her cabin. She understood what he was telling her with his invitation to fish tomorrow. He was setting up the boundaries of their relationship on his terms. He wanted a friendship on the water, not a personal relationship behind closed doors.

Mia closed her eyes and took a long breath, absorbing this, accepting it. So be it, she thought. Charles had looked at her as damaged goods. Her weakness was that she saw herself through his eyes. She would never do that again.

She slowly untied the sash of her robe and let it fall open. She rolled her shoulders and let the fabric slide down her arms to puddle on the floor. Opening her eyes, she looked down at her naked body.

Mia saw her long, lean legs and arms; her flat stomach; her one small breast on the right and the flat, pale scar on her left. She had filled out some in her weeks here. Her muscle tone was more defined from physical work and fishing. Her skin appeared rosy in the firelight. Bringing her hands to her hair, she scratched her scalp and let her fingers comb through the curls. Her hair was growing longer, healthier.

This was her body. And this, she thought as she looked around the small room, was her sanctuary.

This small space in the mountains was her private world.

Mia went to the armoire and pulled out the pile of watercolors she'd painted on artist's paper. On fourteen sheets she had painted the river in different lights. On six of these, she saw that her focus had sharpened, including trees, wildflowers, and birds in her work. Next she went to the kitchen and found the pack of tacks she'd purchased. She felt bursts of excitement as a plan began to form in her mind. She turned the gas on the teakettle, then went to collect her watercolors. The cool night breeze whisked in from the windows but the fire kept her naked body warm as one by one Mia tacked her watercolors up on the wood wall of the cabin. She relished the freedom of her nakedness. This, she thought with a small laugh, was what it must mean to be comfortable in your own skin. When she was done, she stood back and, with her hands on her hips, surveyed her work.

Something was missing. She went to gather her calligraphy pen and ink and some scissors, and spread more paper on the table. Humming now, she gathered Kate's diaries and also brought them to the table. She'd read the diaries so many times she knew exactly where to look for phrases that played in her mind. She chose the ones that most inspired her. Working quickly now, she copied the words verbatim on paper. She started copying down Kate's words, *afraid, scared, timid* . . .

She stopped, then in a rush crushed the paper in her hands and tossed it aside. It was time for something new. She spread out a new sheet and wrote: *strong, audacious, courageous, artistic, fearless, brave.* She smiled, deciding *these* were the words she would say aloud every day. She collected this and the other papers with Kate's words and tacked them on the wall with the dozen watercolors, rearranging them until she was satisfied with the design. By the time she was done the kettle was whistling on the stove like a wild bird.

Mia felt a fluttering of elation as she made a pot of tea, then returned to the armoire and pulled out two place settings of the exquisite, hand-painted china and two settings of silver, and set the heads of the table. Then she carried all five candles to the table and lit each one, enjoying the way the flickering light played upon the creamy paleness of the porcelain plates. She brought cheese and crackers and a fresh peach and placed some on each plate, then poured tea into the two cups. When all was ready, she returned to the armoire and slipped the long, white scarf around her neck. The silk grazed sensually across her skin when she moved. Finally, she carried the blue taffeta gown and very gently laid it across the chair at the head of the table.

Taking her seat at the opposite end, Mia placed her hands upon the arms of the chair and sat far back, settling herself firmly. The wood felt cold and hard against her bare skin as she squared her shoulders. Mia felt like a queen overlooking her realm.

Across the room the dark wood walls had come alive with her colors. They seemed to dance in the flickering light of the fire. She searched out one paper, a stanza from a poem by William Ernest Henley that she'd found written in Kate's fishing diary. She'd copied this selection for her wall because it had spoken to her. She read aloud.

> Out of the night that covers me
> Black as the Pit from pole to pole
> I thank whatever gods may be
> For my unconquerable soul.

Once again she sensed a presence in the room. Nothing she could identify. Perhaps nothing more than her alter ego. She reached for her teacup and raised it in a toast to the empty chair across the table with the blue gown draped over it.

"To us."

Chapter Eleven

In fly-fishing, flies are created to look like
real aquatic insects and are used instead of
bait. A *dry fly* floats on the water's surface to
imitate an adult insect. A *wet fly* sinks below
the surface. Nymphs and streamers are wet
flies.

—KATE WATKINS'S FISHING DIARY

In mid-July a heat wave settled in the south and
everyone and everything was sluggish, including
the fish. But the tourists came to the mountains in
droves. Shaffer's bakery was standing-room-only in the
morning, and the other restaurants were doing a brisk
business the rest of the day. Watkins Mill was in the
thick of the summer season.

After a light lunch on the porch Mia packed her
notebook and shopping list and headed for town. She
passed the deep pool outside her cabin, as was her
habit, to see if she could spot Mr. Big. Most every day
she'd walk over to the edge of the pool and look for that
monster trout. Every once in a while she'd catch sight
of his nose rising from the depths to sip an insect. He

was a magnificent rainbow trout, long and fat and brilliantly colored. Her fingers itched for her rod whenever she spied him. Nothing she cast his way caught his interest. Again and again she was refused. It didn't bother her, though. He was her ultimate challenge. Sometimes she felt Mr. Big knew that.

As she looked into the pool, her mind reflected on the past two weeks she'd spent trying out different rivers and streams with Stuart. He'd come for her that first morning in his red Jeep Wrangler and then several more times after that. He never led her to believe he was anything more than her guide and fishing buddy. The bulk of their conversations had been about how they liked their fishing rods, what flies to use, the fish they'd caught in the past few days, and the fish they hoped to catch in the next few.

Through his eyes, she came to experience the joy of fly-fishing. Each fish caught he declared beautiful, incredible, a miracle. Each moment spent outdoors in the water was treasured. His joy in the sport was like a boy's, and when he smiled his eyes seemed to sparkle in the sunlight.

At other times, they stood a short distance from each other in the water and fished in a companionable silence. Neither felt the need to speak, yet she felt sure he was as aware of her presence as she was of his. On occasion she would look over, content to just watch him cast, feeling the wonder one experiences when watching a great bird soar in the sky or a glistening fish leap into the air.

Mia couldn't help but compare this relationship with the one she shared with Charles. They'd never found something they enjoyed doing together—not a sport or a hobby. They each had their own separate interests and pastimes. If people mentioned the Landans they'd remark how happy they seemed, even how great-looking they were as a couple. Mia and Charles had talked together about their work, the bills, and their families, and when they were with friends they laughed and chatted in a group. But they never talked about their hopes and aspirations, either their own or as a couple. They never focused their gazes on each other.

Looking into the fathomless pool, Mia tried to remember why she'd married Charles in the first place. When she saw in her mind's eye the woman of twenty-eight who had married Charles after a long courtship, she seemed impossibly young. And Charles, he never really wanted to get married in the first place. At thirty-two, it seemed time to commit. Once they'd made up their minds to marry there was no stopping the wedding. The union of two old Charleston families was the wedding of the season. Mia couldn't pinpoint the first time she'd suspected it was a mistake. By the time the cancer was diagnosed and the treatments commenced, however, deep inside she knew. Someday, when she and Charles could talk about it, she'd have to ask him whether he knew he'd wanted to leave before the cancer, or if the disease merely made the decision clear.

A long, silver shape caught her eye. It was that

granddaddy of a rainbow trout cruising around the pool, looking for a bug as if she weren't even there. She'd read somewhere that the life span of a rainbow trout was six years. That behemoth looked double that, maybe more. To her mind Mr. Big was as ancient as the river he swam in, wise and wary. At what price wisdom? she wondered. Had that big trout ever felt the prick of steel in his mouth?

On her way into town Mia stopped at the scenic overlook and made her usual round of telephone calls. Her first call was to Maddie. They chatted about everything and nothing, as sisters often do. Mia felt her muscles ease just hearing Maddie's voice and the details of her life with Don and the children. Sometimes Charleston felt so very far away and Maddie was her only touchstone.

When she hung up with Maddie she returned Charles's four increasingly strident phone messages.

"Hello, Charles. I got your messages."

"Don't you ever answer your phone?"

She explained for the hundredth time how difficult phone reception was in the mountains.

"What's up, Charles?" she asked with a roll of the eyes.

"I'm going to make you a proposition and I want you to think about it before you respond. Take your time, it's important. But please, don't take forever and drag down the divorce proceedings."

"You're wasting time with this preamble."

"I just want you to think carefully about your answer."

"Why don't you tell me what your proposition is?"

He paused, then said bluntly, "I'd like to buy the condo."

"Our condo?"

"Of course our condo. I've thought about it and decided I'd like to stay here. The location is great and it would be a hassle to move."

"And what about my living situation?"

"Well, do you want to stay here?"

Mia saw the sleek, marbled entrance to the building overlooking the Ashley River, the brass fixtures on the elevator, the airy rooms with large windows overlooking the water. It was modern and chic, pearlescent in the twilight when friends stopped by for cocktails before dinner.

"No," she replied honestly. "But this might get sticky. We should sell it outright."

"I know what you're thinking," Charles told her. "That I'll offer you a lowball price."

That was exactly what she was thinking but she didn't say so.

"I wouldn't do that to you, Mia. I know what I've put you through and my timing is lousy and you'll probably never forgive me. So let me do the right thing by you, at least in this one area. I'll be fair. I'll be more than fair. Hell, Mia, I'll be generous."

She looked heavenward, saying a prayer for strength.

She brought her fingers to her trembling lips as water flooded her eyes.

"Mia, are you still there?"

She swallowed hard. "Yes."

"Just think about it, OK?"

"I don't need to think about it."

He didn't reply but she thought she heard a disappointed sigh.

"I'll sell it to you."

"Thank you." His relief was audible.

"Don't thank me yet, Charles," she said, wiping her eyes. "I haven't agreed to the price yet."

It was late in the afternoon by the time she arrived at the *Gazette*. Nada Turner came rushing from her office when Mia arrived.

"Where've you been?"

"I went fishing."

"Oh?" Her expression sharpened with interest. "Where do you fish?"

She never talked to others about her friendship with Stuart. She enjoyed their privacy and didn't want tongues to wag.

"I cast a few into the pool behind the cabin. There's a big ol' trout there that flips its tail at me every morning, just to rile me." She smiled craftily. "But I'm getting better."

"See, that's what impresses me about you. Your persistence. It pays off in fly-fishing." She shrugged. "And in life, too."

"We'll see. That fish isn't caught yet."

"Reading all these articles by Kate Watkins has got me all fired up to go fly-fishing again. I used to fish a lot when I was young, did I tell you that? But over the years I've been so busy with the paper that I just, well, I guess I thought I didn't have the time. But you know what? I'm going to find time. I'm going to dig out my waders and boots and rod and start up again."

"I'm all for that. *Tempus fugit.*"

"Exactly!" she said, seizing the topic. "I got to thinking. If reading Kate's articles got me so fired up to fish, then I'll bet my last dollar it'll make others want to fish, too. Women, especially. The articles are timeless." She looked at Mia with the look of an impending pronouncement. "So I've decided to publish Kate's articles again. I'll run a special column, 'On the Fly,' with her old byline. What do you think? Isn't that a great idea?"

Mia was nonplussed and felt a sudden foreboding. "Publish them? Honestly, Nada, I wish you wouldn't."

Nada's face fell. "But whyever not? I thought you'd be wild for the idea."

"I'm not. Not at all. I never intended to bring her story back in the public eye like this. To get folks talking about her." She looked over to where Missy was sitting at the reception desk, very quiet. She leaned over and said in a whisper, "Can we go downstairs?"

Nada glanced at Missy, nodded in understanding, then led the way to the microfilm room downstairs.

"What's got you so hot and bothered?" she asked Mia when they got there.

Mia leaned against the table. "Not what. *Who.* It's Belle Carson. She's the granddaughter of Kate Watkins."

"I know that."

"Then you also must know that when her mother left town she didn't look back."

"What's that got to do with anything?"

"According to Belle, Theodora wanted to escape any communication with her mother so that when she left Watkins Mill she could start a life of her own in Virginia, without the smear of scandal. Nonetheless, Kate left the cabin and the land around it to Theodora when she died and Theodora passed it on to Belle. Now Belle is making her first tenuous steps back into town." Mia took a breath. In that space of time she said a prayer for absolution for her own part in uncovering Kate's story.

"Belle asked me to keep a lid on anything that had to do with her grandmother. She doesn't want me poking around and stirring things up. The last thing she wants is to have Kate's story brought back in the town newspaper. She's hoping the story died with the two women."

Nada crossed her arms. "So why did you dig into it?"

"Well," she began, dodging the real reason. "Kate

Watkins was an extraordinary woman. I'm impressed not only by her achievements and skill in fly-fishing but by her courage at smashing the image that women don't fish. She broke a barrier for women, like Amelia Earhart. How can I not admire that?"

Nada narrowed her eyes. "Your research goes a little deeper than admiration, seems to me."

Mia puffed out air and looked at her feet. "You're a good reporter, do you know that?"

"As a matter of fact, I do."

Mia sighed. "I'm not sure why this means so much to me. And that's the truth. At first it was an interesting story, a puzzle to work out in my spare time. The more I heard and read about her, the more I dug, and the more the stories didn't fit.

"Somewhere along the line, it got personal. I saw Kate as a mentor and a role model. Her words inspire me and her choices remind me what I could be doing with my life. I have this gut feeling that I owe her. Belle told me not to stir up the mud, but I can't help but think her reputation has been smeared by it. If I don't at least try to find out the truth . . ." She shrugged. "Who else will?"

"That's what a reporter does. She digs deep to find the details that shape the whole picture. For me, the story is paramount to everything else. And this is a good story."

"But we don't know the real story yet, do we? All we have is rumor and speculation. My God, Nada, Phillip Pace tells me Kate never killed anyone. That it's all a lie! Is that possible? Aren't you reporters supposed to get the facts?"

"I thought that's what you're doing."

"I've barely scratched the surface. It's like some mystery and I'm trying to unravel the clues."

Mia went to the table and sat down, taking a piece of plain white paper. She reached into her purse and pulled out a pen. Meanwhile, Nada came to sit beside her.

Mia tapped her pencil against the paper in thought. "Innocent until proven guilty. As far as I know, we still hold to that in our country, right? So, do you know who Kate was supposed to have killed?"

"Someone from out of town. Her lover. What was his name? Delaney? Darcy? No, it was French sounding. Come on, brain . . ."

"I first thought she'd killed Lowrance Davidson."

"Good heavens, no. He was killed in World War I. Everybody knows that." Nada snapped her fingers. "DeLancey. That's his name. Theodore DeLancey. He was some society fella from New York."

Mia wrote the name in her notebook. "When did this DeLancey die?"

"I'm not sure. Likely before nineteen thirty. After that she went to live in the cabin."

"But that doesn't necessarily mean that's when the murder—or rather, the alleged murder—took place." Mia smoothed out the piece of paper and began to draw a chart. "I'm going to start a timeline. That way we can see what we do know for sure. Then I can weed out what is only rumor. OK, let's start with Kate. She was born in nineteen hundred, which means she was in her midtwenties when her first article was printed."

"Twenty-five," Nada said, checking the printed article date.

"We know she lost her house after the stock market crash. So that's nineteen twenty-nine." Her memory jogged. "Wait a minute . . ." Mia pulled out her notebook and leafed through the pages to the information she'd learned in the library. "Here it is. Walter Watkins died in nineteen twenty-nine, too." Her pencil tapped the paper. "I wonder what month."

"That's easy enough to look up."

"OK, she lost the house but she must have kept some land and the cabin to live on. Belle inherited eighty-some acres. In all likelihood, there wasn't any-place else for her to go. It might have been less of a retreat than a practical decision."

"She may have felt hounded, too, by the press and the townspeople after the scandal of a murder investi-gation."

The timeline began to sink in and Mia knew a pro-found sadness for Kate. "That poor woman. She lost her fortune, her home, and her father all in one year. Then she was accused of murder. That's a lot for even the strongest woman to bear. I wonder if she didn't go a little bit crazy."

"The *Gazette* must have covered the case," Nada said. "It was a huge event for the town." She looked at Mia with a slanted gaze. "So, I'm guessing now you want me to dig up that microfilm, too?"

Mia smiled. "Please."

Nada leaned back in her chair, considering. "We're digging into a can of worms."

"We have to keep digging. Which is why I don't think it's time to publish anything about Kate Watkins yet."

Nada took a deep breath and considered this. "Sorry, Mia, I disagree. I'm going to go ahead and print Kate's fly-fishing articles. They're timeless. But I won't run a story on her. Yet. I can stick in some byline info about her being a well-known fly fisher in the nineteen twenties. I'll keep it vague."

Mia shook her head with regret. "Belle is still going to kill me."

"No she won't. The articles will get folks remembering the good about Kate Watkins and not dwell on the old scandal. How could she be upset about that? Look, I admired Kate Watkins. I won't sensationalize her. It's time the town got to know who she really was. Not some hermit or some ghost. The fly-fishing articles will whet the appetites for the true story after all these years."

"Therein lies the rub. How do I get to the true story? Other than newspaper articles, Mr. Pace and Mrs. Minor are the only ones alive who knew Kate. How can you interview the dead?"

Nada's face eased into a self-satisfied smile. "You go to the original sources."

Mia looked up, intrigued.

"Diaries, correspondence, newspapers, photographs—those are the real treasures of the past. It brings history alive. Honey, you came to the right place."

Chapter Twelve

April 18, 1925
Dear Miss Watkins,

   Theodore DeLancey is traveling to Asheville to
fly-fish your beautiful rivers and streams. How I wish
I could accompany him. In my absence, I am giving
him this note of introduction to you. He is a very
great friend and our families have been connected
for many years. He is an experienced fly fisher,
well mannered, and I should add, won our club's
tournament for long distance casting. I've taken the
liberty of expounding to him your great talents as a
guide. I hope you will enjoy meeting him.

   With kindest regards and best wishes to your
father,

                              Very sincerely,
                              Woodrow Nelson

Mia drove along a small road behind Main
Street. Her car climbed sharply up the
mountainside and past houses ranging
from large Victorians to small cottages. Mia stopped
her car before a small, pale green cottage with a
faded, white front porch and trim. It was modest but

tidy behind a cheery perennial border flanked by tall hollyhocks. Mia checked the address she'd written in her notebook. She'd gone directly from lunch to Shaffer's to ask Becky for Mrs. Minor's address and phone number. She glanced at her watch. It was three o'clock. She was right on time.

A little orange Pomeranian dog was chained to the front porch and yapped shrilly while she walked up the steps. "Hush now, shhh," she said as she lowered her hand to the dog in greeting. The petite dog bared its teeth and pumped up its incessant barking. "So don't be friendly," Mia snapped back.

The front door swung open before Mia had a chance to knock. Rising, she peered through the screen to see a wiry woman in jeans and a T-shirt with her black hair pulled back in a ponytail.

"Uh, hi. I'm Mia Landan. We spoke on the phone?"

The woman narrowed her dark eyes. "You the lady who come to talk to my grandmother?" She spoke in a heavy rural drawl.

"Yes, I am. And you're Mrs. . . ." She forgot the name.

"Just call me Lucy," the woman said, opening the screen door. "You hush, Angel," she said, bending at the waist to swoop the dog up in her arms. Angel kept growling, her bulging eyes staring at Mia menacingly.

Angel? More like little devil, Mia thought.

"Sorry about that," Lucy said, jiggling the dog in her arms to settle it. "She just gets testy with strangers."

"Is this a good time for Mrs. Minor?"

"It's as good as it's going to get," she said, letting the screen door slam. Outside, Angel mercifully stopped barking. "Grandmamma's had her lunch so she'll likely be a little more lively. If she's gonna talk it'll be now. 'Fore she takes her nap."

Mia stepped into a darkened living room with weary, large furniture. The old sofa was covered with a crochet throw and a curios cabinet was crammed with statues of angels.

"I've brought some flowers," Mia said, handing the bouquet of cheery summer annuals to Lucy. "And some pastries from Shaffer's."

"My, but Grandmamma will be happy to have these. Flowers and sweets," she murmured, smiling.

"How is she feeling?"

"She's ninety-two and lived a simple life but a good one. She's not doing so good right now, though. Not eating much. It's like she's just dwindling away. But she's a sweet old girl and I don't want anything upsetting her."

Mia heard the warning. "That's not my intention."

Lucy accepted that. "She asked to watch her stories. That's always a good sign. And she'll surely perk up once she smells cinnamon."

"Lucy, how did your grandmother know Kate Watkins? Were they neighbors at Watkins Cove?"

"Yeah. But they knew each other before that. Her mama used to work for the Watkins family, back when they were at the big house. She was the family cook. That'd be my Great-grandmamma Minnie."

"And they moved out to the cabin with her?"

"I don't know what happened, exactly," Lucy continued. "That was a long time ago. I only know that when Miss Kate lost her house and moved out to the woods she gave Great-grandmamma Minnie some land so she and her husband could build a place of their own. That was the first land my family owned outright. It was a right and moral thing to do, that's what my grandmother always says. She says when the chips were down, Miss Watkins could be counted on to stand with you."

Mia followed Lucy down a short hall. They stopped at a closed door to a bedroom and Lucy faced her.

"She might want to talk. It'd be nice to hear one of her stories again. But she might not. Most of the time she just sits in her wheelchair and laughs and sings and mumbles so I can't figure out what the heck she's trying to say. Then out of the blue she'll look at me and know me and we'll have a nice chat. I sure don't understand it. That's all I can tell you." She opened the door. "She's in there."

Mia stepped into a small, lavender bedroom. It was heavily shaded by overgrown yews alongside the house but someone had been kind enough to cut back the dense foliage from one window to allow a shaft of sunlight to pour through. An old woman sat in this sunlight. She seemed to sink into the deep cushions

on her wheelchair. Her black skin was chalky and wizened, and fine gray hair covered her scalp like goose
down.

"Grandmamma, this here's Mia Landan, the lady I
was telling you about. She wanted to meet you." She
stepped closer to the old woman and took her hand.
Then she waved Mia over. "Say hi to Ms. Landan."

The old woman turned her head toward Lucy. Her
dark eyes were clouded with glaucoma and she looked
up uncomprehendingly.

"Do you want to tell her one of your stories about
Kate Watkins? Grandmamma?"

Mrs. Minor's shiny, dark eyes peered over her
shoulder at Mia like a crow.

"Hello, Mrs. Minor," Mia said with a smile.

The old woman scowled, then turned her head to
look out the window.

"Grandmamma?"

The old woman grunted.

"Mrs. Minor," Mia said, scooting lower to be closer
to her face. "I'm Mia. I'm living at the cabin at Watkins
Cove. In Kate Watkins's cabin."

The old woman turned her head back and looked
at Mia. Her eyes appeared sharper as she studied her
face. "What you doin' at the Watkins place?" she said
fiercely. "You ain't got no business there."

"I was invited."

"Huh. No one's invited there. By who?"

"By Belle Carson."

"I don't know no Belle Carson," she mumbled.

"Belle is Kate's grandchild. Theodora's child." Mia paused, hearing her own words. *Theodora's child.* Theodore DeLancey. Another chink fell into place: He was the father of Kate's child.

"Little Theo?" Mrs. Minor's voice brightened. "I haven't seen her in, oh Lord, I can't remember how long. How is that sweet child?"

"I'm sorry. Theodora passed away. Last winter I believe."

The old woman's face seemed to fall into itself. "They all dead now. It's a blessing and a curse to live so long. At least she's with her mama at last. She been waitin' a long time to see her child. God rest their souls."

"What happened between them?"

She waved her hand in dismissal. "Oh, that's a long story. You don't need to know all that."

"I'd like to hear the story. All of them."

"Why you want to know all that? It's all past. Long past."

"It's not past. The scandal is still very much alive."

"Dirty rumors, that's all they is. If you come here for that, then you can go now. You won't hear me bringing up those filthy lies."

Lucy put her hand on her grandmother's shoulder to calm her. "It's OK, Grandmamma. We won't talk about them."

"I'm not here to upset you, Mrs. Minor, or to dig up dirt on Kate Watkins."

"I got nothing to say to you."

"Please, Mrs. Minor. I don't believe the scandals are

true. But the silence over the years has allowed those lies to be perceived as the truth. There aren't many people alive who remember Kate. I talked to Mr. Phillip Pace and now there is only you."

"Why do you want to talk to me? It's not your place. I should be talking to her granddaughter. Belle's her name? You tell Belle to come by soon."

"Belle won't come. Theodora filled her mind with so much suspicion and hate for her grandmother she doesn't want anything to do with her."

The old woman grew agitated. "I need to see Theodora's daughter."

"Mrs. Minor, I'm here because I want to help her daughter. Because I care about her. And . . . I care very much about Kate Watkins."

The old woman leaned forward to peer closer at Mia's face. "You say you're staying in Kate's cabin?"

"I sleep in her room."

Mrs. Minor nodded her head, her eyes gleaming. "She come to you yet?"

Mia's breath hitched. She said carefully, "It . . . It's more a feeling."

"A knowing."

Mia nodded. That was it exactly.

"Mmm-hmm," Mrs. Minor said, and sighed with satisfaction as she settled back into her wheelchair. "If you say you're trying to help Miss Kate . . . I'd do anything for her. People thought she was cold. But she wasn't. She was strong is all. And spoke her mind. People didn't like that in a woman. Not back then."

"Who was Theodore DeLancey?"

The old woman's back went erect in her chair. "What you know about *him*?"

"I only know his name. And that he had a letter of introduction to Kate."

"Humph. If you don't know about DeLancey, then you don't know nothing."

Intrigued, Mia pulled out a copy of the letter Nada had found in the stacks.

"This is a letter of introduction that somehow made its way to the historical society. It's addressed to Miss Watkins and concerns Theodore DeLancey." She opened the thick, vellum paper and handed it to Mrs. Minor.

"I'll need my glasses."

Lucy reached far over to the bedside table and retrieved a pair of glasses with thick lenses. "Here, Grandmamma."

Mrs. Minor slipped the glasses on. They slid down her nose a fraction as she bent to read. Her lips moved over the words.

"So, this here's the letter that started it all. Lord, Lord, Lord, one little letter."

Mrs. Minor adjusted her glasses and looked again at the letter, then let it fall into her lap. "The way the Reverend saw it, a letter of introduction was like a command performance. The Reverend was a gentleman. He surely was. And a gentleman only lives by one code, hear? I don't believe he could've played it another way. That said, I figure if he knew how things would turn out, all because of this letter, well I don't think he'd have made the stand he did."

"Please, tell me what happened."

Mrs. Minor shifted in her seat, ruminating. Mia saw the struggle in the old woman's eyes and waited for her to continue.

"One thing you got to know right from the start. It wasn't just some"—she gummed her lips thinking of the word—"*affair* like people said. When it all came out, folks made it sound tawdry and cheap. It weren't nothin' like that. There was love there. She loved that man fierce and true and went into it with her eyes wide open. That was her way."

Mrs. Minor looked again out the window and her voice grew soft as her mind traveled far back in her memories.

"DeLancey, he come to town in his fancy railroad car. Oh, it was something. The townsfolk were mighty impressed. Everyone who lived in Watkins Cove at that time listened for the high-pitched whistle of the afternoon train. Whenever Reverend Watkins heard it, he said a prayer of thanks. He could remember back to when the train line was built. He was only a boy then but he claimed he'd never forget the high cost that railroad demanded—in lives and dollars. People quickly forget tragedy, though. By the twenties, when that whistle blew the townsfolk ran to the depot to see who might be stepping off onto the platform. On that particular Sunday, the Reverend and Kate were ankle-deep in the Davidson River, as usual. They should've just kept fishing, I always thought, but Kate had a new rod coming in on the train so they went to town."

"Is that when she met DeLancey?" Mia asked.

Mrs. Minor slowly nodded her head. "Him and his fine suit and shoes. Lord, he had money. More money than the Watkins family ever dreamed of having, if that gives you any idea. Not that money made any differ-ence to Kate." She cackled softly. "She used to tease him about it, call him a dandy and a fancy boy. I think he liked that best about her. That she was so feisty and gave him what for. I don't imagine there were too many folk in his life who did. He adored her, any fool could see that."

The old woman sighed again and brought her thin fingers to her mouth. "No, it weren't the money. I know that for a fact. Years after it all happened, Kate and I were sittin' on her porch just watching the sun go down. I remember the sky was all red, like a fire over the mountains. She was in one of those talking moods. You know the kind? It didn't happen often with her. She was tight-mouthed about things close to the heart, so I remember it clear. Might've been she sensed her time was coming, or it just might've been the soft air that night.

"She was rocking and looking far out and she told me when she first saw DeLancey she'd thought he was Lowrance Davidson coming home from the war. She'd stumbled and grabbed hold of her father's arm from the shock of it. DeLancey turned his head and then, of course, she knew it wasn't Lowrance, but she allowed there was some spark in that first connection. Her father did speculate as to how the two men looked alike. Not in the face so much, but in the hair and the way they moved." She shook her head. "It was curious."

"How often did he come to town?" Mia asked, gently steering her back to the story.

Mrs. Minor leaned back in her chair. "For four years he came every spring and every fall. Behind their palms folks used to joke they knew when to change their clocks by when that fancy rail car showed up at the depot. Course, the reason he came was for the fishing. Everybody knowed that. And course, he always got Miss Watkins for his guide. Nobody gossiped, at least not much. I guess you could say the town looked the other way. We all had too much respect for the Reverend. And them two never did nothing that anyone could point a finger at. He rented that fishing cabin from the Watkins family when he came. It was all up-and-up. They'd fish together, of course. I remember Kate had this real pretty white horse. Lord it was a big animal. Testy, too. He scared me half to death. But not Kate. She'd ride that horse most every day in the mountains and when DeLancey came, he rode with her. Once in a while they would come to town to eat dinner. But they never did any of that lovey-dovey stuff. At least not in public. Kate knew how to be proper and DeLancey was a gentleman. But anyone who saw the way he looked at her . . ." She sighed. "And the way she looked at him. Well, you knew. You can't hide a love like that.

"I never understood why her daddy allowed it. I asked my mama once and she said he just knew Kate was different and he wanted her to be happy. I guess we all did. She went all dark inside when her cousin, Lowrance, died in the war. But when DeLancey came she was her old self again."

She shook her head, clucking her tongue. "I'm not saying that DeLancey wasn't a fine man. He was all right. I don't reckon he meant to get caught up in all this, same as Kate. It weren't that he was bad. More that he was . . . weak. My mama said he never should've come sniffin' around Kate's door. Him being married and all. It was bound to turn out bad for Kate. But none of us saw where it was heading. People said afterward that poor DeLancey paid the highest price for his loving Kate. But I say that ain't so. They don't know. Kate paid, all right." Her eyes filled with tears. "She paid and paid and paid."

Mrs. Minor's head drooped forward and her shoulders shook as she silently wept. Lucy wrapped an arm around her slender shoulders, then looked to Mia.

"I think you'd better go now."

Mia nodded in understanding. "I'm sorry. I didn't mean to upset you." She rose and stood for a moment in agony, thinking there was something more she should say.

"Good-bye," she said awkwardly. "Thank you for talking to me."

Mrs. Minor looked up with red eyes and waved her hand. "Now honey, don't be feeling sorry. You did nothin' wrong. I'm an old woman and I feel things stronger. You come back. I want to tell you the whole story before my time is over. I'm just tired now, is all. Come on back and visit with me some more, hear? And bring Belle. I want to see little Theo's daughter."

Chapter Thirteen

Presentation is the placement of the fly on the water. The cast is viewed from the perspective of the fish. The angler's goal is to present the dry fly gently and in a natural manner so that the fish is not scared but will, hopefully, be lured to take the hook.

—KATE WATKINS'S FISHING DIARY

Thunder rumbled overhead, low and threatening. Mia looked up to see a large, angry front of dark clouds coming in from over the mountains, covering the late-morning sky like a lid being slowly pulled over the earth. When she looked upstream toward where Stuart stood, she saw that he, too, had stilled his rod and was checking the weather. A sudden gust of wind swept across the water, bringing cold droplets across her face.

"We'd better get out of the water," he shouted.

Before he'd finished the sentence the first drops of rain fell, icy and hard. She drew her line in as quickly as she could and made her way across the stones and silt, feeling the wind pushing at her back.

Stuart was already at the bank swooping up their

backpacks. "Hurry!" he called to her, and his voice mingled with another roar of thunder, louder this time. Over the ridge lightning lit the underbelly of the clouds, turning them an electric purple and yellow. "It's going to be a downpour. Give me your rod. Let's try and make it to the Jeep."

Mia began to sprint, holding her hat with her hand as the cold wind tugged. The temperature was dropping and looking up she could see a slate gray line of rain moving toward them. All she could think while her heavy, booted feet pounded the earth was *Why did we wander so far from the Jeep?* Stuart was way ahead of her on the path carrying the rods, but though the Jeep was in sight, she knew he wouldn't make it to the car dry.

Lightning flashed, turning the sky white, and only seconds later thunder cracked, shaking the earth. The sky opened up. Cold rain plastered her hair down her face and soaked her clothes. She could barely see the Jeep through rain as thick as fog, but Stuart spotted her coming and pushed open the door and helped her in. When he slammed the door shut behind her, she slumped against the seat and caught her breath. Prying open an eye she saw Stuart leaning against his seat, his mouth open and water dripping down from his hair. When he turned his head and saw her looking at him with the same shock and wonder, his mouth moved to a grin and they both burst out laughing.

"Whoa," he said, mopping his face with his palm.

"That storm came on fast. I thought that lightning was going to fry us."

On cue the thunder cracked seemingly right on top of them. Mia jumped and grabbed his arm, then laughed again.

"You're soaked," he said. "I've got to have a towel in here somewhere."

He climbed up to reach over the seat and scrounged in the back. He tossed a ratty old towel over his shoulder. It smelled musty but it was clean. Mia dried her dripping hair and face while Stuart continued to search the back. His hips butted her head as he stretched, so she pulled back flat against the door. When he slid back to his seat he carried with a look of triumph an insulated bag, a thermos, and a fleece.

"Always be prepared," he said with a self-righteous smile.

The peak of the storm was right over them, a maelstrom of wind, thunder, and flashes of light, but with Stuart she wasn't afraid. Rain battered the black, soft top of the Jeep like a drum, creating a din that they couldn't speak over. She handed him the towel and watched him sweep it across his face and hair. Then he returned it to her, following up with the fleece. She indicated with her hands that he should take it. His eyes flashed like the sky outside and he pushed the fleece firmly her way.

She accepted his offering gratefully. She was shivering in her soaked clothes, and the fleece felt like a blanket around her shoulders. Stuart opened the thermos and she caught the heady scent of coffee, almost swooning when the steam rose from the black liquid. He handed the plastic cup to her and, sipping, she felt the warmth slide down her throat and into her bloodstream. She drank quickly, then handed the cup back to him so he could have some as well. Next he unwrapped peanut butter sandwiches from zip-lock bags and handed her one.

She was having a good time, she realized. She felt snug and safe in the compact space, sitting thigh to thigh with Stuart, feasting on sandwiches and coffee. It was exciting to look out the window and through the sheets of rain to see the power of the wind as it bent the grasses and bowers of trees and swept across the water like a broom.

The storm passed as quickly as it came. The mighty clouds marched to the sea like Sherman's army, the thunder now muffled like the distant boom of cannons. The rain had slowed to a rhythmic patter, and from the northern ridge she could see a slice of blue sky.

She turned from the window to see Stuart still looking out. She stole the moment to study his unguarded face. His thick, dark eyebrows and the scruffy stubble along his jaw made his pale blue eyes shine out like beacons. They were his best feature and always drew her attention.

"Nothing like a good summer storm," Stuart said, turning his head back.

"I've always liked thunderstorms," Mia replied,

settling comfortably against the door to face him. She slicked her hair back from her head and zipped the large olive green fleece high up her neck. Bringing her knees up, she felt like she was tucked under a blanket. "We always used to play the counting game between the flash and the crack of thunder to see how far away the storm was."

"Me, too. And it was pretty close today."

"I know," she said, curling her toes. "The storms seem more violent up here in the mountains than down by the shore. Probably because we're closer to them."

"I remember a storm once when the thunder cracked so fierce a whole herd of cows dropped to their knees. You don't forget a sight like that."

"Did you grow up in the mountains?"

"I did. I grew up in this great old place in the Blue Ridge Mountains. It's part cabin, part house—added on to here and there over the years." His eyes warmed as he envisioned the homestead and he leaned back, tilting his shoulders to face her.

"It originally belonged to my grandfather and his five brothers. What a bunch of characters they were, all fresh off the boat from Scotland. And all of them fly fishermen. They shared the cabin growing up but as the years passed my grandfather bought them out as they lost interest, bought other places, you know how it is. My grandfather worked in insurance but his life was fly-fishing. He taught my father and my father . . . Well, we fish together, but you know how it is sometimes with fathers. They don't always have time to spend with their kids. So my grandfather picked up the slack, happily. He took me out with him every weekend and I don't know who enjoyed it more." His voice grew wistful. "My dad came along when he could. Don't misunderstand. He's a great guy. I come from a close family. My mother and father still live in the house I grew up in. My two sisters live within a day's drive away. So we see each other a lot. But when my grandfather died, I don't know, home just wasn't the same for me."

"What happened to the cabin?"

"It's still there." He took a sip of his coffee. "My grandfather left it to me."

She smiled, understanding how much that inheritance meant to him. "How old were you when he died?"

"Twenty-seven. I was grown up. It was time for me to move on. But I still feel cheated. There isn't a day I'm on the river that I don't feel him with me. He's just casting farther downstream." He refilled the thermos cup and handed it to her. "How about you?"

The coffee steam wafted to her nose as she brought the cup close. "There aren't many of us. My grandparents have all passed on."

"And your parents?"

She sipped her coffee and felt the familiar pang of loss. "My parents are gone, too. My mother died when I was thirteen. My father five years later."

"I'm sorry. That had to be a terrible loss."

"It was. Still is. I've spent my life searching for my mother in one way or another. She died of breast cancer. Back then detection and treatment were not as high-tech as they are today. She had a radical mastectomy, chemo—the works. But she went downhill fast. My father was devoted to her. She was his whole world. After she died, he aged right before my eyes. We all grew older seemingly overnight. She was such fun. She loved packing us all up and going to dinner and a movie on Friday night, or to the beach on Sunday afternoons. My dad had this sailboat and he used to take us out in the harbor. She used to say that he was the captain but she was the navigator."

Mia's heart kindled with the memory, seeing her mother in white shorts and tennis shoes, laughing with her hair in the wind. She'd always wanted a man to look at her the way her father had looked at her mother.

"Were you an only child?"

"No, I have one sister. Madeline." Mia's eyes softened at the thought of her. "Maddie is six years older than I am and she's been more a parent to me than sister. She's coming up next week and you'll meet her then. I warn you, she can be a little bossy, but I guess she's earned the right. She was there for me growing up, then during the cancer. She's my best friend. In fact, she was the one who sent me to Casting for Recovery."

"Does she fly-fish?"

"Maddie? No," Mia replied with a light chuckle. "She's more the tea and antiques kind."

"Hey," he replied with a hint of reproach. "Fly-fishing is for all kinds."

"You're absolutely right. Who would have thought that I would ever be fishing?"

"What did you do, before?"

She wondered what *before* alluded to. Before she came to the cabin? Before cancer? In a sudden flash of insight as searing as the bolt of lightning moments before, she realized that *before*, a storm had rolled over her life in the form of cancer, scattering the water, shredding bits of leaves, and causing beasts and birds to huddle before moving on. And her time at the cabin was like being here in the Jeep, snug in a safe place while the storm passed. But what was coming *after*? That remained to be seen.

Stuart sat across from her, waiting patiently for her answer. He was a good listener, she realized. He didn't feel the need to fire off his own opinions but allowed her the time to fully express herself. It was that quality that made him a good guide.

"I was in public relations," she replied. As she said the words, that life she'd led in Charleston seemed ages ago. She smiled to herself and thought, *Before*. "My job was to manage the talent for an arts festival. It was what one might call a glamour job, but as with all such things, in reality it was still a lot of work. I think I was good at it. But after the cancer, well, let's just say it was easier for everyone if I left."

He was not naïve and let that matter drop. "What will you do next?"

She lifted her shoulders to say, *Who knows?* "That's part of the reason I'm up here. To figure all that out."

Stuart looked out the window at the sky. The rain was now a light drizzle and the sky was clearing up. Shafts of sunlight lit up the river.

"We should go. You need to get out of those wet clothes."

Mia was sorry to leave but nodded her head in accord.

He put the key in the ignition but before firing the engine, he turned to her, his eyes searching.

"What about a husband?"

She hesitated, unwilling to muddy the water by bringing Charles between them. She'd placed him in the *before* category. Stuart . . . she decided to place him in the *after* phase of her life.

"Divorced," she replied, meaning it, but stunned by the finality of her word.

Stuart didn't comment. He faced the road and fired the engine. The Jeep sprang to life and like an old dog it took off across the field, shaking the rain off its back as it headed for home.

The small, gold bell over the door at Shaffer's chimed when Mia walked in. The heady scent of dark, rich coffee and freshly baked pastries assailed her. Like Pavlov's dog, her mouth started salivating.

"Mornin', Mia!" Becky called out in her cheery voice from behind the glass counter. Her cheeks were flushed from exertion but she looked healthy and in good spirits.

It was a busy morning at the bakery. A young woman wearing a pink uniform like Becky's was behind the counter making coffee in the shiny, steel industrial machine. Becky must have hired some help, she thought, and was glad for it. The brunette was buxom and had twinkling blue eyes. She turned to smile in welcome and Mia immediately saw the family resemblance.

Becky looked at the girl with pride pouring out of her pores. "Meet my daughter, Katherine. She's going to help me out for the rest of the summer, maybe even take over, if I can convince her. We'll see."

"You've got some pretty big shoes to fill," Mia told her.

"Don't I know it," Katherine called back before returning to her job.

The air conditioner was struggling against the residual heat of ovens and a half dozen patrons eating at the small tables, each graced with pink flowers in small bud vases. The chalkboard in the front of the store announced cinnamon buns as the special of the day and the front of the glass cabinet was filled with them, each topped with glazed icing.

"Hey, did you see the *Gazette* today?" Becky asked, eager for Mia's response. "They got an article written by Kate Watkins!"

Mia came to an abrupt stop. "It's out already?" She was stunned at the speed at which Nada had printed it. They'd discussed the idea only a week ago. She felt her stomach clench at the thought that Kate's name would be bandied about in every conversation in town that day. And yet she couldn't wait to see the article.

Three people stood in line ahead of her at the counter. The last was Phyllis Pace. She turned and said archly, "I'm guessing you had something to do with that."

Mia turned to Becky. "Do you have a copy?"

A middle-aged, blond woman sitting at a nearby table folded her copy and handed it toward her. "Here, you can read mine."

"Thanks," Mia said, taking it. She went to an empty table and began leafing through the pages, searching for the article. The paper was full of plans for the Watkins Mill town festival and stories about the local sheriff who won a state award and the thirtieth annual Truck and Tractor Pull contest being held on Saturday; there was also a page of announcements of engagements, weddings, and births, with photographs. "Here it is."

Nada had put the article on the front page of the Lifestyle section. Mia sucked in her breath at the photograph of Kate Watkins as a young woman. It was her! Mia bent for a closer look. Her first thought was how beautiful she was. The precociousness she'd admired in the face of the child had blossomed into a regal confidence. Kate's dark hair was pulled back tight and her gaze was slanted to the side, as though watching someone. The severity of her hairstyle accentuated her high cheekbones and eyebrows that arched over dark eyes like butterfly wings. She wore a prim, ruffled collar that rose high on her long neck, but there was nothing prissy about the woman in the photograph. Rather, there was a dare in her simplicity, like Jo from *Little Women*.

It was no wonder that every man in town was in love with her, Mia thought as she gazed at the face. Below her photo there was only a brief byline, as Nada had promised. Mia scanned the article and saw that Nada had selected the one on spring.

"I wonder where Nada found that picture," she said.

"Actually, I found it for her," Phyllis replied. "It turned out my father had some personal photographs of her. After you two had your chat he was awash in his memories. He spent days going through all of his old photo albums. It's been a good project for him. He showed me a few of the old gang fishing together that are quite nice. Come to think of it, I should show them to Nada for her next article. If you're interested, I'm sure he'd love to show them to you."

"Of course I'm interested. When can I see them?"

"He comes to the library with me every Tuesday. He looks forward to the outing but if he knows you'll be there to see his photographs, he'll be all the more delighted. Shall I tell him to plan on it?"

"Absolutely. I can't wait. You know, I've not been able to find any photographs of Kate. Or her father."

"Perhaps other people in town have photos, too," Phyllis added. "I can ask around." She came to Mia's side and looked at the newspaper. "It's a fine article. I know my father is proud to see it. He ordered extra copies of the paper so he can send them to his friends, in case they missed it."

"I'm glad he liked it," Mia replied, remembering the old man's melodious voice as he told his story. "After all, he's the one who first told me that the articles existed."

The bell chimed over the door and Nada came in carrying several copies of the *Gazette* in her arms. She walked in her brisk, no-nonsense manner that always reminded Mia of a drill sergeant.

"Speak of the devil," Mia said.

"Hi, y'all." Nada walked directly to Phyllis and handed her the stack of newspapers. "For your daddy. Tell him there are plenty more where that came from. But don't wait too long. We're selling them like hotcakes. Everyone's talking about 'On the Fly.'" Her eyes were gleaming with triumph. She turned to Mia. "So, how about you? Do you like it?"

Mia released a sigh. "I have to admit, it looks good. I love the photograph of Kate. It's the first I'd ever seen of her as a woman."

"As opposed to a child?" Becky said as a joke.

Mia realized with a start how she'd just made a serious slip. "We were just talking about how there aren't any photos of her anywhere."

"She might've destroyed everything before she died," Nada said.

Mia felt a shudder, thinking of the stark emptiness of the upstairs garret and the absence of any photographs in the armoire, save for the one of Kate and her father in the diary.

"Nah, why would she do that?" Becky said.

"Why wouldn't she?" asked Nada. "Her daughter deserted her. The town turned against her. Maybe she just wanted to disappear."

"If that were the case," Phyllis said, "don't you see publishing her articles as, well, an invasion of her privacy?"

Mia looked at Nada.

"Not at all," Nada said matter-of-factly. "These articles are wise and timeless. They reflect on who Kate Watkins the fly-fisher was, not some scandal. The town needs to remember that person."

"I agree," Becky chimed in. "Says in the paper there are going to be more coming. A whole series of them. That true?" When Nada nodded she added, "Good for you. I reckon most of us forgot that part of her story."

"Forgot?" the woman at the next table asked. She'd been listening in on the conversation. "I never heard of her before. I'm from out of town. I'm here fly-fishing with my pals all week. I loved the article. If you don't mind handing the newspaper back when you're through, I'm going to show it to my club. How cool is it that this woman wrote about fly-fishing back in the twenties?"

"See?" Nada said smugly to Mia. She turned back to the woman at the table. "Did you say you're fly-fishing?"

"That's right. We're part of a club in Charleston called Reel Women."

"A women's fly-fishing club? What do you do?" Nada asked, intrigued. "If you don't mind my asking."

"Not at all. Sometimes we have casting classes, or fly-tying classes, that sort of thing. Mostly we organize fishing trips. It's fun to go with someone else and we found if we organize a trip we tend to get out on the water more often. You know how it goes, once hooked you're a fly-fishing fool."

"In Charleston, you said?" Mia asked. "That's where I live, too. Maybe I should join up."

"Come on by. We'd love to have you. My name's Sheila Northen, by the way. Hold on." She bent to dig into her purse. "Let me write down my phone number. Call me when you're ready to come to a meeting."

"We should have a fly-fishing club here," Becky exclaimed. "I've always wanted to learn but I figured it was a man's sport."

"Oh no, honey," Sheila said, looking up from her writing. She handed her card to Mia. "There are women's fly-fishing clubs all across the country."

"My father always wanted me to learn," said Phyllis. "As a friend of Kate's, he always thought women belonged in the sport. I loved hearing his stories of going trout fishing in the mountains of North Carolina or out west. As I became an adult and had a career, I always wanted to fly-fish but never found the time to learn how. I regret now that I never fished with him. He can't get out on the water anymore and he longs to. Perhaps now I should learn. I could tell him *my* fishing stories for a change. I think he'd like that."

"Count me in," Nada said, her eyes gleaming. "Since I've started digging into Kate's articles I've dug out my rod and reel, too. Maybe we could get Belle to teach us. Imagine, Kate Watkins's granddaughter forming the first fly-fishing club in Watkins Mill. Now that's a headline I'd like to write."

The possibilities excited the women and they looked to Mia for a response. She heard hope in their voices and saw the plea in their eyes. Her first thought was, Oh no, don't ask Belle. Mia didn't want Belle to get involved with this idea at all. If they approached Belle, she would find out about Mia's research into Kate's history and she'd never forgive her. She remembered the look in Belle's eyes when she'd told her not to stir up the mud.

Then Mia looked into the eyes of the women around her. Each had welcomed her warmly into their town. Each had gone out of her way to help Mia in her search. How could she be so selfish as to only think of herself? She also had to give Belle the benefit of the doubt. Nada might be right; Belle might be grateful to learn about her grandmother. And Belle would be a wonderful teacher to these women. Hadn't she hoped to meet the townsfolk, maybe grow her guide business? What better way than with a women's fly-fishing club?

She smiled at them, her new friends, and replied, "I can ask. She's in Europe now but we should go ahead and start a club. That way we'll be organized when we ask her." She turned to Sheila. "Maybe your group can give us pointers how to get rolling?"

"We'd love to," replied Sheila. "That's how we started. Some of us were experienced but a lot of us were green. We went for a crash three-day course and have been fishing ever since."

There followed an intense discussion of the founding of a fly-fishing club, equipment, and such. Mia found herself tuning out and getting swept into her own thoughts. Her research into Kate Watkins's life was having ramifications she hadn't planned on. It was like throwing a stone into a pond and watching the ripples move farther and farther out.

Chapter Fourteen

The Gazette
July 1927
Kate Watkins, "On the Fly"

Whether you catch one fish or many, the joy comes from the pursuit. More often than not, even your best casts fail. Sometimes not catching a fish is fine. Other times, one fish caught after a duel of wits and skill is more satisfying than reeling in dozens. In the end, the quality of the experience matters far more than the quantity of fish caught.

Mia stood on the front porch of the cabin with a mug of coffee in one hand and a brush in the other as she stared out at the early morning sun rising over the eastern ridge of mountains. She felt her soul expand to reach out and grasp the flame red dawn and bring it back inside of herself.

She looked down at her painting to see the colors of that dawn stretch over the lush green of midsummer in the North Carolina mountains. She sipped her coffee and tried to imagine the same vista in the brilliant, fiery colors of autumn. Time was passing so quickly. The cool air would be here before she knew it. Yet it seemed so long ago since she'd arrived in the mountains. How little she'd known then what *wild* was. She looked into the woods beyond the clearing where darkness still hovered in the pale morning light. She'd learned enough to realize that she still knew very little.

Yet in this window of time she had carved out a life that mattered. She was beginning to feel she had her life back. Did she really have only a month left? she wondered. Despite her chaotic beginning, she simply could not envision an end.

Leaving Watkins Cove also meant leaving her new friends. Stuart in particular. She couldn't deny that she was attracted to him, for all that he was only her *friend*. In her mind she had it all sorted out. She was in the middle of a divorce and recovering from breast cancer. The last thing she needed now was to fall in love. And yet she couldn't deny the ecstasy she felt when they were together. The shiver of pleasure when they stood side by side on the water, the flush of joy at catching a fish with him, the melting of her bones when he looked her way with his intense eyes. Could they all be nothing more than the return of her hormones? A sign of healing?

Pitiful, she thought, rousing from her musing. As she gathered her art supplies her gaze swept the outside of the cabin. The cobwebs were gone, the shrubs were trimmed, the porch was swept and tidy, and she'd put one of the rockers out beside a small wood table. By the front door sat a clay pot filled with cheery red geraniums.

The money from Charles for the sale of the condominium couldn't have come at a better time or been more welcome. He'd been very generous, as he'd promised, and that act went a long way to pave the way, if not to forgiveness, to acceptance. The sale had removed the day-to-day worry about whether she'd run out of money for food or supplies. Mia had splurged on creamy white linen curtains to replace the threadbare graying ones. She could see the hems flapping in the breeze of the open windows.

The cabin felt like home now, more than her condominium in Charleston ever had. Mia knew that was because of the personal time and effort she'd spent cleaning and tending the old cabin. There was something about scrubbing a floor on one's hands and knees that bonded you to a place. She hoped that someday Belle would feel the same affection for it. Perhaps once she came to know her grandmother she could reconcile with the cabin.

Before Belle returned, Mia wanted to surprise her with a stone walkway that led from the porch to the parking area. After every rain the front of the cabin became a sea of mud. She'd consulted with Clarence and purchased the stones and equipment to create a simple path. She'd figured if she built it herself, it wouldn't set her back too much. After all, how hard could it be?

An hour later she had succeeded only in digging up the tenacious grass and bits of gravel and grit to form a rough path from the porch to the parking area. She'd thought she was getting in shape with all her walking and fishing, but her muscles ached from digging and from battles with tree roots the size of her arm. She leaned against her shovel, catching her breath. *What was I thinking?* she thought as she surveyed the ragged mess she'd made of the front yard. This job was much bigger than she'd thought. As her mother used to say when Mia had piled her plate with more food than she could ever eat, *Your eyes are bigger than your stomach.*

In the distance she heard the high hum of a car engine coming up the hill. She raised her head and wiped her forehead with her sleeve. Could Clarence be delivering the stone already? She was so far from being ready. A moment later a red Jeep swerved off the road to the cabin. Mia straightened, groaning slightly with stiffness. He *would* come now, she thought, rubbing the small of her back. She was sweaty and scratchy and her arms and legs were coated with dirt and grit.

Stuart climbed from the Jeep and walked to her side. He was wearing shorts and a black T-shirt that made his hair look as dark and glossy as a crow's wing. He looked at her, taking his time as his gaze traveled the long path up her bare legs, then at the collection of tools scattered on the ground around the ragged path, then at her again.

"I guess we're not going fishing today."

"Today? Were we supposed to?"

"I thought so. Must have gotten our wires crossed."

"I'm sorry. I'd love to, but I can't quit midstream."

He arched a brow and pointed to her cheek. "You . . . you've got some mud. Right there."

She reached up to wipe her face and only managed to smear more mud from her glove.

"Here, let me." He took a handkerchief from his back pocket and leaned closer to gently wipe her cheek. He was so close she saw the roughened texture of his skin from hours in the sun and the deep crinkles at the corners of his eyes. Mia held her breath.

"There, that's better," he said, inches from her face.

He had a way of smiling at her with his eyes that was a deliciously odd combination of teasing and flirtation. She never quite knew how to interpret that gaze, or if it was intentional or spontaneous. Yet it never failed to beguile her.

Tucking his handkerchief in his pocket, he looked over at the ragged trail she'd dug into the earth. "What are you making?"

"You can't tell?" she asked, slightly offended. "It's a walkway." Then, feeling self-conscious, she added, "It's nothing fancy. Just something to get from point A to point B without trekking through the slop. I talked at length to Clarence and it seems pretty straightforward."

"Clarence?"

"He owns the hardware store."

"Oh, *that* Clarence."

She tucked a wayward curl back from her forehead. "Yeah, well, he's been a great help. It's just a lot harder than I thought. This isn't exactly the kind of work I'm used to," she said defensively. "I mean, how hard could it be to put some stones together. Like a puzzle, right? Well, it took me forever just to get the path dug out." She looked at her fingers. They were chafed and her nails were deeply embedded with mud. She muttered crossly, "I didn't think I'd run into tree roots."

He covered his smile by rubbing his jaw and came closer to inspect her work. "Well, first of all, you don't want your walk to go near trees, especially not maples. Not only will you run into roots, but new roots will grow close to the surface and destroy your walk." He scratched his head and said, "I see you're going for a curved walkway."

"I thought it was more charming." She saw his expression, then laughed and admitted, "It does look rather like a snake slinking through the trees."

"Are you going to be hauling groceries and luggage along this path?" When she nodded he said, "Then the fewer curves the better. Here, let me show you."

With great relief, Mia stood back and watched as Stuart picked up the ball of string and laid it on the ground to create a simple walkway with only one smooth curve and a distance from any tree.

"Will this design work for you?"

"It's very nice."

"Do you have a garden hose?"

"No, sorry. No call for it, considering there's no spigot. Is there something else we could use?"

He thought a moment, then went to his Jeep. He came back with a can of spray paint. "It's bright orange, but it'll do the job. Now you go make sure the path is three feet in width. You do have a measuring tape?"

"Yes!" She silently blessed Clarence as she trotted indoors to get the measuring tape from her toolbox. While she measured the width he corrected the string position. When they were done, the outline looked ready to dig. She felt hopeful for the first time since she started the project.

"Do you have the sand and stone?" he asked.

"Clarence is delivering it later today."

"Great," he replied, rolling up his sleeves. "Then let's get started."

"Stuart, you don't have to help me. I . . . I can't pay you."

He turned his head and his eyes blazed. "I'm not asking you to." He paused. "Are you always so skittish about people offering to help you?"

Mia looked at her feet. "Lately, yes." Then she looked up, hoping he'd forgive her rudeness. "I'm working on that."

"Good. Now go measure." He started shaking the paint can. "Move over, da Vinci. I'm about to paint my masterpiece."

Stuart was no stranger to hard labor. He worked methodically, and as on the water, he was careful and sure. The morning heat rose with the sun, and sweat caused the black cotton to cling on his back like a second skin. His back was long and his muscles clearly defined. When he bent with the shovel, his shirt lifted and she could see a span of tanned skin between shirt and belt. She turned away from the distraction to focus on the task at hand. Yet while she raked the grounds smooth she surreptitiously glanced over to watch Stuart dig. His arms were very strong. The spade dug deep with each thrust, making clean edges in the dirt. In the same span of time that it took her to scratch the surface, Stuart had carved a complete and defined walkway.

When they were done they caught their breath and surveyed their work. Stuart looked at her and nodded with satisfaction, and in that gaze she felt again the heady sense of camaraderie they shared on the river. Sweat formed on his forehead and he brought his arm up to wipe his brow with his sleeve, leaving a mud streak across his brow. Mia snickered. He looked at her askance. "What?" She pointed to his face. Immediately he understood and pulled out the handkerchief to duty once more, catching her eye and laughing lightly.

"It's getting hot," he said. "The breeze is gone." He went to his water bottle and turned it upside down. "So is my water."

"Let me get you some. I'll put ice in it."

"You wouldn't happen to have a beer?"

"No, sorry, I don't drink beer. I have wine. Diet soda?"

"No, thanks, water will do me fine. Sometimes a cold beer hits the spot."

She made a mental note to buy some. As she led the way up the porch stairs, Mia felt a sudden déjà vu and wondered if he'd come indoors—or if she wanted him to. Then she recalled the many hours they'd spent together on the water, his kindness with the walkway, and she knew in that instant that the old nervousness and awkwardness existed only in her mind.

On the porch she slipped out of her muddy boots.

"If you like, I'll just sit out here," Stuart offered. "I don't want to track mud into your house."

"Don't be silly. You're welcome to come inside and clean up."

"You're sure I won't mess your floors?"

"I can always clean them up again. It's the least I can do to repay your kindness."

"In that case . . ." He kicked off his boots, then slapped them together over the railing to shake off clots into the bushes. When finished he put them neatly by the front door.

He stepped inside and looked around the cabin, his eyes gleaming with appreciation as he turned around to take in the space. She couldn't help but follow his gaze and see the place as he might.

The cabin looked clean and cheery in full light. On the stone fireplace's wood mantelpiece, she saw four of the wildflower porcelain plates she'd placed in stands. To the left was the bookcase filled with Kate's first editions with their gorgeous leather and gilt covers that dated from the turn of the century. A glass vase filled with fresh wildflowers graced the dining table, and in the kitchen a large wood bowl filled with fruit sat on a small white-legged work table covered with an oil-cloth.

Stuart was drawn to the wall where thirty rectangular papers, each with a painting of the river, a local wildflower, a bird, or a line of calligraphy, were tacked up in an attractive display. Mia's breath caught in her throat and she froze. In her spontaneous invitation she'd forgotten about them. She hadn't meant for anyone to see them. She cast him a wary glance. An appreciative smile turned his lips as he studied them. He then walked to the great armoire and admired the stag's head at the apex. When he turned around he put his hands on his hips. "What a great cabin."

She sighed, proud of the place. "I can't take any credit."

"Oh, but you can. I see your touch everywhere. And the watercolors have to be yours."

Mia felt her cheeks burning, glad his back was to her. She felt so exposed. "Oh, those . . ."

"They're very good."

She couldn't speak as the blush deepened. The compliment struck too deep.

"You know, the wildflowers remind me of some paintings I saw on the wall of one of the bedrooms at Watkins Lodge. They were done long ago. More a mural, I think."

Mia's attention sharpened. "You mean the paintings are still on the wall? In a bedroom? My God, they weren't painted over?"

"Apparently not. Why? Do you know the artist?"

"Yes!" she exclaimed, still stunned and thrilled. "They were done by Kate Watkins when she was a little girl. How wonderful that they're still there. Can I see them?"

"I don't see why not. I can bring you over if you like."

"Would you? I'd love that. I can't begin to tell you how much it would mean to me to see them." She was beaming. "When?"

"Well, first I'll have to see if the room is taken by a guest. That's easy enough. We won't finish the walkway till tomorrow, that is if the stone gets here. So, maybe the next day, or the day after?"

"You're going to help with the walk tomorrow?"

"I don't see how you're going to get it done if I don't. The stones can be heavy." When he saw she was going to protest, he looked sternly at her and said, "I thought we'd settled all that."

Mia took a breath. "Thank you."

She walked toward the kitchen, feeling his gaze on her back. "I'm forgetting my manners. You wanted some water. In the meantime, the bathroom is right over there, by the kitchen. Please, help yourself."

At the big farm sink Mia lathered soap in her hands and scrubbed beneath her nails to get the tenacious dirt out. Her khaki shorts were splattered with mud and her cotton blouse was sweaty. What she really wanted right now was a bath. She unbuttoned the top of her blouse and splashed cool water on her face and neck. Droplets of water streaked across her chest. She looked down and saw the softly mounded breast on her right and the padded bra on her left. Beneath, the scar was pale against her skin.

Mia heard a noise, and looking over her shoulder she saw Stuart emerge from the bathroom. His face was scrubbed and the short hair framing his forehead was damp. In a panic she lurched for a towel and patted her face, keeping her back to him while she quickly buttoned her blouse.

"I'll get that water," she called out.

"Thanks."

She had an inspiration. "We worked pretty hard out there and I'm starving. Can I make you some lunch?"

"You don't have to go to all that trouble."

"Now who's not letting someone be nice?"

"OK then," he said, spreading out his hands in mock defeat.

Mia felt a surge of satisfaction as she scrounged through the fridge. The pickings were slim but thank goodness she had some of Becky's crusty whole wheat bread, a wedge of sharp cheddar cheese, and some ripe tomatoes. "How does a grilled cheese sandwich sound to you?"

"Like heaven," he called back from the main room.

She was still smiling as she began slicing thick pieces of cheese. She added butter to the big cast-iron skillet and turned on the heat. As Mia cooked on the stove, Stuart walked around the main room. After a length of silence she stepped back a few paces to look over at him, curious about what caught his interest.

Stuart was standing at the bookcase with his back to her, reading. A fissure of warning coursed through her. She'd not hidden the diaries. With deliberate calm she turned off the stove and walked to his side, clenching and unclenching her fists. Stuart was completely captured by the book and didn't hear her approach. She glanced around his shoulder. Her worst fears were realized. In his hands was Kate's fishing diary. The brilliant colors of her glorious watercolors seemed to leap off the pages.

He sensed her presence beside him and looked at her. "This is unbelievable," he said, his voice tinged with awe. "I've never seen anything like it. Look at the detail on that rainbow trout. And there," he said, pointing to a pencil sketch of a trout leaping from the water. "She's got it exactly right." He turned to Mia, the soft hairs of his arm brushing hers. "Who did this? Kate Watkins?"

Mia froze, her secret uncovered. She reached out to carefully take the diary from his hands, her own hands trembling. She closed it, then went to the bookcase and placed it back into its box. She rested her fingertips on the leather, her back to him, knowing he stood watching her, waiting for an answer. Mia thought through the possibilities. Stuart would innocently mention the diary to someone at Watkins Lodge, and of course they'd want to see it. They'd be mad for it and the inquiries would begin. Everyone would know about the diaries and she'd have no choice but to turn them over. Her only hope was honesty.

Mia wrapped her arms around herself and, mustering her trust, told Stuart about her obsession with Kate Watkins. She began slowly, describing her arrival at the dirty, empty cabin. She explained how she sensed Kate's presence in the cabin from the start, how she'd found the treasures in the armoire. His eyes widened when she mentioned the Payne split bamboo rod, but he didn't interrupt. He listened patiently when she told him how she'd found the child's diary, then later the two fishing diaries. How she'd come to feel like Alice falling down the rabbit hole, and that now she was in this whole new world and how, like Alice, she was chasing her white rabbit—Kate Watkins's mysterious history.

He seemed genuinely moved by her story and took his time responding. "And you don't want me telling anyone about these diaries."

It was more a statement than a question and she appreciated that he understood. Mia nodded, enormously relieved. "They belong to Belle, I know that. I'm going to give them to her when she returns. But I knew if I gave them to her when I first found them she would have taken them away. It would have been her right, I know that. It's just . . . I wasn't ready to let them go. It may sound strange, but I needed them. Kate's words, her spirit—even her fly-fishing tips—have been healing for me. I feel—" Mia stumbled with words, trying to explain what she didn't completely understand herself. "I feel connected to her somehow. Anyway, what started out as idle curiosity about her turned into a quest."

"So, you've stolen a bit of fire, have you?"

"Yes," she replied, delighted with his analogy. She looked up at him with appeal in her gaze. "Please, I'm asking you to keep all this between you and me. I feel I can trust you." She paused. "Can I?"

"I think you know the answer to that, or you wouldn't have told me."

Mia exhaled heavily, feeling her tension slide out on a plume of air. "Stuart, thank you."

"Hey, I love a good fish tale as well as the next guy. I'd like to know more about this lady myself. Anyone who could create a fishing diary like that . . ." He shook his head. "My hat's off to her."

"Her father has one, too. Though not nearly as gorgeous or elaborate. I'll show it to you after lunch. Come on, I can smell the grilled cheese. I'm starving."

She hurried to the kitchen, where the smell of cheese and butter was tantalizing. Sunlight poured in from the row of four windows. She picked basil leaves from the small pots of herbs on the counter, then went to the cabinet to gather plates. He came beside her to take the plates from her hands. Then he reached up to grab glasses and carried them to the table.

"Tableware?" he asked.

"Over there," she replied, pointing to a drawer. He laid out the forks and knives, then filled the glasses with water. They worked in tandem. Mia carried the skillet to the table and served the two sandwiches, which were warm and oozing cheese. Then she cut thick slices of tomatoes, topped them with fresh basil, and set some on each plate.

Mia sat primly in her chair and smoothed the napkin across her lap.

Across the table Stuart looked at her and laid his hand flat on the table, but didn't say anything.

Her heart quickened at the gesture, sensing that his apprehension matched her own that their friendship was inching toward new ground.

"I have to tell you. That's a beauty of a cast-iron stove you got over there," he said, breaking the awkward silence. "In prime condition. Do you cook on it?"

"Me? No, I'm afraid of it."

"Why? It's a great oven, bakes like a charm. My mother loves hers. She cooks on it whenever we go to our mountain house."

"Do you go there often?"

"Not lately, but I try. I've been pretty busy at the shop."

"How are things going at Orvis?"

"Good." He picked up his sandwich and took a big bite. "Delicious."

"Thanks."

While he ate his sandwich, Stuart's gaze circled the room. "That Kate Watkins had a sense of the absurd, didn't she?"

"What do you mean?" she asked, feeling protective.

"The furniture. This grand table, that velvet couch

over there. I wouldn't have picked it myself for a cabin, but seeing it in here, I have to say I like it. It's unexpected."

"I think so, too," she said, brightening. "That's Kate for you. I'm getting the sense that she was a woman who did what she liked and didn't worry if anyone else approved."

"A woman ahead of her time."

"Yes and no. Don't forget that was the era when women were chaining themselves to gates of federal buildings to get the vote, and Amelia Earhart was giving Lucky Lindy a run for the money in the sky."

"So Kate was giving them hell in the rivers."

"Something like that." She set down her sandwich, barely eaten. "To be honest, I've been really bothered by something I learned about Kate Watkins the other day. Apparently she was having a long love affair with a married man from New York. I never thought her capable of that."

"Knocked her down a peg from your pedestal, did it?"

"Yes."

"She was only human. Is it possible you made her out to be something more?"

She took a sip of water, wondering. A few months ago that fact wouldn't have made much of a dent in her opinion. Now that she was on the other side of the bed, so to speak, the wife betrayed, she found thinking of Kate as the *other woman* disconcerting.

She put her glass on the table. "I wasn't completely

honest with you the other day when we were talking in the storm."

His face registered mild surprise and he, too, set his sandwich down. He wiped his fingers on the napkin, then waited.

"I told you I was divorced. I'm not, yet. I'm in the process."

"I see." He leaned back in his chair and asked in a serious tone, "Are you hiding out up here?"

"No, no," she said, rushing to correct what he was thinking. "He never physically hurt me. Never would." She laughed lightly at the thought. "He's far too civilized for that."

"What happened, if you don't mind me asking?"

Where to start? she asked herself. "I got cancer," she replied simply. "We were sailing along and it took the wind right out of our sails. Because my mother died of cancer I didn't think I was going to live." She brought her fingers to her chin, stroking it gently. The memory came as a gush of feeling. "I really expected to die. But I didn't. Then I went through six weeks of chemotherapy. I had the intense therapy. Not everyone can handle dose-dense therapy, but it offered a slightly higher chance for recovery, so I took it. I'm proud that I got through it. It was hard, though," she said in gross understatement. "Very hard. After that came a round of radiation, the hair loss, the fatigue. He wasn't very sympathetic and we grew apart."

She sighed, sorry to feel the undertow of the conversation start to drag her under. "Some marriages make it through that." She shrugged in summation. "And some don't. I came home one day and found him cheating with another woman. It's actually pretty embarrassing to tell you that."

"He's an idiot."

She glanced up at him shyly, surprised by the fury in his eyes. "Yeah, well, it happens. I wasn't the first and I won't be the last."

"It doesn't make it right."

"No," she conceded. "It doesn't." She reached out to trace the drop of condensation flowing down the side of her glass. She felt suddenly very exposed. "What about you? Are you married?"

He laughed shortly. "Me? No."

"Not ever?"

"Nope. This is one fish that's never been caught."

She drew her hand back. "Interesting way of putting it."

"Sorry. It's sort of an old family saying. My father's brother never married and two of my grandfather's brothers—the wild Scots, we called them—were committed bachelors. I guess it runs in the family."

"Being your father's only son, I'm sure he's not too thrilled that his prospects for a MacDougal heir are trimmed."

He only shrugged.

"Do you live at the lodge?"

"Temporarily. They let me live in a furnished condo

for the duration of the project. We're making the carriage house over to be the Orvis shop."

"Where's home?"

"Where I hang my hat, I guess."

"I suppose that's freeing. I mean, to go wherever you want, whenever you want."

"I don't think of it quite like that. It's more I haven't found a place that can hold me."

She wondered if the genes of the wild Scots ran strong in this offspring.

He thought for a moment, then added, "That's not entirely true. The Smoky Mountains . . . they're magical to me." He leaned back in his chair and his voice took on the melodic quality of a southern storyteller.

"Wherever I roam, whether Tennessee, Georgia, or North Carolina, if I'm in southern Appalachia, I know I'm home. I have the MacDougal blood flowing in me and it's the blood of a fly fisherman. My grandfather used to say our blood flows like the streams that course through the Smokies and it will always lead us to trout. I'm luckier than most. I don't work in an office or in a city. I earn my living on the water.

"Spring to me means caddis and mayflies and stoneflies hatching as thick as the violets that grow wild on the shore. Summer is heading to the backcountry where even the highest mountain streams are warming and I'm alone, bare legged and teasing suspicious trout to the lure. Fall comes and the trout join the explosion of color in the mountains. Their red spots blend with the falling leaves that dapple the water. And winter . . ." He paused. "Winter is an introspective season. The landscape is as gray as the smoky mists and even though it's bitter cold I like it because I'm alone—without the nine million kayakers and tubers and anglers who stir the best water in warmer weather. I bring a thermos of hot coffee, wait for the rays of sunlight to warm a few pools, and I'm rewarded with a flash of silver that I know is not ice but very much alive.

"So, I guess I do have a home. If I was married, it'd be to these mountains and the thousands of miles of trout streams that flow between her ridges."

Mia listened, and between the syllables and cadence knew she was falling in love.

He reached over to put his hand over hers. "Have you ever gone night fishing?"

She looked at their joined hands. It seemed an inexpressibly intimate gesture. She shook her head. "No. How can you see your line in the dark?"

"You don't. It's different. Would you like to give it a try?"

"Very much."

"All right, then. I'll take you."

Chapter Fifteen

Time is the substance from which I am made.
Time is a river which carries me along. But I
am the river.

—JORGE LUIS BORGES

The following morning Mia practically flew to town. Stuart was due to come by late morning to help with the walkway, and she had a list of items to scratch off her to-do list before he arrived. She arrived at Becky's so early she had to wait five minutes before her daughter opened the door.

"What's the special today?" Mia asked as she helped carry the large chalkboard out to the sidewalk.

"Pecan roll with caramel icing."

"God help me," Mia said with a soft grunt as they set down the heavy board. "Can you pack up a half dozen for me? And two loaves of honey wheat?" She slapped the chalk from her palms. "Is your mom in?"

"You know her. We can't get her to stay home. She's in back getting the post office opened up. It's a bit warm in there. It'll take time for the air conditioning to catch up with those ovens."

"How's she feeling today?"

Katherine looked in the shop window to see where her mother was. When she turned back her face was sober. "She's better today but yesterday she had a hard time walking. The doctor says she's losing more motor control in her legs and she's started some twitching. I'm afraid the disease is progressing."

Mia saw the fear in Katherine's eyes. She moved forward to hug her and felt the girl's two strong arms around her, holding tight, a signal that there was a lot of worry behind her all-too-ready smile.

"How long do you think she'll keep working?" she asked when they pulled back.

"As long as she can. You know Mom. We hired on another baker and I'm working the front of the store. She's finally accepted that with her legs she can't man the bakery counter. The post office is easier for her because she can sit. She'll hang on as long as she can. I can't imagine her not being here. She'd miss the people."

"She'd miss the gossip," Mia teased.

"That, too."

Mia was glad to see Katherine's reluctant smile. "How's your dad holding up?"

"Aw, he's strong and he loves her. He tells her that every day. Everyone has been so supportive. Like Mama says, you gotta have hope."

Through the front window Mia saw Becky opening the post office window. "There she is. I'll go in and say hey."

"I'll bring you some coffee."

As she walked into the bakery, it was with new humility that Mia realized she could count herself among the fortunate to have had breast cancer that was caught in the early stages. Everything was relative. She recalled those early days after diagnosis when she'd felt profound fear. Hope, she'd learned, was a gift.

She put her smile firmly in place before approaching Becky at the post office counter in the back of the shop.

"You're here early," Becky said.

"I don't know how you can avoid not eating everything that comes out of the oven. The minute I walk in here and smell the goodies I'm ready to sign over my soul for a doughnut."

"Discipline, my dear. Pure and utter discipline," Becky replied archly. Then she stealthily pulled a plate out from under the counter to reveal a pecan roll. "Want one? They're still warm."

"I've ordered a half dozen to go," she said, then quickly added, "but don't get up. Kath is already getting them for me."

Becky delivered a skewered look. "Has Kath been talking to you?"

"About what? I only just arrived."

"Mmm-hmm. Hey, I'm feeling fine. My leg's acting up is all. Oh, you got something here in your box."

"I do?" Mia asked with surprise. She'd secured a post office box for the summer. To date she'd only collected the *Gazette* and junk mail. "Hey, Lennie," Becky called out. "Can you bring me the contents of box thirty-four?"

A thin, young man with his blond hair pulled neatly back in a ponytail, dressed in a white baker's uniform, walked by to hand Becky a large, padded envelope.

"Thanks," she called out. Then handing the envelope to Mia, she said, "Here you go. Looks important. I'm guessing it's from your lawyer."

Mia took the large, white envelope with the return address of Charles's law firm.

"You don't serve any hard liquor back there?" she asked.

"Nope. But I do have some rum cake."

"I'll take one—and hold the cake."

"Aw, go on," Becky said with a wave of her hand.

Mia walked to a small table and sat down, staring at the envelope.

Becky came around the counter, using crutches. Mia was sorry to see it. She sprang to her feet to pull out a chair for her and would have helped Becky sit except that Becky waved her off.

"What you got there?" she asked when she was seated.

"It's from Charles. They're my divorce papers."

"Don't you sign anything without a lawyer looking at it first."

"Charles *is* a lawyer."

"Yeah, but he's also the guy who is drawing up the papers. You can't trust him."

Katherine came by with coffee for Mia and a glass of ice water for her mother. "Do you want your roll now?"

"No thanks. I'll eat it later. I'm kind of in a hurry." Mia put the envelope on the table and sipped her coffee.

Becky's eyes were trained on the envelope. "Aren't you going to open it?"

"Nope. I don't want to think about this today," she replied. "I'm too happy."

Becky's brows rose. "Oh? What's got you so chipper?"

"I'm almost finished building my stone walkway at the cabin."

Becky's face fell. "Oh. Thrills."

"And . . . Stuart MacDougal is coming over this afternoon to help me finish it."

Now her eyes rounded. "Oh? Thrills!"

Mia laughed. "Becky, you're an incurable romantic. You've seen too many movies."

"I've seen your Mr. Stuart MacDougal. He tends to put me in a romantic mood."

"He's not *my* Stuart MacDougal." Yet she couldn't disagree he'd put her in a romantic mood. Since yesterday she found herself singing—in the shower, while doing dishes, and along with music on the car radio. Suddenly the lyrics to songs had great meaning.

Mia told Becky the condensed version of how Stuart came by the day before, how they'd had lunch together, and how he was coming by later that afternoon to help her finish. She couldn't have asked for a more appreciative audience. Becky leaned forward with her chin cupped in her palm, and her eyes widened in appropriate places of the story.

"After we finish work, I thought I might make him dinner. If he'll stay, that is."

"Oh, he'll stay," Becky said with feeling.

"I hope so," Mia confessed. She wasn't as confident as Becky about Stuart's feelings. "I'm going to Rodale's after this to pick up some food. Just in case."

They talked a few minutes with the fervor of young girls about what she might prepare for dinner. When Katherine came over to freshen Mia's coffee, Becky told her daughter to pack up a rum cake to go.

"It's my gift for dessert," Becky said. "It's a winner, I promise you. You just take your hand out of your purse. This cake is on the house, hear? It's no use arguing. This is my shop and I'm still the boss here. All I want in return are the details. No holding back."

Mia left Shaffer's with a rum cake, pecan rolls, and loaves of bread. As she walked down Main Street she saw Clarence in the hardware store. On impulse, she stepped inside and waved at him.

"Just wanted to say the walkway is turning out beautifully. Thank you!"

Clarence hurried over. "Hey, glad it's working out. Real glad. Next I'd recommend adding gravel to the side of the cabin where you park the cars. I'll make you a good deal. Won't put you back much."

"I'll think about that and let you know."

He coughed, then said in a lower voice, "I was surprised to see Stuart MacDougal at the cabin yesterday when I delivered the stone."

"Oh?" she replied. "I can't imagine why. I told you, he's helping me build the walkway." She smiled sweetly and waved. "I've got to go. Just want to say thanks again!"

She escaped smoothly and walked quickly to Rodale's.

"Come see what came in yesterday!" Flossie called out to her when she walked into Rodale's. She led her to a large basket in the front of the store and held forth her arms. The sweet scent of peaches enveloped Mia before she reached them.

"The best of the season. They are gooooood," Flossie said with a roll of her eyes. She reached in the basket and pulled out a ripe peach and handed it to Mia. "Try one."

The fruit was warm in her hand. She bit into the soft lushness and almost swooned.

Flossie laughed with pleasure. "If I don't stop eating them there won't be none to sell. But they are good, aren't they?"

"I'm starving, so my judgment may be askew, but I do believe that's the best peach I've ever had in my life."

Flossie laughed, nodding her head with approval. "I wait all year for them and when they get here I feast. I make peach pie, peach jelly, peach chutney, peach salsa, and canned peaches to last the year. Be sure to get enough to bake yourself a pie. There's nothing better. You still could use a little meat on those bones. A man likes a woman who has something to hold on to, you know? Do you need a good recipe? 'Cause I've got one my mama gave me and it's the best there is. You go on and do your shopping and I'll write it out for you."

As Mia filled the bag with peaches she thought how nice it would be to bake a pie again. She used to love to bake, but while she was working, it always seemed she never had the time. She added more peaches in her bag, realizing that time was the one thing she did have now. Life was too short to squander. This was her time to do the things she loved but had put off. Fishing, painting, gardening . . . why not baking?

Flossie returned and handed her the recipe. "I put my phone number on that, too. It occurred to me that you might not have anyone to call if you need help. You ought not to be so far away without someone to come out if you need." She smoothed her apron, then asked, "So how are things going up there at Watkins Cove?"

"Splendidly. No ghosts to report."

"My kids will be sorry to hear that. You're single-handedly debunking one of the great ghost stories of our town. Speaking of which, I've been reading those articles about Kate Watkins. The whole town's talking about them."

"In a positive way, I hope?"

"Oh, sure. Thing is, though, folks are getting curious. About Kate, you know? Makes us think we really don't know much about her after all. She was famous once upon a time but most of us only know about the murder. Becky tells me you and Nada are doing some research about her."

Mia wondered if this was a misplaced sense of proprietorship the town had for a favored daughter. Or a morbid curiosity over the town's equivalent of a car wreck—everyone wanted to gawk.

"Some. We don't have much yet."

"Well, see, that's what I wanted to talk to you about. My mama knew Theo as well as anyone. Better, most likely. Theo being Kate's daughter and all, she might have a story to share about Kate, too."

"Do you think she'd talk to me?"

Flossie's cheeks flattened as a smile lit up her face. "My mama will be right pleased that you'll stop by. She likes to meet new people and she's been curious about you ever since she heard the old Watkins cabin was opened up. Why not come for dinner sometime next week? Tell you what, say yes and I'll bake an extra peach pie for you to take home with you."

Mia laughed. "In that case, yes!"

By the time Mia returned to the cabin her car was filled with bags. No sooner did she park than she spotted the red Jeep coming from the road, stirring up dust as Stuart turned off for the cabin. He parked beside her sedan.

"Perfect timing," he said as he climbed from the

Jeep. "Looks like you need help carting all these into the house."

"Are you always so chivalrous?"

"It's a genetic trait in MacDougal men. We carry it on the Y chromosome." He bent to pick up two bags and hoisted them into his arms like they were balls of cotton. "Aren't the men in Charleston gentlemen? I'd always heard it was the city of manners."

"It is," she replied, closing the car door with her hip. "And they are. Most of them. I've always thought having someone carry your bags was a matter of timing. My luck has been that I manage to pull into the driveway with a car full of groceries when Charles is gone."

"Charles, is that his name?"

She jolted at the sound of her husband's name on Stuart's lips. "Yes." She hoisted the bags in her arms, then led the way to the cabin, sidestepping the dugout, exposed walkway as neatly as the topic of her husband. Inside, she unpacked the groceries and put on a pot of fresh coffee while he put the peaches into the wood bowl. She could smell their sweet aroma fill the air.

"Try one," Mia said, handing him a ripe peach. She took one for herself. "I've eaten one already but they're so good I just can't resist." She bit into hers. Juice spurted down her lips and her tongue darted to catch the trail.

Stuart's eyes tracked the movement and she felt an exchange of kinetic explosions. She swallowed hard and reached up to wipe her mouth with the back of her hand.

"Be careful. They're juicy," she told him.

His eyes sparked as he bit into his peach.

Mia felt a punch of arousal and set her peach on the counter to gather mugs for coffee. While she busied her hands she wondered if she'd ever felt such a pulsing attraction to Charles when they'd started seeing each other. She was excruciatingly aware that Stuart was standing a foot away, hawking her every move.

"Do you want cream in your coffee?" she asked in a modulated voice.

"I'll take mine black, thanks." He moved over to the wood stove and ran his hand over the enamel. "You know what would taste great with this coffee? Peach pie. I'll bet you could bake a great one in that oven."

"Not me. I don't know how to use it."

"I could teach you."

She swung her head around, intrigued. "You make flies, and you bake, too?"

He shrugged. "I've lived alone for a long time."

"Is it hard to bake in that thing? It looks so unwieldy."

"Not at all. This ol' girl has cooked up countless meals. If you've got some wood, I could fire it up for you. It takes a while to get good and hot. But once you got her going, she stays warm for a long time."

Mia felt like some besotted schoolgirl. Even the

most everyday discussions carried some sexual innuendo in her sex-starved mind. If Maddie were here
they'd exchange a glance and likely burst out laughing.

"I was wondering . . . When we're done with the
walkway, would you like to stay for dinner? I could
make that pie."

"I'd like that."

She smiled and bit her peach. Everything came easily with him. There was no formality between them, as
there had been when she'd first met Charles. He was a
man of pretenses. He enjoyed witty banter over expensive Scotch and important names casually dropped
into the conversation. The makes of shoes and watches
were observed and noted.

After coffee, Mia changed quickly to old jeans and
an old T-shirt. She went back outdoors to find Stuart
already laying the larger rocks into position in the
lined and excavated path. They argued and laughed but
finally settled on a pattern. It took several hours to set
the stones and add the gravel and sand.

Mia looked at the gently curving stone path that
wound around the front of the cabin and it was exactly
like the one she'd drawn on a napkin at Becky's. She
turned to him. Beads of perspiration formed on his
brow and she was tempted to wipe them away with
her palm.

"Thank you, Stuart," she said with feeling. "I love it."

"Looks natural, like it was here as long as the cabin.
In a few weeks' time the grass and moss will grow and

you'll never be able to tell it wasn't. I'm thinking you could plant some of those wildflowers you like so much alongside it. Maybe violets."

"Belle will love it."

He cast her a side glance. "Do it for yourself."

She looked sharply up, catching his profile as his gaze returned to the walk. He was striking, she thought, with his straight nose over that full lower lip. A warrior's profile.

They finished off the project by pouring buckets of water from the river over the stones to settle them. En route they began splashing each other with the cool water, laughing until each was thoroughly soaked. Stuart removed his shirt and shoes, walked into the shallow section of the river, and lay back on his elbows against the stones.

"Come on, Mia," he called to her as she stood watching from the bank. He was smiling and waving her in. "The water's perfect."

There were days not that long ago when she would have readily joined him. In those days she didn't have a prosthesis or scar for him to see. She shook her head and leaned against a tree, flapping her damp shirt in the air, content to watch the racing water wash over the breadth of his shoulders and down his bare chest.

"I hope you have some dry clothes," she shouted out to him.

"In the Jeep," he called back.

"I'm going inside for a more conventional shower," she called out to him with a wave. She turned and walked back to the cabin, all the while knowing that his eyes were watching her as she had been watching him.

Inside the shower she let the warm water sluice over her, washing away what felt like acres of dirt from her body. She washed her hair, too, and when she emerged she took care to apply her favorite lavender-scented cream to her skin. She didn't rush. She dressed carefully in a long peasant skirt that fell down her legs to skim her ankles. Over her head she slipped on a scooped, loose-fitting blouse in the Mexican style. Standing before the mirror she flounced the collar and turned her body left, then right, checking to see that it hid any imperfections of her breasts. She tugged the sleeve down so the elastic would stretch over her shoulders, showing off the delicate collarbones that set off her long neck. Reaching up, she took out the clip and let her hair fall to dry in loose curls around her face and neck. She saw her skin glowing from the exertion. Mia couldn't remember the last time she'd looked at herself in the mirror and actually liked her reflection.

When she emerged from her room he was already dry and dressed in khaki shorts and an olive green T-shirt. He straightened when he saw her and she felt his gaze rake over her.

"You look very nice."

She blushed self-consciously. "So do you."

"Well," he said, turning to the old stove, "it'll take me a while to check this old girl out."

"I'll start the pie."

In short order the counter was dusted with flour and she was having a wonderful time rolling out the crust and slicing the peaches. While she baked and he tinkered with the stove they shared amusing stories about their childhoods and old friends and families, innocently seeking out clues as to who each other was, where they'd lived, went to school, went to church. Or, as her mother used to say, "Who their people were."

It all felt so domestic. As she laid the pliable crust in the pie plate, tamped it down, and filled it with the peaches and cinnamon, she wondered if this comfortable companionship was usual for married couples. She and Charles had spent their Sundays reading the newspapers for hours and drinking cappuccinos but rarely discussing the news. Later she might go shopping on King Street or visit a favorite art gallery and he would play golf. In the evenings they'd go out to dinner with friends or maybe a movie. On summer days she might go to the beach or sit by the pool. He would golf or sail. She couldn't remember a time they ever did simple household chores together, like building a walkway or preparing a meal.

She thought of the divorce petition papers in the envelope lying on her bed. She would sign them, she decided, and post them in the morning.

A loud bang brought her head around. "Are you sure you know what you're doing down there?" she asked teasingly. Stuart was on his back pounding with the palm of his hand.

"I just have to get this stubborn pipe back into place. Wanted to check to make sure all was in order." He pounded the metal back, then slapped the ash and dirt from his hand.

"You're going to need another shower."

"It was actually very clean. This old girl looks good. Except you've got a loose tile here . . . under the leg. See how it wiggles? You ought to fix that. You got some grout handy?"

"No," she said with a short laugh. "I don't think the stove is likely to budge. It weighs a ton."

"I can come by and fix that one of these days."

"OK . . ." She turned back to her pie, feeling grateful to the old stove for getting him to offer to come by again.

"I'm ready to light her up," he told her. "Come watch so you learn how." When she came close he put his arm casually around her shoulders. "The best way is to start with a base of newspaper and small pieces of dry kindling, like that, see?"

She nodded.

He let go of her shoulder to get matches from his pocket. She found she could breathe easier. He struck the match and put it to the newspaper.

"Once you get this burning, add a few pieces of clean, well-seasoned firewood. It's important that the wood you burn has been split and dried properly."

"Oh, I can guarantee mine is. Clarence was very particular about that."

He shook his head and snorted. "Clarence."

"Do you have a problem with Clarence?"

"No," he replied, and he bent to adjust some wood on the fire. "He just seems to take a proprietary interest in you."

Her lips twitched as she watched him stoke the fire.

As the oven heated they sat on the porch and drank the cold beer she'd bought especially for him. He talked about his plans for the new fly-fishing shop. His blue eyes intensified as he emphasized and punctuated his descriptions, and she wondered if Stuart was as passionate about the people in his life as he was about fly-fishing.

When the beers were drunk and the mosquitoes began to hum in their ears they moved back inside for dinner. She put the pie in the hot oven and crossed her fingers, then laughed when he teased her for having so little trust in her formerly rusted friend. While the pie baked and filled the cabin with its sweet aroma, they dined on cold shrimp and pesto with thick slices of ripe tomatoes.

And still they talked. The sun began to lower and they set the pie out to cool. She brought out candles and lit them. He poured more wine. In the flickering light of flames she told him stories and anecdotes about her job in public relations—the foulmouthed, short-tempered restaurateur who didn't understand why he needed public relations; the ego-inflated musician who expected Mia to accompany her on her tour; and the exciting array of international talent that came through Charleston for two glittering, glorious weeks of the Spoleto Festival. He never let his eyes stray from her face as she talked, and she wondered if he was always this attentive, or if perhaps he was as entranced watching the shifting expressions on her face as she was watching his.

She only stumbled once, and that was when she blithely mentioned Charles again. This time, he seized on it.

"You don't talk much about him," he said.

"Why would I?" she replied defensively. "We're in the middle of a divorce. Hardly a happy topic."

"I'm curious, is all. We've been talking for weeks but until recently I didn't even know if you were married."

"Nor I you. I thought we had some unspoken agreement not to get personal out on the river."

"It's kind of a code. The water is neutral territory. Keeps it from getting chatty out there. That's why you always want to be choosy about who you go out on the river with. You don't want to be stuck out on the water with a whiner." He looked at the river. "But we're not on the river now."

"I don't like to talk about him." She averted her eyes and felt the dreamy quality of the evening slipping through her fingers.

"Were you so unhappy?"

"No," she replied a bit sharply. "I was happy. Charles can be very charming and romantic. I won't make him out to be some ogre. But talking about him now only makes me feel bad. I'm done with that. I'm looking to my future now. He's part of my past."

"Not yet. When is the divorce final?"

"I'm not sure. Soon, I expect. I've got a packet of papers I picked up today if you'd like to review them. Do you have any more questions?"

"Just one. Do you still love him?"

Her mouth slipped open in a silent gasp. She hadn't prepared for that one.

"I did love him," she began. "Very much. I loved our life together. That world I was describing earlier, our life in Charleston, was exciting. When I got cancer—" She lifted her shoulders. "Everything changed. I changed. I wasn't the beautiful, outgoing trophy wife who could help him entertain his clients and achieve his goal of becoming partner in his law firm. Instead I became sick and drew inward. I didn't go out at all. Then with chemo . . . Well, you can imagine. He just couldn't handle it. He tried. I have to give him his due. But I wasn't the woman he married. He wanted the better, not the worse. He wanted out."

She reached out to pick at the melting wax that dripped from the candle. "Perhaps if we'd communicated better . . ." She shrugged. "I was angry and hurt at first. Of course. But up here I've had time to reflect and I'm trying to get to the other side of this. I've come to see that the change might just be for the better and I don't blame him anymore. So, the anger is gone but I'm still dealing with the hurt."

"Do you still love him?"

She dug deep for an honest answer and was awash with relief to discover that she truly did not. "No."

He reached out for her hand.

She looked at it, wondering what he was offering. For a wild second she thought he was going to lead her to her bedroom. She wanted him, oh yes she did. But she was afraid. Even terrified. It had been so long since she'd had sex, and she'd never undressed before a lover with her scar. She hesitated, unconsciously drawing back.

"Come on," he said, coaxing, as though talking to a skittish animal. He wiggled his fingers.

With an intake of breath, she took his hand.

He stood and helped her from her chair. "Where's your rod?"

She released a puff of air. "My fishing rod?"

"I seem to remember a promise to take you fly-fishing at night."

"But the pie . . ."

"It's not going anywhere, is it?"

Nonplussed, she went to the closet where she stored her fishing rod and equipment.

"You won't need your waders. We'll stay on the bank. You won't need flies, either. What you will need is a long-sleeved shirt and some mosquito repellent. We aren't going far but there'll be brambles and mosquitoes. I'll meet you at the Jeep."

Mia walked in a daze to her room, still confused as to the sudden shift in mood. She'd been about to ask Stuart if he'd ever been in love. Maybe it was best she didn't ask, she thought as she slipped her fishing shirt over her pretty top. Doing up the buttons, she recalled his tale of his wild Scottish bachelor uncles. Her answer may well lay there.

She changed once more, this time out of her skirt into a pair of fishing pants, and she changed her sandals for tennis shoes. Seeing her reflection in the mirror, she laughed, thinking she certainly didn't expect the evening to end in this manner. She sprayed a bit of repellent, then, feeling like an explorer, went outdoors to join him.

The light was dim when she came down the porch steps. Stuart was standing at the Jeep pulling his fishing rod out from the back.

"Ready?" he asked when he saw her.

"As ready as I'll ever be," she said, looking beyond at the forest.

He laced his fingers with hers and they took off, walking along the river. She took a deep breath and clung tight to his hand. To her left was the river. To her right she could only see the towering vertical shadows of hardwoods. Their feet made loud crunching noises as they walked, and small branches and brambles scraped against her legs. She lifted her face to the sky, feeling the silky evening breeze caress her skin. A Carolina moon was a sliver of silver against velvety black. A smattering of stars peppered the sky, creating a dreamy reflection on the water.

"It's beautiful out tonight," she said.

"The darkest summer nights are the best time for big

fish," he said. "Trout have excellent vision in the dark and they're less wary. And listen to those crickets sing. That's what the big fish are hungry for. If those clouds cover the moon for a while, they'll be hopping."

Before long he stopped and said in a low voice, "This will do." They stood together at a smooth, mossy bend of the river. Over the sound of rushing water the chorus of insects bellowed, and occasionally she caught the whispered sound of bat wings as they lowered to dip in the water. Over this noise she heard an odd splash, but the river made so many noises she couldn't be sure. Then she felt a squeeze on her hand and she knew from Stuart's reaction that her instincts were right and she'd heard the sound of trout jumping.

He let go of her hand to put a small flashlight in his mouth. She came close to watch him attach to her line a "Woolly Bugger," the biggest, bushiest black fly she'd ever seen. His lips turned up in a smile around the metal flashlight when he heard her laugh.

"We'll start out fishing streamers," Stuart said. She couldn't see his face. His deep voice became part of the night. "Just cast down or across into the water, then strip up current."

"But I can't see my fly."

"No, but you can hear. Listen for any odd splash that sounds different and cast at it. And you'll feel the current, trust me."

It was impossible not to hear the river, she thought. In the darkness the gurgles and rushing and splashes all mingled into a roar. And any odd splash she might hear could be made by a fish, a rock, or a bear, for all she knew. But she had to admit it was fun.

She made a short cast into the water and it was anyone's guess where the fly landed. But she felt the strong current capture the fly, just like he said she would, and carry it downstream. She was working more with her intuition than anything else and she knew the fish were out there somewhere. Night fishing wasn't much different from how she'd been spending the past few months, she thought. She was blindly casting her line out to the universe and seeing what took it.

She squinted and tried to see her woolly fly as it drifted away down the river. When, for no real reason, she felt it went far enough, she stripped it in. Then she cast over the water again, up and over, getting a rhythm, enjoying the tugging of the current, flying blind, feeling merged with the river in a way she never had before.

She cast again and this time she felt a distinct heaviness on the end of her line that was different than the current. Instinct told her to jerk her rod high into the air. There was a firm tug in response.

"Stuart!"

He heard her shout and was right beside her, his voice ringing in the darkness with just as much excitement as she felt. "Let go. Give it some line."

The fish took off downstream and she stepped into the river, feeling the cold water soak her shoes. She followed the trout, splashing in the water while the line flowed from her reel.

"He's a fighter," Stuart called out. He was ready with the net.

"I can't see it!" Mia exclaimed, but she could feel it. The connection was visceral.

"Bring it in some," Stuart said, guiding her, speaking low. "Nice and easy. That's right. You've got it."

And she did. Mia's heart was pounding like a drumbeat in the night jungle. She heard the *click click click* of her reel and the music of the insects on the bank. The big fish tugged and she gave him line; then, in turn, she reeled him in, playing him like Stuart had taught her. She could have danced under the stars with this big trout all night. But her partner on the other end of the line suddenly had a surge of energy and bolted into the current again. Mia felt a powerful tug, then the abrupt release as her line slackened.

"Oh, too bad," Stuart said. He pulled the line close to find the fly still at the end.

"No, I'm glad he got loose," Mia replied. "It's so dark I would have had a hard time getting the hook out. He danced with me. That's enough."

Mia stood still and watched the dark water for a moment, wondering where her trout had gone to.

When she lifted her gaze she gasped with surprise. The long line of towering hemlocks formed the silhouette of a bold, black mountain range in the distance. Dancing among them, glistening like twinkling lights, were thousands of fireflies. She'd never seen so many! It was like watching the fairy lights on a row of Christmas trees all come alive. She'd heard fireflies were disappearing from the landscape. But here they were, dancing in the dark, showing the world they had survived.

She looked downstream to where her fish had slipped under the black water to become one with the river again. Standing in the river with the water rushing at her ankles and the light of fireflies in her eyes, she, too, felt part of the river's enduring flow. She heard the gurgles and splashes as the voice of the river and she closed her eyes, listening. *Let go and follow me.*

"Are you OK?"

She opened her eyes, dazzled yet reassured to see Stuart's face inches from her own. "I'm so much more than OK. This might have been the best day of my life."

She heard him breathe in with satisfaction. "Even though the big one got away?"

"Especially because he did. I've never tried to explain this to anyone else but I think you'll understand. I feel truly safe in the river. Like I belong here. Kate Watkins wrote once how we needed to feel part of the river. I'm beginning to understand what she meant.

"Stuart, I know what sickness is. That's where I've come from. And I know what it's like to be healthy. To not live under the shadow of cancer. That's where I want to be again. For the longest time I didn't know how to get from pain to well. I was stuck in this dark place, numb with fear.

"But when I'm in the river I'm living completely in

the moment. Not in the past, not in the future, but in the now. Time swirls together like the water at my feet and I am standing in time and time is a river and I am the river."

He stepped closer and held her shoulders. "I think you're very brave."

"Brave?" she asked, looking into his face. "What choice did I have?"

"The choice to not merely survive. But to live."

The moon had risen higher in the summer sky and her silvery shine was captured in his eyes. They smiled in mutual understanding of attraction, trust, and something more they dared not speak of. The river flowed around their heels, rushing over rocks, music in their ears. He leaned closer so that their foreheads touched. Mia felt his warm breath on her face, the restraint in his tight grip.

"Mia," he said in a hoarse whisper. "Kiss me."

Her breath escaped in a rush. She heard the pulsating river build to a crescendo in her head. She lifted her arms around his neck and pressed her body against his, hip to hip, chest to chest, and with a breath, lips to lips. His scent enveloped her, musky like the earth, tangy like the river's bottom.

Mia was the river. She was water melted from glaciers. Silt and stone dust dredged in her veins. Her current coursed to mingle with his, flooding the banks like the river after a spring rain, racing downward to settle in the delta.

Chapter Sixteen

Shooting line is the releasing of fly line during the cast to allow the line to be carried out by the momentum of the rod. It's all in the timing. It's about knowing when to let go.

—STUART MACDOUGAL

Asheville seemed such a big city after the small-town lifestyle in Watkins Mill. Mia reserved a table at one of her favorite restaurants to meet Maddie. Inside it was like an old tearoom with white-linen-covered tables, dark wood, lush potted plants, and black-and-white photographs of Asheville's people and places. The sun was out and the humidity was low, so Mia chose a table on the covered patio where she could watch the hustle and bustle of the colorful summer crowd.

She ordered two sweet teas and stirred her straw in the ice, the anticipation of seeing her sister again bubbling inside her after nearly two months. In some ways, it felt like she'd lived in Watkins Mill for years. The life she'd carved for herself there was as lush as the mountains that surrounded it. Meanwhile her world in Charleston had receded into foggy memories. Only

Maddie remained a bright touchstone to that other world beyond the mountain ridge.

A blond woman in a pale pink summer dress and a white linen jacket was walking up the sidewalk glancing at the sheet of paper in her hands and checking the address on the building. Mia leaped to her feet and waved ecstatically, calling out, "Maddie! Over here. Maddie!"

Maddie's head bobbed up and her face broke into a wide grin of recognition. "Mia!"

They both bolted, and in another moment they had their arms around each other and were laughing and squeezing tight. In that moment time was suspended and Mia could have been eight years old, or sixteen, or sixty. The bond she shared with her sister was ageless.

"Let me look at you!" Maddie exclaimed, pulling back. Her blue eyes were open wide as they devoured Mia. "My God, you look great!" she said with pleasure mixed with shock. "I was expecting some depressed, thin ragamuffin that I was going to rescue and bring home with me. But look at you," she repeated, shaking her head. "I haven't seen you look so healthy since . . . well, in a long time." She stepped back and surveyed her sister while Mia stood blushing. "You've filled out, your skin is positively glowing, and your hair. Mia, you've got so much hair! It's grown inches and the curls are adorable. I can't get over it. The mountain air really agrees with you."

Mia's chest puffed at the compliments. She'd heard precious few in the past year. She knew from her peeks in the mirror that she was looking better but to hear the accolades from Maddie, who was always her most honest critic, sent her over the moon. Meanwhile, her own gaze was capturing every nuance of her sister's appearance.

Tall like Mia, Maddie had gained some weight to soften her lean edges. Her sister was beginning to look the mother role she'd taken on since she was nineteen. Maddie had cut her long blond hair to chin length and wore it tucked neatly behind her ears, where large pink tourmalines sparkled in the lobes. She'd always been a conservative dresser—knee-length hems; white shoes and white purse; a light jacket to cover bare arms in public; and at her neck a pretty necklace, usually a strand of pearls. Pale pink lip gloss at her lips and blush on her cheeks were her only makeup.

"Oh, Maddie, I'm so happy to see you. I didn't realize how much I missed you until I was sitting here waiting for you to show up."

"Well I certainly missed you every single day."

"You called me on the phone most every day," Mia teased.

"And got your darn answering machine."

"I called you back!"

"Eventually," Maddie said; then she wrapped Mia again in an impulsive hug. "I've been so worried about you." She pulled back. "But I see I shouldn't have been.

You look so . . . happy." She said the word with a tone of surprise.

"That's because I am," Mia replied, realizing how true that was. "Come on, let's have some lunch."

They feasted on southern comfort food. Mia had fried green tomatoes with goat cheese and a spicy grilled catfish. Maddie ordered shrimp and grits in a roasted red pepper sauce, and for dessert they shared some old-fashioned banana pudding. After lunch they linked arms and sauntered along the colorful streets of Asheville, chatting about everything and nothing as they shopped the countless boutiques, steering clear of unpleasant subjects. They both understood without saying the words that this was a special afternoon of sisterly bonding. Mia bought flowers and a quilt. Maddie bought yarn for a sweater, a hand-crafted necklace for her daughter, an Asheville T-shirt for her son, and two bottles of North Carolina wine for her husband.

Later, when their feet were tired and their arms were filled with their purchases, they headed back to their cars. Mia led the way from Asheville to the south-western mountain region and her cabin. As she drove she recalled her first trip down this same road months earlier. That frightened, insecure, pitiful woman was entirely someone else compared to the woman who drove this same car today, she realized. As she ambled along the winding road, Mia knew exactly which turns to take and where she was headed.

She reflected on how in the past weeks her life had

expanded in a new dimension. Stuart had eased his way into her life like the professional fly fisher he was. He'd courted her not with short, erratic bursts of attention but with a series of backward and forward casts, fluid and with care, fully understanding the role of tension in hooking, playing, and landing the fish.

Oh, he was playing her, she thought with a demure smile as she steered her way home. Give and take, give and take . . . she couldn't stop thinking of him. His kisses had ignited her; she felt afire, counting the minutes until she'd see him again. So far, they'd shared only kisses . . . long, lingering, soul-depleting embraces . . . nothing more. She was still skittish, afraid of more intimacy. She knew he was shooting her line, allowing her to decide the moment to completely let go.

When at last she made the final turn off the main road, she checked in her rearview mirror to make certain Maddie was still behind her. She smiled when she saw her sister's turn signal flashing. A few minutes later she was pulling up along the freshly graveled driveway she'd had Clarence install the previous week. It covered the perpetually muddy terrain and led to a parking area at the side of the cabin. Every time she drove on it she'd thought it was money well spent. Opening her car door, she heard the familiar rushing and splashing of the river. It sounded in her ears like it was calling out to her, *Welcome home!*

"Oh, Mia," Maddie exclaimed with feeling as she stepped from her Volvo wagon. Her hand was still on the door frame as she turned her head left to right. "This is the cabin in the woods I've always dreamed of!"

Mia burst into a wide grin of pleasure, remembering the dirty, dark cabin she'd arrived at that first rainy night in June. She followed Maddie up the new walkway, lugging the suitcase while her sister carried a big cardboard box filled with goodies from Charleston. All was ready for Maddie and she was eager to show off what she now considered her home. Stuart had stopped by to help her replace the cracked porcelain sink in the bathroom and hang the cheery trailing plants along the porch. He had taught her how to clean ashes from the grate and replace washers in the faucet.

"I love it!" Maddie exclaimed when she stepped inside. She set the box on the floor and took a quick walk around the room, her mouth open in a wide grin. "And look, did you paint those?" she asked, making a beeline for Mia's watercolors.

The dark walls of the cabin were lit with the brilliant watercolors. A second section of twenty watercolors and select phrases had been tacked on another wall, bringing the total to over fifty. The new ones included the birds that Mia had begun identifying. Their showy plumage mimicked the joy Mia had felt these past weeks.

"You started painting again. Oh, Mia, I'm so glad. I was sorry when you stopped. They're wonderful. Just beautiful."

"They're only on paper," Mia replied, embarrassed

by the praise. She began putting the flowers in a glass vase and filled it with water.

"Can I have one? To bring home?"

"Of course. Take two or three—however many you want."

"I'll have them framed. They'll help me remember this fabulous place."

Mia's smile slipped, for she suddenly realized that there would be an end to her stay here. This wasn't her permanent home, no matter how much she imagined it was. She'd have to remember that.

"Where did you get those porcelains?" Maddie asked in a high voice, hurrying to the fireplace mantel. She reached out to carefully pick one from its stand to investigate. "It's absolutely exquisite. The work is so fine."

"They were here when I arrived. I'm not sure, but my guess is that Kate Watkins commissioned them for the main house and took them with her when she came here. There are a few things here that belong in a grand house." She pointed her finger. "Like that sofa, the pedestal table, and the armoire."

"I couldn't help but notice. I thought Belle was an eccentric."

"Come take a look." She led Maddie to the armoire and swung open its carved wood doors. "There's a set of twelve plates, each one of them different."

Maddie pulled out the china one by one from the felt lining, exclaiming over each design, holding it up and drawing attention to the almost translucent quality of the porcelain. Next Mia showed her the set of silver rolled in pieces of green felt. Maddie untied the raggedy ribbon and opened a bundle.

"This sterling is hardly rustic tableware," she remarked, clearly surprised. She carried the green felt bundle over to the dining room table and spread it open. She picked up a silver fork. It was graceful and sleek, almost modern in design, with the tip pointed and turned slightly under. The initials *KW* were stamped in simple, bold letters, not in the traditional swirling script. Turning it over, Maddie gasped. "My God, Mia, this is Stone silver."

Mia bent over the silver, as if by getting closer she'd understand what Maddie saw. "What's that?"

"It's not what, but who. Arthur Stone was one of the leading arts and crafts silversmiths in America. He had a unique mark. See? It's his name with a hammer going through it. She must have commissioned it."

"Are you sure? She wasn't married. I assumed there must have been some ancestor with the same initials."

"No, that wouldn't be possible. Stone only started producing work under his own name sometime around the turn of the century. So this had to be commissioned between, say, nineteen hundred and nineteen thirty, give or take a few years. I'll look it up when I get home."

"But this doesn't make sense. Why would she have a set of silver made using her maiden initials?"

Maddie pursed her lips in thought, then said, "Because she knew she would never marry?"

Mia picked up a silver fork and slowly turned it in her hand. The fork needed to be polished but it still maintained that gorgeous burnished sheen of sterling. It truly was a lovely piece. The sleek lines of the design were timeless.

"Where was Stone's shop located? In the south?"

"Oh, no. Somewhere up in the northeast. Massachusetts, Rhode Island, New Hampshire. I'm not sure."

Mia shook her head with a rueful smile. "I'll bet this was a gift."

"From her lover?"

"Of course. DeLancey was from upper-crust New York. A man who could afford to travel in a private railcar would have known a silversmith of Stone's caliber." She walked to the armoire and Maddie followed her. She pointed to the blue taffeta gown. "Her dress, his white scarf, the china, the silver . . . DeLancey rented the cabin when he came for his fishing trips."

Mia and Maddie looked at each other and shared a smile of understanding.

"They must have had some very romantic dinner parties," Maddie said with exaggeration. "He probably brought champagne and caviar on his railcar."

"Well, think about it," Mia said with rising excitement. "They couldn't have gone out in public. That would have stirred gossip."

"So they created a world of their own here, where

he could wine and dine her in the manner to which he was accustomed."

Mia sighed and set the silver fork back on the table. She knew it had to be true. She could picture the whole scene vividly in her mind. "He must have loved her very much."

"And she him if she was willing to risk everything— the chance of a good marriage, her reputation—all to continue her affair with him. I could understand if she was poor and he offered her a world she could only dream of. But a woman of her position? Her independence? Why would she do that?"

"Why not?" Mia asked. "She never put much store in the opinions of others. It got her into trouble in the end, true, but early in the affair all she knew was that she was in love with DeLancey. Recklessly so. Maybe even defiantly so."

She walked back to the armoire and pulled out the blue taffeta gown. She shook the fabric to let it fluff out, then held it out in front of her, envisioning the woman who had worn it.

Maddie came closer to press the dress against Mia, holding the shoulder to Mia's, then matching the waists. The hem fell below Mia's ankles. "It fits," she said, tugging at the skirt.

Mia held the gown close. She was beginning to understand the complexities of a real, flesh-and-blood woman better than the one-sided heroine she'd imagined. "I don't think she ever wanted to marry. She was self-sufficient and independently wealthy. She had avid interests, a full life, a doting father. She had the admiration of many men. Why would she give that up to tolerate the demands of one?"

"Spoken like a woman about to get a divorce."

They looked at each other and laughed.

"Well, it's a mystery," Maddie said, returning to the table and putting the silver back into the felt liner.

"Exactly. That's what got me curious about the woman who lived here. You know how you feel when you see a pile of puzzle pieces on a table? You can't help but try to match a few, just to see what fits where." She carried the gown to the armoire, hanging it back up. She remembered her surprise at finding it there that first day in the cabin.

"At first, finding all this finery in the cabin was like being surrounded by puzzle pieces. And I had a lot of free time. So bit by bit I started putting the pieces together."

"And now you want to finish it."

"Yes, I'm getting the picture now and there are a few key pieces still to match up."

"Well, you can tell Belle that this particular puzzle piece will bring her a tidy sum," she said, holding up the felt bundle. "There isn't much Stone silver out there. Most of it is in churches or private collections. And," she added, unrolling the second of many bundles, "it looks to me like she's got a complete set."

"I'm going to ask you a favor. Would you mind taking a sampling of the silver and porcelain back to Charleston with you? I told Belle you knew dealers on

King Street and would get it appraised. She wants to sell the furniture, too. I thought if you could take some photographs and show them to the appraiser, he could let her know if it's worth her lugging it to the city."

"Of course I'll do it. It'll be fun. But I can tell you right now that the furniture is worth taking to a dealer. And the silver? Absolutely. The china is gorgeous but it's one of those quirky items that's either going to be worth nothing or go through the roof."

"That's what we hope the appraiser will tell us." Mia smiled. "And I'm hoping for *through the roof*."

"Belle wants to sell it all? Even though it belonged to her family?"

"Especially because it belonged to her family."

Maddie opened her mouth to say something, then changed her mind. "That's another topic for another time." She grabbed hold of her suitcase. "So, where do I sleep?"

"Upstairs. Follow me." Mia grabbed her purchases and the vase of flowers and led her sister up the narrow stairs to the garret. Her heart was beating with excitement, hoping her sister would like the room she'd prepared for her with care and attention.

She stepped into the long room with the steep, angled ceiling and long row of windows and smiled with pleasure. She'd transformed the once dark and dank space to a cozy guest room. Asheville was a haven of craftsmen, and she'd found a beautiful bed made of polished logs on sale that she knew would be perfect for the room. Walking across the floor, she set the flowers on top of the small, hand-painted pine dresser she'd found in an antique store. It was a bargain she couldn't resist. She pulled the quilt out of the bag and spread it over the mattress. The bright, rosy colors of the crazy-quilt pattern seemed to dance in the sunlight.

"There," she said, looking over at her sister. "It's all ready for you."

"I'm never going to want to leave, either," Maddie said softly, and sat on the bed. Her hand stretched out to smooth the quilt in a wistful movement.

"Oh, yes you will," Mia replied. "You have to walk down the stairs every time you need to pee. There's only the one bathroom. But don't let me hear you complain. At least there's hot water now."

They showered after their day in town, then cooked a meal together like they used to when they were younger and lived under the same roof. They uncorked one of the bottles of North Carolina wine, then the other, with the promise to buy more for Maddie's husband. After dinner Mia lit a fire and they curled up on the blue velvet sofa, and their talk turned, as they knew it would eventually, to more personal matters.

"So," Maddie began, getting right to the point. "How is the divorce coming along?"

Mia brought her glass to her lips and took a long sip. "Well," she began cautiously, her feelings twirling like the wine in her glass. "A few weeks ago he sent me a packet of papers to sign so he could file."

"What kind of papers?" Maddie asked. Mia was quick to recognize the timbre of worry.

"Charles filed the petition for divorce. That's the first pleading filed in a divorce action. Since we don't have children there isn't any custody battle, and as long as we agree on the division of property and the terms of the divorce, we want to get through this with the least amount of damage. All I had to do was sign."

"So, how did he divide the property?" Maddie asked with a frown. "He's living in the condo, after all. Rent free. Does he expect you to just hand it over?"

"He offered to buy it from me. And I sold it."

"You did? For what price? If he lowballed you—"

"No, he didn't. He sent the comps and offered me top price plus the cost of the furniture. I called Charlie Aikman, a friend of mine in real estate in Charleston, and he checked it out for me. I trust Charlie and he said the offer was more than fair, even generous."

"Guilt is a powerful motivator."

"He also divided up the stocks and bonds. Not that we're all that heavily invested, but we've made some gains." She shrugged. "That and our cars were our only real assets. Granted, he's driving a luxury car and I'm driving a cheap sedan, but we bought those before we were married. The terms were fair and I signed my approval. *That*," she said with emphasis, "was quite a moment. But surprisingly . . . I felt much better about the whole thing the next morning. Freer, you know? He's already sent me a down payment on the condo.

Just in time, too. I was down to my last one hundred dollars. Now I'm flush! I've been having a great time. I put in the gravel driveway, bought the bedroom furniture and a few other things I had my eye on. It's been nice to have a few dollars to spend after pinching pennies so long."

"Whoa, slow down, sister mine. Don't go on a spending spree. That's your nest egg. You'll need it for a down payment on your next place."

"Oh, I know, I know," she replied with a weary pat on her sister's hand. "But I'm tired of always being responsible. Let me have a little fun, Maddie. I deserve it."

Maddie's frown of worry shifted to a wobbly smile of understanding. "You're right. You do deserve it. I'm just a worrywart."

"And I love you for it."

"So," Maddie said with an upbeat tone. "When will you be a free woman?"

"The divorce can be finalized as soon as the sixty-day waiting period expires."

"You mean by fall?"

"If all goes well."

Maddie raised her glass with a whoop. "Here's to a fresh start!"

They clinked glasses, laughing.

Mia's thoughts drifted to Stuart.

Maddie uncrossed her legs and clumsily rose from the sofa. "Stay put. I'll be right back. I've been dying to do something."

Mia sipped her wine and stared at the fire while

Maddie hurried upstairs. A few minutes later she heard thumping down the stairs, and Maddie came back into the room carrying her hairbrush and some clips.

"What's that for?"

"I've been staring at your hair all day. Honey, can I brush it? Like I used to when you were little? It was so hard for me to see your hair fall out and here you have these curls and oh, I do love the color. It looks like copper, and you know how I love my copper pots."

Mia backed into the sofa. "I don't know . . ."

"You're afraid it's going to fall out again, aren't you?"

Mia nodded.

"Well don't be. This is your hair and it's healthy and glossy. Let's have some fun with it. I brought some pretty barrettes to play with."

Mia took a leap of faith. "OK."

"Now just relax. You'd think I was going to pierce your ears. I'll be gentle. I've done this before, remember?"

"I remember you used to pull my hair so tight for braids I thought you were pulling it out."

"Those were French braids, thank you very much, and I had to pull it tight. Your hair's not long enough for them, so relax." Slowly, with exceeding gentleness, Maddie began brushing her sister's hair. It was fine but thick and fell in odd layers over her head because Mia hadn't been able to bring herself to cut it. Mia felt the sensation of soft bristles on her scalp. She closed her eyes and let her shoulders droop.

"I guess you'll be coming back home soon?" Maddie asked, brushing.

"Hmmm?"

"Stop daydreaming, we have serious things to discuss. Like when you're coming home."

"I still have to finish my investigation on Kate Watkins."

Maddie stilled her brush. "Mia, you're obsessed! Why are you so into this woman? It's just some local ghost story. Let it go."

"I can't. Not yet."

"This is nuts. I'm getting worried about you."

"Why? I want to finish this. I'm so close to a breakthrough."

"About what? This murder thing? Isn't this going too far for some vacation curiosity? Besides, how do you know Kate didn't kill that DeLancey guy? Did you stop to think that maybe you really were just stirring up the mud?"

Mia grew obstinate, tired of always having to defend this project. "I just do."

"Just so you realize, no matter what you find out, Belle's going to be furious."

"I'm damned if I do and damned if I don't." She hesitated. "Do you think I'm doing something terribly wicked?"

"No, honey, your heart's in the right place."

"Maddie, just look around you," she implored. "We're surrounded by *her* things, evidence of a life lived. Wait till you read her diary—I want you to. You'll understand why I feel so compelled. Kate Watkins was so gutsy, and yet so very human. She deserves to be understood."

"But Mia, you can't put your life on hold until you unravel some mystery that has nothing to do with you. You have some serious decisions to make back home. You need a job, a place to live . . ."

"I know and I will. They'll all be there waiting for me when I get back to Charleston." Mia felt a soft breeze across her shoulders. She shivered and looked around the room with a strange gleam in her eyes. "I don't mean to scare you, but I sense her presence. Do you feel it?"

Maddie drew herself in and looked around the room with a haunted expression. "No. Why? Is she here? A ghost?"

"I don't know if I can call it a ghost. It's more a feeling."

"Oh, God, I'm sleeping with you tonight."

"Don't be afraid. I've never seen her and nothing moves or goes bump in the night. Nothing like that, I promise. Maddie, she's like my friend. Or more, my mentor."

Maddie set her brush down and pulled locks from Mia's head back in a barrette. "Mia, when you were a little girl, do you remember you had an imaginary friend? You used to talk to her all the time."

Mia chuckled, remembering. "Her name was Cha Cha. I know where you're going with this. Whether Kate's presence is real or just a figment of my imagination, it doesn't matter. Kate Watkins has been here for me through some of my toughest moments. She's inspired me to get out of myself and outdoors."

Maddie set the brush down and came around the sofa to sit. "When I signed you up for Casting for Recovery, I thought it would be good for you to be with women who were going through the same experiences you were. I didn't think you'd stay up in the mountains, or become such an avid fisherman. Or woman . . ."

"I didn't either. Maddie, fly-fishing isn't just about catching fish. It's about making a connection. When I'm fly-fishing I can't think about cancer, or the divorce, or needing a job, or all those other things that my mind usually goes over in the middle of the night. You see," she said, looking into Maddie's eyes, "once you're diagnosed with cancer, it's always lurking somewhere in the back of your mind, like the monster under your bed when you were little. You know it's not really there . . . but you're not sure."

She smiled when Maddie laughed. "When I'm fly-fishing I'm only aware of my surroundings and the fish. I'm in alignment with the universe."

"It sounds very Zen," Maddie said, half teasing.

"Yeah," Mia replied with a self-deprecating laugh. Then she added sincerely, "Nowhere else do I experience that peace. And I have you to thank for sending me to the retreat and getting hooked on fishing in the first place. And Kate to thank for teaching me not to be afraid of the dark."

"And how did she do that? Does she talk to you from the other side?"

Mia refused to make light of this. It was too important to her. "Through her diaries, through the articles she's written, the letters, the stories people have told about her. Those are some of her sayings on the wall." Mia rose from the sofa and went to the bookcase to take out Kate's diary and fishing diary. She handed these to her sister.

"Don't take my word for it. Take these upstairs for your nighttime reading. See for yourself."

"She won't come up and haunt me while I'm up there, will she?" Maddie asked. She was only half kidding.

"You should be so lucky."

Early the following morning Mia was pouring two mugs of coffee when Maddie came down the stairs yawning and rubbing her eyes.

"Good morning, sleepyhead," Mia called out.

"Do you always get up so early?"

"I heard you stomping around up there." She handed Maddie the mug of steaming coffee.

"Mmm . . . thanks." She took a sip, then sighed lustily. "That's better. Nectar of the gods. I need it this morning. I was up half the night reading the diaries."

"And?"

"You're right," she said begrudgingly. "She even makes me want to go out and walk in the woods."

Maddie made no secret of her loathing of anything involving the outdoors—hiking, surfing, kayaking. She preferred going to exercise class and treadmills.

"I knew it."

"She certainly was all about fly-fishing, wasn't she?"

"Yes. And soon you will be, too. I've got a little surprise for you. Hurry and drink your coffee. We're going fishing."

Maddie groaned. "I had a bet with Don that you'd get me in the river this weekend. Why the hurry?"

"Stuart is coming to teach you."

Maddie's mug stilled midair and Mia saw her blue eyes narrow over the rim. "Who is Stuart?"

⁂

A half hour later Mia heard the whine of an engine coming up the road. She peeked out the window to see the Jeep's tires spitting the new gravel as it came to a stop. Her heart leaped at seeing Stuart's long legs stretch out from the Jeep and his face emerge, a faint stubble along his jaw. Today was his day off, and he had come to teach Maddie how to handle a fly rod and cast.

Maddie's brows rose slightly when six-foot Stuart walked into the cabin in his tan shorts and fishing shirt, then rose higher when he casually bent to peck Mia's cheek with a kiss hello. Mia knew the mother hen was hovering.

Stuart, in contrast, was relaxed and stuck out his hand when Mia made the introductions.

"I'm glad to at last meet the sister I've heard so much about."

"Oh, God, I can only imagine what you've heard."

"All good," he said with a reassuring smile.

They drank coffee and ate Becky's pastries while standing on the porch, eager to get going. Mia enjoyed watching Maddie struggle to put on the paraphernalia associated with fly-fishing: waders, neoprene socks, felt-lined boots, fishing vest, polarized sunglasses, and hat. She watched her fumble with the gadgets and remembered how she'd felt exactly the same confusion . . . was it only two months ago? It seemed a lifetime had passed since that morning in June.

"Look at me, I'm the Michelin Man," Maddie joked, sticking her arms out and turning around in a circle.

Mia knew her sister didn't need most of that gear on this midsummer day. She'd be in shallow water and Stuart would be knotting all the flies. But Stuart wanted her to have the whole experience. When Maddie picked a rod she liked, he led her to the open area and began with the basics of stance, grip, and casts. He was very patient. Maddie was very nervous. Mia recalled how clumsy and inept a beginner could feel the first time she handled a fly rod. With a quick excuse she left them to sit on the white rocks by the pool.

She dangled her legs, enjoying watching Maddie's first attempts at casting. She couldn't see Stuart's face as his back was to her. She watched as he spoke to Maddie, using his hands to imitate the cast. She could almost make out the words he was saying. Maddie appeared very serious. She had a nice cast and caught on quickly.

After half an hour, the sky began to rumble. Mia looked up and saw angry, dark clouds moving in over patches of blue. Across in the grassy area she saw Stuart looking up at the sky as well. They both knew how fast a storm could roll in across the mountains. He and Maddie began walking toward the shallow section of the river. No doubt he wanted her to try some real casting before the rain.

Mia looked down at the river below her feet, searching the green pool as always for Mr. Big. She peered into the still water for a long while before she saw a dark shadow move behind a large rock. She smiled and her fingers itched for a rod. Quickly she went to fetch her fly rod, then walked down river to where Stuart stood bent at the waist with one arm on Maddie's shoulder and the other pointing to the shadowed pocket across the stream.

"Sorry to bother you, but . . ."

He turned his head. She couldn't see his eyes through the sunglasses but she heard the humor in his voice. "You're after Mr. Big again, are you?"

"Don't look at me like that. You wait. I'll catch him one of these days."

He straightened and said, "That's one wily trout." He studied the river; then he pulled his pack of dry flies out from a vest pocket and opened it, revealing dozens of fuzzy flies of all sizes. Maddie came closer to watch as he poked around the small compartments with his index finger, deliberating.

"Look at all those. How do you know which one to choose?" Maddie asked.

"Well, you—" he began.

Mia interrupted him. "You look at the river then you look at your flies then you poke around with your finger at the mess of flies in your pack, and then you just pick something small, brown, and fuzzy, give it a funny name like Mr. Big's Breakfast, and go for it."

Maddie burst out laughing.

Stuart lifted his sunglasses and met Mia's gaze. They shared a silent, commiserating laugh. He handed her a brown fuzzy fly.

"Here you go. Mr. Big's Breakfast."

"Thank you." She took the dry fly, then, on impulse, stretched up on tiptoe and delivered a quick but proprietary kiss on his lips. Stuart was surprised by her spontaneity. Maddie was floored. She narrowed her eyes with a look of *what's going on?*

"We're going downstream," Stuart told her, his eyes still smiling. "Good luck."

Less than an hour later the sky darkened and thunder rolled closer. At the first flash of lightning, the fly fishers came off the water.

"How'd you do?" Stuart asked as they were taking off their gear on the porch. The first fat drops of rain started falling, landing with splats on the dry dirt and loud taps on the roof.

"You know how I did," she replied.

He only chuckled. "Yep, that's one wily old trout."

"Well, I caught a fish!" Maddie exclaimed. She looked to Stuart for confirmation. "A brown trout, right?"

"Yes, ma'am, all fourteen inches of him."

Mia saw her sister's proud smile and knew that more than a trout got hooked that morning.

The rain came down in earnest with no sign of letting up. Stuart ducked out to give the sisters time alone before Maddie had to head back to Charleston.

"It looks like that storm cloud is just going to sit right on top of this mountain. We're socked in with fog. You'll have to stay another night," Mia told her as she put on a fresh pot of coffee.

"No, it's early yet and that storm is moving fast, heading out to sea. It'll likely keep me company for the whole damn drive home to Charleston."

"Then stay."

"Oh, honey, I wish I could. But I have two kids starting school next week and a husband who doesn't know his way around a shopping list. My kids will go wild with him at Towne Center, buying everything but what they need for school." She lifted her shoulders as though to say *what more can I say?* Maddie took her mug and sat on the velvet sofa. "Besides, you don't need me up here. That's pretty easy to see."

Maddie leaned back against the sofa and stretched out her legs. When comfortable, she patted the sofa beside her. "Tell mama all."

Mia added milk to her coffee, took a sip, then came

around to join Maddie. She tucked her legs under her on the soft blue velvet. "First of all, we're just friends."

"Uh-huh. Do you always kiss your friends on the lips?"

A smile twitched. "I didn't say I wanted to stay friends."

"And what's to keep you from moving forward?"

"I am still married."

"Puhleeze . . . You're on the fast track to a divorce and your husband has already played the infidelity card. "

Mia brought her knees closer to her chest and wrapped her arms around them. "I'm scared."

Maddie's face softened with concern. "About what? The cancer?"

Mia shook her head. "No. Well, indirectly." She looked at her feet and said softly, "I'm afraid of intimacy. I'm terrified that he'll be turned off when he sees my body. Charles was. He never touched my breasts again. He could barely bring himself to look at the scar." She looked at the clouds in her coffee. "He told me he wanted to have sex with me but he just couldn't."

"That's when you might've considered couples therapy."

"I know. We should have talked openly about it, gone to therapy, something. But we didn't. I guess I just expected things to get better in time. But he found his own solution."

"The swine."

"I was devastated. Then angry, ashamed, and

felt my body was unattractive to any man. Even to myself."

"And you're afraid Stuart will have the same reaction?" When Mia nodded she asked, "Does he know about the cancer?"

"He knew Casting for Recovery and figured it out. We met on the river, by accident. We became friends. Fishing buddies. We never talked about our personal lives at first. After a few weeks we moved on to talking more to this stage of, well . . ." She searched for a word to describe it. "Teenage bliss. We're kissing and holding hands and talking . . ." She blushed and put her palm to her cheek. "I'm really like a girl again. I think about him all the time. I dream of him. And his kisses, oh God, his kisses. He's world-class."

"All right, already. I get the picture." After a short laugh Maddie said sincerely, "It sounds wonderful. So what's the problem?"

Mia exhaled a long plume of air. "Me. Though he's never said so in so many words, I know he's not rushing me. He knows I'm not ready. He thinks it's because of the divorce. But it's not. Maddie, I may never be ready. I'm making friends with my body. I can look at my scar without cringing. I even pamper it with creams. But I . . . I don't think I could bear it if he was repulsed by it."

Maddie exhaled, then set her mug down on the table. She looked Mia squarely in the eye. "First of all, Stuart is not Charles. I've only known him for one morning and even I can see that. He deserves a chance."

Mia wrapped her arms around herself. "I don't want to risk what I already have with Stuart by wanting more."

"Honey, if it bothers you so much, why don't you have breast reconstruction? There are so many more options today than there were when Mom had her mastectomy."

"Maybe I should've done something right away. I think it was because Mom died so soon after her diagnosis that when I found out I had breast cancer it felt like a death sentence."

"I know. I was never so terrified in my life."

"I was a mess and Charles wasn't much help. He kept breaking down into tears. The last thing I wanted to think about was another surgery for reconstruction. When Dr. Fiske recommended I wait until I was ready to make a decision I went along. Plus, my insurance company wouldn't pay for it. At least now I have the money to do the surgery if I want to. I just don't know if I can face surgery and pain again."

"Sooner or later, you'll have to either accept your body the way it is or have reconstruction surgery."

Mia raked her hair with her fingers and groaned. "I still can't make up my mind."

"Do you know what confuses me about all this? You've just told me how great this new relationship with Stuart is, how you're going slow, getting to know each other. You positively glow when you talk about him. But what are you afraid of? You're afraid of how your breasts will look. Once again, you're valuing only your body."

Mia blinked slowly, listening but not comprehending.

"Do you remember a while back you told me that the old Mia was gone? That shook me up, I have to admit. Then I got to thinking about the old Mia. Honey, you were always such a perfectionist about your body. And your clothes and your hair. I used to be kind of jealous by how together you seemed. But it was a little off-putting, too. You saw yourself in The Gaze you got from men. If you gained a few pounds you'd exercise and diet until you whipped your body back into shape. That's how you valued yourself, Mia. By how you looked. It could make you brittle at times. I used to think you were just hungry." She smirked.

"Then you got sick and went into some place I couldn't follow and I worried whether I'd ever see the old Mia again. But now I'm sitting here with the new Mia. If fly-fishing did anything for you it brought you out of yourself. You're focused on improving your skill, your art, and learning the names of plants and birds. You're even focused on the story of Kate Watkins. Mia, you're not looking at yourself in the mirror for your reflection. You're looking inward now for authentic signals of who you are. I look at you and see a beautiful, strong, interesting, and creative woman. And hell, you're too young to skip sex for the rest of your life!"

"Oh, Maddie," Mia exclaimed, putting her hands to her face. "What am I going to do?"

Her older sister put her arms around her and held her tight, the way she used to do when Mia was hurt as a young girl.

"You're already doing the work. Keep going. Your instincts were right. Stay here till you find your answers. Sometimes you can overthink these things. Don't listen to what I have to say. Or even what Kate has to say. Listen to yourself, Mia. Trust that you'll know what to do when the time comes."

Chapter Seventeen

You read the water. You study the insects.
You ponder different flies. You do all this—
and sometimes you find you just have to
trust your intuition.

—KATE WATKINS'S FISHING DIARY

The rain persisted through the afternoon and into the evening. Mia prowled the cabin, restless after her visit with Maddie. She missed her already and kept checking her watch, wondering if Maddie had made it home all right in the rain. Her cell phone was useless in the cabin and she couldn't climb the white rocks in the rain. After a light dinner of leftovers she went upstairs to the garret and found some comfort lying on the new bed she'd bought for her sister and read Kate's diary for the hundredth time. But she couldn't concentrate on the words. Her mind kept drifting back to her conversation with Maddie.

Mia was disturbed by her sister's honest portrayal of the pre-cancer Mia. Her sister had been nearer to the truth than she cared to admit. But Maddie had no idea what a roller coaster her body and emotions had been on. Her sister was forty-two and hadn't gone through menopause yet. Even though Mia was only thirty-eight, the chemo treatments had brought on its symptoms. She no longer felt as young and attractive as she did before the cancer. On the other hand, Maddie was right that she was too young to write off any intimacy. For a long while she'd had no interest. Now she had hope, especially lately, that her body was reawakening. When she was with Stuart her senses were heightened and her sexual desire went to hyperdrive.

That night she fell asleep upstairs, wrapped in the new crazy quilt. But her dreams were old ones, filled with searching and longing, and they had her tangled up in her sheets. Sometime before dawn she woke, groggy and thirsty. She lifted herself on her elbows and tried to sew together the elusive pieces of her dreams. Stuart was there, and Charles. She was fighting her way through thick fog, both chasing someone and being chased. She rubbed her eyes, feeling the sense of it already slipping away. The pale light of approaching dawn poured through the row of windows, coloring the wood floors pewter gray. Mia rose and made her way down the narrow stairs to the bathroom, then to her own bed.

When Mia woke later, the light at her windows was bright and she heard the chattering of birds in the trees. Yawning, she stretched, knowing without looking at a clock that it was late. She smiled as she kicked off her sheets, then lay flat on her mattress, her legs and arms spread wide while the soft morning breeze slid like water over her skin. For months after her surgery she'd felt perpetually tired. Even though she slept a lot, she never felt rested. How delicious it was to lie here feeling thoroughly refreshed, she thought. She reached up to run her hands through her hair, then let her finger slide down her neck and down her chest.

Maddie had called her beautiful, she recalled with wonder. In the light of morning, Mia believed her.

She rose, bathed, and dressed in her usual khaki shorts and cotton shirt. Then, grabbing her purse, she drove directly to Watkins Mill. She parked in front of Shaffer's and followed the scent of coffee and hot bread and chocolate into the bakery. The bell chimed but she didn't hear Becky's cheery greeting. Glancing to the back, she saw that Becky wasn't sitting in her usual spot at the post office counter.

"Hey, Katherine," she said as she came to the glass counter.

Katherine spun around from the coffee machine. "Morning, Mia," she called back with her mother's smile. "Sorry, I was fighting this damn machine."

"Where's your mom this morning?"

"She has a doctor's appointment today." Mia's face must have shown her worry because Katherine followed up with, "No need to worry. It's just the usual. But the doctor wants her to take it easier. Not push herself so hard."

"This is the first time I've walked in here and didn't hear her call out my name. Does she want visitors?"

"Maybe not today. Those appointments wear her out." Katherine's bright smile wobbled, but she rallied. "Want your usual coffee?"

"Thanks," Mia replied. She would respect Katherine's request but follow up tomorrow. She looked down through the glass at the pastries. The selection had dwindled this late in the morning but there were a few of the day's special bismarck left.

She carried her pastry and coffee to a table for her late breakfast and phone calls. She took a bite of the bismarck, licked the chocolate icing from her fingers, then checked her cell phone. Multiple voice mails awaited her.

Beep.

Hi, baby sis. Well, I'm home. I was lucky and only caught up with the storm when I hit Summerville. I had such a great time this weekend. We'll have to make a trip to the mountains a yearly event for sisterly bonding. Call me.

Beep.

Mia, this is Charles. Just checking to make sure the money transfer went through all right. Listen, we'd really like to hang on to the Pratt-Thomas marsh painting. I think it's only fair that I keep one and since we bought that one together and well, it looks so great where it is, I'd really like to have it. Let's talk.

Mia cursed under her breath. Of all the contents in the condo, including the china, crystal, and heirloom silver, she'd wanted only the paintings. She didn't think that was asking much. Art was her passion and Charles didn't know a thing about art. It wasn't like they were museum-quality paintings that were worth a fortune. Most of the paintings were done by local artists she knew and admired, so each addition to her collection was personal. That particular marsh painting depicted a moody view of the marsh at sunset and was her favorite. It was also the largest. It hung over their fireplace mantel in the living room. And he'd said "*We'd* like to hang on to it." Mia snorted. If Charles was going to start backpedaling on the agreed-upon divorce settlement, she'd have to get a lawyer, she thought with resignation.

Beep.

Hello, Mrs. Landan? This is Lucy Roosevelt, Mrs. Minor's granddaughter. She's feeling poorly. I don't reckon you should come by today. Is tomorrow OK?

Beep.

Morning, Mia. It's Flossie. Sorry I didn't get back to you sooner about that dinner. Why don't you come by Thursday night? About seven? I haven't forgotten about that pie, neither.

Beep.

Hi, Mia. Stuart here. I followed up with the front desk at the Manor House about seeing the murals. The couple in the room is checking out today. So if you're free sometime after three o'clock, I can bring you up for a look-see. Call me when you think you can come. Oh, and put on a pretty dress. I'd like to take you out to dinner. We have a four-star restaurant here.

She pushed save with a smile. That message brought the sun back into her day after Charles's dark cloud. Then she realized she didn't have a pretty dress up here. Glancing at her watch, she figured she'd have just enough time to buy a dress, do her errands, catch up with Nada at the *Gazette*, and make it to Watkins Lodge before five.

It was nearly five o'clock when Mia passed through a security gate onto the grounds of Watkins Lodge. It was an impressive country estate with a rolling green lawn, meticulously maintained with large beds of flowers. The humidity had subsided so she rolled down her windows to the sweet-scented air. She breathed deep as she drove the narrow, paved road past a medley of historic trees. At the beginning of summer she couldn't have named one. Now she identified each one she passed: beech, sugar maple, tulip poplar, hemlock, Fraser fir. She made a wide curve around a hillside, catching a glimpse of water. Then suddenly before her, rising above a still, blue lake, loomed the steeply pitched, gabled roofline of the Manor House.

The Queen Anne estate sat on top of the hillside like the grande dame of Watkins Mill that she was. The mansion was romantic in design but not fanciful, elegant but not pretentious, regal yet harmonious with her natural surroundings. Ancient magnolias were her ladies-in-waiting, tall, proud, and glossy with creamy white blossoms to adorn the front entrance. An imposing porte cochere that once upon a time gave shelter to carriages that delivered guests to the Watkinses' events now served as the lobby entrance for the Manor House. Behind the house on another hillside she saw a much larger, newer wood-and-stone building. This was Watkins Lodge. To the left of the house was a stone carriage house that was under reconstruction. She supposed that was where Stuart's Orvis shop would be located.

She pulled up under the portico and had no sooner turned off the engine when a uniformed attendant trotted to her door. It had been a very long time since she'd lived in the world of doormen, attendants, maids, and maître d's, and she cursed herself for not washing her mud-streaked Jetta. Slightly embarrassed, she handed over the keys, then took a deep breath and climbed the stone steps to the front porch.

She stepped inside and instantly felt transported back into the previous century. Straight ahead a very wide, bold staircase of dark wood rose to a half landing under a skylight. Rich tapestries, carpets, and upholstery fabrics in gold and neutral tones appeared burnished against the highly polished floors. She could smell the lemon soap and the pungent, clean scent of eucalyptus from the glorious spray floral arrangement at the front desk.

"May I help you?" an attractive young woman at the desk asked.

She opened her mouth to speak when she heard Stuart's voice behind her.

"That's all right, Victoria. She's with me."

Mia turned to see Stuart, and yet it wasn't. She had

to do a double take at seeing him in his dress trousers, an ironed tartan plaid shirt, and a green tie. He smiled and as always her gaze was directed to his eyes. They shone with appraisal.

"You look beautiful," he said.

Mia basked in the compliment. Earlier that day she'd shopped at the only women's clothing store in Watkins Mill. The salesclerk was a young woman about Mia's age, and when Mia told her she needed a dress for dinner, something classic and not showy, the salesclerk brightened. She hurried to the rear of the store, where long dresses with sequins and satin bows hung. Mia's heart sank, expecting to see something fit for a mother of the bride or a prom.

"I thought of this dress the moment I saw you. It's very Audrey Hepburn," the clerk exclaimed as she carried out a slim-cut, black, sleeveless, silk sheath dress. Mia tried it on and felt as chic as Audrey wearing it. She bought the dress and black strappy heels, and, at the clerk's insistence, a strand of faux pearls. Before ringing up the sale, the clever clerk showed her a rose-colored pashmina shawl. "The nights get cool in the mountains," she warned. Mia bought that, too.

She fingered the pearls and looked around the entrance. "It's a magnificent house," she said. "Much more grand than I'd expected. I can't help but imagine how Kate and Walter must have felt living here."

"Did you catch the view they had?"

"The lake? I did, it's lovely. Is it stocked?"

"What do you think?" He took her elbow. "Let me show you around."

He escorted her through the rooms of the main floor.

"I talked to the manager to get a little history. They gave me this," he said, handing her a four-color brochure depicting the history of the property. "In a nutshell, this house has eight bedrooms. The lodge has another fifty and there are condominiums on the other side of the lake."

"I had no idea it was so big."

"They've been mindful of keeping the essence of the estate as true to the original as possible. A lot of the land was put into conservation. That was a condition of the sale, I believe. This is the library," he said, guiding her to a wood-paneled room with arched, paned windows that overlooked the grounds.

Mia imagined she was Kate, born at the turn of the century and living here as mistress of the house at the height of the town's wealth and social life. She would have walked into this room to speak with her father in his paneled library. She'd have read Mr. Nelson's letter of introduction for DeLancey in the living room, perhaps sitting on the blue velvet sofa. The Queen Anne house was asymmetrical. She enjoyed the surprise patios, balconies, and window seats.

Stuart took her for a walk through the house gardens and across the small footbridge that led to the lake. A pair of white swans glided across the serene

water against the bluish-black mountains, like a painting come to life. Even knowing that the estate and
grounds had been greatly improved by the resort compared to when Kate had lived here, Mia was in awe of
the privilege it must have been to be local aristocracy
and to live in this idyllic spot.

After the tour Stuart took her back to the house
to see the paintings on the bedroom wall. "There are
eight bedrooms and each of the rooms is named after
a Watkins family member," he explained as he led her
down the hall of the second floor to the corner room.
Over the door it read *Katherine Watkins.*

"Well, this has to be it," Mia said.

Stuart had the key and opened the door. He
stepped back to allow Mia to walk through. The room
was bright and cheery with lots of windows that
afforded a spectacular view of the lake and grounds.
Yet she couldn't help but be disappointed. It was
not the young girl's room she'd imagined. This was
a typical upscale hotel room. The furniture, though
nice, was reproduction. Still, looking at the queen
bed positioned under the steeply angled roof, Mia
couldn't help but think young Kate's bed would have
been placed in the same spot.

"Over here," Stuart called from across the room.

Mia hurried over and with a gasp of delight zeroed
in on three murals of wildflowers on the wall. They
were done by a young girl, anyone could tell. Yet Mia's
trained eye saw the talent in its execution that Walter
Watkins had seen. The rest of the walls had been painted

a soft yellow color, but the owners had been careful to preserve these murals and had protected them with Plexiglas. Beside the mural was a small framed card identifying them as being painted by Kate Watkins. Mia reached out to place her hand on the Plexiglas over Kate's favorite—the Turk's cap lily—then traced the outline of the six petals. Her mind was filled with the voice of young Kate in the diary, so indignant at having been punished.

"Why are you smiling?" Stuart asked.

"Oh, I was thinking . . . If Mrs. Hodges had known how many people would be charmed by these paintings, she might not have put young Kate to bed without supper."

"Speaking of supper," he said, looking at his watch. "If you're done here, we should go. We have reservations."

She cast a final lingering glance at the murals, then followed Stuart downstairs. Before entering the formal dining room she caught the tempting aromas of garlic, spices, and hot rolls emanating from the kitchen. The dining room was now the Manor House restaurant. Instead of one long dining table there were several small tables, each draped with heavy white linen and covered with white folded napkins, ruby-trimmed china, sparkling crystal, and fresh flowers. The room was empty and Stuart selected a table at the window.

Mia enjoyed the luxury of being taken to a fine restaurant again. She couldn't remember the last time she'd dressed up to go out. She unfolded the napkin, fingering the fine damask linen, remembering a time when such opulence was taken for granted. Her gaze drifted around the room, taking in the heavy brocade wallpaper; the velvet, tasseled curtains; the fireplace with the dentil molding. Over it was a magnificent portrait of a dark-haired gentleman in nineteenth-century clothing. So, she thought, this was Robert Watkins. Despite surviving the agony of the Civil War and the trials of the Reconstruction era, he assumed the typical aloof expression of gentry for his portrait. Suddenly, her eyes widened.

"Stuart, look! In the painting, behind the man. It's the armoire!"

He grinned. "I thought you'd recognize it. After I saw it at the cabin I knew I'd seen it somewhere but couldn't place it. Then weeks later I was having a business meeting here and I glanced up and there it was. I almost choked on my lunch."

"So she *did* bring the furniture from the house. Of course she would. The dining table would have been in here, with all the leaves, of course."

"And the mahogany sofa . . ."

"In the living room by the fireplace."

He was amused. "Is the house as you imagined it?"

"In some ways, yes. I didn't expect to covet living here so much. The house makes me wish I lived in the twenties."

"People always assume if they lived in an earlier era that they'd live in a house like this one. More than likely, most of us would have been in a cramped house without electricity or running water, or the downstairs staff of a house like this one. I'd have been the gillie taking the gentry out fishing."

Mia laughed lightly, thinking of how she imagined she was the mistress of the house. Every girl has dreams of Pemberley, she thought.

"I wonder if Belle has ever seen this house. If the family hadn't lost their fortune, she would have been born here. Maybe even grown up here. Imagine that."

"More than Belle, I wonder if her mother ever saw it."

"Theodora? She must have. At least the outside. Oh, Stuart, imagine how hard that was for her, living out in the cabin and to come here and realize all this could have been hers."

"She'd be bitter."

"I wonder if that's part of the reason why she was so angry at her mother. Even though Kate or her father wasn't to blame. Many families lost their fortunes in the crash of twenty-nine."

"We can see that now, in retrospect. But Theodora was what? Seventeen? That's reason enough."

The waitress came and delivered their drinks. Stuart had Scotch and Mia selected a chardonnay. They took a few minutes to study the menu. Mia ordered the trout but Stuart selected the filet, explaining that, given how he made his living, he had lost his taste for trout. He was committed to catch and release.

Mia sighed and changed her order to the chicken.

"What did you think of Kate's murals?" he asked.

"They're just as I imagined them. The vitality I found in her words was right there in her colors, too. But . . ." She looked around the room, at so much luxury compared to the ruggedness of the cabin. "I don't sense Kate in this house. Not even in her bedroom. Not like I do in the cabin."

"She loved the cabin."

"But she loved this house, too."

"I'd imagine if she's lingering anywhere, she'd be where she had her love affair with DeLancey. She wouldn't have brought him here, not with Dad in the library." He chuckled. "And Mrs. Hodges."

"But there was sadness at the cabin, too."

"Well, we don't really know that, do we?"

She shook her head. There were still so many things she didn't know.

He brought the conversation around to fly-fishing. As always they never were bored with each other's company. The summer sun shone bright through most of their dinner, too bright for the seductive glimmer of candles. It began its slow descent only by the time they were drinking their coffee. Several more diners had joined them in the room, and two more couples were waiting to be seated.

"Thank you," Mia said after Stuart paid the bill. "I haven't had such a wonderful time in I don't know how long. I'd forgotten how much I enjoyed dining at a fine restaurant."

"It's only eight o'clock. If you've got time, I'd like to show you some paintings I've found stored in the carriage house. The old chauffeur's apartment has been a storage facility for the house for years. There's this group of paintings up there that caught my eye. They're all of trout. I liked them and saved them for the shop, but when I saw Kate's fishing diary I was struck by the strong similarity in style between the trout in the diary and the trout in the paintings."

"You think they were done by Kate?"

"They're not signed, but it's a possibility."

"I'd love to see them," she said with barely restrained enthusiasm.

"Good," he said. "Let's go."

The sky had turned crimson over the mountains when they left the Manor House. The lake shimmered with a pearly reflection, its stillness broken here and there with the concentric circles of trout sipping.

The carriage house was an ivy-covered building built for four vehicles. The base was built of stone and the roofline was steeply sloped in the style of the Manor House. Stuart guided her through a heavy wood door. Inside she saw lots of new framing and piles of sawdust, buckets, tools, and other signs of active construction. The floor was made of beautiful stone and she was glad to hear they were keeping it. Stuart described with grand gestures where the clothing section would be, where rods and reels would be sold, and where he would have an entire section dedicated to flies and fly-tying classes. He talked excitedly about the circular wood counter in the middle of the store that he'd designed for customer service and checkout. She saw boyish enthusiasm in his eyes, and as he described the scope of the project she realized that he would be single-handedly responsible for its success. It dawned on her how high up in the management he had to be to take on this operation and it tilted her perception of him.

"Will you stay here once the shop opens?" she asked. "Or will you go back to Orvis headquarters?"

"I don't know yet where I'll end up. This is the third shop I've established and the company is looking at a few more locations. They might want to move me, but I'm tired of traveling around and corporate politics. I put in to manage this one. It's close to home. I'll have to wait and see. The storage is through here. Take my hand. It's dark up these back stairs."

He opened a door and, taking her hand, led her up the dark, dusty, narrow staircase to the second floor. As she followed him, her mind wrestled with the possibility that Stuart could leave the area. To where? she wondered. Orvis was located throughout the country. In her mind he was fixed here, like the other town residents. Even though he'd told her he was a wanderer, she'd just assumed he would always be here.

He opened a narrow door at the top of the stairs. The rooms were dark and she felt a blast of heat from the closed space. "Wait here while I find the light switch," he told her. A moment later light filled the room.

She entered a rabbit warren of small rooms that had once been the chauffeur's quarters and now was filled with clutter like an old attic. Cobwebs hung from the rafters, the small windows were caked with dust, and old furniture and boxes crammed the small space. It was as hot as an oven and she felt her silk dress cling to her skin. Stuart went to open a few windows and let the cooler night air in.

"There's dust and dirt everywhere. I'd hate for you to get your dress dirty."

"No matter," she said, admiring the wood bed frame with beautiful acanthus leaves climbing up the four posts. "I'll bet this beauty is original to the house. It's a shame to see it wallowing in here. Or this bureau."

"Not mine to deal with. I went through the art looking for something I might want for the shop. The paintings are over here."

Her gaze lingered on a standing mirror, a rocking chair, and a wrought-iron garden table as she followed him. I would love to spend a few hours going through those boxes, she thought. Who knew what treasures were there? She joined him in a corner where several framed paintings were stacked against the wall. He grabbed hold and hoisted three frames up and brought them to the wrought-iron table.

"Here they are."

Mia came closer to look. They were oil paintings on paper framed in simple, chipped, black wood frames and glass. She looked around for a cloth of some kind and, finding none, took the end of her shawl and wiped a layer of dust from the glass. The painting was of a glorious rainbow trout leaping with exuberance from the dark water, droplets spraying from its whipping tail. Its rosy band shone across the fish's gray dots.

"The detail and color . . . it has to be Kate's." Excited now, she lifted the first painting and handed it to Stuart. The second painting was of a brown trout as it rose toward a brilliant dragonfly hovering at the water's surface. The bright red dots across the body stood out like neon against the yellow-brown. She lifted this one and Stuart took it.

The final painting was of the wild brook trout, the most elusive of all the trout in the area. In the painting the small brookie was caught by an elaborate dry fly, all bright yellow with spiked hackles. The trout's smooth, dark brown coloring and wormlike markings along its back contrasted sharply with its brilliant ruby-colored belly and fins. The fish was rolling to its side, as though relinquishing the long fight. Kate, she knew, had once compared herself in the diary to a brook trout.

"The glass is cracked on this one," she said, concerned about the condition of the painting. Dirt and insect wings were embedded under the glass, staining the paper. "It has to be cleaned and remounted before it's ruined." She pulled her shawl off and bent over the painting. Carefully she removed the pieces of cracked glass, then used her shawl to gently brush off the insects. She clucked her tongue. "There's mold peppering all of them."

She turned the painting over and began to peel away the cheap cardboard backing. "It's so primitively done. She must've framed this herself," she muttered as her fingers dug in at the corner to tug the old cardboard away from the frame. "Damn," she exclaimed as she scraped her skin against a small nail.

"Careful," Stuart said, coming closer.

"I'm OK, it's just a scratch," she said, determined to see the back of the painting. The cardboard sagged. "I've almost got it." With pressure from the front she pushed out the cardboard and peeled it out from the frame. A yellowed sheet of paper fell from the back of the frame. She caught it in her hand, surprised. It was as light as tissue.

"Look," Stuart said, pointing to the back of the painting. "There it is. She signed it."

In a bold red ink Mia saw the initials *KW* on the back. "You were right," she exclaimed. "They *were* hers." She looked up and in his eyes she saw the shared elation of discovery.

Stuart put down the other paintings and drew closer, curious. "What is that paper that fell out?"

"I don't know." Mia lifted the tinder-dry sheet. Three stanzas were handwritten in a tight script. The ink had paled and it was hard to read, so she had to hold it close to make it out.

"It's a poem," Stuart said, standing behind to read over her shoulder.

"Not just any poem. It's from Dante's *Inferno*. It's one of the most famous cantos, where Francesca tells Dante the story of her love for Paolo."

He shook his head, not understanding the reference.

Mia brought to mind this section of Dante's great epic poem, which she'd always found so poignant. "In the *Inferno*, Dante visits different parts of hell and he comes upon Francesca and Paolo, two lovers condemned to hell for adultery. In life they were reading together the story of Lancelot and Guinevere and they were moved by how similar that story was to their own." Her smile was bittersweet, remembering the words. "They kissed and they didn't read any more that day. It's really a story of love versus lust. Their hell was to spend eternity circling near each other but never to be together."

Stuart brought the thin, yellowed paper closer and read aloud. Mia leaned against him, her cheek against his shirt, moist from the intense heat. She closed her eyes and listened to her love read to her a love poem.

> *Full many a time our eyes together drew*
> *That reading, and drove the colour from our faces;*
> *But one point only was it that o'ercame us.*
>
> *When as we read of the much-longed-for smile*
> *Being by such a noble lover kissed,*
> *This one, who ne'er from me shall be divided,*
>
> *Kissed me upon the mouth all palpitating.*
> *Galeotto was the book and he who wrote it.*
> *That day no farther did we read therein.*

Stuart stepped back. She felt the space open between them.

"Do you think there are more letters in the others?" he asked.

The possibility stunned her. "I should remove them from the cardboard anyway."

He carried a second painting, the rainbow trout, to the table. Once again she clawed at the cardboard backing until she got a corner open and pulled the backing away. A photograph fell from the back.

They both reached for it, their hands touching over the photograph. His hand darted back, as though burned. "Sorry."

Mia picked up the photograph and held it so Stuart could see it. It was a black-and-white portrait of a handsome man in a business suit, just the shoulders and head. His hair was sandy colored and combed back from his forehead in the style of the day. He wasn't smiling but she felt the power of his personality in his eyes.

"It has to be DeLancey," she said.

She looked up and saw the thrill of the hunt in Stuart's eyes. They both turned simultaneously to look at the third painting. Stuart lunged for it and this time he tore off the back cardboard. Mia's heart was pounding, wondering—knowing—some treasure had to be there.

His hands tore back the moldy cardboard. This one fell back readily.

She gasped when folded pieces of paper fell from the back. Like the poem, these papers were yellowed and dry.

Stuart picked up the papers and handed them to Mia. She wiped her hands on her shawl, then took the papers and unfolded them. At the top of the stationery a family crest was embossed. It was a dragon with claws out and a star at each corner. The fine script was the same as for the poem. "It's a letter," Mia said breathlessly. "To Kate." The pages were filled with a fine script in ink pen. She flipped to the second page for the signature. "Oh my God, Stuart, it's from DeLancey."

He came close to look over her shoulder. "Read it."

Mia lifted the pages closer. Every nerve ending came alive in the heated room. She could feel Stuart's hand on her shoulder, the heat of his body beside her, and his warm breath against her hair as he bent his head to read along.

My darling Kate,

    I am alone, riding the train north. I hear the hum of the rails beneath me, feel the rocking of the car as it carries me miles away from you. I am desolate. Each time I leave you my course is harder. I close my eyes and see your dark hair spilled against the pillows, your eyes shining with love, your arms stretched out to me in welcome. This vision tortures me and yet I return to it, over and over. I am as doomed as Paolo to circle around

you, never able to have you—my Francesca—day
after day, year after year, throughout infinity, in
this, my beloved Inferno. Over the cabin door I
should erect the sign: Abandon all hope, ye who
enter here!

Except that upon entering, I am in paradise.

I know you do not want to discuss that I am
a married man. You accept that I will never leave
my family. Ah, Kate, what I am asking of you is too
much. It is wrong. I should ride this train north and
never look south again. Yet I am too weak. When I
am away from you I am in hell. Being with you is the
only heaven I desire.

I love you. I love you as much in the heart as in
the mind. I love you as much on the river as in my
bed. I love you when the sun rises and when it sets.
My love for you is all-consuming.

So knowing that I must pass through the flame
before entering Earthly Paradise, I will return in the
fall.

To you, my Francesca . . . my Kate.

DeLancey

"Oh, Stuart," she said, feeling a rush of emotion. "It
all makes sense. DeLancey's letter, the poem. This is
how they saw themselves. As Paolo and Francesca, two
lovers damned to be near each other but never able to
touch. Their hell was having no hope that it would ever
change. It's all so beautiful. And so sad."

Mia lowered the letter, swept away by the powerful emotions swirling inside of her. She felt Stuart squeeze her shoulder. Looking up, she saw DeLancey's passion in Stuart's eyes.

Mia folded the letter in crisp movements, then busied her hands to deflect her nervousness, smoothing the painting, moving the pieces of broken glass.

Slowly, tentatively, Stuart brought his hand up to stroke her hair, then let his hand move down her back, gentling her with tenderness. His hand trembled. Mia's hands went still on the table and she closed her eyes.

Stuart lifted her hair from her neck and lowered his lips to gently caress the tender skin. She felt her senses come alive, so powerfully it bordered on pain. His kisses traveled along her shoulder; then he buried his face in her neck. She shivered, then froze when she felt his hands move across her arms to her chest, cupping her right breast in one and her prosthesis in the other.

"Shh . . . ," he murmured, gentling her, murmuring words she couldn't make out in her terror, aware only of the sensation of a palm against her nipple, caressing in circles on one side. And on the other side, though she felt nothing, she was intensely aware that this hand moved over her body in rhythm with the other. He turned her to press against her as he wrapped strong arms around her. "You're beautiful," he told her.

She looked away, her face against his chest. He

cupped her chin and tilted her head. When she raised her face to his she read the question in his eyes.

Enough of reading and long kisses and swirling in hell, she thought. She relinquished and offered him the desired smile. He took her hand and led her from the sweltering room, out from the carriage house and across the sweet-scented meadows to his bed.

Chapter Eighteen

Fly-fishing is a celebration of the senses and
the spirit. On the river you feel whole again,
ready to say *yes* to life.

—BELLE CARSON

Mia blinked heavily in the piercing sunshine,
then brought her hand up to shield her eyes.
Gradually she moved her palm, growing
accustomed to the light, and looked about the room.
The curtains were drawn and the sun shone freely
through large, expansive windows revealing a brilliant
blue sky.

Dazed, Mia realized those were not her cabin windows. Awaking fully now, her gaze darted around the
strange bedroom—at the taupe walls, the large television, a long dresser and mirror. She turned her head on
the pillow. Stuart was lying on his stomach, his head
turned away from her, his dark hair rumpled on the pillow. The long length of his tanned back was exposed
and the white sheet lay across his hips.

Memories of the night before returned in a flood.
She closed her eyes for a moment as the rush of feel-

ings washed over her. Sighing, she felt a shiver of contentment. The passion from DeLancey's letter had
ignited their own. It was an explosion of desire and
they'd moved to his room, groping and kissing, unable
to keep their hands from each other. There had been
only one awkward moment. When he'd started removing her dress, her hands shot up and clung to the silk, a
last, wretched gesture of panic.

Stuart had taken her face in his hands and compelled her to look into his eyes. Their gazes locked and
his hands moved to gently tug the dress from her. It slid
like water down her legs. Whenever he sensed her shy-
ness he brought her gaze back to him, over and over,
until she was caught in his rhythm and released the last
remnants of hesitation and doubt in a cry of release
ripped from her heart.

She smiled and felt the sunlight swirling inside of
her. She looked again at the man beside her, feeling so
grateful. She had not been sure that she'd ever feel again
the passion, or the fulfillment, she'd felt last night. She
longed to reach out and run her fingers along his beautiful, tanned skin and the dark hairs along his soft arm.
She put out her hand and held it over his back, then
withdrew it, not wanting to wake him.

Instead she slowly, carefully rose from the bed. She
looked for a robe and, finding none, she went to the
bathroom and wrapped a large towel around herself.
She tiptoed from the room and closed the door soundlessly behind her.

His condominium was handsomely done in mountain decor. It was sophisticated and not cabinlike thanks to its lofty ceilings, a stainless steel and wood kitchen, and rich, colored palette. He'd told her the resort had arranged for him to stay in this furnished condo for the duration of his job. Outside the windows the steel blue lake glistened in the morning sun, and beyond, his beloved mountain range was cloaked in every conceivable shade of green.

She prowled through his kitchen, surprised to find the cabinets nearly empty of any food save a few condiments and nuts. His fancy refrigerator held only a few bottles of beer and water, some old cheese, and a half bag of withered carrots. She began to worry when she found the coffee machine in the cabinet, pristine and obviously never used.

"Good morning."

She jerked her head from the cabinet to see Stuart leaning against the granite counter looking disheveled, a navy cotton robe loosely tied around his waist. Dark stubble lined his jaw and lip, and his hair stuck out in spikes.

"I was going to make you coffee," she said.

"Never drink it."

"I figured that out," she said, rising slowly. She tightened the towel around her chest, feeling suddenly awkward.

He reached out toward her and wiggled his fingers for her to come closer. Relieved, she closed the distance and he wrapped his arms around her and held her tight against his chest. She felt enormously reassured and took a deep breath, exhaling a long plume of air.

"You were lovely last night," he said in his gruff morning voice against her head. "*Are* lovely this morning."

She smiled, enjoying the feel of his soft, furred chest against her tender lips.

"I'm hungry this morning," she replied, unable to remark on the night before.

"I don't cook but I can take you to a proper country breakfast. Grits and eggs and bacon. And coffee."

"At the inn?"

"That's what I usually do. They serve breakfast on the patio."

"Don't you think they'll notice I'm wearing the same dress I wore last night?"

She felt his shoulders move with his chuckle. "I'll gain some points. And it will make you very exotic. A wanton woman on a one-night stand."

She didn't reply, uncertain about the one-night stand element of the comment.

He moved back so he could see her face. "Except it's not a one-night stand, is it?"

"Isn't it?" she asked, looking up at him.

"What do you think?"

She nestled her head in the crook of his arm and softened her spine. He tightened his arms around her again. She heard his heart beating, felt his chest rise with a deep inhalation of breath.

"What about if I drive you back to your cabin, you

shower and change, and then we'll drive to Shaffer's for coffee and breakfast. How does that sound?"

"Sounds like a plan."

Things went according to plan with a few minor changes. Stuart drove Mia to the cabin, where she quickly showered. When she returned to her room dripping wet he kissed her, and one kiss led to another. Later, en route to town, they stopped at the overlook outside Watkins Mill. Mia was feeling expansive and wanted to share with him the view that had brought her so much pleasure over the past months. The distant mountain peaks were visible in the clear sky. Below, the wide, verdant valley showed off its earthy greenery.

Mia sat on the small bench at the overlook. Her long, tanned legs extended far out before her on the grass. Stuart's longer legs, in jeans, stretched out next to hers. They'd been sitting here for several minutes, shoulder against shoulder, silently staring out. Mia tapped his sandal with hers.

"What?" he asked.

"So, what do you think? Isn't it wonderful?"

"It's nice."

"Nice?" she asked, feigning insult. "Is that all you can say? This is the finest view anywhere for miles. I can see clear to Tennessee from here."

"That far, huh?"

"Really, Stuart, it's marvelous, isn't it? It's my favorite haunt. I have to pass here every day to get home from town. It's so high up I feel like an eagle perched on some ledge overlooking her domain."

"It's high enough, I give you that."

She tucked her arm under his. "Sometimes I stop on the way back home and sit here to make phone calls. Sometimes I come to sit here and just think. And sometimes I'm drawn here for no reason at all. It's so majestic. So powerful. I feel so small and insignificant before all *that*." She raised her hand to indicate the vista. Lowering her hand, she sighed. "Looking at this sight helps me believe there is a God."

He turned his head and cast a sidelong glance her way. "Did you stop believing?"

She laid her head against his shoulder, feeling the coarseness of his cotton shirt against her tender cheek. Looking out, she nodded. "There were times it was too hard to believe."

"And now?"

"Now it's easier to believe than not believe. I'm thankful He let me live to see this," she said, expressing more to him in those few words than she'd confessed before. "To be here with you. At this moment."

She lifted her head to see him looking at her, his gaze penetrating. She reached up to gently stroke his jaw with her palm, then lowered her hand and tucked it back under his arm. "That's all I'm asking for," she said quietly, her eyes looking out to the distance.

When they walked into Shaffer's, the bell chimed and Mia heard Becky's cheerful voice ring out, "Mornin', Mia!" Becky's smile froze when she saw Stuart walking in behind her. She was sitting at a table with Flossie and Phyllis, all of whose eyes were fixed on the tall man behind her.

"Good morning, ladies," Mia said as she walked up to their table. "Have y'all met Stuart?"

Their eyes devoured him as he came forward and smiled. "Ladies."

Mia moved her hand to indicate the tall man beside her. "Stuart MacDougal, meet Becky Shaffer, Flossie Barbieri, and Phyllis Pace."

"You're the fellow who's setting up that Orvis shop up at the lodge, right?" Becky asked.

"Yes ma'am."

"How's it going?"

"It's coming along, thank you."

Mia saw Phyllis's eyes narrow in speculation. Flossie, she was shocked to see, was tongue-tied.

"Y'all having a coffee break?" Mia asked. It was unusual to find all three women sitting together for coffee midmorning.

"I guess you haven't heard," Becky said.

"Heard what?"

"Mrs. Minor passed away yesterday."

Mia felt a stab of regret. "Oh, no. I hadn't heard. I would have liked to see her again."

"She was feeling poorly," Flossie continued. "Her granddaughter said the doctor had been out several times in the past few days. At her age, you never know when the Lord's going to call."

"She lived a good life," Phyllis added. "No one can say she was cut down before her time. God rest her soul."

"When is the service?" Mia asked.

"Saturday morning at ten o'clock," said Phyllis. "My father and I will be there."

"I'll be there," Mia replied.

"I'll go with you," Stuart told her.

Hearing this, the three older women shared a knowing glance and reached for their coffee, smiling.

The white, Gothic Revival Presbyterian church was the bulwark of the western side of Main Street. At ten a.m. the church bell in the spired tower tolled mournfully for Louise Minor. The small church filled slowly with family, friends, and acquaintances of a woman who had lived all of her ninety-two years in Watkins Mill. When the tolling ceased and the church quieted, the eulogy told of a woman who had witnessed her small town endure the poverty of the Depression; the long, lean years during which the town struggled to pay back its debt; and the recent resurgence of popularity and new wealth as tourists returned again to the area. She had seen the final horse-drawn carts replaced by cars, electricity put into all homes, and her children, grandchildren, and great-grandchildren grown. It had been a full life.

Mia sat with Stuart in the back of the church and looked at the pointed, arched windows, saddened to have learned that Kate Watkins had not had a public funeral in this church that her father had served so many years. She'd talked briefly to Phillip Pace outside the church and he had informed her that Kate had a small, private service attended only by Mrs. Minor's family and his own immediate family. Afterward, she was laid to rest beside her father in the Watkins family plot. Mia thought of the young woman who had walked so proud on these streets during her young life, who sat in the front pew on Sundays watching her father preach. Had she fallen so low that she was quietly buried, an outcast, forgotten or ridiculed by the town that once celebrated her fame?

A tear fell down her cheek. Stuart, misunderstanding her grief, reached over to hold her hand.

After the service Mia stood at the back of the church with Becky and Skipper. It was the first time she'd seen Becky not wearing her pink uniform. She appeared solemn in a dark brown suit. Skipper held her arm and was exceedingly attentive to her, worried lest she stand too long. Mia was moved by their tenderness toward each other. She looked up to Stuart. He stood separate from the group, staring out the double doors toward the sky. The sun shone clear and sunny, like a light at the end of a tunnel.

"Excuse me, Mrs. Landan?"

Mia turned her head toward the voice. Lucy

Roosevelt stood beside her, looking regal in a black suit and a large black hat with a silk rim and bow.

"Lucy, I'm so sorry for your loss."

"Thank you. My grandmother enjoyed her visit with you. She mentioned you several times before she died. She wanted to see you. She had something she wanted to give you."

"Give me?" Mia asked. She couldn't imagine what Mrs. Minor had for her, unless it had to do with Kate Watkins.

"Well, not for you, exactly. For Miss Carson. Theodora's daughter. Will you be seeing her?"

"Yes. I'm sure I will."

"Good," she replied with relief. "See, a long time ago Miss Watkins gave my grandmother a letter and asked that she send it to her daughter if she died. I reckon she tried to mail it to her, except she didn't know where to send it. Well, after Miss Watkins passed, my grandmother and my mother both tried to find Theodora. But they didn't know where to begin to look. They called people and looked in phone books. We're simple folk. We don't have the means to hire a detective. So my grandmother just hung on to the letter, hoping that someday she'd find out what happened to Theodora, or hoping that she'd come back to town. That was a while ago and to be honest, we kinda forgot about that letter. Then you came by and my grandmother had me go up in the attic where I keep her things that she brought from her cabin. I went through all her stuff. Lord, there were a lot of knickknacks. There are some old pictures of her and Miss Watkins and Theodora, too, that she thought Belle might like. I found this."

Lucy handed an envelope to Mia. It was thick, and yellowed from age. Mia looked at the writing on the front. In bold script was written the name: *Mrs. Theodora Watkins Carson.*

Mia ran her fingers over the script. She turned it over and saw that the envelope was sealed.

"Would you please deliver that letter to Miss Belle Carson when you see her?" Lucy asked. "My grandmother wanted to ask you to do that favor for her but she took sick before she could. She loved Miss Watkins and was a true friend to her. She never felt right that the letter wasn't delivered. It's too bad it never reached her daughter, but she'd be grateful to know that at least it reached her granddaughter. It'd mean a lot to all of us."

"Of course," Mia replied. "I'll give it to Belle. I promise."

Chapter Nineteen

Knots are important in fly-fishing. Anglers must take care to seal the knot tight and secure. Many anglers rue the day they lose a fish because of a poorly tied knot.

—KATE WATKINS'S FISHING DIARY

"Poor Theodora . . ."

Mrs. Amanda Rodale was a large woman. She filled the upholstered chair by her front window. The soft rose and blue floral pattern matched the fiery sunset Mia could see lowering over the distant mountain. Flossie sat on the chair next to her mother, and Mia sat on the striped sofa across from them. It was Thursday night and they'd feasted on a home-cooked meal with the family and were enjoying coffee and the famous peach pie in the living room. The husbands had muttered excuses after dinner and conveniently disappeared, leaving the women alone to talk.

"Why do you call her poor Theodora?" Mia asked Mrs. Rodale. "Was she mistreated?"

"Heavens no! My mama used to say Theo was likely the best-cared-for child in town. She ate fresh food and had plenty of exercise with all that walking."

"Then why do you say *poor*?"

"Because I've never known any child who wanted to be part of the norm as she did. I guess part of it was the old grass-is-greener thing. But it's more than that. See, she was a Watkins, with all the baggage that name carried. Good and bad. Her mother, Kate, didn't come to town much. The Minor family did a lot of shopping for her and folks were kind and did deliveries out to her place. But when she did come in it was like she parted the waters. Nobody got in her way. It wasn't that she was uppity. Though she had that upper-class air about her. She was born to class so she came by it honestly. No, it was more that she had this shell around her that she didn't let nobody get through. 'Cept maybe Phillip Pace and Mrs. Minor.

"Theo, though, she was different. More a shadow of the woman her mother was. Where Kate was strong and regal, Theo was weak and flighty. I've heard folks say Theo was more like her father, though I never met him so I can't say.

"The way my husband puts it is Kate Watkins was hardwired for being alone in the woods. But her daughter, Theo . . . she was wired different. Theo liked being in the town and wearing pretty dresses. The times she was allowed to come to our house, all she wanted to do was stay inside, listen to our radio, and try on my dresses. And eat candy. Oh, she loved her sweets. Every time she came my mama went to the grocer's and stocked up. We all used to wonder if she'd get sick, she stuffed so much in. I think if she'd lived in town, she would've been normal. For sure she would've been a real social-ite if the family hadn't lost their money and position. It had to be hard on a girl like her to live way out in the middle of nowhere knowing what the family once had. I remember once she cried and begged my mama to let her live with us. She didn't want to go back to the cabin."

"Did your mother ever look into why? Did she talk to Kate?"

"Of course she did. My mother was about the only friend Kate had in town. Like I said, Kate did a fine job raising her child all on her own. She lived modest but decent out there. They weren't starving or anything like that. And this is important to know. Theo loved her mother. Loved her something fierce. If anyone said anything bad about her in Theo's face, she'd tear into them. Though she might've blamed her mother some for choosing to live so far out. If there was anything like abuse at all, I'd say it was the town that was at fault. We weren't neighborly, not the way we ought to have been to that child. Especially seeing how things were. I still feel badly that me and my friends didn't go out there to see her when we were old enough, or invite her into town for parties."

"I thought Theo came to your house?"

"When we were little she came by after school. I pretty much did what my mama told me to do. But as we got older, well, you know how teenage girls are.

They form cliques. Country girls are no different than city girls in that way. By the time we were old enough to learn the gossip about Theo's mother, we excluded her from our circle."

"You mean she was an outcast?"

"That's a strong word, but yes, I reckon I do mean that."

"What was the gossip back then about Kate?"

"No different than it is today, only it was fresh and the stink of it was stronger. First off, there was the tittle-tattle about how Kate had an affair with a married man and got herself pregnant. That would've been enough to make Theo unpopular. The boys called her the *b* word for illegitimate when she was little. But it was the scandal about the murder, and worse, that maybe it happened out there in that cabin, that shot Theo out from just being different to weird."

Mrs. Rodale's pale blue eyes stared out vacantly for a moment while her mind searched her memories. Flossie looked a lot like her mother. They both were overweight and pale yet looked lovely in the summer dresses they wore for the occasion. The sweetness to their expressions mirrored their affability, no doubt also passed down. Mia imagined Mrs. Rodale's mother had been very much like them.

"To be totally honest," Mrs. Rodale continued, "we girls had another reason not to like Theodora Watkins. She had to be by far the prettiest girl in town. Now, there's pretty and then there's so pretty you just stop and stare. Theo was that kind of pretty. The boys started calling after her like tomcats. The problem was, none of them would have married her on account of her reputation. Or, rather, her mother's reputation. Do you get what I'm telling you? You could say those rascals hoped the apple didn't fall far from the tree."

"Did Theo fool around?" Mia asked, thinking that certainly would have been a cause for mother-daughter fights.

Mrs. Rodale laughed, then shook her head. "No. I don't think she could have even if she wanted to. For all the stories those fool boys heard growing up, I reckon none of them heard the story about what a crack shot Kate Watkins was. Come one night she fired off a few rounds and sent them tomcats running, which only served to spark more talk about how Kate Watkins was crazy and a killer. You know how that kind of talk spreads in a small town. Looking back, we all knew that if she'd wanted to shoot one of those boys, even nip 'em, she could've. She was just sending them a message they could understand."

Mia smiled to herself, thinking that even a formal letter written on thick vellum with the Watkins crest would hardly have had the same effect. "I imagine by that point Kate was beyond caring about protocol and reputation."

"Oh, sure. She wrote us all off. Some said she'd gone wild out there alone."

"And you? What do you say?"

"I say Kate was as far from wild as any woman I'd ever known. She was an outdoors woman. That's different from wild."

"Yes, it is," Mia replied, understanding the difference now. "And Theo? How did she respond to all that shooting and gossip?"

"She run off. I have to reckon she just couldn't stand living out there. One day some guys came through town and they weren't familiar with the rumors about ol' Kate. One of them, a fella by the name of Daniel Carson, took one look at Theodora and fell head over heels in love with her. His friends moved on but he stayed for a few more days. When he finally left on the three o'clock train headed north, Theo went with him. We've never seen her in this town again."

"And Kate? What did she do?"

"That's the saddest part of this whole story. When Theo didn't come home that evening Kate came driving straight into town in her old motorcar, worried and scared like any mother would be when she discovers her young'un is gone missing. She went to our house first and talked to my mama. After all, I was the only one who was Theo's friend. My mama called me into the living room and I'll never forget as long as I live the night I had to stand in front of Kate Watkins."

"So you did meet her," Mia said, leaning forward. "What was she like? Was she striking?"

"She wasn't striking. She was . . . exotic. There was no escaping her gaze."

"Go on."

"It was late fall. I remember it was unusually cold that day. She had this long, black men's coat that went clear down to her ankles. It was old and worn but it was good quality wool, you could tell. I thought it might've been her father's or that DeLancey fellow's. And she wore this white silky scarf looped around her neck. Her hair was dark and pulled up into a loose bun and though she weren't wearing a shred of makeup her cheeks were reddened by the cold. Most of all I remember her eyes. They were dark and seemed to snap at me. Even though I was right nervous, I remember her face like it was yesterday. Thinking on it—" Mrs. Rodale counted on her fingers. "She had to be in her late forties, and that's not old, hear? Anyway, Kate had a way of looking at you that could see right through nonsense. I remember how she pinned me with those dark eyes."

March 1948

"Amanda," Kate said in her clipped voice. "Do you know where Theodora is?"

I clutched my skirt and looked away. "I, uh, I'm not sure."

"Tell Miss Watkins what you know," my mother prodded. She stood next to me and in her eyes I saw that she was nervous, too.

"Yes'm. Well, some guys came to town about a week ago. On the train. They stayed at the Riverside Inn. One of them was quite taken with Theo."

"How old would you say he was?" Kate asked.

"Older than us, but not old. Maybe twenty?"

Kate's expression grew wary. "Go on."

"He and Theo started hanging out a lot in town. She skipped school and I saw her with him."

"What were they doing?" Kate asked in a sharp tone.

"Nothing bad. Just walking and maybe having something to eat. They went to the movies once. You could see she was sweet on him, too."

"Do you know this young man's name?"

I hesitated, not wanting to get Theo in more trouble. There's an unspoken loyalty the young have, especially when confronted with an angry parent.

"Amanda," Kate said, and her voice was tinged with pleading. "Please understand. Theo is gone. She's only seventeen years old. She could be in serious trouble. Please, tell me everything you know."

"Tell her everything, dear," my mother urged.

"His name is Daniel Carson. Miss Watkins, I saw them get on the train together."

"When?"

"Today. The three o'clock."

Kate's face paled and I saw a vulnerability in her expression that I didn't think her capable of.

Kate drew up, trying to compose herself. "Thank you, Amanda," she said, and I could tell it was from the heart. I . . . I felt sorry for her.

She spoke with my mother by the door for a few minutes more. Then, before she left, my mother, who was an emotional woman, burst forward and hugged

Kate. It was one of those quick, spontaneous hugs I'd seen her give other women in tough times. I knew then that my mother had been a better friend to Kate Watkins than I had any knowledge of.

It was already dark outside. My mother stood by my side and watched Kate walk down the street, her head bent to the wind and her hands clutching the coat around her neck. My mama's hand tightened on my shoulder and though she was still looking out the front door she said to me, "Don't you ever leave me like that, hear? You'd break my heart same as Theo just broke her mother's."

Mrs. Rodale's index finger rose to swipe a tear from her eye. "I never tell that story without getting emotional myself. I get that from my mother, I reckon."

"Did you ever see Kate Watkins again?"

"Yes. After that visit she came to town often to talk to the sheriff to see if any word came about Theodora. She opened up a post office box in hopes Theo might write, and she'd always check that. As the weeks turned into months and no word came, she didn't come in so often. The town gave her wide berth, knowing how things were. She'd come in to check her mailbox at holidays, like Christmas. It was real sad. Anyone who looked at her couldn't help but feel her pain. Before Theo left I wouldn't have said she was lonely. But after?" She shrugged.

"My mother went out to the cabin to see her a

couple times. Once when she was feeling poorly she brought her some chicken soup. She died not too many years later. I was married by then to Mr. Rodale. I might even've had my Flossie already when word came that she was dead."

"How did she die?"

"Why, she drowned. She was found in the river that runs up to the cabin. Kate knew her way around a river better than anyone but she was getting older and they figured she must've slipped. Her waders were filled with water. It was Mrs. Minor that found her. Thank God. With her living alone up there, who knows how long it might've taken before anyone realized she was gone. Still, I always thought it was a blessing that she died doing something she loved so much."

Mia closed her notebook with an overpowering sense of grief. "Thank you, Mrs. Rodale."

"I hope I've been helpful."

"Very. I appreciate your time."

"Before you go, I just want to say I'm real glad for what you're doing here. Telling people about who the real Kate Watkins was, not the crazy woman that the town folks make her out to be. I'm old enough to have lived through the war and 'women's lib,' and the young ones today, they don't know what it was like to be a strong woman like our Kate back when. So she was smart, strong willed, and opinionated, and throughout she showed us all how to hold our head high. I'm real pleased that the newspaper is running her articles so the town can be proud of Kate Watkins the famous woman fly fisher. But I'd like to see an article about Kate Watkins the woman. Period. She'd be an inspiration for our young women today."

"I take it then that you don't believe she killed DeLancey?"

"No I do not! Nor does Phillip Pace, and he knew her better than anyone. He was at the investigation, you know."

Mia didn't know that. "And Theo? Any last thoughts about her?"

Mrs. Rodale's face softened to sorrow. "Poor Theodora . . ."

Chapter Twenty

The Gazette
November 19, 1929
INVESTIGATION OF MISSING PERSON
ORDERED

An investigation will be held in Watkins Mill
to examine the circumstances surrounding the
disappearance of Theodore DeLancey of New York.

Mr. DeLancey, 39, was last seen late November
9. Police received reports of sightings of DeLancey
in town and later on the road but extensive searches
failed to find him. The coroner, Paul Miller, has now
called for public assistance in an investigation that
will be held on November 21 at Watkins Mill
Court.

Sheriff Michael Dodds says family members
and others will give evidence but he hopes some
new information will be received. "We are appealing
to the public, to people who may have some
information and have not yet come forward."

Anyone who believes they may be able to assist
can call Watkins Mill police.

Mia sat on the rocking chair of the cabin's porch. The sun was a slice of crimson over the purple mountain range. Nearby, the river raced. She could hear the omnipresent sound of rushing water. From somewhere in the surrounding trees the Carolina wren was crying out its strident whistles. She searched the foliage for the small, buff-colored bird with white streaks at the eyes. From off in the woods, another wren returned its call. She leaned back in the chair, enjoying the calm of the twilight hour as serenity settled in the mountains.

It was deceiving. A hurricane was hitting the Gulf coast and was expected to travel north toward North Carolina. Mia felt a tempest of emotions in her heart, as well. She held the yellowed envelope addressed to Theodora Watkins Carson. Since the moment it came into her hands it had been the bane of her existence. She turned it over and ran her finger over the seal. The side edges of the envelope had opened over the years. It would take but the slightest pressure from her finger in the center to raise the seal and open it.

The temptation was overwhelming. In this letter she might well learn from Kate herself what the truth of her story was. This was her final letter to her only child. Her last chance to express all that she'd harbored in silence for so many years. What would she say?

Mia longed to know. She had gone this far in her search; what was opening one more letter, she rationalized?

She rose and walked back indoors, tapping the

letter against her palm. She paced once around the room, deliberating. Then she made a beeline for the bookshelf. Finding Kate's diary, she put the envelope inside of it and placed the book back on the shelf.

Her mind was made up. The diaries, the conversations, the news articles—all of those had been open and available to her. The seal on the envelope was a moral line she could not cross. To break it would be the equivalent of opening Pandora's box.

The following morning Mia drove to town to see Nada. The hurricane and its projected path was the hot topic on every news station. When she arrived at the *Gazette*, the office was busy. A special be-prepared edition was going out that afternoon. Nada was on the phone in her office but she signaled for Mia to take a chair and wait.

Two minutes later Nada hung up the telephone and shook her head with disbelief. "You'd think a category five was hitting Watkins Mill."

"How bad is it?"

Nada rubbed her face with her palms, then looked down at the map spread out across her desk. "Hurricane Nicholas is still a category two, but that water is warm and it's predicted to gain strength. Hurricanes not only affect the coast, they can move inland and drop buckets of rain. A single hurricane can wallop a large area. I remember back in 2004, hurricanes Frances and Ivan passed through the North Carolina mountains within a two-week time span. The rivers and streams flooded. Mudslides took out roads, cars, houses . . . a real mess. That's what we're worried about. In your neck of the woods, you should be, too."

Mia felt a flutter of panic. "What do I do?"

"Make sure the cabin's sealed up good and tight and get some provisions to last you for three days or more. If the road goes out, you could be up there for days before they clear it up. Mudslides are the big threat up here. We've had an unusual amount of rain lately and the ground is saturated. That's when trouble starts."

"I'm going directly to Rodale's after here to get supplies. But I got your message. Sounded urgent. What did you want to see me about?"

"Oh, that!" Nada's face brightened with recollection. "I found those articles about the investigation. The articles dated November, nineteen twenty-nine. They're here somewhere." She rifled through stacks of papers on her desk and the credenza. Then she called out, "Missy!"

The young girl poked her head in. She had pink streaks in her hair and heavy kohl around her eyes. "Yeah?"

"Where's that file for Mia? The one about Kate Watkins."

"I'll get it."

A minute later Missy sauntered into Nada's office carrying a manila folder bulging with papers. Mia couldn't help but notice her violet nail polish.

"Thanks, dear," Nada said, taking the folder from

her. "Oh, and will you tell Bob I need that article? Right away, please?"

"OK," she replied with a bored expression.

When she left Nada shook her head with frustration.

"That's a new fashion statement for her, isn't it?" Mia asked.

"That's one girl who's not set her cap on the newspaper world. I swear, nothing seems to light a spark in her. Not even a hurricane."

Mia was anxious to see the articles. She pulled her chair closer to the desk and sat down as Nada opened up the file.

"I printed out copies of all the articles I could find. Once I got started, I traced back to copies of newspapers that printed the story in other cities. Let's see . . . New York," she said as she passed a printed article to Mia. "Here's Boston. New York again."

Mia read through a few of the headlines: *Information Sought on Missing Person. Wife Demands Investigation. Inquest Ordered for Missing Man. Love Nest Uncovered. Murder or Mayhem? DeLancey Declared Missing Person.*

"Some of these headlines read like tabloids," Mia said, flipping through them.

"It was a sensationalized story at the time. But I hadn't realized it was covered in out-of-town newspapers. What with the scandal, that would have explained why Kate's column was discontinued."

Mia brought the copies to the small table and settled herself to read. The minutes passed as she quickly scanned the articles, and with each one Mia felt her heart race faster with shock and indignation. When she went through them all, she tossed the last sheet on the table and leaned back in the chair.

"But Nada," Mia said, incredulous. "There isn't any proof there was a murder at all! It was just an investigation. There wasn't even a trial!"

"Right! There never was a body. DeLancey's case was a missing person investigation. Despite some very public accusations and very harsh criticisms of the police concerning improper handling, the sheriff's office determined that insufficient evidence had been provided to declare Mr. Theodore DeLancey dead. He remained a missing person."

Mia was stunned. Her mind whirled with the injustice of it all. "So all these years the stories about Kate Watkins killing her lover were nothing more than rumor and scandal?"

Nada nodded her head. "Appears so. I've been in the news business and a historian for many years and one thing I know is that, sadly, it wouldn't be the first time. It was mostly the out-of-town papers that made all the assumptions about a love triangle and the murder motives," she added with a tone of defensiveness. "The *Gazette* didn't point that finger."

"But it didn't defend her, either."

"No. But that's not a newspaper's job." She drew herself up. "I thought they did a decent job of being impartial in a very emotional case."

Mia didn't want to get into a battle over the quality

of the *Gazette*'s reporting of the case. "No matter what paper," Mia said, "the innuendo that Kate Watkins murdered DeLancey was allowed to fester and grow until it became accepted as the truth. Why didn't anyone speak up for her? I thought she was so beloved by the town. She must have felt so betrayed," Mia said, understanding that particular emotion so well. "Where were her friends? Where was her family?"

"Her father died immediately after the investigation. His obituary is in that pile of papers for you. As for her friends . . ." She shrugged. "I can't say what anyone might have said or not said. I wasn't there and it wasn't recorded in the paper."

Mia squeezed the bridge of her nose as she tried to collect her thoughts.

"I'm going to talk to Mr. Pace."

"I thought you said he wouldn't talk about the murder."

"I'll show him the articles. Beg him on my knees. I've got to try. He's my last hope."

Chapter Twenty-one

The Gazette
May 1926
Kate Watkins, "On the Fly"

Rivers and streams can have dangerously swift currents. Remain alert and cautious when stepping foot into any moving water. Once in the water, stand with your feet shoulder-width apart and one foot slightly in back of the other. Once anchored in your position you can concentrate on your cast. A stable stance is a must in strong currents. As any dancer knows, the secret is balance.

"I've lived many, many years and in all my memory no disappearance in this part of the county has prompted so much speculation as that of Mr. Theodore DeLancey."

Mia sat across from Phillip Pace in the library. Rain streaked the windows in sheets driven by a fierce wind. The storm had hit the coast and the weakened tropical depression was now making its way north. Though it was midafternoon, the sky was dark. Inside, small pools of light flowed from table lamps like halos.

"How could Kate have been so vilified?" Mia asked. "In her own town?"

"What you got to remember," Phillip said in earnest, "is that it wasn't a normal time for this town. Not anywhere in the country. Everything was in a tizzy. October of nineteen twenty-nine. Does that date ring a bell?" He gummed his lips, and hands large and gnarled gripped the sides of his chair in agitation. "You're all so young I don't know what you kids know or remember anymore."

"Yes, sir, I know about the stock market crash," Mia replied. "October twenty-ninth, nineteen twenty-nine was Black Thursday. It marked the end of the Roaring Twenties and the beginning of the Depression."

He nodded his head with seriousness. "What goes up must come down. That's what people said a lot back then, trying to make sense of it. Asheville had the highest per capita debt of any city in the country. I'll bet you didn't know that."

"No," she admitted. "I sure didn't."

"Our town was booming in the twenties. When the stock market crashed, it was a hard hit. Those of us who lived through the Depression were changed forever. We learned to do without. An old suit, a bit of string—everything has some use left in it. Some, like the DeLanceys and the Watkinses, lost fortunes. The rest of us just hoped we could get our cash out of the bank. Folks were panicking. I'm telling you, it was a bad time. Emotions were high, folks weren't themselves.

"On top of all that, we were having a spell of serious

weather. Rain, rain, and more rain, like now. Mudslides were so bad folks couldn't get to town for supplies. Every able-bodied man was out clearing roads. So when word come that Mr. DeLancey was missing, I reckon the sheriff just put that on his list."

"Who reported him missing?"

"I don't rightly remember who reported it. Everything got all muddled. Sheriff Dodds was a good man but he caught a lot of chaff for his handling of this case. It weren't his fault. If DeLancey had gone and disappeared even a month earlier they'd have conducted the search in a timely manner, grilled the people they needed to, and reported it in the accepted, straight-out way of doing police business. And you can bet your last dollar this whole DeLancey case would've been cleaned up without scandal if it had involved average people at an average time."

"You mean because DeLancey was from a wealthy family?"

"That. And the fuss she made."

"Kate?"

"No! Mrs. DeLancey. Camilla, I think her name was. She came to town with her lawyer in tow and smoke coming out of her ears. She went straight to the sheriff's office to demand he investigate her husband's disappearance. She started making all kinds of accusations against Kate Watkins, and they were of a nature that if it got out the sheriff knew the newspapers would have a heyday with it. He did the right thing, trying to calm her down some."

Mia leaned far forward, not wanting to miss a word. She didn't know that DeLancey's wife had come looking for him.

"Right off, the town didn't like Mrs. DeLancey. Not just because she was from out of town. She was an uppity kind of woman, you know the type? She lifted her nose at you like you had a bad smell. We're always wary of pushy northerners anyway, but this woman was attacking one of our favorite daughters. So the town stood strong in support of Kate Watkins. The DeLanceys might have been important in New York, but in Asheville, the Watkins family mattered.

"But Mrs. DeLancey's wealth and influence was not to be denied. She and her lawyer called the investigation sloppy and forced the sheriff to begin a formal search. Did I tell you some reporters came to town, too? Yes, ma'am, they did. Once whiff of the story got out, they were like a pack of hyenas on a scent. A three-ring circus it turned out to be."

Mr. Pace adjusted his seat and Mia sat with her pencil ready. She could see in the old man's eyes he was going back in time.

"It was raining like the Lord's flood. Nobody could remember a fall before or since with so much rain. Route Nine out of town was gone. It slid right off the mountain. That didn't stop the folks from coming into town, though. Everyone was milling about, eager to hear any word about the investigation.

"Now, this wasn't any inquest or formal court proceeding, mind you. The sheriff just called together the main people so he could get his story straight. And to appease Mrs. DeLancey's lawyer, I reckon. Let's see," he said, rubbing his jaw and trying to recollect. "Mrs. DeLancey was there, of course. And her lawyer. Some insurance fella was there, too. Kate, of course. And her father, the Reverend Watkins. I was there. Kate asked me to come and wild horses wouldn't've kept me away. Paul Miller the coroner was there, too, just in case. Course, there wasn't a body, but he was there. A few reporters muscled their way in. Sheriff Dodds was an honest, polite man, respected by everybody in town. I don't know if anyone ever saw him lose his temper, so we knew he could keep an even keel on this procedure. Still, he shouldn't have let those reporters in. It was standing room only. The air was thick in there, I remember. And it didn't have nothing to do with the rain and humidity."

November 21, 1929

"I'll try to make this brief," Sheriff Dodds said to Mrs. DeLancey. "Tell me, please, when you first realized your husband was missing."

Mrs. DeLancey was tiny and fragile looking, like some porcelain doll. Anyone could see she was upper class, and when she spoke in that breathy voice, she sounded like a Brit. She was dressed in black mourning, which a lot of the local women thought was jumping the gun seeing as how her husband hadn't even been pronounced dead yet.

"My husband had left for North Carolina on the eleventh of November. He usually was gone for a week, maybe two, on his fishing trips." She said the words *fishing trips* as though she meant something else. "So I was alarmed when I received a phone call from you, Sheriff Dodds, a few days later asking me if my husband had returned home."

"And had he returned home?"

"No. The last I saw of Teddy, I mean, Mr. DeLancey, was when he left his home in New York. You proceeded to tell me that my husband had not returned to his hotel room or checked out. The bill was as yet outstanding. The hotel staff found my husband's clothing and some personal belongings still in his room."

"What did you do next?"

"You can imagine my state of mind. I immediately called the Watkins family."

"Why the Watkins family?"

"My husband rented the Watkins cabin for his fishing expeditions," she explained. "I assumed this continued to the present."

"How often did Mr. DeLancey rent the cabin?"

"He came to Watkins Mill twice a year in the spring and the fall. For four years. I used to wonder why he stopped fishing the Battenkill. We have a place of our own on that river, you see. Or why he didn't accompany his friends on trips out west. He was determined to return to western North Carolina every year, two times a year. My husband was passionate about fly-fishing.

However—" She paused and tugged at the handkerchief in her hand. "I must admit I did not understand his passion for this particular cabin in Watkins Cove."

"But our records show he had a hotel room at the inn and did not stay at the cabin," prompted Dodds.

"Yes. When I was informed of that, frankly, I was confused. I knew you were getting a lot of rain. I thought perhaps there was flooding. The truth is, I didn't know why. So I called the Watkins house, in hopes they could shed some light on my husband's whereabouts."

"I see. Who did you talk to?"

"Their housekeeper, I believe. A Mrs. Hodges answered the phone. She informed me that my husband was not there."

"She knew Mr. DeLancey?"

"Apparently so. She didn't stumble over his name."

"Did you ask to speak to anyone?"

"I did. I asked to speak to Miss Watkins and was told she was not at home, but that the Reverend Watkins would be returning home at five. I left my number and requested that he call me back immediately. That it was of the utmost urgency. I waited several days and received no reply. I grew frantic, as you can imagine. My suspicions were aroused and not knowing where else to turn, I called my lawyer, Mr. Michael Morris. He urged me to take immediate action."

"Your suspicions were aroused? What suspicions were those?"

Mrs. DeLancey drew back her shoulders. They

were tiny but straight as steel. She looked at her hands clenched tightly in her lap. The room hushed and everyone leaned forward in their seat.

"I knew for some time that my husband was having an affair with Miss Kate Watkins," she said.

The room broke out in rumbling and all heads turned to Kate. All this time she sat in her chair straight and silent, staring out like she wasn't even there. She was dressed in a plain gray suit—with her usual pants, I might add. Her dark eyes were trained on some point in the distance and no one could tell by looking if she'd heard a thing that was being said.

Sheriff Dodds frowned at that and his voice grew censorial. "How did you know this?"

"When my husband's trips extended to two weeks or more at the cabin I consulted his fishing friends and they told me that they had never accompanied him to North Carolina. In fact, they complained how they missed his company on their customary trips."

"The rivers of North Carolina are known for exemplary fly-fishing," said Sheriff Dodds. "Is it not likely that your husband found a place he preferred to all others and continued to return here, year after year? I think most men in this room fish in these waters and never seek to go elsewhere."

Mumbled agreement sounded from the local men. Morris glared in his seat.

Mrs. DeLancey, however, did not lose her composure. "As I said, we have our own property on the Battenkill River, which is well known for its superb fly-fishing. No, I suspected that there was another lure at this particular spot. I learned that each time he went, he engaged the services of Miss Watkins as his personal guide. I remember her name because she was a woman guide and that's not usual, in any state."

"Miss Watkins is a nationally respected fly-fishing guide."

Mrs. DeLancey's brow rose. "Miss Watkins is also not the grizzled old mountain woman I had in my mind but an attractive, well-bred, young woman."

"Excuse me, but what do your unfounded suspicions have to do with your husband's disappearance?"

More murmuring from the observers.

"Before my husband left for this trip, I confronted him."

"Are you saying that Mr. Theodore DeLancey admitted to an affair with Miss Katherine Watkins?"

"He did not deny it."

The room burst with comments from the gallery. Kate stared straight ahead as though made of stone.

"Mrs. DeLancey, forgive me, but I still fail to see what your husband's real or imagined relationship with Miss Watkins has to do with his disappearance."

Her lips tightened with annoyance. "I'm sure you are aware of recent events in the stock market. What you might not be aware of is that my husband lost his family's fortune in the crash. He speculated wildly and lost. He was desolate. Inconsolable. I'd never seen him in such a state." She dabbed at her eyes with her handkerchief.

"Yes, Mrs. DeLancey," Dodds said in a conciliatory tone. "We all have experienced loss and can only imagine the magnitude of your own."

Mrs. DeLancey mustered her resolve. "The point I wish to make is that my husband and I were brought closer together. He begged my forgiveness and pledged his undying love. He swore he was going to Watkins Mill for the last time, to break off his illicit relationship with Miss Watkins."

Everyone's head turned to Kate. Her dark eyes flickered with a glimmer of reaction as she slowly turned her head to gaze at Mrs. DeLancey. Kate's face revealed neither disbelief nor anger. She just stared at DeLancey's wife as though she were trying to make up her own mind whether to believe her.

"Why would he come all the way to Watkins Mill to tell her this?" Dodds persisted. "He could have wired. Or telephoned."

"You may not know my husband also speculated in the market for Miss Watkins. He no doubt promised great returns, as he did with others." Her voice was tinged with bitterness. "My husband could be very persuasive. In the end, Theodore lost the Watkinses' money as well. He felt obliged to tell her this in person. My husband was not blameless. I know that. But the fact is Miss Watkins was the last person who saw him alive." Her voice rose with emotion. "She had passion and motive."

"What are you implying, Mrs. DeLancey?"

"What am I implying?" She lost all her composure,

pointed her finger at Kate, and screamed, "I am *telling* you Kate Watkins murdered my husband!"

The room erupted in angry shouts. Kate's father, sitting beside her, silently held her hand. Amid the roars, Mrs. DeLancey and Kate stared at each other like two lionesses about to pounce, one hysterical, the other as silent as stone.

Mr. Pace sighed and leaned back in his chair. Mia thought the memory might be tiring him. She handed him his glass of sweet tea and waited while he sipped some. When he was done, she waited patiently until he was ready to come back to his story.

"Afterward, nobody thought it did Kate any good to be so stoic," Mr. Pace continued. "I never in my life saw Kate cry, but I thought a few tears might have done her some good that afternoon. I felt the shift in public opinion. People walked into the room saying 'Poor Kate' and walked out saying 'Poor Camilla.' In matters of the heart, sympathy usually goes to the wronged wife."

"Who else made statements that day?" asked Mia.

"None that day. But the sheriff had already talked to several other folks. The hotel maid remembered seeing DeLancey that night. The trainmaster collected his ticket. I guess he didn't have his fancy rail car anymore. Most notable was that waiter, Arthur . . ." He scratched his ear. "I can't remember that fella's last name. He worked at the inn for years. He was a lean, rangy man, nervous at being questioned." He sighed and let the name go.

"Apparently Kate and DeLancey had dinner at the inn that night. He claimed they often had dinner together when Mr. DeLancey was in town. Said how they were always polite. Never any hanky-panky. Except that night, they'd been arguing. She said some angry words at him, then took some piece of jewelry from around her neck—a pendant or locket—and threw it at him. He remembered that. She just threw it at him and left. Arthur made it crystal clear that Kate Watkins left the restaurant alone that night. And Theodore DeLancey remained at the inn drinking."

Mr. Pace sighed heavily and he looked at Mia with cloudy eyes. "That summed things up right then and there as far as I could see. Kate left for home. DeLancey stayed at the hotel. End of story."

"But it wasn't the end, was it?"

"No, ma'am, it was not," he conceded. "Just like the rain, the rumors and gossip kept coming. Everyone was told to go home. The next day Sheriff Dodds said there wasn't enough evidence to declare Theodore DeLancey dead and that he'd be listed as a missing person. This wasn't welcomed by Mrs. DeLancey, to be sure. Her lawyer went on about favoritism and incompetence. They left in a huff. Good riddance, that's what I thought. We had enough of our own problems to deal with. The Central Bank in Asheville had just closed its doors."

Mia sat back in her chair and went through in her

mind all she'd just heard. "I'm confused, Mr. Pace. With this ruling, how did Kate get the reputation as a murderer?"

He answered in the manner of a man who had been asked this question many times over many years. "That's the thing about gossip and small towns. There are facts and then there's what the public chooses to believe. This case was tried and the verdict delivered not by the sheriff but by those out-of-town reporters— from New York, Philadelphia, Boston. They didn't listen to the evidence. They heard a lead or a juicy tidbit and then sensationalized it in their own version of the truth. You heard of yellow journalism, haven't you? These guys were as yellow as it gets. They wrote about the seamy side of the story. The juicier the story the better, because scandals sell newspapers. The papers had headlines about the big fight DeLancey and Kate had the night he died and Mrs. DeLancey's pointing her finger at Kate and saying she murdered her husband. Changed a lot of folks' minds about her. I always figured that was her intent from the beginning. Revenge, if you catch my meaning."

"Why did they attack only Kate?" Mia asked, feeling the injustice of the woman always being the target.

"Oh, they went after DeLancey, too. The newspapers portrayed him as some rich playboy and made Kate out to be some wild mountain woman. Cartoons showed him like some dandy, Kate in rawhide pants and her dark hair flying. Camilla DeLancey, with her gold hair and pale skin, was the ideal vision of the wronged, saintly wife.

"Found out a lot about DeLancey, though. They made him the poster boy for the rich, pampered society boy of the twenties brought low by the crash. He was richer than I'd ever imagined, and I'd imagined a lot. I don't know if you young people today can imagine the splendor of that time. The Vanderbilts and the Groves, folks like them lived that kind of life right here in Asheville. It's never been the same since. Not anywhere in this country."

Mr. Pace scrunched his face and waved his hand in dismissal. "I saw it for what it was. Idle gossip to take the people's minds off the real trouble they were in. Banks were closing everywhere. Those reporters didn't give a damn about DeLancey or if he was ever found. They sure didn't care about Kate Watkins or her reputation."

"So, DeLancey's body was never found?" Mia asked.

"Nope. No one ever found out what happened to that poor fellow. There were reports of him being spotted in California, but that was months after. Crazy stuff. Never proved." He shrugged and his whole body sagged with the effort.

"What convinced the sheriff to drop the case?"

"No evidence, plain and simple," Mr. Pace replied. "Again, you got to remember the times. Men who lost their money were checking out. We'd hear tell about how some men jumped out the window in New York.

There were eleven suicides by noon on Black Thursday. A lot of others slowly drank themselves to death. But some others just disappeared."

"What happened to them?"

"I mean they just left!" he said in exasperation. "They couldn't make it in the new life that fate dealt them and took off. It was the Depression and a lot of men became hobos, going from town to town, riding the trains, looking for handouts. A few of them were men keeping one step ahead of the insurance investigator looking for them. They just disappeared and no one ever saw or heard from them again."

"Do you think that's what happened to DeLancey?"

"Could be. I'm sure the sheriff considered that possibility. As for me? No. I knew him. I don't think he could've left Kate. His wife, yes. I didn't believe for a minute that hooey she said about him leaving Kate to return to her. She said that for spite. I never knew a man love a woman as much as DeLancey loved Kate."

"Then what do you think happened to him?"

He shrugged again, noncommittal. Mia got the sense he was keeping his own counsel on this topic.

"You don't think she killed him?"

Mr. Pace shook his head firmly. "No," he said quickly. "I knew Kate Watkins as well as any person and she would have killed herself before she killed him." He sighed. "But she couldn't do that, either."

Mia suddenly understood. "Because she was pregnant!"

"Right."

Mia reflected on Kate's silence in the courtroom, enduring in silence the slurs on her reputation and the accusations of DeLancey's wife. "Did she know throughout that she carried his child? Did DeLancey know?"

"I don't know. I would've married her," Mr. Pace admitted. "I was just a kid, barely out of college, but I truly loved her. I always had. But she wouldn't have me. She told me she wouldn't let me ruin my future by tying myself to her. She tried to be brave and spare my feelings, but I knew the real reason was because she still loved DeLancey." He wiped his eyes and seemed embarrassed. "Forgive an old man's tears. I never told anyone that before. Must be losing my mind in my old age."

Mia was deeply moved by his admission. She looked at Mr. Pace and tried to see him as a young man of twenty-three, stricken to see his dear friend and idol's reputation in tatters, loving her enough to harbor dreams of rescue. Chivalry was the noblest of sentiments, she thought.

She blinked and Phillip Pace aged again in her eyes, becoming the very old man who had given her his time generously. He was, she realized with sadness, the only person living today who knew the characters in this saga. He was looking off, seemingly preoccupied. His shoulders slumped and his eyelids drooped over opaque eyes. She was about to thank him and say good-bye when he surprised her with his final thoughts.

"Kate's silence was her own worst enemy. She never spoke up in her own defense. You hear me? Not once. She was silent throughout. I never understood it. The headlines read: *What's She Holding Back?* Soon, that's what the folks around here were asking as well. Eventually, they arrived at their own conclusions. The public believes what it wants to believe. That's the way it was back then. And the way it is now. The result of all the fumbling of the investigation and the later accusations was to start gossip, launch rumors, and spread suspicion thick as glue."

"And it stuck," Mia said in conclusion.

"Yes, young lady. It did."

"But she didn't kill him! He was a missing person."

"You can't prove she didn't kill him, just like you can't prove she did."

"What can be done now?"

"Missy, without a body, you're right back in nineteen twenty-nine." He indicated the rain streaking the library windows. "Rain and all. You don't have any evidence—you don't have any story."

There was a long silence in the room. Mia slumped back in her chair and let her notebook slip to her lap. Her hands lay still over it. She looked up at the ceiling, her lips pressed tightly together to stop any embarrassing tears. She'd spent months searching for answers to this puzzle. She'd interviewed people, researched the library and the newspaper microfilm, enlisted the help of others. And despite all her digging she really had uncovered nothing solid. Why had she been so drawn to it? She'd gone after this story despite Belle's request that she let it lie.

Mia closed her eyes as her heart sunk. Belle was on her way home now and she was going to be furious with her. She would find out that Mia had been snooping around, getting everyone talking about her grandmother. Mia put her hands to her eyes. She had been so sure she would find some evidence that would exonerate Kate Watkins once and for all. But she'd run out of time. She'd failed.

There was no proof that Kate Watkins did kill Theodore DeLancey. But neither was there evidence that she did not. All the parties involved were dead. The truth was buried with them.

Chapter Twenty-two

There are times when the storm clouds roll in
and lightning flashes above that you have to
use common sense and get out of the water.

—BELLE CARSON

Belle came in like a hurricane. Her eyes were
dark thunderclouds with lightning bolts flashing from them and Mia stiffened as she walked
into the cabin, feeling the cold gust of confrontation
whipping in with her.

Mia wanted to run for shelter. She'd been curled up
on the velvet sofa, sipping tea and reading *Reel Women*,
by Lyla Foggia, a book about heroines in the history of
fly-fishing. She'd heard the crunching of tires coming
up to the house and had thought it would be Stuart.
He often stopped by unexpectedly. She'd unwound
her long legs, set aside her book, and rose to her feet
to open the door.

Belle was polite when Mia welcomed her in but
her stiff smile, her cool, controlled voice, and her body
movements as she walked past her into the cabin were
all red-flag warnings of a storm coming. Mia stretched
her hands at her sides as she joined Belle in the center

of the room. Belle stood with her arms crossed against her chest. She wore khaki pants and an olive green shirt with her business logo emblazoned across her pocket. Her red hair was braided and looped tightly around her head. She didn't even look around the room and Mia felt a sting of disappointment that she hadn't noticed any of the improvements she had made. The rainy day made the room darker, so she went from lamp to lamp, turning on lights.

She returned to stand a few feet before Belle, clasping her hands tightly in front of her. "So, Belle," she said with forced cheer. "Did you see the gravel drive? And the walkway? What do you think?"

Belle appeared nonplussed to be asked. "They're nice," she said bluntly. "I thought you didn't have any money."

Mia was caught off guard by the ungracious response. Her mind stumbled for a reply. "Well, my husband—Charles—bought my half of the condo. That gave me some cash. I . . . I wanted to do something to say thank you to you for letting me stay here."

"You didn't have to do that."

"I know. I wanted to." She smiled again and lifted her arm to indicate the cabin. "How do you like the place? Looks good, don't you think?"

Belle remained stationary but she moved her head to look briefly around the room. Her gaze lingered on the watercolors, but she didn't comment.

Mia felt herself stiffen as she walked to the fireplace mantel, unnerved by Belle's fractious attitude. Picking up one of the hand-painted china plates, she said, "My sister came up and she took a sample of the china and silver back with her to Charleston. The china dates back to the twenties and the dealer believes it was done by a local artist. He's checking into it further, but it might well be valuable. And the silver! Belle, you have a treasure there. Estimates are coming in, but you stand to do very well."

She pressed on, talking nonstop. "The furniture is good, too. They'll need you to bring it into the shop, however, so they can inspect it to make certain that it's straight—unaltered or refinished," she amended. "Maddie says to tell you it's definitely worth the effort. Oh, and Belle," she added, drumming up enthusiasm, for Belle seemed uninterested and unimpressed with her report. "I saw a painting at the Watkins Lodge Manor House of your great-grandfather Robert Watkins. Right behind him, in the painting, is the armoire! So you have a record of its provenance." She paused as Belle's face grew tight. Her stomach clenched, realizing too late that she had opened the door to the storm.

"So, you went to Watkins Lodge?"

Mia nodded.

Belle ruminated, pursing her lips and choosing her words. "Mia, do you remember that conversation we had here, before I left for Scotland?"

Mia's stomach rose to her throat, choking her. She swallowed hard.

"I asked you at that time not to look into my grandmother's life. I thought I was very clear. Yet today, when I went to Watkins Mill, I picked up a copy of the *Gazette*. And what do you think I saw staring out at me on the front page? Something tells me you know." She made no effort to hide her scorn.

"And when I asked about it, I learned the newspaper has been running a series of the articles for weeks." She continued, her anger ringing in her words. "People couldn't stop talking about them. No matter where I went my grandmother's name was on everyone's lips. And all of them told me that it was you that started it all. *You*." She flung the last out accusingly.

"The articles are good," Mia said defensively. "They let people know who your grandmother really was. Not the monster they thought she was."

"You had no right to do this!" Belle exploded. "I'm so upset I can't even articulate what my feelings are, they're so raw. You came to me. You asked for my help and I took you in, let you stay in my cabin. I was there for you. And all I asked of you was to lay low. I didn't want my family business stirred up. You went behind my back while I was out of town and did exactly what you wanted to do. I can't begin to understand this invasion of privacy. I thought we were friends."

"I did it for you!"

"No, you didn't. You didn't do this for me. You did it for yourself."

Mia stepped back as though struck. This was so close to the truth she had to own it, but it also stirred her up enough to stop cowering and speak her mind.

"Yes, in time, I did," she replied. "You invited me

here to help me, I know that. I'm eternally grateful. When I arrived I had no idea who your grandmother was or any interest in her." Mia stretched out her arm indicating the cabin. "But here I was, surrounded by her things, and you have to admit, there are some incongruities here that make one wonder who your grandmother was. So I started looking around. I had no agenda."

"And then I asked you not to pursue it. Mia, that's a weak argument."

"You're right. But that was just the beginning. It grew and took on a life of its own. That same day you told me—I'll never forget it—you said that your grandmother was nothing but a shame to get past. I felt a shiver go through me, it was so cold. But you went on and told me your story and how your mother never sold this property. How she paid taxes on it, even though she didn't have much money. Do you remember what you said then? You said you were going to hang on to the property for a while until you could figure out why she did that."

"So you were going to find out the answer for me." Belle's sarcasm was a sharp swipe.

"Yes. And for me. I thought if I could uncover the truth, find Kate's true identity . . ."

Belle lost her patience. "You're looking for Kate's identity? Come on, Mia. Whose identity are you really looking for?"

Mia felt herself numbing up.

"I know your type," Belle said bitterly. "You try on

new identities like you try on a new outfit. You wanted to be a fly fisher and you put on the clothes and the gear and think that's all there is to it. This whole thing with Kate Watkins was just a new thing for you. Some sport. You didn't think about how all this would affect me. It was all for you."

The injustice of the accusation was so sharp Mia felt stabbed by it. The pain literally took her breath away and for a moment she couldn't speak. Then her own fury rooted in her core. It swirled up in a fulcrum and tore from her throat.

"That's a lie! Another lie! There are so many lies in this town everyone is blinded by them. You told me that fly-fishing is all about the senses. But you're so shut down when it comes to your family, you won't hear the truth, won't see it when it's standing smack in front of you. Look around you. This place is filled with clues to your grandmother and you won't even look at them. You want to throw them all out. Belle! Pay attention! The townspeople are not talking scandals about your grandmother. They're celebrating her. They aren't pointing fingers at you, they're opening their arms."

"Celebrating her? They call her a frigging murderer! They drove my mother out!"

"A long time ago, yes. The town chose to believe the scandals and lies about your grandmother rather than the truth. They were wrong to do so. But you condemned her, too, based on the stories your mother told you. I don't know why your mother left but it wasn't because she was mistreated. It's only her version of the truth."

"Who are you to tell me about my mother? Or my grandmother? They're not your family."

"She might not have been my grandmother but I've come to love her. And let's talk about family. Your mother didn't defend her. And you didn't, either." Her anger flung out the accusation with more intensity than she'd intended.

Belle bowed up. "No, I did not," she roared back. "Why would I? Do you think I haven't thought about what my mother went through? I had to live with those painful memories all of my life. Day in and day out. I don't want to go back there!"

"But you did come back!" Mia cried.

Belle's face contorted and she turned and walked to the window to look out. Mia could feel her lion's struggle for composure. It helped her regain her own.

"Both you and your mother turned your backs because of your hurt and your pride," she said gently. "Don't turn your back now. All families struggle with truth and lies. Family secrets. Your family is no different, only more public because of your family position. My mother told me there were three sides to every story. His, hers, and the truth. I was only trying to get to the truth."

Belle didn't reply.

"Give Kate a chance. She's your grandmother. She really was amazing. You don't know who she really was. And it's a shame. Because you're so much like her."

Belle spoke evenly, her back still to Mia. "You speak as if you knew her. You don't know her."

"Yes, I do. She's here. If you opened your heart you would know she is. She's crying out from the grave."

Belle turned around. Her face was cold but her dark eyes gleamed like volcanic glass as she flung out one final insult. "You're plumb crazy. Hearing voices—"

"I'm not hearing her voice," Mia replied. "I'm reading her voice."

The time had come. Mia took a breath and walked directly to the library shelf. She had to give up the diaries now. Belle needed them more than her. She opened Kate's diary and took out the sealed envelope from Mrs. Minor. Then lifting all three volumes she walked to Belle and handed the books to her.

"What're these?"

"Kate's diaries."

Belle looked stunned. "Where did you find them?"

"Here. In the bookshelf. They were always here. One is a diary written by Kate when she was a girl of twelve. The other is her fishing diary. It's a marvel and it spans over twenty years. When you read them, you'll hear her speaking to you. The last is her father's fishing diary. That's more perfunctory, but still, it was done by your great-grandfather, Reverend Walter Watkins."

Belle lifted the cover of the diary and perused the girlish script. As though the emotion was too strong, she snapped the cover shut and looked at Mia. Her dark gaze was unreadable.

Mia reached out. In her hand was the long envelope, curled at the edges and wrinkled from time stored in a box in Lucy Roosevelt's attic.

"And this is a letter that was written by your grandmother to your mother. It was never delivered. Old Mrs. Minor held on to it for years. Unfortunately, she died before she could give it to you. Her daughter asked me to do that, so . . ."

Belle looked at it, then stuck out her hand and took it. She looked dispassionately at the envelope. Then Mia saw a faint softening of her features as she ran her finger across her mother's name. She turned it over and saw that it was sealed.

"I'm surprised you didn't open it and read it."

It was a low blow, but not altogether undeserved. Mia didn't reply.

Belle put the letter into a diary, then looked up, her face impassive. "This doesn't change anything," she said. "It's time for you to go. There's a storm coming, but when it's passed, I'd appreciate it if you'd pack up and leave the cabin. Right away."

Mia felt like she'd been punched and was trying to catch her breath. A silence fell between the women. Mia looked at Belle and found her unrelenting.

"Thank you for the time you gave me," she said sincerely. "I'm sorry I caused you any pain. That was never my intent. I'll leave as soon as the storm is over."

"That would be good. I'd appreciate it if you left the key on the table."

Belle was gone. Once again, Mia was alone.

She went to the bookshelf and ran her hand along the empty space where the diaries had lain. Only an outline of dust remained on the shelf. Mia felt their absence like a pall. She looked around the room at the watercolors that were her visual diary of her time spent here. Each one spoke to how she showed up every day saying yes to the universe.

One by one, Mia removed the tacks and took the watercolors down. She stacked them neatly on the table. They resembled pages of a book, and she knew someday in the future she would look at them again and read the story there with fresh eyes. Looking around, she thought the cabin felt void, empty without them, as though she were already gone. She felt that Kate was gone, too. She no longer sensed her presence in the cabin. Mia wrapped arms around herself and walked from room to room. On the final round she stood in the middle of the cabin and called out, "Kate? Kate, are you here?" She looked at the empty space on the bookshelf, the unadorned wood walls, and the rain streaking the windows like tears.

"I'm sorry. I'm so sorry I failed you."

Mia grabbed her purse and went out the door, slamming it behind her. There was nothing here for her any longer.

Chapter Twenty-three

I cannot put into words all of the heartfelt gratitude that I have for making this one of the best experiences I've ever had—and it was not just about fishing! You brought meaning to everything we did and learned. Thank you seems so little to say for all that you gave me.

—TO BELLE CARSON
from a Casting for Recovery participant

Mia's small, dented car sliced through the wind to Watkins Lodge, where she found Stuart standing in the carriage house, bent over blueprints. The plastic sheeting was billowing loudly in the wind and a drill was humming, so she couldn't call his name. He looked up and saw her standing at the entrance, her slicker soaked and her strawberry blond hair plastered to her face. He abandoned his work to walk directly to her and wrap his arms around her.

"What's wrong?"

"I have to leave," she said against the soft corduroy, not knowing if he heard. She closed her eyes and buried her face in his chest. She was enveloped in the scents of sawdust and sweat.

He held her tight a moment, then lowered his cheek to her ear. "Wait here."

Letting go, he went to the other side of the room to speak to the man working with the drill. The high hum ceased and Mia saw Stuart's hands move in the air as he spoke. The other man looked up at her, then nodded. Stuart walked across the room to grab his Barbour jacket and keys off his work table, then returned to her side.

"Stuart, I didn't mean for you to stop work. I'll get some coffee at the inn and wait."

"It's OK. We're about done. We're just battening down the hatches for the storm."

"I'll wait," she said again.

He took her arm and said, "I don't want you to."

Like that first night they'd spent together, he curled his fingers in hers, then led her to his Jeep parked outside the carriage house. He swung open the door on her side, then sprinted around the front to hop in. The Jeep sprang to life and Stuart drove the narrow road around the lake to the handsome arts-and-crafts building he lived in.

"This damn rain is relentless," he shouted.

Mia could only nod and grip the door handle, feeling an ache of embarrassment that she'd come to him with her sad story.

When she stepped inside his condo she felt again the mild surprise that this earthy man lived in such a high-style, professionally decorated space. It always threw her, and she stood at the entrance with her dripping Gore-Tex jacket, unwilling to step across his polished hardwood floors.

"Come in," he said, stripping off his jacket.

"Your floors . . ."

"Oh, for God's sake, come in." He walked over to help her with her jacket. He held tight to it for a moment, looking at her, then turned to hang both jackets on a tree stand made to look like antlers, while she mopped her wet hair from her forehead.

"Why don't you go in the bathroom and dry off. I'll make a pot of coffee. I bought some especially for you. That rain has a cold bite and you look wet to the bone." He looked at his watch. "I could order us some dinner."

She shook her head. "No, thanks. I couldn't eat a thing. But coffee sounds great."

"OK. Go on, dry up. There's a robe hanging on the door. Help yourself."

She walked across the room, feeling undone by his kindness. She closed the bathroom door and leaned against it, wrapping her arms around herself and bending at the waist. She felt this wild shriek circling inside of her, gaining strength like the hurricane that was battering the coast.

"You like milk in your coffee?" he called.

She shivered then uncurled, taking a breath. "Yes, thanks," she called back, trying to force her quaking voice to sound normal. Methodically she stepped from her wet clothes and wrapped herself in the dry terry robe, tying it tight at the waist. The man's size large was far too big for her. The shoulder seams trailed down her shoulders, but she felt like she was wrapped in a warm blanket and curled the collar high up along her neck. She came out barefoot and with her damp hair brushed back from her face.

He handed her a steaming mug. "You look better."

She took a long sip of the hot coffee, feeling its warmth spread through her veins. Over the rim of the mug she saw him watching her.

"With your hair brushed back like that, the dimple on your chin is pronounced," he said. "You look like a little girl."

She reached up to touch the depression in her chin. "It's genetic. My mother had one."

Mia walked to the far end of the brown leather sofa while he clicked a button on the wall beside the fireplace to ignite the gas logs for an instant fire. She curled her legs underneath her in the cushions. Once more her gaze scanned the massive fireplace of river rock that climbed to the ceiling. Across from it the storm was streaking sheets of water against the tall plates of glass.

Stuart came to sit beside her. He stretched his long arm out across the back of the sofa and with the other took hold of her hand and drew her out from the corner to him. She set her mug of coffee down on the table and crawled into the nook of his arm. Once more she rested her chin against the soft corduroy.

"Now what's this about leaving?" he asked.

Stuart did exactly as she knew he would—he listened. Mia opened up the floodgates, telling him with unrestrained fury how angry she was at Belle for kicking her out, and more, how hurt that she'd do it with so little concern or feeling. Belle had always been a little intimidating, but at least Mia had thought she was fair. She carried on like the storm outside, blowing hard and without restraint. When she finished her story she sighed, spent. He stroked her hair from her temples, curling it around her ear. The rhythm of it was even, like his casts on the water, and she sighed.

She'd come mostly for this, she realized. The silence between them. She simply needed to be with her best friend.

They sat for a long while, listening to the storm. Mia's eyes grew heavy and her mind wandered. Where was Belle at this moment? Did *she* have someone to confide in? Or was she alone reading the letter from her grandmother? With her anger spent, Mia grew concerned for Belle and the confusion and pain she might be going through.

"I'm worried about Belle," she told Stuart.

"Do you know where she is?"

Mia shook her head. Her cheek rubbed against a button on his shirt.

"She's a resourceful woman. I'm sure she's OK."

Mia reached up to pick at the button and wondered if that were true. The tallest tree fell the hardest.

"What are you going to do now?" Stuart asked her.

"Go back, I guess."

He hesitated. "You could stay here in Watkins Mill."

"I don't have a job."

"You could get one. Mia . . ." He paused. "Why go back to Charleston?"

She slipped the button disk out from the buttonhole. "It's not just about getting a job." She moved her hand to the next button and played with it. "I've got to go back to Charleston. I have unfinished business I need to tend to. My divorce will be final soon. I have to move my things from my condo." Her fingers released the second button. "My doctors are in Charleston, too. I'm due for my checkup. And . . ." She opened a third button and slipped her hand underneath the fabric. She felt his chest rise as she ran her fingers through the fine hairs, letting her nails softly skim from shoulder to shoulder.

"I'm considering breast reconstruction."

"Why? You look beautiful the way you are."

She shifted her head to look up at him. His face was inches from hers. "You make me swoon. They should clone you. I know a thousand and one women who would steal you in a minute to hear the things you say to me."

"I'm serious, Mia. Why do it now? Why go under the knife again?"

She tucked her head back in the crook of his arm. "Because maybe I want to look normal again? Whatever that means. Every time I see that empty space on my chest I'm reminded of the cancer." She brought her lips to his chest and kissed the smooth skin. "Maybe I won't. I don't know. But that's a decision I'm ready now to face. I remember something you said to me a while ago. You were talking about my reading the diaries and you said I was stealing the fire. Remember?"

"Yes, vaguely."

"I remember it vividly because it was perfect. It's exactly what I was doing. Kate Watkins showed me the fire and while I was here she helped me conquer my fears. I know who I am better now than before the cancer. I know now that being a survivor means I've got my life back. I see things more clearly. I'm stronger and I know I can take care of myself. My time at the cabin—and with you—changed me."

"But . . ." He stopped and his hand stilled on her head.

Mia closed her eyes tight, hearing the subtle plea in his silence. He couldn't ask her to stay. He knew she had to go back. And yet, if he did ask, she might do it.

She raised herself from his shoulder and moved to sit cross-legged before him. They sat for a moment, eye to eye. He'd been working long hours and her loving eyes picked up signs of his fatigue: the chalkiness of his tan, the dark stubble on his jaw and upper lip, the faint shadows under his eyes.

Over the past few months she'd had a crush on this man. He'd made her body come alive again after a long hibernation. During the summer months she'd experienced the giddiness of romantic love, the gushes of a girl complete with self-doubt and uncertainty.

But this man sitting before her was real, not a summer fantasy. She knew with him the infatuation could grow, in seasons, to love. What could she bring to love? she asked herself. She had to settle issues within herself before she could answer that question. Mia had to go home for those answers.

She reached out to bring her hand to his jaw, cradling it. "Stuart . . ."

His hand flew to cover hers on his cheek. His eyes blazed. "I know."

She shivered and he grabbed her arm to pull her to him, not gentle this time but rough and full of need. Her body fell against him, feeling the pressure of his desire. Their lips pressed hard, hungry and probing. *Steal the fire* kept running through her mind as her fingers fumbled at the remaining buttons of his shirt. He spread open the terry robe, exposing her chest, bringing his mouth to her nipple. Her hands froze for a moment, stunned as always by the exposure. She bent her head and saw that his eyes were closed and he wasn't looking at scars or voids. She closed her own eyes and relinquished as his lips traveled up her neck, his breath warming her skin as he moved to claim her mouth. They knelt together, his hands clasping her head while he kissed her fiercely, possessively.

I could love this man, she thought, holding him tight. He leaned against her, pressing her back against the sofa. She felt the cold leather against her back, then looked up as he tore the shirt from his body and threw it on the floor. She watched him wrestle with his belt and send it flying, heard the hum of his zipper. She lifted her arms in welcome and felt the weight of him on her, flesh against bone, heart beating against heart.

When he entered her she closed her eyes and once again they were moving in perfect synchronicity, back and forth, slipping into a natural rhythm. When at last she arched to meet him she cried out from her depths. Then, with a shudder, she was released.

Tropical depression Nicholas was loaded with rain and headed straight for Asheville. The rain was falling at a steady rate from a slate gray sky as Mia made her way back to the cabin. The windshield wipers were clicking feverishly but couldn't keep up with the sheet of water on her windshield. Mia had to lean far forward and squint to see the slice of road through the water. Her hands gripped the wheel tight. Her little sedan cut through the rain on roads that were slippery with mud. It was like driving on ice. She crawled at a snail's pace around Route 9, then up the back mountain road that led to her cabin. Alongside the road, the river roared like a racing lion.

When she arrived at the cabin she was alarmed to see how high the river had risen. The pool was nearing the top of the banks and it was only a matter of hours before it overflowed them. She drove her car to the far back of the cabin, to the highest ground. She had to steer around the green truck parked beside the cabin. It was emblazoned with the sign *Brookside Guides*.

Her first thought was relief. Belle would know what to do if the river overflowed. Her second thought was, What is she doing here? She yanked up the parking brake, pulled her nylon hood over her head, and took a deep breath before pushing open the door. The wind attacked her, knocking her hood from her head and billowing her rain jacket. The rain slapped her face with stinging cold so she ducked her head as she ran along the stone path, mentally thanking Stuart for his help with the project. Around the walkway the ground was a sea of mud. Mia climbed the stairs and ducked under the porch roof. She caught her breath, then shook the rain from her jacket like a dog and mopped her face.

Mia hesitated, her hand on the door handle. She couldn't imagine what Belle was doing here again, so soon, with a storm raging. She'd said she could wait until after the storm to leave. Could she possibly be kicking her out now? There was nothing to do but face the music.

Pushing open the door, Mia stepped into the cabin. Belle was standing at the pedestal dining table, bent over her stack of watercolors. Her head bobbed up and she straightened the minute she heard Mia enter.

"You're back," Belle exclaimed.

"Yes," Mia replied guardedly. She took off her dripping jacket and set it on the tree stand by the door. Walking across the room she felt Belle's eyes on her. Her muddy boots thumped on the wood floors, and Mia was keenly aware of the trail of mud she would have to wash off later. She reached for the kitchen towel and began drying the rain from her face and hair. She looked over to Belle.

Belle appeared self-conscious. She was still in her rain slicker and her long braid fell like a damp rope down her back. "Were the roads bad?"

Mia nodded and set the towel on the counter. "Very. They're getting muddy." A sudden gust of wind rattled the windows, emphasizing the point.

"I better go," Belle said, and began walking toward her. "I just came by to give you this." She handed Mia an envelope.

Mia recognized the yellowed envelope immediately as Kate's letter. She took it in her hands and stared at Kate's flowing script. The name *Theodora* was smeared with drops of rain. She looked up with uncomprehending eyes. "Why are you giving this to me?"

"I thought you deserved to read it. And I was ashamed."

Mia's breath hitched as she saw Belle's implacable face crumple with grief. She wanted to reach out and hug her but Belle held herself so rigidly Mia sensed that to touch her would break the composure she was fighting for. Mia recalled the gentleness that Belle had shown her that day she found Mia sobbing in the car. She stepped closer to Belle.

Belle was still looking down as she spoke. "I spent the evening reading the diary. I couldn't stop," she said, looking up at Mia. "It was like listening to her voice." She released a short, pained laugh. "My grandmother's voice. After all these years. You can't know what that meant to me."

"I think I might."

Belle sighed and shook her head. A droplet of rain shaken from her hair trailed down her forehead. She swiped it away, then rubbed her eyes. "What I'm trying to say here is you were right. I didn't know who she was. Not at all. I wish I did. I would have liked to have known her."

"Belle, you're so much like her. Strong, independent, and a hell of a fly fisher. I'm sure she would've been so proud of you."

Belle's face softened. "You know what's weird about all this? My mother never taught me to fly-fish."

"Then how . . ."

"She had all this gear, so she must've fished a few times before she gave it up. So one day I just borrowed it and went to the river. The minute I cast onto the water I knew I was home."

"Genetics won out."

"Had to be."

"When did you learn your grandmother was a fly fisher?"

"Not till years later. I read her name in some article written about women fly fishers who paved the way in history. I about fainted and I never faint. I was teaching at the university at the time but my passion was fly-fishing. At Thanksgiving I came home and showed the article to my mother. I was prepared to go toe to toe with her on it, but it was one of the few times I heard pride in her voice when she spoke about her mother.

"Right then and there she told me about the Watkins family and this town. Not in a bad way, like before, but like some history lesson. Can you imagine how I felt? Me, who grew up not knowing I had any relatives at all to learn I came from some historical family a town was named after?"

"I imagine you were pretty proud."

"I was, but it took a while for me to accept the reality it was my family, not some people in a book somewhere. I wonder if that's how my mother felt, living as an outcast in a town that bore her name. She told me that when she was young and still lived here, she used to go to the Manor House and just stand outside it and stare. It was somebody's private home at that time and she wasn't welcome in. She used to dream what it might be like to live in it instead of the cabin. To be rich and respected in the town, instead of poor and rejected."

"That's such a sad image."

"She blamed Kate for their lot in life, like it was her fault the family lost their money." She shrugged. "Maybe it was, to some extent. She did gamble in the stock market with DeLancey. But they'd have likely lost the house anyway in the Depression. Who knows? My mother must've realized that in time because I didn't hear the old bitterness in her voice when she talked about Watkins Mill and Kate's success in the sport. It was a turning point for her."

Mia raked her hands through her damp hair, feeling

the tension ease. Dropping her hands she said, "You know, Belle, when you think about it, all of us—Kate, Theodora, you, me—we're all just women trying to do the best that we can in tough times."

Belle stared at the rain hitting the window and her eyes filled with tears. "All my grandmother asked for from her daughter in that letter was a little compassion."

"And what is compassion but sympathy for the suffering of another?"

"Doesn't seem like much. But it is." She slumped against the counter. "I feel so bad that my mother couldn't find compassion in her heart."

"You never know. Maybe she would have gone to see her mother but put it off, thinking she'd have time. Kate died so young. Theodora might have missed her chance."

"Regret is a bitter pill to swallow."

Mia nodded. "Maybe it wasn't bitterness she felt, but sorrow."

Belle sighed heavily. "I'll never know. She wasn't real good at talking. She kept a lot bottled up. Everything with my mother was a secret." She snorted. "If she'd have told me she was the illegitimate daughter of some foreign prince, I'd have believed her."

"Well," Mia said with a crooked grin. "She sort of *was* considered that in this town."

They both chuckled at that.

"So I reckon you nailed it," Belle conceded. "Somewhere in my subconscious, that's why I came back here. To learn where I came from." She reached out to indicate the letter in Mia's hands. "I came to deliver this letter to you because you deserve to read it, Mia. I think you'll find your answer in there. I know I did."

Mia looked at the letter with warring emotions. "I don't know if I should. You were right, too. I took this thing too far."

"Aw, go ahead," Belle said. "You can't read a story and not find out the ending." She smiled and pushed herself from the counter. "I gotta go if I'm going to get out. This storm is a hellion." She came forward to wrap her arms around Mia in a firm hug. "Listen, you be careful up here. You're still on my watch."

Mia's tension flowed from her as she hugged Belle in return. "I'm glad at least this storm is over."

"Me, too." Belle walked across the room, zipping up her jacket and flipping her hood over her head. She paused before opening the door to the storm. Belle was tall and lean and the hood covered her red hair, so only her obsidian eyes shone from beneath it as she took a final sweep around the cabin. Lightning flashed outside, and in that moment Mia saw Kate come alive in her granddaughter.

"She is here, you know," Belle said to her. "I felt it, too."

By midnight, the storm bore down in full fury. Mia went from window to window double-checking the locks and putting towels where water leaked through the seals.

The little cabin was well built and held firm against the battering wind, but the roof leaked in the add-on kitchen, so she placed two buckets beneath a steady drip of water.

There was nothing left for her to do but wait it out. The electricity had gone out hours before. She lit a strong fire and made a picnic dinner of cheese and bread and carried it and a bottle of red wine to sit on the velvet sofa. Wrapping herself in a blanket, she brought Kate's letter close. Her fingers trembled with anticipation as she stared at the envelope.

She'd read young Kate's words and come to love her. But these were the words of Kate as a woman nearing the end of her life. What would she have to say in these pages? Mia ran her hand across the writing on the envelope. Did she want her image of the brave, confident, headstrong girl to be tarnished by the ramblings of a defeated woman? What changes had a tumultuous forty years wrought on the young girl's optimism?

A thunderous cracking of branches sounded from outside as another tree lost its footing in the wet earth and toppled over. Mia jumped at the crashing thud not far from the house. She tightened the blanket around her shoulders. Inside the cabin she felt safe. Yet she also sensed Kate again. Her presence was very strong, almost tangible in the close smoke from the fire.

Mia looked again at the envelope in her hands. Belle had said Kate asked for compassion in this letter. Kate wasn't some goddess on a pedestal, some one-sided heroine in a tragic story. She had been a real, flesh-and-blood woman with strengths, weaknesses, and flaws, like anyone else. Who was she to deny her that compassion?

Mia settled back against the cushions and tugged the paper from the envelope. She smoothed out the folds from the paper, tilted it to the rosy light of the fire, and began to read.

Chapter Twenty-four

November 9, 1952
Dear Theodora,

Darling child, I am writing to you across the miles praying that, wherever you may be, you are safe and warm and content. I am sitting by the fire on the velvet sofa. Do you remember how you loved to cuddle up together on it when you were a child? The wind is whistling, rattling the windows as a cold front moves in. Fall has come to paint the trees and the trout are frisky in the cold waters. If you should come to Watkins Cove today you'd see that nothing much has changed since you left. Except, perhaps, me. I am older now. Gray streaks my hair like the shadows across the river as I reach the sunset of my life.

My dearest Theo, you were always my sunshine. Since you've left, my life has been filled with darkness. I miss you terribly and long to see your face. In the fullness of time I've come to understand why you left. Once the hurt passed and my heart healed I was able to see with a mother's eye that you left Watkins Cove—not me. I know

how you longed for town life. I was not deaf all
those years to your pleas to leave. I didn't, perhaps,
appreciate your desperation. Nor do I understand
why you feel the need to cut off all contact with
me. Perhaps now, as a grown woman with a child
of your own, you, too, can finally release the hurt
and comprehend the many reasons why I could
not leave this place of refuge.

News of my darling grandchild reached
me—and such news! Geraldine Rodale came to
tell me that you had a daughter and named her
Isobel after your grandmother. Thank you for
asking her to let me know. I planted a tree for dear
Belle and whisper hello to her every time I pass it.
It is a magnolia because I remember that was your
favorite tree. It sits prettily beside the river where
you and I used to fish. I pray that someday you will
bring my granddaughter to Watkins Cove to meet
her grandmother. I would so love to share with my
granddaughter my love of fly-fishing. She carries in
her a long, proud legacy of fly fishers. Oh, Theo, I
have so much I'd love to teach her!

It is in this spirit that I write to you tonight.
Not to ask for forgiveness but for understanding.
For with understanding comes compassion. So
often you asked me why I chose to live at Watkins
Cove and why I would never leave. I was asked
countless times why I kept my silence after
DeLancey's disappearance. It is my intention to
explain that to you in this letter. To once and for

all purge myself of the memories that have both
sustained and haunted me these many years.

I hardly know where to begin. "Begin at the
beginning," my father used to tell me. Oh Theo,
what is the genesis of this story?

It must begin with Love.

I have loved and been loved in my life, Theo.
What more can anyone hope for? A woman does
not need to live among many people to be content.
She needs but one true companion, one soul mate
with whom to share this long journey we call life. I
have known one great love and it has sustained me
through the years.

My youth was filled with great moments. Much
has been said about my achievements in the sport of
fly-fishing. In my twenties the town that now scorns
me celebrated my fame. I was called confident,
headstrong, determined—descriptions which, in
my time, were usually attributed to a man. Women
before me have made great advancements in the
sport and women after me will continue, ending
once and for all the misconception that women do
not fish. I admit, one of my greatest pleasures in life
was breaking down that male barrier. If life were a
river, men would shuttle women off to fish the riffles
of small streams. I've always sought the deeper, fast-
moving water.

I tell you this so you know who your mother
was the day she met your father.

From the moment I first locked gazes with

Theodore DeLancey I felt the universe move into alignment. It was not something I'd planned or even wished for. I've come to accept it was our fate. Or, perhaps, it was ill fated. I was caught in the current and I surrendered to it, body and soul.

Theo, I loved your father with an all-consuming love. And he loved me equally. This is the bedrock of our story and the seed of your conception. There is no shame in love.

There are, however, regrets.

We were discreet. I knew he was married and committed to his wife and children. I never sought to disrupt that sacred union. Nor did I care a whit for his fortune. He came to Watkins Cove in the spring and fall and I never demanded more. We might have gone on for years in this manner but fate had other plans. First was the stock market crash of 1929. DeLancey had speculated with his fortune, and with mine. We gambled and lost. Second was you.

Teddy came to see me one night early in November. Outside a storm was raging, and inside Teddy raged too. I'd never seen a man so desperate. His marriage was a facade. He had nothing to go back to. He kept telling me again and again how much he loved me. How I was his life. Despite his pain, I confess I was overjoyed.

I cared nothing about my lost fortune or his. Quite the contrary, I was thankful for the stock market crash. I thought it freed him from his obligations. I had girlish dreams that we'd be happy

living a simpler life together at Watkins Cove. Even
as I write these words the old woman of experience
in me shakes her head at the folly of innocence. But
forgive my naïveté. I was pregnant, emotional, and
prone to mood swings. I chose not to tell him that
night of my pregnancy. He was too indisposed.

The following night we ate dinner at the inn.
The storm continued and the road to the cabin
grew dangerous. DeLancey secured a room at the
inn and I planned to go home to the Manor House.
I was filled with my news and waiting for the best
moment to tell him. During that dinner DeLancey
told me, with a calm that was chilling, that he could
not live the life that now lay before him. I could not
grasp his meaning until he held my hand and called
me his Francesca. The blood drained from my face.
Instinctively my hand went to my belly.

Looking at DeLancey that evening, his eyes
wet with tears and his face slack with emotion and
drink, I fully understood that I was stronger than
he was. I was repelled that he would rather end his
life than give up the lifestyle he'd lived in New York.
And I was so very hurt and angry that he could care
so little for me—for us. I rose from my seat and
threw my locket at him, ending it. I said words to
him that to this day fill me with shame.

I left the restaurant alone. Had I known how
violent the storm would get, I might have returned
to the Manor House. That night, however, I was
bereft. My one thought was to return to the cabin.

It was a miracle that I made it safely. The roads were more stream than road and there were many times my wheels slid perilously in the mud.

That night was the worst night of my life. The heavens unleashed their fury. The devils howled and the angels wept. Trees bent to the wind and branches banged against the cabin like fists. I huddled on the sofa, struggling to keep the fire lit, and waited for DeLancey. Despite everything, I prayed he would come to his senses and return to me. I kept vigil for him all night, rehashing every line spoken at that horrid dinner. I prayed as I'd never prayed before.

Then, very late in the night, the storm abated. The quiet was intense in contrast to the roar of the storm. Of a sudden, I had the overwhelming sensation that DeLancey was with me. It was so strong that I stood up and called his name. As God is my witness, DeLancey's presence was in the room with me. I shuddered as a cold breeze went through me and the room was filled with his scent. I knew it so well—sandalwood and lime. I was cold and went to stand by the fire's warmth. A pale light glimmered not six feet away from me. It was not the flickering light of the fire or the flash of lightning from outside. Nor was it a ghost. But I knew without doubt it was him—my DeLancey—circling near, saying good-bye.

The storm returned in full fury and my howls matched the wind. I knew in my heart that he was dead. I threw myself upon the sofa and cried till the storm passed and there were no more tears left in me to shed.

The following morning I rose early. In the light of day I doubted what I'd seen the night before. I got in my car, desperate to see him. I drove only partway to town when I saw that the road had been destroyed by a mudslide. It was three days before I could make it down the mountain to town.

I never saw my DeLancey again. I stayed in my room for days, eating only out of obligation to my child. Some time later Sheriff Dodds paid me a visit and informed me that Mrs. DeLancey had come to town in search of her husband. She was making some dangerous charges and he hoped I could set her straight.

Theodora, I have kept my silence for years not to be obstinate or headstrong, nor to snub the town or his family. Quite the contrary. My silence was to protect DeLancey and his family. I believe Theodore DeLancey, your father, committed suicide the night of November 9, 1929. He died and his soul came to me to ask my forgiveness. It is I who beg his forgiveness. I knew I was stronger and I blame myself for not helping him through his depression. If I had but shown compassion and not scorn, perhaps he would not have felt so desperate. I believe he would have found his path again, even if that path led away from me. That terrible night he was holding tight to the one thread that held him to this earth—our love—and I threw it back at him.

My anger and my pride killed him. My shame and my guilt silenced me.

I vowed I would not destroy his family's faith in him nor his reputation. Had I voiced my belief that he had committed suicide the insurance company would not award his family the money they so desperately needed.

My father alone knew the stand I was taking and he supported me in this as in all things. My dear darling father … I fear he gave the last of his strength to me, for he died soon after the horrid investigation trampled the proud Watkins name, sullying it forever. I shall carry the burden of that disgrace to my grave.

Before he died, my father held my hand and told me how he, too, had been devastated after my mother died. He couldn't look at anyone or anything that reminded him of her. Not even his infant daughter. He told me how at his lowest point he'd turned to a favorite psalm—Psalm 23. Reading it, he said, was like hearing the voice of God.

The Lord is my Shepherd; I shall not want
He maketh me to lie down in green pastures:
He leadeth me beside the still waters.
He restoreth my soul.

"Kate, go to the cabin," he told me. "Go lie beside still waters. Listen to the river. It will bring you peace."

I've always trusted my father's advice. I packed up a few cherished treasures, negotiated to keep Watkins Cove, and moved from the Manor House. I knew I could never return so I never looked back.

That, Theodora, is my story. It is not a sad one. Tragic, perhaps, but not without hope. My love perseveres. You are the living symbol of our love. And now dear Belle lives on as well.

The river calls to me now. I hear her voice and soon the time will come when I will lie down in her embrace and she will carry me to join DeLancey and my father and my mother and Lowrance and all who have gone before me into the current. I will do as I've always done. I will follow the river home.

If you should choose not to visit me, or if something should keep you away, I understand silence better than most. The bond between mother and daughter can never be broken. Love is stronger than death. So if I should pass before I see you again, please know that I will be standing in the river of time, waiting with open arms for you to join me, dear, darling Theodora.

With greatest love,
Kate

Chapter Twenty-five

A hatch is a cycle in which insects emerge
from eggs and swim to the surface to dance
on top of the water. They fly up to swarm in a
mating frenzy, then drop eggs over the water.
During each stage of the dance the fish join
in to feed. It is the circular dance of nature,
the complete cycle, as old as the river.

—KATE WATKINS'S FISHING DIARY

The air held that astonishing freshness of a
morning after a storm. Mia thought it was as
though God took the mountain, gave it a good
washing, shook it out, then set it out to dry in the sun.
The trees stood taller, the leaves of shrubs and plants
rose higher as though in thanks, and the birds were
chirping and jumping from branch to branch with
relief as much as joy.

Around the cove, broken branches and leaves littered the ground like confetti. The river had overflowed
its banks to within feet of the house. There was a tangy
odor in the air of drenched and soggy soil. Mia was
relieved that she'd parked her car on the high ground

in back of the cabin—until she'd seen the tree that had fallen on it.

The memory of the thunderous cracking and falling played again in her mind and in one breath she thanked God that the tree hadn't fallen on the cabin. Then, in her next, she cursed her bad luck while she pulled branches and leaves aside to check the damage to her car. Her little sedan sat nestled in a blanket of green but was miraculously spared serious damage. Only the tips of the maple cloaked her car, scratching it at best, denting it at worst. As long as it could drive, she thought as she began tugging away broken branches.

The echo of someone calling her name distracted her. Turning her head she saw a man hiking up the road in a red baseball cap and a black backpack. As he drew near she recognized his long, lanky form.

"Stuart!" she called, waving her hand in an arc over her head. She trotted down the driveway and waited at the edge of the gravel.

He trudged through the sea of mud and water, his blue eyes blazing and fixed on her. When he reached her side he swooped low to gather her in his arms, press her tight against him, and kiss her profoundly.

Mia wrapped her arms around the breadth of his shoulders. He smelled of soap and sweat, tangy mud and green leaves. His lips were as cool as the morning when they touched hers, but heated with the lingering kiss. When he released her he leaned back and cupped her face in his hands and his gaze devoured her for a long minute.

"What?" she asked breathlessly.

"Last night I wasn't sure I'd see this face again," he said. "If you don't mind, I'm enjoying the view."

"Stuart, I . . ."

"Wait. And listen. I'm going to stay in Watkins Cove. I've made up my mind. I know you've got to go back to Charleston, but not for forever. I'm going to be here waiting for you to come back. Do you hear me?"

Mia's smile trembled as she stepped back, trying to take it all in. "Yes."

"Good." His face relaxed and he wrapped an arm around her shoulders, then looked around the cabin. "Looks like the cabin held up OK. I'd feared the worst."

"How bad was the storm out there?"

He looked incredulous. "You couldn't tell?"

"Well, yes, sure, but this cove protects the cabin from the worst of it."

"Nicholas packed a punch. They're saying it dumped between twelve and sixteen inches of rainfall over twenty-four hours and triggered at least twenty isolated landslides. Highways are blocked, houses are damaged or destroyed. And you know that bit of road with the overlook you're so fond of?"

Mia nodded her head.

"Gone."

She blinked, not sure she understood. "Gone?"

"Yep. The whole side of road slid right off the mountain. If you were sitting there on that bench, you'd be in Tennessee about now."

"Oh, no," she said with a soft moan. "I loved that little spot."

"It's a goner. That's why I hiked over the ridge from Watkins Lodge. It's the only way in or out of the cove. The state bulldozers are already clearing up the mud so they can open up the road and that's the only road that leads to Watkins Cove. It could be days before you can drive out of here."

"You can say that again." She looked over her shoulder and lifted her arm toward her car buried under green. Bits of silver peeked out from the dense green.

Stuart released a sinking whistle as he walked toward the car. He poked through and lifted branches to get a better look at the damage. They flung back with a shudder when he released them. He wiped his palms on his shorts. "You might've gotten off lucky. Looks like a good chainsaw and some muscle will set things to right. We can come back with tools when the road is clear. But for now, mountain girl . . ." He curled his fingers with hers. "Pack up a few essentials in a backpack and put on your boots. It's going to be a muddy hike."

Hours later they cleaned up and headed to Shaffer's for coffee and news. Main Street was filled with locals milling about and Mia assumed they were all in town to pick up supplies at Rodale's Grocery and Clark's Hardware after the storm. Everywhere, she saw signs of damage. Yellow tape blocked off the western edge of Route 9 that led to the overlook and Watkins Cove. A high-pitched hum contrasting with the low growl of engines rent the usual peace of the small town as bulldozers, dump trucks, and other state machinery worked at clearing the roads. Even state troopers had their lights flashing as they blocked traffic from approaching.

Shaffer's was full of townspeople talking excitedly. A long line traveled all the way to the door. Becky was ringing the register while Katherine and even Skipper manned the busy pastry counter. Mia and Stuart took a place in line, and she heard snippets of conversation from the people in the shop as they moved slowly forward. "Lost that purty maple in my backyard." "I prayed to Jesus all night long." "I was a-scared, all right. The river, it come lappin' at our door." When she heard someone say something about "bones," she turned her head.

She felt Stuart's hand on her back and he bent to say in her ear, "Look back there. Your friends are waving."

Mia looked over to where he was pointing and saw Phyllis Pace and Nada Turner waving her over. Nada jumped up to snatch two spare chairs from empty tables and bring them over to their small circular one. Mia smiled and nodded in acknowledgment, thinking as she did so that it was the first time she'd heard these women described as "friends."

When she finally got to the counter she heard Becky call, "Mornin', Mia! Sure is good to see you this morning. We were worried the river was going to wash that cabin away like it did the road."

"Nope. Still here," she called back. She was glad

to see Becky so full of energy. "Sure is busy this morning."

Skipper came up and smiled his hello. "It's all the excitement."

"About the road?" Stuart asked from behind her.

Skipper looked surprised that they hadn't heard. "No. About the bones!"

"What bones?" Mia asked.

From the table in the back Mia heard Nada call out, "Quit holding up the line. Come on back here and we'll fill you in."

Mia looked behind her with a guilty eye to see a long line waiting for a chance to grab a coffee and a pastry. *Sorry,* she mouthed, and the people smiled kindly in response. Lennie came in with a fresh tray of hot, iced cinnamon buns, and her knees almost melted when she caught their sweet scent. She ordered two with two large coffees and slapped bills on the counter before Stuart could grab his wallet.

"It's standard pay for rescues," she told him as she snapped her wallet shut.

They carried their buns and coffee to the table and squeezed into the tight space. Stuart's jeans rubbed against hers under the table.

"What's this about bones?" Mia asked.

Nada and Phyllis leaned over the table, their eyes bright with excitement.

"They found bones on Route Nine while they were clearing the mud," Nada reported. "That's why the police are involved."

"Do they know whose they are?" Stuart asked.

"No, it's too early for an ID," she replied. "They're still searching. They'll bring them to the coroner's office once they've finished. Right now they're picking through the mud to make sure they get them all and to see if they can find anything that will help identify who it is. You know, like a driver's license, bits of clothing, that sort of thing."

"Do they have any suspicions?" asked Stuart.

"No, not yet."

"How old are they?" Mia asked as the ghost of an idea began to take shape in her mind.

"Can't tell. Pretty old. There's only bones there, if you know what I mean."

Mia mulled this over as she sat back in the chair. She stared down at her coffee while her mind went over the letter she'd read from Kate to Theodora. She must have read the letter a dozen times and with each read she heard Kate's voice as though she were speaking to her in the same room. There was such love and compassion in her words, especially for the granddaughter she'd never met. How could Belle not have been overcome by reading it?

There were also specific descriptions in her letter of the night DeLancey disappeared. Or, rather, died, as Kate believed. Mia had read the letter so many times she could recite it verbatim. *I drove only partway to town when I saw that the road had been destroyed by a mudslide.*

What if Kate were wrong about DeLancey? she wondered with mounting excitement. What if for all those years she'd thought he'd died by his own hand, when, in truth, it had been an act of God?

"Mia?" Stuart asked, drawing her attention.

Mia startled, brought back to the conversation. "Oh, sorry, I was just . . ." She sat forward. If she needed a support team right now, the two women at the table were her best bets. "Girls," she said, feeling adrenaline pumping in her veins. "This is really important. Can anyone get their hands on a geological survey that goes back to nineteen twenty-nine?"

Nada narrowed her eyes. "That's easy enough. What's going on in that brain of yours?"

Phyllis tapped her chin with speculation. "I know where she's headed. You think those bones could be DeLancey's?"

"Yes," Mia declared.

"Mia," Phyllis said with slight exasperation. "This time I think you're stretching too far."

Mia leaned closer and kept her voice low. "Huddle up."

The two women raised their brows but brought their heads closer. Stuart brought his ear close as well.

"Cone of silence, OK?" she asked. The women's eyes gleamed as they nodded. Stuart smirked. "Last night I read a letter that Kate Watkins wrote to Theodora."

"Where'd you get that?" Phyllis exclaimed.

"Oh hush, Phyllis," Nada whispered heatedly. "Ask your questions later. Go on," she said to Mia, as alert as a hunting dog pointing at the brush.

"It's no secret," Mia answered. "Don't you remember the letter that Lucy Roosevelt gave me for Belle?" She saw Phyllis frown in stern disapproval. Mia quickly shook her head to dispel her suspicions. "No, I didn't open it. I gave it to Belle. Yesterday Belle gave it back to me to read."

"What did it say?" Nada asked.

"I'll let Belle decide how much to share, but what's to the point today is that Kate wrote about the night DeLancey disappeared." She heard the intake of breath at the table. "She wrote that there was a terrible storm that night. I remembered that your daddy, Mr. Pace, remarked on the same thing," she added to Phyllis. "How it rained like the Lord's flood that whole week." She leaned closer, her whisper hoarse with excitement as she spoke each word with deliberation. "In the letter, Kate wrote that the road was washed away and that she was stuck in the cabin for three days before she could get to town."

Nada drew back. "And you're wondering if a mudslide took away Route Nine that night."

"Right," she replied. "The only road from town to Watkins Cove is Route Nine. All we know is DeLancey disappeared the night of November ninth, nineteen twenty-nine."

"But they found bones," Stuart argued. "Not a car."

"But he didn't have a car," Nada remarked. "He took the train in."

"He wouldn't walk to Watkins Cove," he said.

"The fact is, he was drunk and upset when he disappeared," added Mia. "Let's just say his judgment was impaired. What if he was desperate and didn't have a car so he just started walking back to Kate?"

"And the poor guy was caught in a mudslide." Nada shook her head. "I can believe it."

"Yes, but will the sheriff?" asked Phyllis.

Nada rose from the table like a shot.

"Where are you going?" Mia asked, surprised.

"*We're* going to see the sheriff. He'll need to know all this. But we need to lay it all down for him nice and clear. First we'll go to the *Gazette* and gather up all those articles we dug up. And Phyllis, you get that geological survey. You can do it if anyone can."

Phyllis jotted down the date, her brow knit with concentration. "I'll get right on it and call you the minute I find anything out." She looked up and her usually skeptical eyes were wide with hope. "Oh, Nada, do you think this might be it? An answer, after all these years . . ."

Mia reached Belle by phone and gave her a brief account of their conclusions and told her of their plan to go to the sheriff. After a stunned silence Belle replied, "I'll meet you there. I'm on my way."

Sheriff Rusty Rhodes was an affable man. He was average height and build with an all-American face and red hair that gave him his nickname. He had an easy manner and good looks that inspired confidence. Mia figured he was likely the dreamboat of the local high school in his time. His belly was a little paunchy now, and his cheeks fleshy in his middle years, but he still charmed when he smiled, as he did now.

"Well, that's an interesting story," he told the assembled group after they'd told him of their suspicions that the bones found might be those of Mr. Theodore DeLancey. Mia stood by Nada in front of the sheriff's broad wood desk. Behind her, Stuart, Phyllis, and Becky formed a wall of support.

"It's no story," Nada snapped back, all six feet of her straightening in offense. She prided herself on being a top-notch reporter, and the last thing she tolerated was anyone doubting her facts. "Theodore DeLancey of New York was declared missing by this very office in November of nineteen twenty-nine. His body was never found. We've got here a copy of a geological survey that shows Route Nine had a mudslide the very night DeLancey disappeared."

"Here it is," Phyllis said as she stepped forward with the papers in hand. She set them on the sheriff's desk with a flourish.

"Thank you, Miss Pace," Sheriff Rhodes said, taking them in his hands. He put on his glasses and studied them, then raised his eyes over his lenses speculatively. "So, you think this here DeLancey fella was taking a stroll along Route Nine that night? In the pouring rain?"

"We have reason to believe he was on his way to Watkins Cove," Mia added.

He squinted, as if trying to place her, then removed his glasses. "Are you referring to that story about ol' Kate Watkins and the killing at the cabin?" He shook his head ruefully. "That's an old chestnut."

Mia snapped her mouth shut in frustration. Sheriff Rhodes was a parody of Sheriff Andy of Mayberry trying to talk sense to the poor, confused townsfolk.

"You listen to me," Phyllis Pace said sharply, pointing a finger at the sheriff. "I remember you running naked in your mother's yard, so don't you dare talk to me in that patronizing tone of voice."

Mia turned her head to see Stuart's eyes twinkling.

Phyllis puffed up and Mia could well imagine high school boys cowering under that steely gaze. "You see before you representatives of some of this town's oldest and proudest families. Nada Turner is the editor and publisher of our newspaper. We speak for the town when we say that we demand an answer to this scandal that has clouded our city, spawned malicious gossip, and smeared the reputation of the Watkins family for two generations. I call on you to do your duty, as the town failed to do in nineteen twenty-nine. If this *is* the body of Theodore DeLancey, then this town has the right to know. The Watkins family has the right to know. And frankly, Sheriff, *I* want to know. This *story*, as you put it, must be put to rest at last."

Mia felt a stirring of pride for Phyllis. Sheriff Rhodes appeared chastened, though Mia knew as a politician, he was wise enough to see which way the wind would turn if he ignored this request.

"Well, now, Miss Pace," he began in a conciliatory tone. He looked up to include the group. "Ladies. Sir. This isn't the kind of thing we can get an answer for right away. See, here's how it goes. We've got searchers out there this very minute working in difficult terrain. Some of them guys are in mud knee-high to chest-high in spots. We're picking through to find not just bones, but shoes, a jacket, and any other clothing or jewelry that could have been stripped off with the mud as it tumbled down the canyon. Now that alone takes time."

Mia heard a door open and close, felt the stir of air rustle through the room.

"Next the bones are cleaned and assigned an identification number," the sheriff continued. "Then the victim's teeth are X-rayed, any clothing and jewelry carefully packed away, and a sample of his DNA taken.

"But you get into another problem now. What do you compare this DNA to? In a crime scene you've got DNA at the scene and a suspect you're trying to link the crime to. The best way to make an ID with DNA is to have living blood relatives, a parent or a child, to come forward and offer to have their DNA tested and compared. It's basically like doing a paternity test."

He leaned forward in his squeaky chair and pointed his index finger on the desk. "Now, see, here's the stick-ler as I see it. Supposing we get the DNA. Where are we going to get the DNA sample to match it with?" He spread open his palms. "Where's his family today?"

"Here."

All heads turned to the rear of the room, where Belle stood by the door. She was dressed in khakis and a coral-colored fishing shirt that complemented her red hair. She walked forward to the sheriff's desk and stuck out her hand.

"My name is Belle Carson. Belle Watkins Carson. If that body is Theodore DeLancey, then he's my grandfather."

Chapter Twenty-six

The Gazette
September 13, 2007
OLD SCANDAL LAID TO REST

Today the remains of Theodore DeLancey were laid to rest, ending nearly eighty years of speculation and scandal.

DeLancey was first reported missing in 1929 by his wife, Camilla DeLancey, now deceased. After a brief and some say flawed investigation, the sheriff officially declared Theodore DeLancey a missing person. Later, the state of New York, where his family resided, declared him legally dead. Unfounded and wild rumors and accusations concerning the nature of Mr. DeLancey's death plagued noted fly fisherwoman Miss Katherine Watkins (Kate) for the remainder of her life. Miss Watkins had frequently served as Mr. DeLancey's fly-fishing guide.

The discovery of bones at a mudslide on Route 9 this week was a huge break in this unsolved mystery. Following confirmation of DNA tests with his granddaughter, Belle Watkins Carson, the coroner declared DeLancey's death accidental.

With the burial of Theodore DeLancey the town of Watkins Mill will, at long last, lay an old scandal to rest.

The Gazette
September 15, 2007
TOWN TIDBITS

The first meeting of the Reel Women Fly-Fishing Club will be held at the Public Library on Thursday, Sept. 15, at 7 p.m. Ms. Belle Carson will give an overview of the sport and provide a casting demonstration. The meeting is open to all interested in joining.

The Gazette
October 1, 2007
Nada Turner, Editor in Chief
EDITORIAL

This will be the last editorial I write for the *Gazette*. With the recent developments concerning one of our town's most famous citizens, Kate Watkins, I can now retire a happy editor.

I've been a reporter for this paper for 20 years and an editor for another 25. One of my first assignments was to cover the death of Kate Watkins. I had the honor of writing her obituary and as a young woman I was struck with her long list of accomplishments in the sport of fly-fishing, not the least of which was helping to break down the barriers against women in the sport.

Up until that point I'd only known of Kate Watkins from the rumors and gossip that had flown about town for years like the dirt that blows off a mountain on a windy day. You know what the rumors were. I'll not credit them by printing them in this newspaper again.

At long last that unfair and unfounded scandal that plagued Kate Watkins and her family has once and for all been silenced. Truly, the truth set her free.

As the editor of the paper that helped fuel the scandal by its reporting of the investigation into the disappearance of Theodore DeLancey in 1929, I would like to offer an apology to Miss Kate Watkins and her family. In an effort to help restore her proud name in our community, my last act as editor will be to run a series of articles on the life and accomplishments of our town's favorite daughter beginning Monday, October 8.

Further, as the chairperson of the Watkins Mill Historical Society, I shall propose the town erect a statue in her honor as a testament to the legacy of Kate Watkins—and women—in the sport she loved so well—fly-fishing.

See you on the river—I'm going fishing!

Chapter Twenty-seven

The Gazette
October 1928
Kate Watkins, "On the Fly"

In autumn the heat of summer is past and the faithful angler is rewarded with a cornucopia of color in the mountains. Bits of reddish orange and bright yellow dot the rivers that run low but steady. It is the spawning season and the trout get showy as they seek a mate. Brown trout are hefty and their vibrant red spots gleam on their shiny, olive brown courting suits.

As another fly-fishing season draws to an end, I sometimes abandon my rod and walk my beloved hills to search out waterfalls and color instead of trout. I roam the valleys with the ghosts of loved ones, harvesting memories for the long winter ahead. It restores my soul.

I t was a beautiful autumn. Everyone in Watkins Mill thought it might be the prettiest fall in years. Fall was always Mia's favorite season. It was an introspective time of year when her thoughts turned inward. She took long walks, her chest expanding at the wonder of color and treasuring each warm moment before winter descended with its cold winds to chase her back indoors.

Autumn had come early and quick this year. Seemingly overnight the trees in the cove exploded in color, replacing the dense green with a tapestry of ochre, rust, tawny orange, and vivid yellow. Birds migrated overhead but the Carolina wren outside her window, that boisterous, perky, warm-colored neighbor, would stay for the winter and be there to welcome her whenever she could return.

Mia sighed and closed the window, turning the lock and drawing the curtains. Fall was also a season of endings, she thought. She'd come to this sanctuary in the woods in the spring when her tears flowed like the rain. It was a time for renewal, and she dug deep and carefully planted seeds that had taken root in the long days and nights of summer to flourish and mature.

Mia walked from window to window, shutting and locking each as she prepared to close up the cabin for her return to Charleston. With each thump and click the silence closed her in. Silence had a sound, she realized. It was the sound of emptiness.

She knew this day would come but she didn't know how hard it would be to leave. Her fingertips lingered on the window latch, remembering how she'd unlocked the windows and flung open her arms in welcome to the night. She was closing the windows again not in fear but to secure the cabin, tucking it in till another pair of hands—Belle's—raised them up again.

In the upstairs garret she'd left the furniture she'd purchased. Belle had told her it would be her room, waiting for her anytime she wanted to return. Downstairs all was tidy. The western sun cast slanted light into the kitchen, illuminating the polished enamel of the cast-iron stove. She walked slowly into the main room, her careful eye catching every detail to tuck neatly away in her mind like a photograph to pull out at a time in the future when she needed it.

Mia had selected two of the many watercolors she'd painted of the river to frame and hang over the fireplace. One when the sun was setting and turning the still water of the pool the colors of stained glass; the other of the shallow riffles when the morning sun shattered the water into sparkling crystal. She smiled to think that a part of her would stay behind in this cabin that had sheltered her through so many storms.

She felt emotion welling from a deep source. She stood in the center of the room, inhaling the scents of pine oil and soap, breathing deep as if she could somehow absorb the soul of the cabin to carry with her. When she exhaled she opened her eyes and looked once more around the shadowed room.

The soul of the cabin was gone, Mia realized. It was bittersweet not to feel the presence of Kate Watkins in the cabin. Not even the return of the diaries to the bookshelf had brought her spirit back. Whatever force had held her to this piece of earth had released her. She was free.

From outside she heard the rumble of tire against

gravel, and going to the window she saw Belle's truck roll to a stop. She rushed to the door both surprised and delighted by Belle's arrival. She'd thought they'd all said their farewells at the party the night before. Nada, Becky, and Phyllis had joined forces and thrown a combination *Welcome Belle! Farewell Mia!* shindig at Nada's house on Main Street. Nada had given her a tour of the house, explaining room by room how in her retirement she was going to turn the big, old Victorian into a bed and breakfast at long last. "You," she'd told Mia, "will be my first guest when you return."

Mia swung open the door, then hurried to the porch railing to lean far over and call out, "Hey, I'm not running off with the silver!"

Belle laughed as she walked along the stone path and up the steps, her hands tucked into her jean jacket. "Better not be. I'm planning on keeping that silver." She reached the top of the stairs and added, "And the china and the books and anything else that belonged to my grandmother."

"Really? I'm glad. Good for you. It's irreplaceable, no matter what the monetary value."

"I know it. And thanks to you I had a second chance to think it over. Though," she said, rubbing her arm, "last night I promised to hand over Kate's diary to the historical society. There are some important comments in there about the times and topography."

Mia smiled to herself. So many times over the summer she'd been tempted to at least show Nada the diaries. It was Belle's place to make the grand gesture.

"Nada must be over the moon!"

Belle chortled. "She is. She also caught me after one too many beers."

"What about the fishing diaries? Are you donating those, too?"

Belle walked to the edge of the porch and looked out across the cove. A shaft of light revealed every line on her weathered face as she squinted. Her red hair shone like a sunset and her dark eyes, the Watkins eyes, were as dark a brown as the pool's bottom. Mia thought she never saw her more beautiful.

"I don't know what I'll do with them," Belle confided. "I only know I can't let them go." She turned to look at Mia, her eyes questioning.

Mia tilted her head. "I know exactly what you mean."

"Figured you might. We have that in common. Our love for Kate Watkins. Genes have no claim on love."

Mia closed her eyes and said nothing for a moment. She just wanted to absorb the compliment, to feel this bond, like sisters.

Belle leaned back to rest against the porch railing. Her long arms held on to the wood at her sides.

"Hey, I came for another reason entirely. Sheriff Rhodes came to call on me the other day. Now that the investigation is over and the bones interred, he was free to give me the few items they found with DeLancey's remains. There was his signet ring," she said, and she held out her hand.

Mia took the hand and brought it closer to her eyes.

On Belle's middle finger was a large gold ring with the family crest engraved into the circular plate. Mia recognized the handsome dragon with its foreclaws raised and the four stars, one on each corner of a shield. It was the same crest she saw embossed on DeLancey's letterhead. "It's beautiful."

"It is, isn't it? I don't wear much jewelry, but I'll wear this. There's one more thing," Belle said, and she dug into her bag. She pulled out a small box wrapped in tissue paper and tied with a bright red ribbon. "There's no way I can ever thank you for what you've done for me and for my grandmother. I know I gave you a hard time about digging in the mud, but as it turned out, that's exactly what you needed to do. Literally!"

They laughed quietly, thinking how life could sometimes be filled with irony.

Belle sighed. "You know, I only wish my mother were alive to witness all this. She'd be basking in her glory, that's for damn sure. I can just see her strolling through town with her head held high." Belle looked up and Mia was surprised to see Belle's eyes moist with tears. "If she were here, she'd thank you, too."

"I didn't do it for thanks. It's I who should thank you."

"Let's not get into that or we'll be thanking each other till the spring thaw. Here," she said, and without ceremony handed the box to Mia.

"What's this?"

"Open it and find out."

Mia tugged at the red ribbon and it slipped loose.

She tore the tape from the tissue, then pulled the wrapping back and opened the box. A gold locket lay nestled in a wad of jeweler's cotton. Her heart leaped to her throat because she knew instantly what it was. With shaky fingers she removed the locket from the box and let it slide into her palm. The locket was the size of a half dollar and made of burnished, antique gold. It hung from a chunky chain of the same rosy hue. The metal was dented in spots but it only added to the locket's charm.

"They found it clutched in his hand."

"Oh, that's so sad. Can't you just see it? DeLancey fighting through the storm, clutching this locket, desperately trying to make it back to Kate. And she sitting here, alone, feeling such guilt. My God, Belle, she died thinking she should have saved his life. That thought haunted her. If only he could have made it. If only she could have found out the truth before she died."

Belle shrugged. "If only . . ." Then she looked at Mia. "In the end the only life we can save is our own."

Mia pressed her lips together. "Belle, are you sure you want me to have this? It doesn't seem right."

"I thought you should have something that was hers. But if you're going to get all weepy about it I'm taking it back."

Mia closed her hands around the locket and tried to think of something that could even touch the depth of what she was feeling. She'd heard so many platitudes over the past year when she was battling cancer that she'd thought simply masked people's aversion to sickness and death. She knew now she was wrong. There was a reason cultures created pat phrases for moments of intense emotion. *With deepest sympathy. Congratulations. I'm sorry.* Thousands of years of universal emotions were encapsulated into a few select words of meaning because no string of creative, clever, brilliant language could ever express the depth of feeling.

"Thank you," Mia said softly.

"You're welcome," Belle replied.

Belle took the locket, then stood behind Mia and fastened the chain around her neck. Mia turned to face her, settling the locket on her chest between her breast and scar. They hugged as women do when emotions are so high that no words, not even pat phrases, are enough. When Mia released Belle, she turned toward the cabin and delivered a grandiose wave.

"She's all yours now. I hope she's as good to you as she was to me."

"It'll always be here for you. I'm not going to rent it. I thought I'd stay here for a while. See how I like it. I may be more like my grandmother than you know!"

Mia smiled and looked to where water cascaded from white rocks into a deep pool. The mist rose from the waters, curling like smoke, and from somewhere they could hear the rat-a-tat-tat of a woodpecker seeking a meal. It was a sight Mia had seen and painted every day of the summer. She would, she realized, have to seek out a new source of inspiration now.

Belle looked at her, as though reading her thoughts. "That river has flowed through this cove for thousands of years. It's not going anywhere. When you're done doing whatever it is you have to do down in Charleston, you just follow the river home."

Mia nodded her head. "I just may do that."

"Do you have everything you need for the trip? A full tank of gas? Directions? I've got bottles of water in my car you can have."

"Hey, thanks, but I can take care of myself now."

"I expect you can." Belle looked at her in her brown fishing shirt and pants. "You look real natural in those clothes now. They fit you well."

"They do, don't they?" she replied with a smug smile. That compliment had been hard won from a tough teacher.

"How's the rod and reel treating you?"

"Real good," she replied. Belle had sold her the Temple Fork Casting for Recovery rod she'd been using all summer. They both knew a fly fisher grew attached to her rods, and Mia had a world of experience attached to that one. "In fact," she said, turning toward the stairs, "I thought I'd take it out one last time before I go."

Belle twisted her lips in a smirk and, putting her hands on the railing, she leaned over and called out to Mia's back, "I reckon you're going to meet Stuart?"

Mia hauled her fly rod and reel out from the sedan, careful of the delicate tip. She looked up with a sly smile. "Yep."

"He's a good man," Belle replied. "Even if he is the competition."

Mia closed the car door and faced Belle with an ear-to-ear grin on her face. "Honey, you're the granddaughter of Kate Watkins in Watkins Mill. You don't have any competition!"

She waved, then turned and began walking the path that led past the deep pool. As was her habit, she took a quick scan of the depths. She thought she saw a sliver of movement but she wasn't sure. That wily trout. Of all the fish she caught, she knew she'd remember the one she didn't catch the most.

"Hey," Belle called out from the porch. "You ever catch that big trout?"

Mia shook her head, chuckling softly to herself, then turned once more toward the cabin. Her smile wavered. Belle was standing on the porch, tall and lean, her long braid falling over her shoulder. She stood with a proprietary air and, for a flash, Mia thought she could be Kate Watkins.

Mia walked the well-worn path along the river, deeper into the backcountry. The forest swallowed her as she hiked steadily through a medley of trees to where the air cooled and the dew was wet on the vegetation. She was surrounded by surreal color and she kept her head tilted toward the trees, mesmerized by the foliage. Underfoot she heard the crunch of fallen leaves that created a new layer of compost on the forest floor. The air smelled of ripeness and rot, sweet and pungent, that made her think of apples and pumpkins. Resident birds flitted in a thicket of mountain laurel and plump, chatty squirrels were in a frenzy of gathering for the long winter ahead.

She came to where the rhododendron clustered, feeling as she always did at this point that something wonderful was just around the bend. She walked a little farther and the vista opened up to reveal a grassy knoll, golden now, overlooking a wide curve in the water. Standing on the banks, like the first time she saw him, was Stuart MacDougal.

His tall form stood relaxed on the river's bank, dressed in his tans and browns. He wore his fishing hat and Mia could just make out bits of vivid yellow, dark brown, and bright orange of the dry flies looking like fallen leaves hooked along the band. He cast smooth and tight loops over the water, the line stretching farther with each stroke, then presented his fly gently to the trout holding in the pocket.

Her mind drifted back to the night before when he'd held her in his arms. They didn't talk. They had already said their good-byes. When he rose above her and she wrapped her arms around his shoulders she thought of the mountains that he loved and called home and the rivers that laced their sloping sides like tears. She drew him closer, feeling lost and eager to bury herself in the granite and stone and firs, drowning in the streams.

From the ridge, Stuart had spotted her and was waving her over. Mia lifted her arm in a high arc, then came out from the woods and felt the warm afternoon sun on her cheeks. She stood by Stuart's side at the river's bank and spotted some big browns cruising the shallows. Their bright red spots stood out against the pebbly bottom.

"What are you fishing?" she asked, opening up her packet of flies.

"A Booby Nymph," he replied, straight-faced.

Mia chuckled at their private joke and pulled out a tiny, brightly colored fly and held it up.

"Or a number twelve Adams," he amended.

"Me, too."

He chortled at her answer, then held out his hand. "Want me to tie it?"

"I can do it."

"Yeah, sure. But I don't think the trout will wait that long."

"You go on, then," she replied with a stubborn jutting of her chin.

"Yes ma'am," he replied, backing off and heading downstream.

Her fingers moved with dexterity as she tied the minuscule fly to the thin tippet at the end of her line. One of her goals this summer was to become an independent angler. The least of it was being able to tie her own knots. She brought the line to her mouth, feeling the slender plastic thread slide between her lips as she moistened it, then slowly tightened the knot. Done.

She looked up to see Stuart watching her. He touched the rim of his hat in homage.

Mia felt a surge of emotion as she looked out over the water, assessing the river and her mood. Slowly she moved upstream, her felt-soled boots sliding over the slippery pebbles as she made her way to the middle of the stream. When she reached the center she stopped and felt the gravel shift and settle in the silt beneath her feet. Lifting her chin, she took a good look around.

On one side the current ran quick and strong in brilliant, shallow water. On the other side dense shrubs that hung over the edge of the bank provided cover where fish could hide and feel safe. She remembered back to when she was sick and thought she might die. It was like standing in the middle of a river, wondering which bank she needed to prepare for. On one side life moved on. On the other, all was stillness. She had felt so alone and afraid, not knowing to which bank she would drift.

Now she was standing knee deep but steady in the river, facing the current head-on, her rod at the ready.

Mia cast her line far out to the fast, moving water. The line unfurled slowly, moving like liquid on wind to present her fly. Her breath held as she watched a trout rise then sip her fly down. Instantly she felt the electric current of life travel up the filament to the rod directly to her heart.

It was not a large fish; there wasn't a great struggle.

Mia played her gently to the net. She bent to meet the fish at the river's surface and held the trout with hands as cold as the water, crooning assurances as she removed the tiny hook. Dark eyes stared back as the brookie went still in her hands.

Mia's head filled with the voice of the river, pulsing loud in her ears as she felt the timeless connection with the fish, the water, and all living things. Opening her hands the fish remained still in the water, her spots shiny against the gravel. Then in a flash, she was gone.

Mia rose slowly and looked out at the river that rolled on through time. She was going to make it, she knew that now. She was a real fly fisher. She was a survivor.

She turned and headed back toward Stuart in the deeper water of the pocket. He was aware of her beside him but he didn't speak. The wind gusted, rippling the water and showering them with colored leaves like confetti. They set their casts out over the water and together slipped into a four-count rhythm. Side by side they moved in tandem. Their lines whispered through the air and their flies danced on the rushing stream. With each cast she felt her worry of leaving flow from her heart down the thin line to disappear into the river.

It was time. Quietly, in the silence Mia had come to cherish between them, she drew in her line and unhurriedly walked away over the striated rocks and through the current, leaving Stuart alone in their private space. He paused, eyes on the river. Then, with an upswing, he cast forward again.

Before leaving the river, she bent to dip her hand into the cool waters.

"Remember me," she murmured, sending her spirit to join the infinite flow of death and rebirth, of beginnings and endings, into the current. Mia lifted her face to the final moments of this perfect day, welcoming the last rays of light.

READERS CLUB GUIDE

1. What does the title, *TIME IS A RIVER*, represent for you? What characteristics do the passing of time and the flowing of the river share? Why does the river come to mean so much to Mia?

2. The road to healing does not always follow a straight course. Often, emotional healing takes two steps forward and one back in a circuitous route to recovery. The opening of the book reflects that forward and backward movement. Cite the small steps forward Mia takes and the subsequent setbacks as she gradually gains strength and purpose. Discuss how the back-and-forth movement of casting symbolizes this pattern of healing.

3. Mark Nepo's poem "Holding Each Other Up" opens the book. Discuss this poem's significance to the novel.

4. Discuss Mia's relationship with her sister Maddie. How is Maddie like a mother to Mia; how is she like a sister? How like a friend? What is the difference?

5. At the start of the novel, Mia is in need of rescue and Belle is there for her. How do their roles reverse by the end of the summer? Discuss how friendships are strengthened when each person both gives and takes.

6. Did you notice that important events seem to happen during a downpour? Being that nature is so important to Mia, could this be nature's way of acting as an actual character in the story? Discuss how nature affects the plot.

7. When it is time to leave the cabin at the story's end, Mia "[breathes] deep as if she could somehow absorb the soul of the cabin to carry with her" (page 454). In what ways does the cabin have a soul and a spirit? Have you ever felt that a place or an object has a personality or a soul?

8. When Mia begins exploring the cabin she finds not only Kate's diaries, but an armoire filled with treasures: hand-painted china, priceless silver, split bamboo fishing rods, and beautiful clothes (page 56). If you were to fill a hope chest today with your most prized possessions, what would you include? What would these things say about you should somebody find them fifty years from now?

9. Discuss Mia's relationship to her body throughout the course of the novel. On page 61 the narrator tells us that Mia felt as betrayed by her body as she did by

Charles. How does her time in Watkins Mill affect her feelings toward her own body? Has she made peace? How has Stuart played a role in this?

10. Kate and her granddaughter Belle have quite a bit in common, even though they've never met. A love of fly-fishing "ran through their bloodline as sure and strong as the currents in a river" (page 134). Do you think preferences like this are innate or learned? What hobbies or preferences do you think you have inherited from a relative?

11. Mia learns much of Kate Watkins's history directly from the people in town—through stories passed down through generations, or from Kate's old friends who are still around to share. How does this technique of telling the story via an oral history affect the credibility of the narrative? In an age in which almost any information you could dream of is available at the click of a mouse, how does the unraveling of the history of Kate and of Watkins Mill through hard-earned research, from firsthand sources, seem more credible?

12. Mia nicknames the giant, and elusive, rainbow trout "Mr. Big." On page 210 she thinks, "Mr. Big was as ancient as the river he swam in, wise and wary. At what price wisdom? she wondered. Had that big trout ever felt the prick of steel in his mouth?" What do Mia and Mr. Big have in common? How does Mia's

relationship to him develop? Why do you think she still has not caught Mr. Big by the end of the novel?

13. When Mr. Pace tells Mia the story of DeLancey's disappearance and the trial that followed he says, "People walked into the room saying 'Poor Kate' and walked out saying 'Poor Camilla.' In matters of the heart, sympathy usually goes to the wronged wife" (page 391). Being a wronged wife herself, how do you think Mia maintains her feelings of kinship with Kate after learning she was having an affair with a married man? Do you think Kate's story helps Mia to see her own divorce in a new light?

14. "Genes have no claim on love" (page 456). By the end of the novel Mia feels love toward Kate, and toward Belle. Are there any women in your life who have been so meaningful to you that they feel like family? Who has been like a sister to you? Who like a grandmother?

15. "Each step she took into the woods was a step away from her old life. Was it any wonder great fairy tales took place in enchanted forests?" (page 114) Classic fairy tale structures are included in the novel. Find examples and discuss each: 1) the old wise woman, 2) the magical hut or sanctuary, 3) feminine solidarity, 4) dressing as a male, 5) a caring lover, 6) transformation, 7) a restored, renewed world order.

Turn the page for an excerpt from
the next novel by

Mary Alice Monroe

LAST LIGHT OVER CAROLINA

Coming soon from Pocket Books

Chapter One

For three generations the pull of the tides drew Morrison men to the sea. Attuned to the moon, they rose before first light to board wooden shrimp boats and head slowly out across black water, the heavy, green nets poised like folded wings. Tales of the sea were whispered to them in their mothers' laps, they earned their sea legs as they learned to walk, and they labored on the boats soon after. Shrimping was all they knew or ever wanted to know. It was in their blood.

Bud Morrison opened his eyes and pushed back the thin, cotton blanket. Shafts of gray light through the shutters cast a ragged pattern against the wall. He groaned and shifted his weight in an awkward swing to sit at the edge of his bed, head bent, feet on the floor. His was a seaman's body—hard weathered and scarred. He scratched his jaw, his head, his belly, a morning ritual, waking slowly in the leaden light. Then with another sigh, he stiffly rose to stand. His knees creaked louder than the bedsprings and he winced at aches and pains so old he'd made peace with them. Standing, he could turn his knee to let it slip back into place with a small *pop*.

Wind whistled through the open window, fluttering the pale curtains. Bud walked across the wood floor to peer out at the sky. He scowled when he saw shadowy, fingerlike clouds clutching the moon in a hazy grip.

"Wind's blowin'."

Bud turned toward the voice. Carolina lay on her belly on their bed. Her eyes were still closed.

"Not too bad," he replied in a gravelly voice.

She stirred, raising her hand to swipe a lock of hair from her face. "I'll make your breakfast." She raised herself on elbows, her voice resigned.

"Nah, you sleep."

His stomach rumbled and he wondered if he was some kind of fool for not nudging his wife to get up and make him his usual breakfast of pork sausage and biscuits. Lord knew his father never gave his mother a day off from work. Or his kids, for that matter. Not in shrimping season. But he was not his father and Carolina had a bad tooth that kept her tossing and turning half the night. She didn't want to spend money they didn't have to see the dentist, but the pain was making her hell on wheels to live with and in the end, she'd have to go anyway.

He'd urged her to go but she refused. It infuriated Bud that she wouldn't because it pointed to how he was unable to provide basic services for his family. This tore him up inside, a kind of feeling only another man would understand. They'd had words about it the night before. He shook his head. The woman could be stubborn. No, he thought, he'd rather have a little peace than prickly words this morning.

"I'm only going out for one haul," he told her. "I'll be back by noon."

"Be careful out there," she replied with a muffled yawn as she buried her face back into the pillows.

He stole a moment to stare at the ample curves of her body under the crumpled sheet. He fought an urge to crawl back into the scented warmth of the bed he'd shared with Carolina for nearly thirty-five years. Even after all that time there was something about the turn of her chin, the roundness of her shoulders, and the earthy, fulsome quality of her beauty that still caused his body to stir. Carolina's red hair was splayed out across the pillow and in the darkness he couldn't see the slender streaks of gray that he knew distressed her. Carolina was not one for hair color or makeup and Bud liked her natural, so the gray stayed. Lord knew his own hair was thinning and gray now, he thought, running his hand over his scalp as he headed for the bathroom.

Bud took pride in being a clean man. His hands might be burned and scraped, his fingers broken with discolored nails, but they were scrubbed. The cotton pants and shirt he put on were scrupulously laundered, but no matter what Carolina tried she couldn't get rid of the stains. Or the stink of fish.

As he brushed his teeth he thought the face that stared back at him looked older than his fifty-five years. A lifetime of salt and sea had navigated a deep course across his weathered face, long lines from the eyes down to his jaw telling tales of hard hours under a brutal sun. A quick smile brightened his eyes like sunshine on blue water. Carolina always told him she loved the sweet smell of shrimp on his body. That it was his own special vintage of Old Spice. He spit out the toothpaste and wiped his smile with a towel. What a woman his Carolina was, he thought, tossing the towel in the hamper and cutting off the light. Carolina's face was dusky in the moonlight. He walked to the bedside and bent to kiss her cheek goodbye. Then, not wanting to wake her, he drew back and instead lifted the sheet higher over her shoulders. Soundlessly, he closed the door.

He rubbed his aching knee as he made his way down ancient stairs to the kitchen. The old house was dark but he didn't need a light to navigate his way through the narrow halls. White Gables had been in Carolina's family since 1897. When they weren't working on the boat, they were working to infuse new life into the aged frame house, repairing costly old woodwork and heart pine floors, fighting an interminable battle against salt, moisture, and termites. His father once chided him about it, telling him it was like throwing more sand on a beach with a strong current. In his heart, Bud knew the old man was right but Carolina loved the house. Even in the dim light he saw evidence of it in the shine of the brass doorknobs, the sparkle on the glass windows, and the neat arrangement of the inherited, threadbare sofa and chairs. Every morning when he walked through the silent, old house, he was haunted by the worry that he'd cause Carolina to be the last of her family to live there.

Bud went straight to the kitchen and opened the fridge. He leaned against the cool metal, staring in, searching for whatever might spark his appetite. With a sigh he grabbed a six-pack and shut the door. The breakfast of champions, he thought as he popped open a can of beer. The cool brew slaked his thirst, waking him further. Then he grabbed a few ingredients from the pantry and tossed them into a brown bag: onions, garlic, potatoes, grits, coffee. Pee Dee would cook up a seaman's breakfast later, after the haul. He tossed in the rest of the beer.

At the door he stuck his feet into a pair of white rubber boots, stuffing his pant legs tightly inside the high rims. The Red Ball boots with their deep-grooved soles and high tops were uniform for shrimpers. They did the job of keeping him sure-footed on a rolling deck and preventing small crabs from creeping in. He rose stiffly, rubbing the small of his back. Working on the water took its toll on a man's body with all the falls, twists, and heavy lifting.

"Stop complaining, old woman," he scolded himself. "The sun won't wait." He scooped up the brown bag from the table, flipped a cap on his head, and headed out of the house.

The moon was a sliver in the dark sky and his heels crunched loudly along the stone walkway. Several ancient oaks, older than the house, lined their property along Pinckney Street. Their low, sagging branches lent a note of weary melancholy to the dark night.

The air was soft this early in the morning. The rise and fall of insects singing in the thick summer foliage sounded jungle-like. Bud glanced up at the sky again. He wasn't fooled by the seeming serenity of the drifting clouds. His experienced eye knew they were the tips of a rain front likely to hit sometime later that afternoon. At least he hoped the rain would hold off. God knew he desperately needed a good haul today to pay bills and it would be easier to get in and unloaded before the first drops fell.

He drove a few blocks along narrow streets. McClellanville was a small, quaint village along the coast of South Carolina between Charleston and Myrtle Beach. There used to be many similar coastal towns from North Carolina to Florida back when shrimping was king and a man could make a good living for his family. In his own lifetime, Bud had seen shrimping villages disappear as the value of coastal land skyrocketed and the cost of local shrimp plummeted. Docks were sold and the weathered shrimp boats were replaced by glossy pleasure boats. Local families who'd fished these waters for generations moved on. Bud wondered how much longer McClellanville could hold on.

His headlights carved a swath through the inky darkness, revealing the few cars and pickup trucks of captains and crews parked in the lot. He didn't see Pee Dee's dilapidated Ford. Bud sighed and checked the clock on his dashboard. It was 4:20 a.m. Where the hell was that sorry excuse of a deckhand? he thought.

He followed the sound of water slapping against the shore and the pungent smell of diesel fuel, salt, and rotting fish to the docks. Drawing close he breathed deep and felt the stirring of his fisherman's blood. He felt more at home here on the ramshackle docks than in his sweet-smelling house on Pinckney Street. Gone were the tourists, the folks coming to buy local shrimp, and the old sailors who hung around retelling stories. In the wee hours of morning the docks were quiet save for the fishermen working with fevered intensity against the dawn. Lights on the trawlers shone down on the rigging, colored flags, and bright trim, lending the docks an eerie, carnival appearance.

His heels reverberated on the long avenue of rotting wood and tilting pilings that ran over mudflats spiked with countless oysters. Bud passed two sixty-foot trawlers—the *Village Lady* and the *Miss Georgia*, their engines already churning the water. The early bird catches the worm, he thought, lifting his hand in a wave. Woody, the grizzled captain and an old mate, returned the wave with his free hand, eyes intent on his work. There were fewer boats docked this year, dwindling from fifteen to seven in as many years. Of these, only five would be heading out today. The soaring cost of diesel fuel this summer had docked the others.

Bud continued down the dock, sidestepping bales of rope, holes in the planks, and hard, white droppings from gulls. As he passed the boats he took note of one boat's chipping paint, another's thick layer of rust. Every boat had a distinctive look, depending on how much money and how many hours the captain and his crew could afford to give. Each boat had a unique story.

"Hey Bud," called out LeRoy Simmons as he passed. "Looks like rain coming."

"Yep," Bud replied, looking up to the deck of the *Queen Betty* where LeRoy was hunched over his nets. "Wind, too."

LeRoy grunted in agreement. "We oughta get a day's work in."

"A half day, at least."

"At least. I'm hopin' the rain flushes the shrimp down."

Bud waved and walked on. There wasn't time for small talk. Bud had known LeRoy all his life. LeRoy was second generation of a McClellanville family of African-American shrimpers. As captain of the *Queen Betty*, a big, sixty-five-foot trawler, LeRoy could bring in more shrimp on a blustery day than most other boats on a good day. Bud knew it took a lot more than luck. A good captain knew the unchartered bottoms of the sea like the back of his hand—where the rocks hid that could snag and tear his nets, where the sunken vessels lay like dangerous skeletons, and where the tall grass could swamp his engine. The captain knew, more than any fancy, high-tech equipment, where the shrimp were. His tools were experience and instinct.

Time was, a captain with the reputation of bringing home the shrimp had his pick of top crew because the strikers got a percentage of the day's catch instead of salary. Now the catch was unpredictable, if not downright pitiful. Too often, the crew got little money and drifted off to higher-paying jobs on land. It was damn near impossible for a captain to hire on decent crew.

In this, LeRoy was more than lucky, too. Bud glanced back at the *Queen Betty* to see LeRoy and his two brothers nimbly moving their fingers over the nets, searching for tears. The Simmons brothers worked together like a well-oiled machine. He scowled, thinking of his own nets and the work that needed to be done before he could shove off. Where the hell was Pee Dee?

Peter Deery was born to a dirt-poor farming family on the Pee Dee River and the nickname stuck. For all the damage booze and drugs had done on his brain, poor guy, he thought, Pee Dee was clean and sober on deck, as nimble as a monkey on the rigging, and worked harder than two men. And he was his second cousin. A man couldn't pick his family but a captain could pick his crew—and Pee Dee was somewhere in the middle.

Bud's frown lifted when through the mist and dim light he spied the *Miss Carolina* waiting for him at the end of the dock. His chest expanded as he took the sight in.

The *Miss Carolina* was a graceful craft, sleek and

strong like the woman she was named for. He'd built the fiberglass and wood trawler with his own hands and knew each nook and cranny of her fifty-foot frame. He spent more time with this boat than any woman alive, and his wife often complained that the *Miss Carolina* was more his mistress than his boat. He'd shake his head and laugh, inclined to agree. Every spring he gave *Miss Carolina* a fresh coat of glistening white paint and the berry red trim that marked all the Morrison boats. Yes, she was a mighty pretty boat. His eyes softened just looking at her. All captains had their families, children—and loved them dearly. Yet there was a special love reserved for their boat.

The morning's quiet was shattered by the roar of an engine coming alive. Bud swung his head around to see the *Queen Betty* making her way out to sea, her green light flashing. LeRoy would have his nets dropped by sunup, he thought with a scowl. Damn, and he'd get a good spot, too. He quickened his pace and climbed up the boat.

Fifteen minutes later the *Miss Carolina*'s diesel engine was growling and Bud had a mug of hot coffee in his hand. He sat in the pilothouse, breathing in the scents of diesel fuel mingled with coffee, and listened to the marine radio for weather reports. The boat rocked beneath him, warming up. After finishing his coffee he began his chores. There was always one more job needed doing, one last repair he had to see to before he could break away from the dock. Today's disaster revealed his trynet was beyond mending.

Bud put his back to it. With each chore he ticked off his list, each muscle spasm, each minute that Pee Dee didn't show up, Bud's anger was stoked till it fired a burn in his belly. He knew in his heart that Josh wasn't being a smart-ass and that he was likely right that Pee Dee was on some bender. He ground his teeth, feeling the betrayal of the no-show.

The roar of engines sounded and he rose to look out over the bow. The final three shrimp boats slowly cruised past along the narrow creek to the Atlantic. Josh's small but sturdy forty-five-foot *New Hope* followed in the bigger boats' wake. Clever boy, he thought. With his smaller boat and his ideas for niche markets, he might do all right, Bud thought with grudging respect. Shrimping always was a young man's sport.

Bud cleared his throat and spit into the ocean. But there was a lot of life left in this salty old dog, he thought. He'd match his experience against some young Turk any day. Bud pressed the small of his back while his brows gathered. At times the pain was so severe it felt like a hot iron was being jammed into his lower lumbar.

Time was wasting. He crossed his arms while he mulled over the pros and cons of the decision that faced him. The dawn was fast approaching. He couldn't wait for Pee Dee any longer. Could he go it alone? Sure it was a risk to take a boat this size out alone. But he'd done it before, hadn't he? He cast a wary glance at the gathering clouds. Maybe not with the wind picking up, but he'd only be out for one haul. He'd be back in dock before things got rough.

He brought his arms tight around his chest and narrowed his eyes. To his mind, a man worked hard to take care of his family. He did whatever he could, whatever toll it took. With or without a crew, he was the captain of this vessel and it was his duty to bring home the shrimp. He leaned forward, gripping the railing tight, and stared out at the docks. He only needed to bring in one good haul to pay the diesel fuel bill. One good haul, he repeated to himself, and he could keep his boat on the water.

What choice did he have? Failure would mean the loss of everything he'd worked so hard for.

Bud tugged down the rim of his cap, his decision made. "Well, all right then."

With experienced swiftness he untied the ropes, then hurried to the pilothouse. Grabbing hold of the wheel, he carefully maneuvered the *Miss Carolina* away from the dock. He looked back. Under the dull light over the warehouse, he saw Old Tom step outside and wave. Bud lifted his hand. The *Miss Carolina* was the last of the shrimp boats to leave McClellanville that morning, but she was on her way at last. The dark water gurgled low, rumbling like a truck in first gear. He knew the narrow creek as well as the narrow stairwell of his home. A guard of gulls flew in sloppy formation around the *Miss Carolina* like tugboats.

He motored through Jeremy Creek and the Intracoastal Waterway in the quiet darkness, past barrier islands with their maze of winding creeks and lush acres of marshes. Then, suddenly, the vista opened, and in a breath he was on the Atlantic. The pitch of the engines rose and the fumes of diesel fuel filled his nostrils as he throttled up. The wheel vibrated with the power and the water churned whitecaps and froth in the wake. Above, the gulls began their raucous screaming.

At long last, Bud released the ear-to-ear grin he'd held in check throughout the early morning hours. This was the moment he lived for. This was what he rose each morning in search of. Freedom!

Out here, all the problems with his house, all the worries of money owed, the fights with his wife, the struggles with his father, his brother, Pee Dee—all that was behind him on shore. All that lay ahead was the majesty of a dawn breaking across a horizon that went on forever. Out here, he was his own man. Bud wasn't looking back. He was rushing forward, standing wide legged with his chin up and his hands firmly clasped on the wheel. Bud took a long, deep breath, then laughed out loud, feeling the saltwater flow in his veins.

Bud passed other boats with their nets already in the water. Their lights twinkled in the distant darkness. He pushed the *Miss Carolina* hard, racing against the pink rays of dawn breaking through the periwinkle blue sky. At dawn, shrimpers all along the coastline could drop their nets.

"They'll be catching all the shrimp around here," he muttered in frustration, pushing the throttle up. He had a place in mind, farther out than he usually liked to go. It was his secret spot. A treasure trove to which he was pinning his last hope.

Bud pushed the *Miss Carolina* faster and harder than he should have across the rolling water—and the wind pushed back. The boat was hitting the chop hard. The nets swung violently on the outriggers, spitting out bits of entangled dead fish and creaking almost as loud as the gulls. Bud locked his jaw and cut his course through the black water, leaving a wide, ruffled wake behind. Overhead, the sky grew lighter by the minute.

An hour later there were no other boats in sight. The gulls above and the occasional dolphins racing at his side were his only company. Bud slowed his speed and flicked on the marine band radio. Instantly he heard the crackle, then chatter between shrimpers. He smiled, recognizing Woody's twang, then LeRoy's gravelly voice. It was comforting to hear friendly voices out in the middle of nowhere. Usually Bud joined in to exchange jokes and trash as much as important information. This morning, however, he didn't want anyone to know where he was headed. They may have been friends, but when it came to making a living, each man was on his own. So he sat back in his chair and steered with one foot, stealing a precious moment to sip hot coffee and chuckle at one of Woody's off-color jokes.

A short while later the water changed to a murky

green. Bud sat up and tossed the cup in the trash. Dead ahead a series of hammocks clustered in a semicircle resembling an island. A brisk wind was rustling the palm fronds. He looked at the screen of the depth recorder and checked his radar, then slowed his engines. This was the spot he was looking for.

Alone, Bud had to work twice as fast. He tied the wheel in place, and hurried out on deck to the winch that rolled cable around a steel drum. Slowly, he lowered the new trynet into the water. The net blossomed like a flower, bellowing out in the slow drag.

Now he had nothing to do but wait. Bud walked across the deck, checking the ropes, cables, chains, and nets that were neatly stacked. A gust of wind rocked the boat and had him grabbing for a rail. Bud grimaced as his knee twisted and an old injury flared up. He cursed his luck on this day and, ignoring the pain, he limped back to the winch.

When the trynet rose from the sea, dripping water, he hurried to reach out with a long metal pole and retrieve the bag and pull it to the deck. Bud untied the knot at the bottom, and with a *whoosh*, the catch spilled out into a squirming mess on the deck. He quickly bent and sorted through the pulsing, flipping, swarming mess of jellyfish, bottom fish, sea slugs, a small shark—and shrimp.

Bud kicked the bycatch to the side with his rubber boot and anxiously counted the shrimp. He sat back on his haunches. Ninety-two! He pumped the air with a fist as his face broke into a grin revealing the hope that the good number sparked. This could be one of his best hauls of the season. Bud rose and, looking out over the sea, laughed out loud, congratulating himself on his decision to go it alone this morning.

Now it was time to lower the big nets.

He moved quickly, eager to begin trawling. The sun was getting higher in the sky even as more clouds moved in. Every minute counted. He shoveled the bycatch over the edge of the boat. Instantly the gulls' screams rose to a crescendo and they began diving and vying with the dolphins and each other for the free meal.

Bud moved to the main winch and his thick, calloused hands gripped the lever and shifted. He smelled the pungent grease and heard the whine as the cable rolled around the drum. The great steel outriggers slowly lowered over the choppy water. He smiled, thinking how Carolina always said that they looked like folded butterfly wings opening up.

Maybe it was his eagerness, or perhaps it was because lowering the big nets was usually a two-person job. And just maybe it was because his mind drifted for that instant to Carolina. But when the wind suddenly gusted, Bud's gimp knee gave in and he lost his balance. His hand slipped into the drum.

Bud jerked his hand back but it was too late. His world became a black, crushing, vortex of pain, shattering his thoughts, shooting up his arm to his brain where it exploded—white, blinding, incomprehensible, hot. He threw back his head, stretched his mouth wide and bellowed like a gored bull, a horrendous, gut-wrenching, primeval howl ripping from his lungs. It echoed over the ocean, scattering the gulls, then silenced into the vast loneliness.